PARK
OF
WONDERS

DARBY ANN CLAIRE

ISBN 9798371348760 (paperback)

This is a work of fiction. Any names or characters, businesses or places, events or incidents, are fictitious. Any resemblance to actual persons, living or dead, or actual events is purely coincidental.

Cover and interior design have been created by David Provolo

Follow me on Instagram @ darby.ann.claire

Dedicated to
James E. Kendall

"We all have our time machines,
don't we? Those that take us
back are memories…And
those that carry us forward,
are dreams."

— H.G. Wells, *The Time Machine*

TABLE OF CONTENTS

PART ONE

Chapter 1
UNKNOWN
September 1996

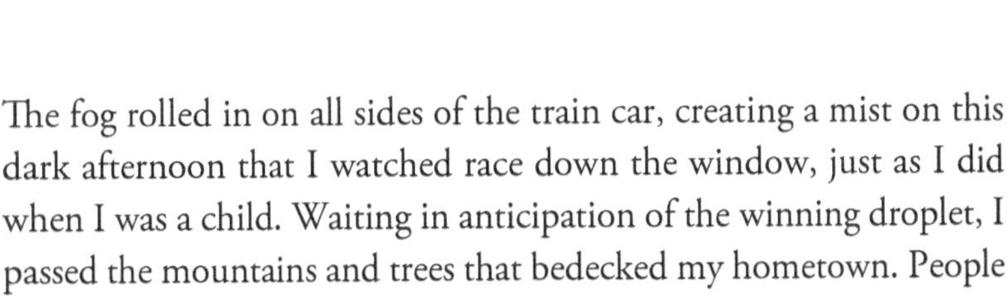

The fog rolled in on all sides of the train car, creating a mist on this dark afternoon that I watched race down the window, just as I did when I was a child. Waiting in anticipation of the winning droplet, I passed the mountains and trees that bedecked my hometown. People say there's something just not right about the small town of Fathorne; some even say there lies something almost sad in its grounds.

I love the unknown, and I don't want to know the facts or the truth, because if you know everything, there would be no mystery. I guess I have an obsession with the weird. The fog was so intense with its gray abnormality that you couldn't see two inches in front of you. Most people took the train to work or wherever they were going to miss the gray mist. On occasion, I'd see figures dancing in it; they seemed happy, but I couldn't see their faces. Today I saw a man and a woman, no older than me, probably around twenty years of age. The woman had hair so blonde it was almost white, and the fog seemed to make her skin radiate with beauty. Her yellow floral dress twirled with her. The woman was taken in the arms of a man who was as handsome as she was beautiful; he had defined, sharp cheekbones, hair as dark as a raven's feather. Every day, they were in the same dust-covered field, dancing to an unheard melody or an imaginary rhythm. The couple looked at each other like they were the only two people on Earth. I looked back, and they disappeared. Some say maybe they are ghosts or possibly just my imagination.

I often get in trouble for my imagination, for it distracts me from my daily tasks, but I can't get on without it. In the distance loomed perhaps the most mysterious place in all of the secret little town of Fathorne—Fayland Park. I saw the old arch that was decaying away with time. The red paint chipped away, along with its few remaining letters. Nature had grown around the decaying remains, while the wood rotted away with each tick of the clock. It's beautiful how the vines and forestry take over after people abandon their creation, and it's sad that some places are just forgotten and left to die. I passed the park every morning and every evening, wondering what lay behind that old white wood that makes the arch. Many rumors go around the town on why it closed, and supposedly, an unknown individual burned most of it to the ground, killing nearly every visitor of the park that day. The unknown killer was said to have burned the place down out of hatred, but perhaps it could have been an accident. In the nearly forty years since its abandonment, it has rotted away with dark kept secrets.

Just then, I had a vision of the white arch, its white paint wholly stripped of its former glory, blood smeared on the sides, the red liquid covering the grounds. Spelled across the entrance were three words, "Don't be afraid." At least forty bodies of all ages, men and women spread along the front of the arch and across the land. A blurred figure stood in the center and put his finger up to his lips as if he were trying to silence someone. It gave a cruel smile and yelled something I couldn't make out. That was when the train's intercom woke me.

"You okay, dear?" asked a woman behind me.

"I think so; I must have fallen asleep."

That's not the first time I've had that vision, but it was the first time anyone has spoken to me in weeks in public. The people in this town all wear sad faces and dress in drab clothing. No one gives a smile or says hello; they mind their own business and keep to themselves. I guess this town has that effect on me too, as I looked down at my ripped black jeans, gray hoodie, wine-red combat boots, and fishnet stockings. I looked at my reflection in the window, just another sad face looking back at me, happiness drained by this small town, dried up and forgotten. My messy black hair was pulled back into a ponytail with black lace, contrasting my diamond-blue eyes. The only compliment I ever get is about my eyes and how rare they are. My skin is pale and covered in freckles; chipped black nail polish covers all my fingernails. I looked back at the dust-covered field where the beautiful couple danced, and although I didn't even know if they existed, I hoped that someday I could be that happy.

The train came to an abrupt stop into the train station of Fathorne's town square. I was on my way to work at the corner coffee shop. As usual, the streets were filled with only a few people, and the silence was unsettling. I walked these same gray, cracked concrete sidewalks every day with the fear in the back of my mind that someone would suddenly jump out and attack me. I walked into the coffee shop, with its dark brick and haunting atmosphere, its usual people sitting alone or in small groups, sipping their coffee in a melancholy way with sad, red, tired eyes. They talked about their workdays and families; small talk, I guess, is what you would say. I didn't want to be a waitress serving nearly cold coffee and stale muffins, but I couldn't handle college with my overactive mind. My focus has always been terrible. I want to be a writer; I think it's appropriate, with this imagination of mine.

"Kimberly!" my boss, Mrs. Cummberlins, yelled as I nearly fell.

Unfortunately, the day had just begun, so I put on my apron and an "I care about my job" face. I walked around the restaurant, pouring coffee for nearly three hours for the dismal strangers. I walked behind the blue chrome counter to get more coffee, and when I turned around, everyone was gone; the people seemed to have vanished into thin air. I looked straight ahead as the fog came rolling in from all sides of the coffee shop, the bricks growing long black vines, blood dripping off their spikes into the floor. Standing at the entrance door was the figure, his face a blur, his eyes almost red, and I saw a long scar stretching across his face. He placed his finger on his out-of-focus lips, gave me a devilish smile, and reached for my throat. I screamed out for help.

"What is wrong with you?" screeched Mrs. Cummberlines. "Get up, you worthless thing! If I ever catch you having one of your stupid delusions, you're out of a job!"

I stood up and forcefully yanked my shoulder out of her stubby hands. "There won't be a next time, because I quit!"

I threw my apron onto the damp ground and marched out of the shop. As I turned the corner in a rage, I ran right into someone. I looked up and saw who the idiot was who was not paying attention, and to my surprise, I looked into two large, bright-green eyes. My heart raced, feeling like it fell two stories to my stomach, and sweat dripped out of my every pore. It was Asher, my next-door neighbor.

"Hey, Kim!"

"Hey."

"What's up?"

"Nothing, well, I just quit my job. Please excuse me."

I got out of his sight and ran to slam myself against a wall and exhale deeply. I guess it could've gone worse; I could have thrown up on him. When my mind wasn't wandering about the strange mishaps in this town or imaginary killers, it was always on him. I didn't want him to see me so angry and on the verge of tears. Coming back to my senses, I started to head to my home.

The barista job was the third job I'd lost in three months; I guess you can't get anything done when you always have delusions that someone is trying to kill you. I can't explain these visions that keep recurring, or even when they began; they just happened. I call him the man in green. What I can see of him is an olive-green suit and fedora that he wears with bloodstained green gloves. When I was a teenager, I used to go to a therapist, and I would explain these strange visions with every detail, but she couldn't explain them either, so I just quit going altogether.

Since I was going home so soon, there was no train for another hour, so I decided to walk. I knew it wasn't smart, but I wasn't going to stay in the streets of the town square. As I walked briskly with my hood pulled around my face, I passed people with blank, depressed-looking faces staring at the cracked concrete, not once looking up to make eye contact. I also passed the lines of stores with an endless amount of *for sale* and *for rent* signs. Just like Fayland Park, they were rotting away from their once-golden days.

I passed dark alleyways that separated the stores, hearing whispers in the darkness that made me nervous, but I knew I wasn't going to see who or what was making the nearly silent chatter. The rain started in, and the fog intensified. Now unable to see, I had to navigate by listening to my surroundings. I began to hear footsteps; they got louder as the fog rolled in, until I was in a cloud of the white smoke. I could hear the faint sound of a violin playing sad music far off in the distance. It was strange, but I didn't question it. The music seemed out of tune and forced but also peaceful, as the unknown person playing it probably found solitude. I had finally reached my small apartment, just outside downtown Fathorne.

My building was made of old wood and brick, looking as though it would fall in at any moment. After climbing the long staircase to room four, I opened the door to my one-bedroom apartment, staring at the leaking roof, cracked walls, and faded wallpaper.

"Home, sweet home," I muttered to myself, trying to stay positive.

My apartment building used to be a Victorian home, which was renovated into four apartments. I lived alone, but I knew Asher was just beside me in his apartment. I pushed my white striped curtains back to look out the window, which had fogged up, and the rain raced down the glass. I saw the neighbor who lived below me, an older man, sitting outside, smoking a cigarette. Smoking was his daily routine; after he finished, he put it out and stared into nothingness, perhaps missing a loved one, reliving an old memory, or waiting for something remarkable to happen.

The trees swayed with the wind, and the town was covered in gray. I picked up the weekly newspaper that I received this morning, to look for job listings. I couldn't believe what I saw. The *Fathorne Post* was hiring investigative journalists and interns. All these years of wanting to become a writer and reporter for the newspaper had finally come to me. I decided that I would go in the morning to apply but dreaded going into town and not staying in the comfort of my own home. All my dreams were about to come true. And I guess, to accomplish what I wanted, I must back away from what made me comfortable.

The following morning I had never felt such excitement, The sun seemed to shine brighter than usual, and the air had a sweeter smell. I walked onto the train platform with a feeling of optimism, which I had never felt getting on the train. The train car held only a few people, much to my liking, for I don't prefer crowds. I sat in my usual seat with its outdated pattern, along with a few stains, under a dusty window. As the train moved past the mountains and the endless number of trees, it soon passed Fayland Park again. This time, it was just the arch and its faded paint and the pink roses that twisted up the sides. Before I knew it, we were in the town square, not far from the Fathorne newspaper building. I walked up to the old building with its dust-covered windows and the red doors at the entry. As I entered the dimly lit building, cigarette smoke filled the air, making my lungs feel assaulted, and I had to cough to release the tension.

At the front desk, the receptionist was wearing a pink jumpsuit; she was the source of the smoke. She had packed on blue eyeshadow and uneven pink lipstick.

"Can I help you?"

"I'm here to apply for the job opening and was wondering if I could set up an interview."

"Oh yeah, sure, Mr. Leeran can take care of that. He's right through there."

I headed to the door she pointed out and entered an old-style office with wood paneling and red shag carpet. I felt as though I was walking into a 1970s time capsule. Mr. Leeran, who was in charge of the newspaper, looked as if he had walked right out of the same era as the office. He was a rather large man with a mustache and long, dirty, blond hair.

I gave him my resume, and he greeted me with, "Hello, how are you today?"

Before I could answer, he told me to take a seat, and we started my interview. The interview was moving rather quickly, I thought, and I hadn't even applied yet.

"At this time, there are no other applicants, but we are still going to hold interviews over the next week. Tell me, why do you want this job?"

I looked at him, and I came up with the quickest answer I could. "Well, I have always been skilled at writing and paying attention to details, things most people miss. If I wrote a news article, I wouldn't leave anything out, and I promise that it would be well written."

"Typically, we don't hire people without the proper college degrees, but it's not mandatory; it depends on if your topic is interesting and how good the article is. We want someone to write articles about the events and the history of Fathorne. We are trying to get more people interested in this small town." Mr. Leeran looked at me, not looking overly impressed, and he stroked his mustache. "I would like you to write an article, just to see your skill. If you were to write about something in this town, what would it be?"

I couldn't think of an intelligent answer, but I thought about the most mysterious place. "I've always been fascinated by the mysteries that surround Fayland Park."

He looked doubtful, even giving me a glimpse of worry. "That old dump, why would you want to write about that?" As I started to answer, he interrupted. "Do you realize the criticism you would receive? People want to forget about it."

I quickly responded, "But that place was a huge part of our town, and maybe I could discover the mysteries behind the place."

"The burning has been unsolved for years, how are you going to solve it?"

"I don't appreciate your lack of confidence in me, I could do this, and it would be one hell of an article."

He stared at me with his beady eyes and then answered, "All right, I'll give you the opportunity. Don't screw it up. And if I like your article, then you will be welcomed to the team."

When I got home, I felt my heart race with anticipation. I threw myself on my bed and covered my face with my hands. I looked past my curtains, which had green and maroon stripes, into the clouded white world. The town I always saw as dismal and the reason for my dread began to fill with opportunities and possibilities. I closed my eyes and pictured what was beyond that old white arch, as I did every day riding the train to a job that I wouldn't keep for long. As I was drifting on into my imagination, I was startled by a knock at the door. It was a terrifying occasion when someone knocked on your door in this town.

I looked through the peephole and saw Asher. My shaky hand reached for the door to let him in.

"Hello, Kim!"

I gave him a quiet and nervous hello back. "What are you doing here?"

"I baked you a clementine upside-down cake because I know they're your favorite, and you couldn't hide that smile if you tried. I saw you walking up the stairs smiling, and I thought I should con-gratulate you."

"I must have fallen asleep in my room; I didn't even know that I had been home for so long." I almost asked him how he knew about clementine upside-down cakes, and then I remembered the first day I moved in, and he asked what my favorite dessert was, I replied with a clementine upside-down cake because my grandmother always used to make them for me. The very next morning, he surprised me with one.

"So, what are we celebrating?" he asked.

"Well, I interviewed for an investigative journalist job, and I may end up getting it," I said with a flirtatious smile.

"That's great!" He nearly knocked the dessert out of his hand as he hugged me. He smelled like cologne as his wavy brown hair grazed my forehead.

We sat and talked awhile as we watched television on my old floral couch. Asher liked to ask random questions, but I enjoyed answering them because I felt like I got to know myself better in a way. He asked me, "If you could travel anywhere in the world, where would it be?"

I sat and thought awhile, not because I couldn't think of where to go, but I couldn't just say one. I answered that I would love to sit in an old corner bookstore in London while I read a book as the rain makes music on the rooftops.

He stared at me and said nothing, and I replied, "I know that sounds boring, but I see the happiness in it."

"That's not boring!" he said. "I've been to England, you know. I've been to twenty-five countries." I looked at him in astonishment; I had never known this about him. "My parents traveled all the time when I was a kid, and they still do."

I couldn't understand how he could stand being here after seeing all the things he must have seen.

I couldn't help but ask, "Why are you staying in Fathorne if you could go anywhere or even stand the boringness of this town?"

He sat and thought for a while like he was trying to come up with a reasonable explanation. "I guess there is no place like home, is there?"

"I guess not," I replied.

We watched television for the next several hours. I fell asleep, waking with my head on his shoulder. He didn't question it, and I just sat up quickly without saying a word. I finally got up the courage to tell him, "I'm about to do something idiotic, and it could put me in a lot of danger."

Asher's eyebrows raised, and his face grew to look worried. "What are you talking about?"

"I have to prove I'm a worthy writer for the newspaper job, so I'm doing a story on Fayland Park. It means I have to uncover the secrets and probably have to go there to see what I can find, because no one knows much about it, besides the ones that do will sit in silence without a reply."

"If you go there, I'm coming with you."

I looked at him, puzzled as to why he wanted to come with me. "I couldn't ask you to do that. I can't put that burden on you."

"I want to go; I want you to be safe, Kim." He sat there staring at me for a moment and said, "It would be an interesting article, but the number of people who go missing around those woods and the rumors of that place are too much for a young woman to wander."

"I know it's risky, but you know how I feel about the unknown and how much this job means to me."

He then said, "All right, how about tomorrow around noon?"

"Okay."

I placed the rest of the clementine upside-down cake in the refrigerator. He then walked to the door and turned around and took my arms into his. Asher looked into my eyes, his green eyes reflecting off my blue. He held me for over a minute, but I remained speechless. His eyes then moved down from my eyes to my lips. My mind was internally screaming. As he moved closer, my only thought was he was going to kiss me.

I closed my eyes and prepared for our lips to meet, but instead, he put his lips to my ear and whispered, "Be safe. This town can take away that ambitious spirit of yours." He then walked out the door without saying another word.

I went to my bedroom and started pacing with my arms crossed, wondering why he told me that. Asher was one of the few people who would smile and act somewhat alive in this dull town. It sent chills down my spine, feeling his hot breath in my ear with a voice that didn't even sound like his own. The apartment had gotten much colder and the rain much louder. The thunder startled me with its loud cracks. I finally lay in bed, trying to go to sleep, and the rain and wind twisted together to create a vicious swirl of water. I kept the lamp beside my bed on throughout the night. The lampshade was crooked and made the light reflect on my wall. I started to faintly hear a violin playing its eerie melody. I could hear the whispers in my closet that I always heard in the alleyways. I could then hear my heartbeat going along with the voices. I took caution to look out the window, and there he was, the man in green. His long scar and pale face looked more ravaged than usual. A sinister smile spread across his face, and his hand was reaching toward me, covered in scars and burns. I don't know what happened next, except I woke up the next morning lying in the kitchen, wrapped in pink rose petals stained with red.

Chapter 2
FLORENT'S DREAM
November 1925

Florent looked out the frost-covered window and felt the frigid air trying to come in. The fireplace crackled in the background as its light glared on the wall. He was disgusted at how everything had changed since he was a young child. The closet was no longer an entrance to another world. The forest no longer held mythical creatures. The underside of his sheets was no longer a submarine, and his stuffed animals were just now meaningless objects that sat in a closet collecting dust. The monsters under his bed, the blackness of his room, the midnight whisperings, and his fear remained still. The world was a dull place, an unhappy place.

Florent passed the time reading books, especially novels that took him to new worlds and freed him from his boring reality. He had just turned eighteen a week ago, and he could not wait to live a life of his own and have some independence. He no longer wanted to be a part of his mother's tea parties or social gatherings; at times, he felt like an object in his mother's social rank festivities. Florent had graduated top of his class and was highly intelligent, but he was not interested in college or expanding his education. He had other plans, but they would take significant measures to accomplish.

Florent looked around the dark room that was lit only by the fire burning brightly in the corner. He walked to his bed and sat on the red velvet covers, placing his head on the handcrafted headrest. His black hair fell over his eyes, and he dreamt of when his father was alive.

He was eight years old again, looking around at the rides as his father placed him on his shoulders. The carousel spun around at a fast but graceful pace, with its hand-painted horses and paintings of European countries on every corner. The Ferris wheel stood tall by the lake, and the smell of caramel corn and cotton candy filled each nostril with childlike wonder. The chatter and excitement were all Florent could think about, along with the smiles, the glory, and worry-free attitudes that happened each year at the fair. It was his fondest memory.

Then his memories turned black and into a much darker place, to the night that changed his life forever. It was a frosty night, much like this very night, and the house seemed quieter than usual. Florent heard banging downstairs, along with many other mysterious noises. He heard his father and mother scream as three gunshots went off, resulting in a tremendous crash. A man who had not liked his father had broken into their mansion, shooting his father in the chest, leaving him dead on his parents' bedroom floor. Florent remembered he stood in the hallway with his red pajamas, watching people take his father out of the house covered in a white sheet and the press following while flashing their cameras. Florent was young, but he understood death. His mother was standing in the doorway wearing a white satin gown covered in blood. Tears rolled down her cheeks, and the diamond necklace she always wore was gone.

It took only an abbreviated time for the press to share the breaking news on the famous surgeon, Horace Fayland, who was tragically shot. Florent tried to run after them, watching his father being taken from him and his mother pulling him back. Florent had the greatest memories with his father, even though their time together was short.

"Florent, it's time to come downstairs. Are you ready?" his mother yelled from the hallway.

"Yes, Mother."

He looked in the mirror at his outfit, which was expensive and overpriced. It was red with white pinstripes. The fancy outfit was not who he was, and he found it repulsive. Florent never felt like the aristocrat type; he felt much more than being tied down to society's standards.

He could hear gossip among his mother's so-called friends. He walked down the long wood-and-marble staircase to the main living area. Seven women sat around in green sofa-like chairs, holding their cigarette holders with pride. These women were commonly in his home, sharing their gossip about the people in town, except one red-haired girl who was about Florent's age. Florent's mother smiled and walked in a glitzy manner.

"Florent!" Nearly yelling, she took him by the arm and brought him to the ladies' circle. The ladies sitting in his living room all wore extravagant gowns and pricey accessories. Florent stood silent and still, actually quite tense while his eyes stayed glued to the floor. "Florent, there's someone I would like you to meet," his mother said too enthusiastically. "This is Lottie, and I think you should get to know her."

Lottie had rather unpleasant features. Florent found her appalling and couldn't look at her. All the women in the room looked at Florent, waiting in anticipation. They wanted to see what was to become of their planned romance. Florent stood silently and played with the bottom of his dress shirt. He gave a shy nod and took a seat by his mother. This arrangement was not the first and probably not the last time his mother would try to plot a marriage for him and plan out his future. Florent would never marry if it were arranged; he wanted to find love of his own. He never actually thought about falling in love much; it was foreign to him. Lottie looked at Florent, and she gave him a shy smile.

Florent decided to stare at the wallpaper covering the walls, with its yellow tint with birds sitting on the flowering branches. He had zoned out, though he did sip his tea and nod his head several times, just trying to pass the time. He heard his name called by Lottie's mother as she asked what his plans were for the future.

Florent started to sweat; no one had asked him this before. His mother never asked for his opinion. If she commanded him to do something, then that's what he had to do. He took a deep breath and decided to reveal the truth finally, and he opened his mouth.

"I don't know. I thought of maybe opening an amusement park of my own."

He could feel the eyes on him and the silence getting louder. Florent's mother looked at him as she wanted to slap him in the face for embarrassing her. All the ladies looked around at each other and started to whisper.

Lottie's mother looked confused. "What a childish idea. I would imagine that you would want to be an acclaimed surgeon, just like your father."

Florent's mother made direct eye contact with him, "Why didn't you tell me this dream of yours?" she asked harshly.

"Because, Mother, I knew you wouldn't approve." Florent fled to his room, not raising his head once, and he slammed the door, locking himself inside.

The hours passed, and Florent's eyes were red and in pain from the tears that had streamed out of his eyes for hours. His mother finally came up and knocked.

"Florent," she said softly, "can I please talk to you?"

"I suppose."

She entered, and her beads glistened from the dim light. He could see her feather headband dancing on top of her head. Her black bob fell in front of her eyes just the way Florent's hair did.

"Honey, why do you want to own an amusement park? There's

no shame in it; it's just I wondered why this is what you want to do with your life. It seems like a waste. It would just be difficult to become successful following that path. You're smart, dashing, and I could afford to get you into any school you would like."

Florent looked at her with disbelief. "Remember when Father used to take me to the fair every year?

"Yes."

"Well, it was the happiest moment of my life. It was the trivial things like how the sun would shine off the Ferris wheel and how the air smelled like cotton candy and kernel corn. Dad placed me on his shoulders, and I felt like I was on top of the world. It was just him and me."

A tear rolled down his mother's cheek, ruining her blush. "I miss him too. I remember how he would come home and always kiss me softly; then, he sang me a love song while holding me in his arms."

Florent smiled. "I want to make people happy. I want to give people the feeling I had as a child, before I …" He stuttered on his words.

"Before you what?"

"Before I grew up."

Florent's mother looked at her son for just a moment. "You'll always be my little boy, and your father will always be with us." She got up and left the room, leaving the door slightly cracked open, and with those words, Florent fell into a deep sleep.

The next day, Florent woke exceedingly early, just before the sunrise. He walked downstairs to eat breakfast the house staff had placed out for him, and then he dressed. He sneaked out of the house to get some fresh air. As soon as he was outside, he just kept walking down the brick driveway. Snow-covered trees made an arch, and the driveway was so long to his house, it was impossible to see the end. The fog danced by his feet as he took each step, and he kept his hands in his pockets.

Florent had heard the story of his aunt and uncle's tragedy on this same brick lane. The Faylands had lived in the mansion for generations, which was the home to his aunt and uncle before his father took over. It was late, the fog fierce, and blackness surrounded the property. They were coming down this driveway to get to the mansion. Their carriage crashed into a tree, killing both of them instantly. No one knows the real story, but legend has it that the entire Fayland family was cursed somehow.

After their deaths, Florent's father was granted the estate. Sometimes he could hear their screams on the anniversary of their death and see a confused man along with a woman walking down the road. Even with Florent's overactive imagination, he didn't believe in ghosts or the supernatural. He thought that the mind made you hear and see what you feared.

The sun was coming up brightly above the trees, and silence reined through the forest. Florent had finally reached the busy town square, where shoppers paced and people went on with their daily lives. Granted, he didn't get out much, but he saw a new flower cart sitting in the middle of the square. The flowers were quite beautiful in the stand, displaying all the colors imaginable.

Florent decided to get a closer look at the flowers' beauty, and a soft voice said, "Can I help you find anything?"

Without lifting his head, he said, "No, thank you, just looking."

When he looked up, he saw a young woman, probably around his age, with white-blonde hair that went down to her waist and the brightest blue eyes he had ever seen. She was beautiful; there was no other way to describe her. Her yellow floral dress swung along her bare feet, and her cheeks were blushing red.

She sweetly said, "I grow all these plants on my own in my garden. My favorite are pink roses."

Florent seemed to have an extra skip in his step when he was walking home as he carried a bouquet in his hand, along with a lone pink rose. He was no longer thinking about the conversation he had with his mother the previous night; all he could think about was that girl. He didn't even ask for her name because he was caught in the moment and taken by her beauty. This girl's hair made the sun look dim and the water from the stream that ran in his backyard seem lifeless. He knew he would go back the next morning to talk to the girl and buy more flowers, to be near her.

His heart was racing, and his shortness of breath started to worry him. He had read many stories and poems that talked about this feeling. He wondered, could this be love? Was he in love with this girl he had just met? That was impossible, he thought; desire at first sight was ridiculous and just a delusion, but he knew that just maybe it could happen. It wasn't just her looks; it was her sweet voice, the way she smelled, and only the thought of holding her in his arms that made him get a twist in his stomach.

Florent finally reached his house and walked up the broad staircase to the main entrance, where the butler let him in.

"Mister Fayland," he said, "are you all right? You are acting strange."

Florent looked down, as he was walking rather fast, and his head raised instead of slumped, and he had a smile on his lips.

"What do you mean?" Florent asked, again with a smile.

"Well, sir, you seem, well … happy."

"Trust me, it's strange to me too, but I think I like it." Florent gave his butler a purple flower.

"Thank you, sir." He seemed as if he was in shock at this kind gesture.

Florent then joined his mother in the atrium, where the sun illuminated the room from the glass-domed ceiling.

"Where did you get those?" she asked.

"There is a wonderful new flower stand in the town square."

"They are rather beautiful." His mother smelled them and smiled. "They are absolutely lovely. You can place them there on the table, and the gardener will care for them." Florent did as she had said, except he kept the pink rose in his hand, avoiding the thorns. He walked up to his room and placed it on the nightstand by his bed.

The next day he rushed to get his clothes on and ran out the door while avoiding his mother. He noticed he was almost running, and his heart was racing; he almost tripped over his own feet. It was strange, but he could smell her honeyed scent and hear her joyous voice, even though she wasn't near him. He could feel the tightness in his chest. It was painful, yet he liked this new feeling he had never felt before. When he reached the town square with the bustling shoppers who were completing their daily errands, he spotted her in the mass of people, selling a bouquet to a young couple. He walked swiftly toward her, almost knocking two people down along the way, but it did not matter to him. He finally got to her, nearly short of breath, and she was wearing the same yellow floral dress. The girl still wore no shoes, and mud covered her feet.

"Oh, hello," she said softly, "you're back soon."

Florent was still short of breath and stumbled on his own words. "Hello, yes, it's just, you're so beautiful. I mean, the flowers are so beautiful."

She smiled, and what sounded like a small laugh came from her perfect pink lips.

"I'll take … um—" Florent was dying to ask her over to his house but couldn't seem to get it out.

"Are you all right?"

Florent then realized he had zoned out and said, "Yes, sorry, I'll take a bouquet of pink roses."

She didn't say anything but smiled and went to the side of the cart to grab them. "Here you are."

Florent gave her the money and started to walk off, knowing he would regret it. He abruptly turned around and asked awkwardly, "Would you like to come to dinner at my house tonight?"

She gave him a surprised look. "Why do you want me to come to dinner?"

Florent didn't know what to say. "Well, I just thought it would be nice, and I appreciate your services in the flower business." *Services in the flower business?* Florent wanted to slap himself in the face, that was so stupid for him to say.

To his surprise, she said, "I'll be there," and a smile spread across her face. "But I don't even know what your name is."

"It's Florent, and yours?"

"Althea."

She still looked confused, but he couldn't hold his excitement. "I'll meet you. May I have your address?"

"No!" she exclaimed. "I'm sorry, could you just meet me in the square by the fountain?"

"Of course. Is seven o'clock all right?"

She nodded, and Florent headed home.

The evening had come up quickly, and he had spent all day preparing for his special dinner. Fortunately, Florent's mother had left for a short trip to a nearby city to purchase some new gowns and jewelry for herself. Florent wondered how they had any money left with her irresponsible spending—though he knew his father had left a vast fortune behind, large enough for Florent and his mother to live their lives in luxury. He knew if his mother were home, she would not accept having a girl over; she didn't approve.

Florent was in charge of everything in the house when she was away. He had their chef make the finest dishes he could cook, and the housekeepers were informed to make the dining hall very presentable. *Althea*, the name ran over and over in Florent's mind, and it sent shivers down his spine and his heart to beat abnormally. He walked into the dining hall and felt a considerable amount of prestige. Purple velvet drapes hung from each window; the fireplace burned bright, which was the only source of light in the room, along with the candles set in the middle of the table. The table had all the right silverware placement, set up for two. Florent looked up at the grand chandelier and could see his reflection. The way it glimmered in the darkness didn't even compare to Althea. The time had come for him to meet her, and he left the house in anticipation.

Florent got into the automobile that usually sat in the garage, but this was a special occasion. He opened the glossy black door and got behind the wheel into the red leather seat. Florent reached the town square, where a few streetlights dimly lit the street. He parked on a side road and decided to walk to the fountain. He turned the corner, and she was at the fountain, picking the petals off a flower on the ground. She sat on the side of the large fountain with her legs swaying while she whispered something to herself. She looked up and was startled by Florent's sudden appearance.

Florent noticed she wore the same dress, but had shoes, though they looked too small and very worn. She also had no coat and seemed to be shivering.

"You scared me," she said.

"Are you ready?"

"Yes."

"Are you cold?"

"No."

She would not admit to it, even though Florent noticed her shaking and her pale face. He took off his trench coat and placed it around her shoulders. She looked up at him with her big blue eyes, and Florent could tell how thankful she was.

"Thank you," she said.

Oh, how beautiful she is when she says even the simplest phrases. "Of course," Florent replied.

They turned the corner, where a single streetlamp lit a small circle in the street. The sun was beginning to go down, and the darkness was emerging. They both reached the car, and Althea looked shocked. "You drove?"

Florent did not know why she asked that, but he replied, "Yes, why?"

"No reason," she said as she put her head down. Althea reached for the door, but Florent jumped in front of her to open it for her.

"Oh, thank you very much, quite the gentleman."

Florent started the car and headed toward his house. When he looked over, Althea was feeling the seats and slowly moving her hand down the interior of the car, but she never said a word. Florent didn't know what to say, so he stayed silent as well.

Florent turned down the old, long driveway to his home as the fog rolled in on them. "Sorry about the unwelcome, terrifying, never-ending road into nothingness"

"That's okay; it's quite peaceful."

He had never thought about his family's grounds, but the starry sky and the quietness with just her were somewhat like a haunting dream from which he didn't want to wake up. Florent then saw the black gates that wrapped around the property like vines.

"This is your house?" Althea asked, sounding as if her breath had been taken from her. She looked up at the house in complete astonishment, at a loss for words.

Florent pulled around the circular driveway at the front entrance and opened the door for her. They headed for the door, and Florent grabbed her hand, hoping he wasn't rushing things, but her fingers intertwined with his. They walked up the stairs, and the butler opened the door for them. Althea gazed up at the three grand chandeliers that hung in the entrance to the house. "If you don't mind me asking, what do you do for a living to afford such an extravagant place?"

Florent smiled. "Actually, my mother owns the place, and my family has owned this land for generations. My father was a surgeon, possibly the best one in the world. People paid him top dollar to get his surgeries. He owned a line of medical equipment that was the best in the business, and doctors all over bought his supplies. Unfortunately, I lost my father many years ago, when I was only eight. My mother was in show business before she met my father. She was a ballet dancer and a beautiful singer, but she gave it all up when she became pregnant with me."

"That's fascinating," Althea said.

"Enough about me, though. I'm sure you're starving."

Florent, still holding Althea's hand, led her to the dining hall. He let go as soon as he pulled out her chair, where she gracefully sat down. He took his seat at the other end of the table. He made fake binoculars with his hands to see Althea better, making her laugh.

Quickly realizing there was too much distance between them, he picked up his plate and placed it in front of the chair next to hers. They sat and ate their food quietly and made small talk. Every word out of Althea's mouth was like sweet nectar spilling from her lips, making his heart swell. He had never felt this way for anyone in his life; just the thought of her leaving him to go home made him feel depressed. Althea ate at a fast pace but still quite proper.

After they finished eating, Florent led her to the large living room, where his mother and her friends had their weekly get-together. They sat down on the red velvet couch and put their hands to the fireplace to warm themselves. Florent had placed the pink roses he had purchased earlier into a glass vase on the center table. He realized when Althea saw them because she had a broad smile. The house was eerily quiet, and the fire in the fireplace made for a comforting atmosphere. If there were a time Florent was going to kiss her, it would be now. But he sat in anticipation because he didn't want to rush anything or make her feel uncomfortable. He didn't even know how to kiss. After about thirty agonizing minutes, he decided to attempt it, and he slowly placed his hand behind Althea's neck and pulled her closer to his face, then put his lips on hers and continued to kiss her passionately. Althea slid her hands on his and kissed him back just as hard, but then she pulled away.

"I'm sorry, it's just that we …" She cut off her sentence, and her voice started to crack. Tears began to roll down her face, and she started to sob.

Florent was scared. Had he done something wrong?

"I'm so sorry, what did I do?" Florent panicked and feared he'd made her feel discomfited.

"Nothing," Althea replied.

"Then what is it?"

"This can't happen."

Florent was very confused. "Why?"

"You know why."

Florent looked at her with concern on his face.

"I have only read about men like you in fiction books, where the handsome prince comes to rescue the damsel from the dragon, then they marry and live happily ever after. But this is no fairytale; this is real life, where there is no happily ever after, just tragedy. You're extremely handsome and wealthy, and as soon as you get tired of me, you'll throw me to the side, like some stray dog that wandered into your home."

Florent sat down closer to her and took her hand in his. "Althea, that will never happen. I would never do that to you."

"You've known me for two days. How can I trust you?"

"Money means nothing to me. It doesn't make me happy, but you do. Money could never bring my father back or bring back the days I had with him. It sure hasn't made my mother any happier. When I first saw you, I felt something I haven't felt in a long time— the kind of feeling you can't explain, but you know it's right. I know I have only known you for just this brief period, but in a way, it's like I've known you my entire life. It's as if when I cried when I was a child, your presence was there, or whenever I felt alone in the world, you were there to fill that void."

"Florent, it's not going to work. We're from completely different worlds."

"We're not that different."

Althea's head dropped, and her voice got quieter as she spoke again. "Florent, do you know why I wear the same dress with no shoes, while my feet are covered in mud? It's because I have nothing, absolutely nothing. My mother died when I was thirteen, and my father was bedridden from a fatal injury. As soon as my mother passed away, I was the only person my father had, so I took on the responsibility to care for him day and night. I dropped out of school and all the activities that I had once enjoyed. Despite everything, I don't regret it. I'm glad that I got to spend all the time I could with him and make his last days a little more cheerful by reading and singing for him. It's crazy how fast five years just went by and took him from me."

Althea's eyes were drowning in her tears, and her face was bright red. She never made eye contact with Florent but instead kept them focused on the window. "I couldn't keep up with the payments on my father's farmhouse, so I took our flower cart and kept walking. I tried looking for help; I went to every house. I just needed to ask for a place to sleep for the night. It was one door in my face after another. Eventually, I ended up in Fathorne, the next town over from mine, and something told me to stay, that this is where I belong.

"I was nearly starved when I arrived in town. I went to the first place I saw and knocked on the door; it was a small house just west of the town square. A man, his wife, and their two little boys live there. Never in my life did I think someone would look at me with such sympathy, and that's when I realized how much life as I knew it was gone. They offered me their extra bedroom and a section of their greenhouse to grow my flowers so I could make a profit. They never asked for rent, but I give them most of my income.

"Those people made me realize that there's still hope for humanity. Even when the world seems chaotic, there's always someone out there, somewhere that will comfort you while it's falling apart. This world is a dark, cold place, but all you need is someone to light the way for you. Not long after all this, you came and bought flowers from me. At first, I thought you were an illusion, a figment of my imagination. I was embarrassed by my appearance because you looked so put-together and elegant. My head told me it would never happen; no one would love me this way. But my heart told me there may be a chance, even just a small one, for you to feel the way I do. I loved your kindness and the way your pitch-black hair fell perfectly in front of your eyes. Then, when I saw your home and your luxurious belongings, I knew you wouldn't be able to accept me. What would your family think of me if they saw this dirty girl who is a nobody standing in your home?"

Florent took her hand and pulled her up from the couch. He placed his hand on her back and started to sway. He just started dancing, and although Althea stumbled a few times, Florent didn't mind and helped her find her way back to the rhythm. Althea's tears had dried from her eyes, and she placed her head on Florent's chest. The house was dead silent; they were dancing to no music but found the melody within themselves. Florent knew that sometimes no words had to be said, just the feeling they felt when they were with a person they cared about dearly.

"Althea?"

"Yes?"

"I know it sounds crazy, but I'm in love with you."

Althea lifted her head and stared into his eyes, "I'm in love with you too."

Chapter 3
REMAINS
September 1996

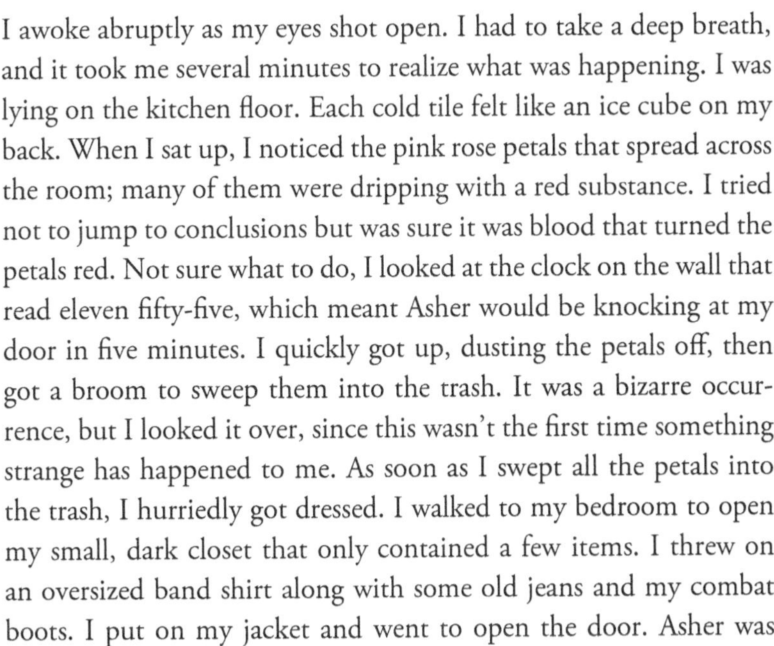

I awoke abruptly as my eyes shot open. I had to take a deep breath, and it took me several minutes to realize what was happening. I was lying on the kitchen floor. Each cold tile felt like an ice cube on my back. When I sat up, I noticed the pink rose petals that spread across the room; many of them were dripping with a red substance. I tried not to jump to conclusions but was sure it was blood that turned the petals red. Not sure what to do, I looked at the clock on the wall that read eleven fifty-five, which meant Asher would be knocking at my door in five minutes. I quickly got up, dusting the petals off, then got a broom to sweep them into the trash. It was a bizarre occurrence, but I looked it over, since this wasn't the first time something strange has happened to me. As soon as I swept all the petals into the trash, I hurriedly got dressed. I walked to my bedroom to open my small, dark closet that only contained a few items. I threw on an oversized band shirt along with some old jeans and my combat boots. I put on my jacket and went to open the door. Asher was standing outside with his hands in a fist as if he was getting ready to knock.

"Hi," I said.

"Hello," he replied.

"We can take my truck there; it's safer than walking."

"Okay."

We walked down the steps to the back of the apartment building. Asher's truck, a yellow 1985 Chevy pickup, was by some trees. I opened the door and got into the passenger seat, where there was an abundance of soda cans on the floor.

"Sorry about that. You can just push them to the side."

The rain had finally stopped after such a vigorous storm the previous night—many places flooded from the enormous amount of water. I was looking at my pale hands and then looked out the window. Again I stared at the gray world in which I was raised. I had never called anywhere else home, even though I found this small town was dilapidated and dull. It was once a place of happiness, a place where families would come together and enjoy everything the town had to offer. That all changed when Fayland Park became an unsafe place, where families got torn apart. Through the years, numerous people went missing, and until this day, never were found. The kidnappings never had any ties to the amusement park, or at least there was no proof. Many of the missing people's posters still hang on the side of buildings. They were forgotten and fading, like the memories of all those who were gone.

I jumped when Asher started talking to me. "Why are you doing this, again? I mean, I know it's for the newspaper. I just don't understand why you're putting yourself in this situation. No one goes on those grounds; you know the rumors about that place."

"They're just rumors; it doesn't mean they're true." Just as I had finished my sentence, we turned onto the dirt path to what used to be a parking lot, now overgrown with grass. Asher pulled into the large grassy area and turned off his truck.

"Asher thank you, for doing this, but I don't want to put you in danger. I wish you wouldn't come with me, because I don't want you to get hurt."

"Kim, I'm coming with you whether you like it or not." Asher pulled out his backpack from behind the seats and pulled out a knife. "This is in case we get in any kind of trouble."

Asher and I began our journey toward the woods; the fence that had once surrounded this place had fallen over many years ago. I could see the train tracks that I took almost every day and, to be on this side of the glass was a weird feeling. As soon as I got closer to the trees, goosebumps erupted on my neck, and the air seemed colder.

"What's that smell?" Asher asked.

"I don't know," I replied.

The smell was strong and had a musty odor of machines and dead animals. It was almost too much to take.

"I need to find pictures, artifacts, maybe old newspapers, or anything that would be some evidence of the history of this place."

"We'll see what we can find," Asher said. The air was very chilly, but the sun came through the trees like a spotlight in a theater and hit us like we were the stars. The trees were nearly bare, half of them looking blackened and dead. The leaves crunched under our feet from the trees that still had life. The further we got into the woods, rose petals started to appear under each step.

"Where are all these petals coming from?" Asher asked. I just shrugged my shoulders and didn't tell him of the incident I had in the kitchen. They looked the same, pink rose petals, but without the blood. Before we knew it, there were roses everywhere, vining around everything, just like the ones on the front arch. It was almost like walking into a pink cloud as a garden of the flowers surrounded us. After being overcome by this scene, I looked to the right and saw a Ferris wheel sticking out from the forest. It must not have been caught in the fire, as it was only damaged by time, nothing else. The carts were made of white-painted wood. The backs of the carts had painted vines with cherubs holding up the flowers. It was extraordinary architecture with so much detail, even after all these years.

Asher stood looking, dumbfounded at everything that surrounded us.

"I know this place has a messed-up, psychotic past, but who would abandon something like this? I always thought this place would be just a junky old amusement park, but who knew such a strange place could be so—" He struggled to find a word.

"So beautiful," I replied.

"Yeah."

I stared at the circle of trees above us that only showed a small amount of sunlight. We kept walking for at least ten minutes until we came upon another decaying attraction. I almost walked right into the water, which had boats shaped like birds, white cranes, down the stream. I could tell it was a water ride; the remaining water was green and full of algae. The cranes were a beautiful structure, and I noticed something strange written on the sides in cursive lettering. The word spelled out Althea, which I didn't understand; perhaps it was someone's name.

"Who do you think Althea is or what it means?" Asher asked.

"I don't know."

Fayland Park was a large part of Fathorne's history, but the records got destroyed, and no one dared ever to mention anything about it. The owners remained a mystery; the only known fact was their last names were Fayland, the same as the park. We continued to walk where trees and overgrown forestry surrounded us. To our surprise, we looked up to see a large structure out of place. It was a house, a mansion technically, that was blue with gold trimmings around every corner. "What is this place?" I muttered out loud.

"I never expected a castle to be in the middle of an abandoned amusement park, but here we are," said Asher.

I got closer to this massive structure and stepped onto a white marble staircase that led to a wraparound porch. Asher was right; this was so large and grand, it could have been a castle. The building was too detailed to be an attraction; this used to be someone's home. I started to get closer to the house when I got a sharp pain on my leg, and I noticed it got cut on a thorn from a rose. The rose was just one out of a massive garden of them. They stretched as far as I could see, even more than earlier. The land was covered pink from the flowers on every corner.

"Are you okay?" asked Asher.

"Yes, I'm fine."

I was bleeding, so Asher gave me a tissue out of his backpack to soak it up. "Thank you."

"I guess we should go inside."

I walked up to the grand doors that stood tall with broken glass. The house wasn't even locked; the door was cracked open. I pushed open the door as some of the glass fell to the ground, and what I saw in front of me was incredible. The inside was phenomenal, and though it showed evidence of abandonment, the decay made it more beautiful. I looked up to see a glass dome that, just like the door, had broken glass. The holes in the dome created streaks of light that shone all through the room, almost looking like lasers. A grand crystal chandelier hung behind the glass dome, which was in the center of a square glass frame. I heard rustling close by and was startled as a bird flew out of one of the rooms, scaring both Asher and me. I ran to him, and he grabbed me while I buried my face in his chest. We looked at each other and laughed at the incident.

"I hope that's the only other thing in here with us," said Asher.

Two grand marble staircases met in the middle, leading upstairs. I started to walk up the stairs; each step was another crack. The handrail was broken and wobbled when I tried to hold on to it. I had reached the second floor, with its long, dark hallways; the only light came from the sunlight. The painted ceiling was like Italian art, consisting of angels, clouds, and cherubs. More crystal chandeliers hung from the ceiling in a straight line down the hallways. No pictures of the family who may have owned this house were on the wall. All the furniture looked ripped to shreds, as if by an animal. Asher handed me a flashlight from his backpack, and I noticed the furniture was not the only thing that had been cut. The wallpaper on the walls was peeling and had diagonal cuts as if someone took a large knife to it.

The wooden floorboards had been destroyed with scratches, but I could not tell if claws or a knife had done the damage. I went into the first room on the left; the door was already cracked open.

The room was just as beautiful as the rest of the home, and everything in it was untouched. It seemed as if the inhabitants of this room had just left, leaving all their belongings. The room was illuminated in a pink glow, as the sun came in from the large window and bounced off the walls. The side the bed was on had striped wallpaper, but it was in good condition, unlike the other wallpaper. The huge bed had a white headrest and a pink comforter that included lace and frills, and about five throw pillows. I went over by the window to see if I could see anything else on the property. I pushed the lace curtain open to find a tiny cemetery that consisted of only two gravestones. Perhaps it was the family who had owned this extravagant home. I tried to see if I could read the names on the gravestones, but from the corner of my eye, I saw something moving.

I then saw it more clearly; it was a disembodied figure of a woman. This woman was very petite and was wearing a white satin gown. Her features were blank; she appeared not even to have a face. She swayed more than walked; each step was very graceful. She slowly stopped right by the gravestones and stared straight ahead. Then she slowly turned her head and faced me. I started to breathe slowly and was frozen with shock. The woman's head was slightly at a slant, and her strawberry-blonde hair was cut to her jawline and curled to perfection. She stood there facing me with an eyeless stare for at least a minute, as more fog started to roll in. She began to sway oddly. A line of blood started to run from the top of her head, down her blank face. I wanted to run away from the window or scream, but I couldn't move. I was forced to watch her entire head stained red. I then saw two large pieces of glass lodged into her neck. Then, without notice, she turned to mist and was carried away with the fog.

I let go of the curtain quickly and backed up slowly, backing into a vanity. I knocked over a few of the items, and I noticed a photograph fell to the ground. I picked it up and couldn't believe my eyes; the photograph showed what may have been an inhabitant of the house. The picture was torn at the bottom and covered with dust, just another forgotten memory. There were three people in the photograph, and their clothes suggested that it was taken in the 1940s. They were standing in a garden filled with distinct types of flowers. Two were teenagers or at most their early twenties. What caught my attention was the third person in the photograph, a small boy, but his face was marked out entirely. It looked like someone took a sharp object and scratched it out completely. I looked up to the vanity to see the photo album that the photo had fallen from; I opened it up to see if I could find any more photographs, but it was blank, covered with dust. I looked around at the empty room, everything untouched as if it was waiting for someone to come back someday.

"Kim?" I jumped as Asher entered the room.

"Did you find anything?" I asked.

"No, you?"

"Just this picture." I handed Asher the photo, and he stared at it.

"This is very strange," he said.

"I'm going to see what else I can find."

I walked into the dark, destroyed hallway and walked to the very end to two large doors. I opened them to an enormous bedroom. Another glass dome let the light into this room, illuminating a giant bed, a beautiful fireplace, and a marble floor. This room, just like the other, was untouched and frozen in time. I looked around to see what I could find and heard a crunch under my foot. I had stepped on a broken picture frame, which held another photograph. I knocked the glass off as I picked it up. A young man and woman were holding hands and smiling at the camera. The couple looked happier than anyone I had ever seen in my entire life. I examined the picture harder and recognized the floral dress and the girl's long hair. I saw the man's dark hair, but I could see their faces, unlike when they danced in the field. I was in shock when I looked into the girl's eyes; though the picture was not in color, I could tell she had lovely eyes. I turned the photograph over and found writing on the back, which read, "My dearest Althea," but the rest was marked out. I thought of the two pictures that were both detailed but gave no explanation to who was in them. I suppose they were someone's painful memories that they wanted to be forgotten forever.

Chapter 4
THE DANCING FIGURES
November 1925

Florent had awakened from a short nap, realizing he had fallen asleep on his living room sofa. He looked down to see Althea resting on his chest, entirely still. He looked up at the ceiling and smiled, then placed a kiss on Althea's head. He got up from the couch while slowly placing her down and laid a blanket over her. Althea made a small movement then went back to sleep. He glanced at her one more time then quietly walked away. He walked down the dark hallway to his bedroom but stopped halfway to look at the large painting of his father. Florent looked up at him, a well-respected man. Most people saw Horace Fayland as a business tycoon, intimidating and powerful. Florent just saw him as his loving father, the person who would read him a bedtime story and comfort him when he had a nightmare. It was all in the past, though; the happy endings never happened, and the monsters had tortured Florent for years. Something was removed from his heart the day his father left, leaving him with a void.

Florent changed into his pajamas and got into bed, and he realized something. When he held Althea his arms, the pain healed, and for the first time in a long time, he couldn't wait for tomorrow.

When tomorrow came he quickly jumped out of bed, checked the mirror to fix his hair, and changed into the clothes his maid had placed out for him. He ran down the long staircase to get to the kitchen to grab some muffins and threw them into his jacket pockets. He then went to the living room to find Althea on the couch, but she wasn't there. *That's impossible*, Florent thought. *I didn't dream what had happened the previous day.*

"Good morning, Florent."

Startled, he turned around and saw Althea smiling at him. Florent quickly ran to her, putting her hands in his and kissing her on the cheek.

"I'm sorry. I shouldn't have left the living room or went anywhere without your permission," Althea said.

"You're my guest; you may go wherever you please."

"I was just admiring your mother's plants and flowers in the atrium. They are very lovely."

Florent guided Althea down a hallway. "Come on, there's something I want to show you."

They walked out one of the back doors and down the steps from the porch. Althea looked at the fountain centered in the backyard, which had a mermaid sculpture in the middle. They walked into the woods that surrounded the house. "Florent, where are we going?"

"On an adventure."

They walked into the woods, which Althea found eerie, so she squeezed Florent's hand tightly. They then came out into an open field surrounded by the forest. The sun shone brightly over their heads and bounced off Althea's hair. They ran, still holding hands, to the center of the field, laughing and smiling at one another. "I used to come here as a child and let my imagination run wild. I even came here when I was still in school, to clear my thoughts. There's something else I need to show you." Florent walked back to the forest as Althea followed him and came up to a square object with a large rectangular cloth. He pulled back the fabric to reveal a playhouse made of wood. "This was my castle, my ship, or just whatever I wanted it to be. My dad and I built this with some wooden planks, and we would play pretend games for hours."

"The child mind is one of the most beautiful and purest things ever to exist ," said Althea. Florent took her hand and opened the small cloth door, watching not to hit their heads. They crouched down to the tiny space inside, just enough room for the two of them. Florent reached inside his pocket to pull out the muffins and gave one to Althea.

"Thank you," she said politely. Althea looked around at all the drawings that Florent must have drawn when he was a child.

"I haven't been here since my dad died; I guess it was too painful to come back. Also, when I grew up, I don't know, the spirit I once had was gone. The day my dad passed, I felt so empty, and I felt as if a piece of me went with him. I seemed always to be walking down a pointless path, and every ounce of happiness was drained from me."

"You and your father must have been very close."

"Yeah," Florent said as he gave a weak smile. "He was my best friend."

"I know how you feel, but I know everyone we lose will somehow find their way back to us. There are no endings, just new beginnings."

Florent looked up at her and smiled. When they finished the muffins, they both ran to the center of the field again. Then Florent placed his hand on Althea's back and placed his other hand in hers until they were dancing a type of ballroom dance just like the night before. They extended their arms and spun in a circle while laughing. Florent spun Althea around one last time; then, he dipped her down, kissing her harder than the first time. Althea placed her hands on both sides of his face and kissed him back vigorously. Florent lost his balance, and they both fell. "Althea, I'm so sorry, are you okay?"

Althea looked at him and burst out laughing.

"I'm better than okay."

Florent laughed back, picking himself up then extending his hand to help Althea up from the ground.

They walked back up to the house and in through the back door. Once again, Florent took Althea's hand and led her up the grand stairway. He opened the door to his mother's room.

"Just sit down here for a minute."

Althea did as Florent said and sat down on an ottoman by a large mirror on the wall. Florent walked toward the back of the room and then opened a door leading to another room, disappearing. Althea looked at herself and started to lose all her confidence as she looked at her old, stained, yellow dress, which was covered in holes. She knew she loved Florent; she loved him with all her heart and gave him all her trust. No matter how kind he was to her or how many times he kissed her, she felt like she wasn't enough for him. *Why would a man like him love a girl like me?* she wondered. Althea looked up to see Florent carrying a large box and coming toward her.

"What's that?"

"My mother throws all her clothes that she no longer wears in this box and usually just ends up throwing it all away when she gets tired of them." First, Florent pulled out a green dress with gold beads strung from top to bottom, and it looked like it was ready for a flapper. "You should go try this on."

"What? I can't take things that don't belong to me, and it's too fancy for someone like me to wear."

"You're going to look beautiful in it. Really, it's okay, my mother doesn't wear this anymore."

Althea hesitated but then took the dress to the closet where she could change. Not long after, she opened the door to where Florent could barely see her. "Can you come closer? I want to see it."

Althea walked closer to Florent, and the gold beads shimmered as she walked. Florent remained silent as he just stared at her. The dress was a bit large for Althea, but she somehow made it look stunning.

"Oh, my," was Althea's reaction to seeing herself in the mirror.

"You look gorgeous. I want you to keep it."

"Florent, I can't just take things from you."

"Really, it's okay." They walked down the hallway to the grand stairway, and Florent took Althea to a part of the house she had never seen. She then went to grab her yellow dress, and Florent grabbed her hand to take her somewhere else.

Florent walked down another long hallway to two large wooden doors. He opened them, which led to an enormous ballroom. Everything was covered in dust, but that did not take away from the beauty. As in the rest of the house, three crystal chandeliers hung from the ceiling. Long, red velvet drapes hung from each tall window, which was closed, making the room dark. The wooden floors shimmered.

"My father used to have parties in this room, inviting almost everyone in town. This room hasn't seen a party since he passed away." A large phonograph was at the side of the room, which Florent went to and started to play a song. He danced to the music and sang the lyrics as he pulled the drapes back one by one. The sunshine throughout the room was almost blinding. Althea laughed at his performance. This was behavior she did not expect. Florent took Althea's hands, pulling her to the center of the room. It was just like he did in the field and sang along with the song. Althea was giving a profound smile. Florent then released Althea's hands, "Come on, flapper girl, let's see you dance."

"I'm embarrassed ... though I would love to show you my Charleston, if you don't mind."

"Let's see it."

Althea started to do her dance, and the tassels on the bottom of her dress swung with her every move. One foot went behind the other and turned every five seconds. Florent thought it was rather impressive. Althea then fell when she took a wrong step.

She started to laugh. "Why are we both so clumsy today?" Florent helped pick her up and leaned in to kiss her, but then the door opened.

"Mister Fayland, your mother has returned from her trip."

"But she wasn't supposed to be back for two more days."

"Well, she decided to return early."

Worried, Florent grabbed Althea's arm as fast as he could.

"What's going on?" Althea said, almost out of breath.

"My mother will lose her mind if she finds out you're here." She grabbed her dress, and Florent grabbed her hand, rushing to get out of the room.

Florent ran out the back door of the ballroom and turned every corner of the house very sharply. He had finally reached the carport where his car was parked. "Sit in here until I return."

"Okay."

Florent left Althea in the car by herself and ran to the front of the house to greet his mother. As he turned the corner, the chauffeur was helping her out of her car. She turned to Florent and smiled.

"Hello, dear, why are you so red?"

"I just went out for a stroll."

"In your good suit?"

"Yes. Why not? You taught me to always look presentable." Florent couldn't think of any other excuses. "If you don't mind, Mother, I need to drive into town to pick up some things."

"Well, okay, but don't take too long. Dinner should be ready soon."

"Yes, Mother."

He didn't know how many times he had said that in his lifetime; he was tired of living by his mother's rules. Fortunately, this time she didn't ask him as many questions about where he was going or what he was doing. Florent ran back to the carport and saw Althea was still sitting in the passenger seat. He got in and started the car immediately, then quickly pulled out of the carport.

"We have to keep this secret, don't we?" Althea asked sadly.

"No."

"Then why did you sneak me out and go crazy when your mother came home?"

"I'm going to tell her about us tonight, and it doesn't matter what her opinion about it is, because I can make my own choices. It just wasn't the time to tell her. She can be quite scary when she doesn't get her way. Now, where does the family you stay with live?"

"About twenty minutes out of town."

Althea gave him the directions the rest of the way, and they sat in silence for most of the trip. She pointed to a small, yellow house that was surrounded by farmland. Florent pulled into the rocky driveway to let her out. Before getting out, Althea gave Florent a quick peck on the cheek. Florent smiled and placed his hands on Althea's chin, pulling her closer, then kissed her. "Thanks for the ride," she said with gratitude.

"Of course."

Florent felt the tightness in his chest and the beating of his heart. He knew these were feelings of nervousness. He dreaded telling his mother about Althea, knowing it would go against her wishes. He knew that his love for Althea was more durable than his cowardice. He decided he would tell her over dinner, and his hands started to become sweaty. As soon as he drove down the long, dark driveway, he parked and entered his house. Florent played the conversation he would have with his mother over in his mind like a broken record. He entered the dining room, lit only with a few candles, where his mother sat at the far side of the table.

"Hello, dear, what did you get in town?"

Florent sat down in the chair opposite hers, and now his hands were positively damp with sweat.

"Mother, there is something I need to tell you."

"Are you all right? You look ill."

"I'm better than all right. I'm … I'm—" Florent struggled to get the words out as he watched his mother's concerned face. "I'm in love."

"What are you talking about?"

"I met a girl in town a few days ago, and she's the most beautiful person I have ever met.

Florent's mother stared at him. "Who's her family?"

"Well, she doesn't have one. She sold me the flowers that I brought home the other day."

"I demand you stop seeing her right away."

Florent stood up and walked toward his mother. "I'm sorry, but you're going to have to accept that I can make my own decisions."

Florent's mother stood up as well, meeting Florent eye to eye. "This family has rules, and you will not break them. You are the heir to the Fayland fortune and the heirlooms, meaning you must marry into a family of our quality."

"Just because she doesn't have money or a title does not make her any less of a person, Mother. That's your problem—you don't know what it's like to have nothing. You have been given everything since you were born and probably will until you die!"

"How dare you speak to me like that! I listened to your ridiculous future plans, and I accepted them, but you will not go through with this. I'll give you two options: stop seeing her or get out of my house!"

"Well, Mother, I guess this is goodbye."

Florent's mother was completely red in the face, and he knew she was furious. He had seen his mother fire help because her beef was a little undercooked or a speck of dust was left behind. He knew his time would come soon enough when he got tired of her orders. He couldn't believe that he had a pleasant conversation with her not so long ago. Florent stormed out of the room and slammed the grand doors to the dining room. He could taste the freedom just beyond his house; he could do anything and go anywhere he pleased. He ran up to his room, pulled out two large suitcases, and packed as many outfits as possible into their limited space. He went to the back of his closet and opened the secret vault where he had stashed all his allowance and birthday money and placed it into one of the suitcases. Florent headed to the entrance doors. As he looked back at the only place he had known as a home, he saw his mother standing at the dining room doors.

The thunder outside shook the walls of the house, and a flash of lightning spread across the sky. The rain was coming down hard, thoroughly soaking Florent's clothes. He quickly left and headed for his car. He threw his suitcases into the trunk and drove off that dark, long driveway for what he thought was the last time.

Florent came up to the little yellow house where he had dropped Althea off. He knocked on the white screen door, and a woman came to open it. "Can I help you?" the woman asked.

"I'm here to pick up Althea. Could you tell her to pack up her things?"

"Why don't you come inside. You're soaking wet." Florent stepped into the house, which was neat and put together. "Can I get you anything, tea or water, perhaps?"

"No, thank you."

The woman went up the small staircase located by the door. Florent sat on a sofa for half an hour. He looked at the photos placed on the wall of the family who lived there. Their children had happy faces in every photo. Florent knew one day he wanted that. Althea came down the stairs, back in her usual dress.

"Florent, what's going on?" she asked. She sat on the sofa next to him.

"Come away with me."

"What?"

"I told my mother about us, and as I suspected, she was not fond of the idea. She told me if I didn't obey her wishes, then I had to leave."

"Florent, you can't leave your mother and everything you know for me."

"This is my choice. For the first time in my life, I'm going to decide what *I* want. I love you, Althea, I want to spend the rest of my life with you."

Althea stared at Florent for a short time. "I want all those things too, but where are we going to go?"

"I have a decent amount of money, and I'm thinking about

selling my car. We will be able to live off those funds for a good amount of time before I can figure everything out."

Althea kissed Florent's cheek and went back up the stairs. Instantly she came back down with one small suitcase. Althea hugged the woman and thanked her for everything she had done for her.

Florent placed his suit jacket around her and gave her his shoes.

"Florent, you don't have to do that."

"Yes, I do. You'll freeze."

Florent opened the car door for Althea, and he got into the driver's side. "I know a small inn. We can stay for a few days, just outside Fathorne."

Florent drove for about thirty minutes before coming to an out-of-date building. He pulled into the small grass lot with only one other vehicle. Florent got out to open the door for Althea and got out all their luggage. They opened the door to a small lobby that smelled like must; dust covered all the furniture.

"I need a room for two nights, please."

The lady at the desk gave him a key for room 114 and gave him a very depressed-sounding, "Enjoy your stay."

They walked down a hallway to their room. The room was decent sized with a small bed. Old furniture filled the room, along with as much dust as the eye could see. Florent placed the luggage into an old armchair.

"I've never stayed in an inn before," Althea said as she walked around the room, soaking it all in.

"I have once, when my mother and I went to Cuba."

Althea threw herself on the bed. "This is wonderful!"

Florent found her enthusiasm for such small things as part of her charm. He personally thought the place was dingy, but it did make Althea happy, and that was all that mattered to him.

Florent exited the room, leaving Althea. He wanted to see where the dining room was so they could get breakfast in the morning and see what else this place had to offer. He felt an eerie feeling as the hair on his neck started to rise. He began to walk faster down the hallway when suddenly he ran into someone.

"My apologies," said a man. He was very tall and buff, and Florent found him intimidating. "Well, I'll be! You're Florent Fayland!"

Florent cleared his throat. "Yes, I am." He extended his arm and shook his hand.

"My name is Roger Merriam; I was a huge fan of your father's work. It's a shame what happened to him."

"Yes."

"Tell you what, I'm having a sort of a party at my home, and I would love it if you would come. You could be my guest of honor."

"That's okay; I don't want to intrude."

"No, of course not. It would be a real pleasure to have you there." The man was smiling at Florent until he gave him an answer, his large mustache curving upward.

"Okay, I'll come."

"Great!" he said with a big smile. He handed Florent an invitation from his coat pocket as if he was expecting him. It held all the details, including the address and time. Florent forgot about looking for the dining room. That man was genuinely nice, but there was something off-putting about him. Florent went back to the room and noticed that Althea had fallen asleep on the bed with his jacket still on. Florent went to close the curtains, and he noticed the man standing outside, looking in, smiling at him. His long, black coat was swaying in the wind, and the rain was pouring down on him. Florent closed the curtains and walked over to the bed. He looked at Althea and smiled; even sleeping, she was radiant. He pulled the blanket over her and got in on the other side, pulling the blanket over himself. He turned and put his arm around her while kissing the back of her head. Florent closed his eyes, but he felt Althea put her hand in his, and they were both fast asleep.

The next day, Florent woke up and saw the brightness coming through the curtains. He reached for Althea, but she wasn't there. He sat up quickly, looking around the room for her, when she swiftly walked through the door, carrying a bouquet in her hands.

"There is a beautiful field filled with wildflowers right next door." She placed the flowers in a glass sitting on the dresser in the corner of the room. "There, now it feels more like home." She got on the bed next to Florent, putting her head on his chest. He placed his arm around her, feeling her warmth.

"It's strange, isn't it?"

"What?" Florent asked.

"Just a week ago, I was just some lonely girl with no money, friends, or family. Now, here I am, in love with the most wonderful person I have ever met. I guess that just proves how your life can change in such a short time. I feel like I can't even blink or I might miss something."

Florent knew what she was talking about; not long ago, he was suffering in his room, just having his thoughts for company.

Althea got up and started to walk toward the bathroom when she noticed the invitation on Florent's bedside. "What's this?"

"Some strange man invited me to his house for a celebration. He knew my father, said he was a fan of his work, and wanted me to be his guest of honor. So, I guess I'm going. When did it say it was?"

"Tomorrow night."

"Althea, I hope you're planning on coming with me."

"No, I have nothing to wear, and I look like a mess."

"We'll go out today, and you can get what you need. We're going to make you the belle of the ball," Florent said, leaning over and kissing her hand.

Althea smiled. "I've never been the belle of anything."

They left later in the day to get Althea an outfit. As they were walking out of the inn, a man with a camera stopped them. "I'm taking photos today for only five cents. Would you like one?"

"Sure," answered Florent.

"Could we get in front of that field just over there?" Althea asked the man.

"Absolutely."

They walked over to the area to make wildflowers their background. The man snapped the photograph. "Here's my card with my office address; this should be ready for you in the next few days."

"Thank you," Florent said while giving the man a nickel.

Florent took Althea to a small clothing store in the middle of town. He had brought all the money he had collected, minus the money he had spent at the inn.

"My mother and I used to shop here to get my school outfits each year, and I believe they have a broad selection of party dresses."

The clerk came from behind the counter and bowed down to Florent as if he was a king. "Mr. Fayland, what can I help you with today?"

"May I see your party dresses, please?"

"Certainly."

Florent, holding Althea's hand, followed the clerk to the store's back end. Dresses made each aisle sparkle and look very colorful. Althea picked out the dresses she liked most and took them to the dressing room, as Florent sat on a sofa outside. Althea came out in a baby-pink dress with gold jewels and tassels that swung just above her knees. She had picked out some gold shoes with a small heel on the bottom. Florent looked at her and was mesmerized by how her figure fit perfectly into the dress.

"I think this is the one. Florent?"

Florent realized he had been distracted with her beauty. "Definitely."

Althea also picked out some gold earrings and makeup to match the outfits. Florent pulled out his cash and went to the counter, taking the items with him.

"Is this all for you, sir?" the clerk asked as Florent set the outfit on the counter.

"I believe so."

"That will be fifty dollars."

"Florent, you can't pay for these things. They're too expensive. I can find a cheaper outfit," Althea said, grabbing on to his arm.

"No, it's okay, you're worth every penny." Florent paid the clerk with cash and put the remaining money back into his jacket. He gave Althea the items and placed his hand on her back, leading her out the door.

The night of the party, as the sun was going down behind the mountains, Althea had been in the bathroom for nearly an hour, putting on her makeup. Florent sat on the bed, waiting for her and dreading having to go to this party. The man had seemed anxious for him to go; he felt he should, since he was an admirer of his father. This night could also be a way for Althea and him to have fun outside of a drab room. Althea came out in her new attire; she twinkled from head to toe. Florent was shocked when he looked at her hair. Half of it was gone. "I cut my hair; I hope it looks okay."

Her white-blonde hair was in a bob around her face with just a small amount of curl. She wore pink eyeshadow along with pink lipstick. Her rouge gave a pop of color to her face, and her eyebrows had been drawn to perfection.

"You look stunning." Florent kissed her cheek, not wanting to mess up her lipstick, and then took her hand. He looked in the mirror one last time, pushing his black hair out of his face and fixing his suit.

"You look very handsome," Althea said, causing Florent to smile.

"Are you ready?"

"Yes," she said excitedly.

They got into his car and drove to the address on the card. They pulled onto a road, which gradually went up a hill. On top of the hill was a white mansion. It featured four pillars in the front, and every light was shining from each window. A man came up to the car window and offered to park the car and opened the door for Althea. Florent gave the man the keys; then she grabbed on to Florent's arm. Together they walked up to the steps to the main entrance. As soon as the door was open, the sound of clinking glass, laughter, and music roared from the main lobby. There were people everywhere, catching up on each other's lives, dancing, and enjoying the ritzy atmosphere. Florent handed a man the invitation and led them into the ballroom, which was smaller than Florent's but just as elegant. Roger was talking to a couple dressed just as fancy as the room. "Please, excuse me." He walked toward Florent, extending to shake his hands. "It's truly a pleasure to have you here. And who is this lovely young lady?"

"This is Althea."

"You're a lucky man."

"Yes, I am."

Althea's cheeks turned red and smiled as she looked to the floor.

"Please help yourself to anything on the food table, and perhaps I could give you a tour here shortly."

"Sounds great," Florent answered.

They walked over to see the endless line of food from lobster tails to steak to chocolate cake. Florent grabbed a plate, then one for Althea. He placed some lobster tails on his plate and a couple of sides, whereas Althea just got some vegetables and fruit. They sat down at a round table by themselves and ate their meals. Roger got up on a platform in front of the room and grabbed a microphone from the band playing.

"I would like to thank all you folks for coming out tonight to celebrate my new home. We have a special guest with us tonight. Florent, can you stand up, please?"

Florent stood up, turning red and feeling very embarrassed. "Florent here is the son of the world-acclaimed surgeon, the late Horace Fayland." Everyone in the room cheered, but Florent did not know why; he wasn't his father. The band began to play again, and Roger left the stage and walked toward Florent. "May I give that tour we discussed?"

"Yeah, sure."

"I'll just stay here and finish my food," Althea told him.

"All right."

Roger led the way through the house, showing Florent all the spectacular rooms. They came upon a large room, which was dark and only had a few pieces of furniture. A chandelier hung from the ceiling, and the outside lights illuminated the inside from the window. Florent looked to one side of the room, where a painting of a young woman hung on the wall. She wore a purple dress with white pearls, and her long brown hair was neatly put up.

"Her name was Annette; she was my wife and my world. She was taken from me too soon. She suffered from heart problems."

"I'm very sorry to hear that."

Roger stared at the floor, looking like he was going to cry, "Shall we go to the next room?" he asked.

They walked down a narrow hallway to get to the next part of the house. They came upon a balcony that overlooked the ballroom where they could see the entire party right below them. "So, a man with your reputation and money must have big plans for his future."

"Well, everyone thinks I'm crazy, but I want to own an amusement park."

Roger lifted his eyebrows. "That's not crazy. The only crazy thing is not having a dream at all. Besides, the world could use a little more amusement."

Florent smiled. "That's for damn sure."

"That Althea is quite a girl, where did you meet?"

"She sold me flowers; she's a florist. I instantly fell in love with her from the first moment I saw her. I didn't even notice the flowers; all I saw was her. Somehow, she made the flowers look dull when she stood next to them. I constantly had dark thoughts that haunted me; I just didn't feel alive. But when I met her, all those thoughts were taken over by her. I haven't been this happy since I was a kid."

"That, my boy, is true love. Make sure you hold on to it and never let it go, because it's rare. It can be taken from you at any time. I could tell you two love each other by the way you look at each other; you see less and less of that these days."

Florent looked down at Althea and smiled and again felt the butterflies in his stomach.

"My mother kicked me out of the house when she found out about her. She cares too much about social status; she doesn't understand that I just want to be happy. I have a decent amount of money that I have saved over the years, and I plan on selling my car. It's just Althea and me now; she's the only family or friend I have in this world."

Roger just lifted an eyebrow and had a faint smile on his face. They walked back down to the ballroom, and Florent joined Althea at the table.

"How was the tour?" Althea asked.

"Fine."

The band on the stage began to play. Everyone immediately got out of their seats to head toward the front of the room to dance. Florent got up and extended his hand toward Althea. "May I have this dance?"

Althea took Florent's hand, and he pulled her up. "Yes, you may, Mr. Fayland."

They ran to the center of the floor and began to dance. They danced for nearly an hour to all the popular dance crazes, not caring what the others thought of them. They stumbled over each other and laughed each time at their ungainliness. Many people gave concerned looks at their behavior. Eventually, the band played a slow song for all the couples in the room. Florent looked into Althea's eyes, and they both stopped smiling and just stared at each other. Florent placed his hand on Althea's back and put the other hand in hers. They started to sway, and eventually, they blended with everyone else in the room, picking up the pace. Though there were many people around them, Florent felt the peacefulness and isolation he had felt in the field and his living room, except he didn't miss a single beat. Althea looked up at Florent.

"Florent, were we stupid to come here?"

"What do you mean?"

"I mean we just look so out of place. We're just kids among all these socialites."

"I don't care where we are, as long as I'm with you."

"I guess we're just two stupid kids in love."

Florent looked down at her and grinned. Althea returned a smile and placed her head on his chest. Everyone else in the room became a blur; it was just him and her. All the weight he had felt all these years suddenly lifted from his shoulders. She was there in his arms, captivating in her every movement. Florent remembered their conversation from earlier and realized how his life had changed so fast. Finally, the music stopped, and the celebration was over. Florent put his suit jacket around Althea's shoulders to keep her warm. As they were heading toward the door, Florent felt a hand grab his shoulder. He turned around quickly to see Roger, who bent down to whisper in Florent's ear.

"I think your idea for an amusement park is brilliant and could benefit our small town. I would like to meet with you to discuss business."'

"I told you I have no money."

"That's just it—I want to help you accomplish this. I could help you get started financially."

Florent looked at him, puzzled. Why did this man he just met want to help him with his childhood fantasy?

"Can we meet next Wednesday at five?"

"Yeah, sure." Florent knew his life was about to change once again.

Florent and Althea had made their way back to the inn. Florent pulled out the key with the hand that wasn't holding Althea's. He sat down on the bed and smiled; his life started to make sense after so long.

"What did Roger want?" Althea asked from the bathroom.

"He wants to talk to me about some future endeavors of mine. He told me he would help me out financially."

"What future endeavors?"

Florent realized he never once mentioned anything to Althea. "I guess I haven't told you; I want to open an amusement park."

Althea poked her head out of the bathroom and stepped out back in her yellow dress. "Florent, that's wonderful!"

"You think so?"

"Yes, absolutely!"

Florent looked up at her and smiled, then he pulled her onto the bed, and she fell backward. Althea landed on top of him, and she kissed him back. She stopped to push his hair out of his face. She got off the bed and went to the other side to get under the comforter. "Good night, my love."

"Good night, Florent."

Florent placed one last kiss on her forehead, and they were both asleep for another night.

Florent got up incredibly early the next morning, just before sunrise. He realized he was still in his suit from the night before. He got his jacket that Althea had left on a hook in the bathroom and walked out the door. What Florent was about to do sent mixed emotions though his head and most of all, he was quite nervous. He got into his car and started to drive. He couldn't help but smile, and his leg was shaking with anticipation. He drove to a small store just a few miles from the inn. His mother had bought jewelry here before, and she would sometimes bring him along. Strangely, they opened exceedingly early, around seven in the morning. Florent looked down at his watch, which read seven fifteen. He parked and walked toward the door.

"Mr. Fayland! What an honor. Is your mother wanting some of our new collection?" a woman behind the counter nearly yelled.

Florent swallowed hard and started to sweat. "Actually, I'm here to see what engagement rings you have."

The woman's mouth dropped open. "You plan on marrying? Is it Lottie McCoy? Your mother mentioned her and said she was from a very extravagant family."

"No, it's someone else."

"Well, whoever she is, she's truly fortunate. I'm surprised I haven't read anything in the paper."

"I haven't told anyone."

"Well, let me show you what we have."

Florent looked at every ring, but none of them seemed good enough for Althea. "Do you have anything else?"

"We do have one that we keep in the back; it's very classy. I'll get it for you." The woman came out with a red-velvet box. She opened it to reveal a unique piece. The ring had a gold band, and diamonds covered the entire ring. The center of the circle held an emerald that reflected into Florent's face.

"This is the one," Florent said.

"Excellent choice, Mr.Fayland! You must love this girl very much."

"More than anything."

He took his remaining money out to pay for the ring, leaving him with nothing, but he knew it was money well spent. Florent mulled over where he would propose. He had noticed on their first-night stay at the inn there was a gazebo just in the back. He would take Althea there and ask for her hand. On the ride back, he couldn't hold back his smile. Florent parked his car and entered the building to go to his room. He had the ring in his jacket pocket. As he walked down the hall, he heard music in the distance. The noise sounded like a violin; it was hauntingly beautiful. It got louder as Florent got closer to his room and realized it was coming from inside. He opened the door to Althea playing the violin on the bed, her back facing the wall. "Althea?" She jumped.

"Why didn't you tell me you played violin?"

"I'm not exceptionally good, so I don't like playing in front of people."

"Are you kidding me? That was beautiful."

Althea blushed. "It was hard to get my violin into my bag, but I knew I needed it. Playing releases tension and makes everything feel a little better. I woke up, and you were gone. I was afraid you had left me."

"Althea, I will never leave you; I promise. And I can prove it to you. Come with me; there's something I need to do."

Florent grabbed Althea's hand, and they walked out of the inn together. Florent led her to the gazebo in the back.

"What are we doing here?" The floral field was just behind her as she beamed with elegance.

Florent took both her hands in his. "I know we have only known each other for a short time, but this just feels right. Althea, you completely changed my perspective on life; before I met you, life was dull and senseless. When I first saw you, the sun shone for me once again, and the darkest parts of my mind filled with sunshine." Florent got down on one knee and pulled out the ring. "Althea, will you be my wife, spend the rest of your days with me, and most of all, will you be my forever sunshine?"

Althea looked down at him, looking extremely shocked. Florent started to get nervous at her reaction. A tear inched down her cheek, and she lit up in a smile. "Yes! Oh, Florent, I'm completely blown away!"

Florent stood up and placed the ring on her finger; then she kissed him, almost knocking Florent down. He knew it might have been too early, but if you genuinely love someone, what's holding you back? The sun was coming up from the mountains, and for once, the world seemed just a bit brighter.

Chapter 5

THE MEETING

November 1925

Wednesday evening had come quicker than Florent expected. He did not know if this man was to be trusted, but he may have been his only hope. He never received a time or location for this "meeting" that Roger had mentioned. Roger had only been kind, but Florent saw something strange about him. It made his hair curl thinking of that smile he had given the night they met; it was as though he held secrets behind his lifeless eyes. Florent went over to see Althea sitting at the vanity in their room, looking luminous as usual, wearing her engagement ring.

Their time here was almost up, and Florent had no more money. They had been living on the food they received at breakfast time; he needed help more than ever. He was startled by a knock on the door. Althea got up to answer it, but Florent jumped in front of her and pushed her behind him. He firmly held Althea's arm, making sure she was safe. He opened the door to two men in black suits and dark sunglasses, much like the attire Roger wore, but neither of them was him.

"Mr. Fayland, Mr. Merriam has called for your presence at his office."

"Yes. Can you give me just a minute?"

"Certainly."

Florent shut the door and walked toward the bed.

"Florent, are sure this is such a good idea? Doesn't it seem a little suspicious that he wants to help you so badly?"

"Maybe, but it may be my only chance to get a start on my dream. Besides, maybe he wants to help me because he was a fan of my father and feels sympathy for my loss."

Althea kissed him and took his hands. "All right, just be careful."

"I will, I promise." Florent opened the door, and the men got on either side of him, walking him down the hallway. A large, black car was parked on the street in front of the inn. One man got into the car, and the other held the door open for him, then got inside beside Florent. The two men were sitting on either side of him in the back seat. The man driving wore a black hat and all-black attire as well.

The ride was completely silent; no one said a word. Florent felt like he was one his way to be killed, but if Roger wanted him killed, why hadn't he already done it? Roger knew that he didn't have any money, so that couldn't be the reason to lead him to his death. There wasn't much time to think of his real intentions as they reached the destination.

The driver pulled into an empty lot to an old warehouse, which looked completely abandoned. There were no windows on the building, and there was one small door in the front. The man on the right of Florent got out and held the door open for him, and the other ran to get the door to the building. They led Florent to a small room in the obscure-looking building.

In the room, Roger sat in his all-black suit, smoking a cigar. The small room contained frames with newspaper articles. Florent finally realized what Roger did; he owned factories. The newspaper clippings showed his businesses' achievements throughout the years, but they looked fake, like someone pasted the articles together. His legs were crossed and up on the desk. He quickly responded to Florent's presence and got up.

He gave Florent a strong handshake. "Hello, my boy! How was the ride?"

"Very quiet."

Roger looked at the men. "We would like to be alone, please." The two men bowed and walked out the door in an orderly fashion.

"I appreciate the hospitality, but I could have come here myself, I don't want to be a bother."

"Nonsense. Anything new since we last talked?"

"I got engaged."

Roger's eyebrows lifted. "Really? Congratulations, that's wonderful!"

"Yes." Florent smiled.

"So, when's the wedding?"

"We haven't discussed it."

"I see. I think it's time to get down to business now. I will provide everything, including construction, funds, and all the stressful aspects of ownership."

"I appreciate you doing all this for me, but why are you?"

"I see something in you that I don't see in many people anymore."

"What's that exactly?"

"Ambition. I have always said a man with a head of stone, a heart of passion, and a stomach full of ambition is already halfway to success." Roger stood up and put his cigar out. "Tell me your plans for this grand amusement park you dream of."

Florent looked down, and he thought of everything that he had planned in his head since he was a child. It all started to come together in his mind. "I want a Ferris wheel with a magnificent view, a roller coaster that will be able to see over the tops of the mountains, games with the largest stuffed animals, and most of all I want the entire park to smell like cotton candy, coming from a large number of food stands."

"You have thought this through."

"Yes, ever since I was a child."

"Truly a remarkable vision."

Roger gave him paperwork that explained everything to the last detail, stating that he would take care of everything. Florent just needed to tell him how to do it.

"Well, I guess this concludes our meeting. It was nice talking to you."

"It was nice talking to you too," Florent replied.

"If I begin the work now, the park should be up and running in about two years," Roger said.

"Wow, that's very soon."

Roger shook Florent's hand, and Florent headed out the door.

"Oh, Florent, you told me you wanted to sell your car?"

"Yes."

"I can take it from you; I'll give you a great price on it too. It's a gorgeous piece of machinery."

"It is. I received it on my eighteenth birthday, so it's practically new."

"I'll give you thirteen thousand for it."

"I can't accept that much."

"No, that is my offer. It will allow you to pay for your wedding and get out of that dingy inn. And I will get an admirable car. I will pick it up tomorrow, and let me write you the check."

Roger went over to his desk and wrote the check and gave it to Florent.

"Thank you for everything. I appreciate this, and listen, when I get back on my feet, I'll find a way to pay you back."

"Nonsense! It's no problem at all."

Florent met up with the two men waiting outside the door like guards. They led him to the car and took him back to the inn, just as silently as before.

The black car pulled into the inn, and Florent got out, taking the paperwork with him. He felt optimistic about this plan with Roger, and he considered him to be a potential friend. When Florent got to his room, he described to Althea that Roger was going to provide all the work, and Florent just needed to tell him what to do.

"That's incredible. So, this is going to happen?" said Althea.

"Yeah, I guess so. Also, we are leaving this dump tomorrow. Roger bought my car and gave me a decent amount of money for it. He also said construction would begin soon. I will do some rough sketches of what I would like done."

Althea kissed Florent on the cheek.

"We can afford our wedding now; you may do whatever your heart desires," Florent said.

"I don't want a fancy wedding, Florent; it's just not who I am. But I do have one request."

"Anything."

"There's a small church on top of the mountains; it's where my family used to go." She walked to the window and stared out of it as she talked. "It has a gorgeous view; you can see God's creation for miles."

"That sounds perfect."

Althea turned around and gave Florent a shy smile.

For a whole month, Florent had not talked to Roger and didn't know how much progress he had put into his plan. Althea and Florent were looking for an affordable place to live during this time. They had almost given up until they found a small, one-bedroom house right in the middle of town. It sat between a department store and a drug store, and though it was in a odd location, it was a lovely place. They had put an offer on it but had not yet heard of their decision. Fortunately, with Florent's money he had gotten from Roger, they were able to stay at the inn for much longer than they had expected. Florent read the contract Roger had given him. It stated that Roger would be co-owner and take on responsibilities of any repairs or finances that needed attention. Florent signed the agreement; sharing ownership was not a problem since Roger was paying for everything to be done.

Florent had also reserved an evening at the church Althea had requested. Althea had bought a dress, but of course, Florent hadn't seen it, as she kept it hidden in the wardrobe in their room. The wedding was only a week away, and Florent felt nervous and excited. They didn't even have a guest list, but they thought of inviting Roger, since he was the only friend they had. Florent thought of his mother, but he knew it would be a waste of an invitation. She wouldn't dare come to see him marry someone she didn't approve of.

Florent watched Althea at the dresser taking out her hair accessories and putting on her gown.

"Althea, there is still something we haven't discussed."

"What's that, dear?"

"Where are we going to go on our honeymoon?"

"Florent, we don't need a honeymoon, just as long as I'm with you on our wedding night."

Florent thought for a while and remembered that his family used to go to Fathorne Lake just outside of town on his father's sailboat. He remembered how stunning it was, especially in the evening with the sunset in the background.

"What if I rented a houseboat, and we spent a night on the lake?"

"That would be fun!" Althea got up and sat on the bed next to Florent; then she kissed him.

Florent got a piece of paper. "I'm making an invitation for Roger if that's okay with you."

"Absolutely, he has changed our lives."

At that moment, there was a knock on the door. Florent went to open it, and one of Roger's workers was standing there with a piece of paper.

"Mr. Merriam would like to schedule a meeting on the twenty-second of December at two in the afternoon to discuss business. Does this time work for you, Mr. Fayland?"

"Uh, yes. Could you do me a favor and deliver this to him for me?" Florent handed the man a small envelope with their wedding invitation.

"Yes, that will be done."

Florent shut the door as the man walked down the hallway.

"It's strange how every time we mention him, they show up," said Althea.

"It does seem that way." These strange appearances only added to the creepy demeanor Florent thought Roger had.

Night came, and Florent started to feel fatigued. He felt this often from all the planning in his life. He could tell Althea had felt the same way as he noticed the dark circles under her eyes. He lay back with Althea under his arm, and he thought that everything in his life was finally starting to fall into place. Everything that he had once dreamed of was coming to him.

Florent opened his eyes and awoke in a dark room, not even realizing he had fallen asleep. Darkness entrapped him. He tried to move, but he couldn't; his arms had been tied behind him, and his legs were strapped down. He appeared to be bound with the kind of straps that would hold a mental patient. The dark-brown straps were so tight, they were cutting into his skin. The metal buckles were digging into him like knives. Florent was sweating, but the room was freezing. He heard footsteps coming toward him and whispers in his ears. He couldn't tell what they were saying, but it made him feel a wave of anger he had never felt before. A bright light lit up one small spot in the room and revealed a woman. It wasn't just a woman, it was Althea, and she was crying. Through the tears, she was singing a song, but Florent couldn't understand the lyrics.

A pink rose, which Florent thought she was just holding, was impelled into her hand. Her blood was dripping onto the ground on the rose petals that surrounded her. Florent felt rage fill his entire body; whoever did this to her was going to regret it. Florent struggled to get out to save her, but the straps got tighter.

"Althea!"

She turned toward Florent with a distressed look, then a silhouette of a person came from the shadows. Their entire body was a black mist, and it came toward him. Someone else came from behind and pulled on the straps, dragging Florent nearer to Althea.

Florent kicked, but it did no good; whoever was dragging him was much stronger. He was inches away from Althea; when he got closer, she extended her hand without the rose toward Florent. Her face was just an emotionless stare. He tried to break loose just to hold her hand and tell her everything was going to be okay, even if it was a lie.

"Florent," a small whisper said behind him. He turned to see his father standing there.

"Dad!" Florent started to sob.

His father started to approach him, but as he got closer, blood began to drench his father's clothes, and his brain was halfway outside of his head. He screamed in a fury of tears. He then turned to see a gun pointed at Althea's head. Florent tried to warn her, but nothing came out of his mouth. A gunshot vibrated off the walls, and Althea's blood covered Florent's face. Florent screamed and jolted up.

He looked around, and he was back in the inn. Althea was beside him, alarmed at his outburst.

"Florent, what's wrong?" She was breathing heavily and looked frightened. He pushed her down on the bed and put his hands around her neck. He threw himself off her as soon as reality started to settle within him. Florent couldn't come to his senses; he continued to take deep breaths and panic; he noticed his entire side of the bed was covered in sweat. Florent had a panic attack; he felt an uneasiness in his stomach and quickly ran to the bathroom. He vomited into the toilet and was finally able to calm down. The sweat remained all over his body, and he noticed Althea standing in the doorway looking terrified. Florent went back to sit on the bed. Althea sat beside him, placing her hand on his back. He tightly embraced her as his tears soaked her clothing.

"Florent, what is it?" Althea asked gently.

"It was a nightmare. "Im so sorry. Are you hurt?"

"No. I am startled more than anything. Dreams aren't real; they can't hurt you."

"No, but *I* could hurt you. My past haunts me still. My father was shot and killed in my own house. I can still hear the gunshots and my mother's screams. Sometimes, just hearing a small noise that sounds like a gun will send me into a panic attack. I have had these nightmares about my father before, but this one was different."

"How so?" Althea said as calmly as she could while stroking Florent's back.

"You were there this time. Althea, I will never let anyone hurt you, that I promise. If I lost you, I'd completely go mad."

"Florent, I'm not going anywhere. I'm not in any danger."

"I can't be so sure about that, not in a world that has taken everything else from me."

Althea wrapped Florent in another loving embrace. She wiped Florent's tears from his cheek while pushing his hair out of his face.

"No matter what happens, I'll always be there with you. Do you promise you'll always be with me wherever I'll be?"

"Of course," Florent replied.

"Then this world will never tear us apart." With a last kiss on Althea's cheek, they both went to sleep.

After waiting a short time, Althea and Florent received a call they had finally got the house. They packed all their belongings and made their way to a new chapter of their lives. They couldn't be happier. The walk was long from the inn, but they had finally made it to the front of their new house. The sidewalks were bustling with shoppers and workers in town, though no one seemed very lively. They walked down the busy sidewalks with all their luggage in their hands. Florent needed his privacy, but he adored the crowd, compared to being secluded in the mountains, where he had lived all his life. Florent took Althea's suitcase and violin.

"Stay here; there's something I want to do." He ran into the house, placing all their belongings down, and ran back out quickly. He swiftly picked Althea up off the ground, and she gave a small shriek along with a giggle. Florent carried her into the living room and set her feet down on the floor.

The house had a living room, kitchen, one bathroom, a short hallway, and a bedroom. It was everything they needed. It was smaller than Florent was used to, but he did not mind. There was some furniture that came with the house, all the things that would be necessary.

"Something is missing," said Althea. She pulled out a flower from her suitcase. "I had some flowers in our room; I thought I would bring them along." She took a mason jar that was sitting on the counter and placed it inside. "That's better."

Florent smiled at her, and that small flower made this place feel like a home.

The week leading up to the wedding was a blur. Florent became more anxious with each tick of the clock. He wanted everything to be perfect; he wanted Althea to have the greatest day of her life. He knew she would be the prettiest bride ever to walk down the aisle, and he was the luckiest groom. Florent received a letter from Roger that expressed his gratitude and his verification that he would be attending. Roger would also have to be their witness, for he was their only guest. Althea was getting ready in their bedroom, and Florent was in the bathroom. A taxi was going to pick up Florent and drive him to the church; then, a follow-up cab would pick up Althea just minutes after. Everything was going to plan so far. He took a deep breath to steady his breathing. He could hear his heartbeat inside his chest, which was very unsettling. He looked up in the mirror to see a young man full of hope. He pushed his black hair out of his face, revealing his hazel eyes. He put on some cologne, headed for the door, and stood outside, waving to a passing taxi. Fortunately, it stopped.

Florent got in the cab and started to twiddle his thumbs.

"You look familiar may I ask you name?" The driver asked.

"Florent. Florent Fayland."

"Florent Fayland, it's an honor to drive you. Where are you headed?"

"Could you take me to the church that sits in the mountains? I apologize I don't know the exact address."

"Actually, I know where you're talking about; I went there when I was growing up."

"You wouldn't happen to know Althea Angelos, would you?"

"I do! She was such a pretty little girl; she was about five years younger than me. She was very quiet, never said a word, but she was always so polite. She stopped coming when her mother died. It's such a shame that happened to her. How do you know her?"

Florent just looked down at the floor and smiled. "I'm madly in love with her. I'm marrying her this evening."

"That's exciting! Congratulations!"

They drove up the mountains, a lengthy and unnerving drive. They finally reached the church, which was just as elegant as Althea described. It was simple and made of gray brick, with vines growing on both sides. Florent walked inside where the pastor was standing in the front. The stained-glass windows shone into the small room, and the colors illuminated a purple glow throughout. Roger sat in the front row, where he nodded and smiled at Florent as he came in. Florent looked out the window and saw the entire town of Fathorne with the rolling valleys around it; he had never seen such a glorious view.

After a few minutes of waiting for Althea to arrive, Florent heard a taxi pull up. He ran to the front of the room on the platform, waiting for her. The door opened, and she was as charming as ever. She smiled at Florent and looked down while her cheeks turned a glowing red. The dress was made of white lace, and tassels hung at the bottom. She looked like a star twinkling in the midnight sky. She pulled down her veil, which went all the way to the ground to cover her face. In her hand, she held a bouquet of pink roses. The organist played when she started to walk down the aisle. Florent watched her come up to him, unable to hold back his smile.

At that moment, everything became a haze; all he could focus on was her. He pulled the veil off her face and let it fall behind her.

The sun was coming through the stained-glass window with an angel above them. The light bounced off Althea's rosy cheeks, and her face was beaming. He cleared his throat. "Althea, I know I have said this before, and I will say it for as long as we live. The darkness that I once lived through is gone; to be honest, I haven't felt myself smile since I was a kid. I thought there was no way I could be happy again, but you prove me wrong every day. You were right about needing that one person to be your light to see life just a bit more clearly. You are that person." Florent could see Althea's teary eyes under her makeup.

She took a deep breath in and said, "Florent, I haven't been my happy self since I was a child either. I don't know what to call it—fate, destiny, luck. All I know is there was a reason you came to my flower cart that day. Truthfully, I didn't even believe in love; I thought it was just some made-up word in fairytales. I didn't believe in happily-ever-afters. All that changed when I met you, though, because if there is ever a time where I don't believe in any of those things, I'll look at you, and I will be a believer once again."

After a good amount of time the ceremony began to come to a close. The pastor said his final words to complete the ceremony. "Do you, Florent Fayland, take Althea Angelos to be your wife?

"I do."

"Do you, Althea Angelos, take Florent Fayland as your husband?"

"I do."

He continued to say his last words, followed by, "You may now kiss the bride."

Florent dipped Althea and kissed her intensely. Roger clapped loudly and gave a genuine smile. Florent took Althea's hand, and they ran out of the church. The taxi that brought Althea was waiting to take them to the lake, where they would spend the night. As soon as they got in the cab, they embraced and kissed each other as hard as possible. The taxi driver, not as friendly as the one he had before, looked in the mirror at them with a disapproving look. They stopped but were laughing.

"I love you, Mrs. Fayland," Florent whispered.

Those words gave Althea a flutter in her chest. "I love you too."

The evening was coming to an end. The sun was going behind the mountains for another night when they reached the lake. They had just arrived in time to see the sunset that Florent remembered seeing as a child. Althea had her head on his shoulder and her hand in his. Florent saw the houseboat he had rented sitting on the dock, ready to be taken out for their next adventure. Florent paid the taxi driver and led Althea out of the cab.

"Oh, Florent, it's beautiful. This was a wonderful idea."

"Just wait until the stars come out."

Althea grinned, and they walked toward the boat. The helmsman greeted them on the dock and just gave them the rules and safety measures; then he went to drive the boat, disappearing for the rest of the night.

Florent and Althea pulled out some extra blankets from storage and put them on the deck area. The stars came out instantly just after their embarkation; they looked like glitter in the sky. No star in the sky compared to Althea's smile, Florent thought.

Althea looked out over the lake and saw the cranes standing in the shallow water. "They are so beautiful. Back at my father's farmhouse, he used to have cranes on a small lake on his property; I was always fascinated by them." They lay down on the blankets and held hands.

"My father used to know every constellation in the sky. He told me about every one of them with so much detail. I loved it when he talked about the things that he felt passionate about. He loved outer space and loved things that were pretty much unknown to man. Every day he was finding new ways to expand his knowledge by learning something unusual. His eyes would twinkle when he talked about the things that interested him." Florent smiled. "I used to have such an imagination, but it somehow faded away when I grew up."

"I don't believe that's true."

"What?"

"Your imagination cannot fade away; it's something that is part of you. I just think when we get older, our mind gets occupied by other things, and we have to take on adult responsibilities. When I was young, I believed that all the stars in the sky were people who have left this life. They are our loved ones that watch over us. I still do, somewhat. I think my parents are there watching me. I think they would be proud."

"I think my dad would be proud too, because I followed my heart my whole life. He was different from my mother; he didn't care about social class or living a luxurious life. He wanted to save people when all hope was lost, and he did that. He did what made him feel joyous. The only reason we have such an exquisite lifestyle is because that's what my mother wanted. He did everything that would make me and my mother happy. I just hope I can do that for you. I am trying to be the best person I can be."

"Florent, I told you, you have made me the happiest I have ever been in my life."

"I still don't think that's good enough for someone as wonderful as you." Florent looked into her eyes and kissed her until it was like a rhythm in a song, and he could hear the water gently being pushed on the sides of the boat by the wind, and the moon illuminated the sky.

Chapter 6

PAINTINGS OF A TIME FORGOTTEN

September 1996

I looked at the photograph, and it made me sad. Has this been the young couple I saw slowly dancing in the fog? Their clothes and physical characteristics very much suggested this. A million questions turned over in my mind, but the main question was, what had happened to them? These two happy people stuck by some tragedy were much more than I could bear. I placed the photo in my jacket pocket. I didn't want to take anything from this place, but it may be evidence of who once lived here. I looked around the room to try to find any more archives, but it was no use; there was nothing else in the room. I walked over to the closet to see if there was anything hidden in there. There were just basic things you would find in a closet—a large number of dresses and shoes that probably dated back to the fifties. I grabbed a wooden box that I thought may have something inside. I opened it to reveal a time capsule of old hair accessories and a hairbrush.

My luck changed when I found a heart-shaped locket, which had two pictures in it. I could tell it was a man, but his face wasn't scratched out. The man had a scar, which gave me a tight feeling in my chest. I threw the locket back into the box and put it back where I found it. I would return all these belongings as soon as I finished my research. I started to shut the closet doors until something caught my eye. I trembled when I realized what it was—the same olive-green suit that haunted me. The suit was tucked away and neatly put on a hanger; it looked like it was ready for someone to wear. I saw the green hat and gloves on the dresser beside the bed, which sent chills down my spine. I stood there in complete confusion and wondered if this man I always saw was connected to this house.

I turned around and noticed the bed was neatly put together and dust free, whereas the pink room was tidy, and the bed remained made, but it was covered in dust as if no one had touched anything in the room for years. Has someone been living here after all? I quickly shut the closet doors and ran out of the room. I was no longer going to stay here to find out if someone was here other than Asher and me. I ran into the hallway and searched for Asher.

"Asher!" I began to panic and sweat as I ran through the halls. The house was like a maze; there were as many hallways as there were doors. I heard footsteps getting closer and closer to me, so I started to run.

I ran into one room and shut the door, locking it. I turned around to find a room that was much different from the rest of the house; it was a library. The bookshelves reached to the ceiling, one placed on each wall. I started to walk and heard the crunch of dead plants underneath my feet. I looked up at the painted ceiling, just as it was in the house's main area. The sunlight gave it a natural glow through the broken window. The wind was blowing the long, red curtain in every direction. A large desk sat in the corner with a maroon leather chair and a green lamp. I saw papers on it, so I decided to investigate what they were. Maybe they would offer a clue of some kind. The papers were a burst of color from corner to corner. There were several types of paintings. One had a spring scene with a little girl on a swing facing a sunset. The back of the paper just read, "waiting." I wondered why the girl was waiting.

The paintings were beautiful and filled with many details; they almost looked like photographs. Another one that caught my eye was one of a woman with a beautiful face. It wasn't long before I realized she was the same woman I saw outside the window. She had soft brown eyes in the picture and strawberry-blonde hair, but it seemed more vibrant in the painting. The back read, "Sisterhood." There were four paintings on the desk. The other two were much darker in theme than the previous two. One had a man in a dark room, sitting on a chair, facing a broken carousel. The back said, "all is lost." Again I looked back at a familiar face in the last painting. It was in black-and-white paint. He was a young man; his scar went from the top of his forehead, down the side of his neck. The back said, "my brother." I heard footsteps getting louder and louder; I left the paintings on the desk and hid under it.

A voice outside said, "Kim?"

I got up quickly and opened the door. Asher was standing there, looking flushed in the face. "Asher, are you okay?"

"We need to leave now."

"Why?"

"We just do."

He grabbed my hand and started to run; we promptly took each corner, almost running into the walls and furniture that was scattered in the hallway. I didn't say anything; I honestly wanted to leave too, so I didn't question him. At least I had some evidence that could lead to something. We ran out of the house and looked back to see the blue, rotting exterior. I saw a man standing in the distance, his head down toward the ground. I forcefully inhaled deeply and let Asher lead the way. I almost tripped over the roots of the trees. I began to hear a violin playing and smelled something strange. It was the smell of rotting wood and burnt flesh. I eventually tripped on a root that stuck out of the ground.

I looked up to see a circle of people standing around me, and they started to get closer, where I could see them more clearly. Their burnt skin looked like it was melting from the bones. They started to grab me when suddenly I was awakened by Asher shaking me.

"Kimberly! Kim!"

"What happened?" I was sitting on the passenger side of his truck when I woke up.

"I'm not sure. We were running, and you just passed out and fell to the ground. You fell pretty hard; I hope you don't have a concussion."

"I think I'm fine."

"Are you sure about that?"

"Yeah."

"You look pale; maybe we should take you to the hospital."

"I'm fine. I just had a vision."

"A what?"

"They're not visions; they're, well I don't really know what they are. I see things that aren't there, but it's all in my head. I'm pretty sure."

Asher looked at me; I assumed he probably thought I was crazy.

"What did you see?"

I was surprised by his response, but I answered him. "It happened very fast, but I'll try to piece things together. I was lying on the ground, where I was surrounded by a group of people standing in a circle. I heard what sounded like a violin playing softly in the background. The people had burns down their bodies, and they all looked horrified. Then they started to come near me, and then you woke me up. The most common one I have, though, is a man in a green suit; he has strangely long black hair and a ..."

"A scar across his face"

I was taken by surprise when Asher finished my sentence. "You've seen him too?"

"I saw him standing outside the house. He wasn't wearing a green suit, though. His clothing looked almost too small for him.

He was wearing a sweater and black pants. He turned around and saw me, and that's when I ran. I didn't know who he was, and I didn't want to know, so I got the hell out of there." We didn't say anything after that. I put my seatbelt on as Asher got in the driver's seat.

Heading back to our apartment building, Asher finally decided to speak again. "Did you find any evidence while we were there?"

"Not really, just this picture." I pulled out the picture of the couple. "I've seen them before too, not at the park, but in a nearby field. I know it's them; it looks just like them, down to the very last feature."

"This picture looks like it's from years ago; that couldn't possibly be them. I know this sounds far-fetched, but what if you saw spirits of some kind?"

"That's not far-fetched; I thought the same thing. I need to figure out who these people are. Could you take me to the library?"

"Um, yeah, sure."

We pulled into the parking lot at the Fathorne Library. "I'm going to see if I can find any records or possibly some newspaper articles." Asher came with me into the library; inside was just one other person. It made me sad that no one came here much; the library was a large part of my childhood.

"Can I help you?" the librarian asked.

"I was wondering if I could find any records or possibly newspaper articles on Fayland Park and the Fayland family."

The librarian gave me a skeptical look. "Why?"

"I'm researching its history to write an article for the newspaper."

"All right." She got up and had a look of concern and even anger on her face. Why was everyone in this town so oblivious to that place? I know it's horrifying, but strangely, that's what draws me toward it.

She came back with two single newspaper articles that had been cut from the original newspaper. "Here you are," she said rudely and threw them toward me. I happened to glance at her name tag, and it read *Irina Welsh*. "If I were you, I would not be doing any type of investigation on that hell hole. I would also never go near that place. You'll see when you read these." Then she walked off in a fury.

I was confused as to why she was so mad until I read the articles. The first article dated back to 1960 and was about the fire. Two hundred fifty people were thought to have lost their lives that day. An unknown criminal started the fire and made it almost impossible for anyone to get out. It went on to say that the three Fayland children, Lawrence, Clementine, and Vincent, had all died in the fire. They weren't children at the time of the fire; they all had to be in their twenties or early thirties. Their pictures were all in a row, and they were very beautiful people. But I was struck by Vincent's picture. It was *him*, the man in green. He had that long scar that went all across his face and the blackest hair I had ever seen. He was the son of the owners; that was something I found very surprising.

Has my fascination with this mysterious place been for a reason, and is all this connected somehow? Was there an explanation as to why I always had visions of him? The article explained that the fire department came soon after, but it was too late. Some of the structures remained untouched, including some attractions and the Fayland residence. The pictures of the sections that burned down were tragic and were so unsettling, it made me want to cry. The other article was dated a little earlier the same month. It was about three teenage boys who had been murdered on the property. Their bodies were found by a family riding the water ride, what was left of them anyway. It described the bodies were cut so severely it was difficult to identify them. Their names were Jack Darcin, Bobby May, and Dean Welsh.

"Do you think Dean was related to the librarian?" Asher asked.

"It would explain why she was so angry at us for looking this up." I looked back, and she was back at the desk. I got up and walked toward her.

"Did you know Dean Welsh?"

She looked up with sad eyes and then looked back down. "He

was my son. My wonderful little boy who was taken from me when he was too young."

"I'm so sorry."

She kept looking at the floor as she talked to me. She took a deep breath. "They never did find his killer, but I have my theories. I believe it was the youngest Fayland boy. My son said he was always quiet, never said a word. He said he would see him walking by himself at night, always playing the violin, and had that nasty scar. I only saw him a few times when I went to pick up Dean from school and always thought he was rather odd. I saw the way he looked at Dean; it was always a glare of hate. I never understood why he hated him; my boy would never do anything to harm anyone. The entire Fayland family was strange, including Florent. He never left his house. The last time people saw him was before his wife died. I bet his son killed him too, and then he burned the place to the ground just for fun and then locked himself in that place so he would never have to face his crimes. He can burn in hell for all I care. That boy was trouble, and I should have him locked up in a mental institution before he could hurt anyone else. As for Clementine, his sister, she painted everything day to night; she too had a strange demeanor. I never liked her, and she would …"

"Wait, did you say she liked to paint?"

"Yes, why?"

"That small detail might help me in my research. Thank you, and I'm sorry about your loss."

"I appreciate that, but those are the only records you're going to find. Those newspaper articles are out of my own personal archive; all the other records got destroyed years ago."

I ran over to Asher and told him about the paintings; I knew who may have painted them. I had no one to ask. Everyone who was once affiliated with that park is gone.

"I feel like I'm at a dead end."

Chapter 7
THE MEMORY CHEST
April 1926

The sun was shining through the windows as the birds were singing a sweet melody just outside. Florent had just woken up and turned over to place his arm around Althea, but she wasn't there. He smelled something sweet from the kitchen and ran his hand through his hair and got out of bed. He placed his matching slippers on. The morning was young, and Florent was still half asleep. He had spent weeks, day in and day out, on the construction site of his amusement park, which was being built at a fast pace. He purchased a decent parcel of land to begin the construction. The land was very close to his mother's home; he even recognized some of the property and woods surrounding the area. He had gotten his license to be able to operate the park, meaning everything was a go.

Florent walked into the kitchen to Althea cooking. Althea pushed her blonde curls out of her face, growing back from when she cut it into a bob. They had been married for five months, but every morning, he wondered how he got so fortunate.

She wore her pink satin nightgown, which twirled with every movement. She looked frazzled, like she had been up a long time and working extra hard.

"Good morning, angel."

She turned quickly toward Florent as she was mixing the batter in a bowl, almost splattering it on herself. "Good morning, Florent!"

"What's all this for?"

"Well, I know you have a big day today, so I thought you might need extra fuel to keep you going. I made pancakes, eggs, bacon, oatmeal, biscuits, and freshly squeezed orange juice."

"You didn't have to go to this much trouble, even though you know I love your cooking very much."

"It was no trouble at all! Besides, I wasn't feeling well this morning, so I stayed up and started breakfast."

"Are you okay?"

"Yes, I'm fine."

"Are you sure?"

"Yes." She seemed distracted about something and didn't seem fine. She had batter on her cheek, so Florent grabbed a towel and wiped it off.

"Oh, thanks." Althea said with a blush. Florent kissed her as she leaned back on the counter. She let out a small sigh.

"All right, if we don't stop, you're going to be late. Now get to eating, mister."

Florent smiled and sat down at the table. "Yes, ma'am."

"Sorry, I didn't mean to sound bossy. I just want this to be a perfect day for you."

Florent put a piece of pancake in his mouth. "It's pretty perfect so far."

Althea sat down with a bowl of oatmeal and bacon. She looked timid and didn't even look up to make eye contact with Florent.

"Althea?"

"Yes?"

"Nothing, it's just you seem to have something on your mind.

I can tell it's troubling you. You know you can tell me anything." Florent reached across the table and grabbed her hand.

"It's nothing, really."

Florent decided to stop asking her, and he didn't want to annoy her or make the situation worse.

He had eaten everything on the plate, even though he felt extremely bloated and couldn't possibly eat another bite.

"That was amazing. Thank you, sweetie."

Althea smiled as Florent bent down and kissed her on the cheek. "Well, I guess I'll be on my way. I love you."

"I love you too."

"Are you sure you don't want to come with me? I mean, this amusement park is yours too."

"No, I have errands I need to get done."

"Okay, goodbye, dear"

"Bye."

Florent put on his jacket and hat, then headed out the door. He motioned a taxi to pick him up. He got in the cab and told the driver the address.

Florent sat anxiously, and he noticed he was shaking his leg and breathing hard. Today was the day he was to go around and make final decisions along with last-minute tweaking, including choosing an opening date. He couldn't believe how fast the construction had gone. He knew Roger had his workers constantly working on his project. To this day, Florent still didn't know why Roger had done everything for him; perhaps he wanted this town to have more ostentatious features; it was a very dull place.

Florent visited the park once a week to check on the progress and share his ideas with Roger, but now it was completely done. Florent's imagination was now built into a material world. The other part of his mind was on Althea; she was acting very strange. He was concerned about her health and mental state. He hoped that spending time away was not affecting her.

Florent looked up, and he saw the white arch, the entrance to his accomplishment. "Thank you." He paid the driver and got out.

Roger was standing at the entrance, waving to him. "Hello, my boy! Are you ready to see your dream become a reality?"

"More ready than I've ever been."

"Well, great, let's get started on the tour, shall we?"

The white arch sat like a blank canvas; Florent saw many possibilities on that white wood. "We need to have something catchy for the entrance. Any ideas?" Roger asked.

"Well, I was thinking of big red letters that say Fayland Park."

"I love it!"

"Are you sure you don't want your name in the park's title? I mean, you did pretty much all the work."

"No, now I told you I wanted this project done, and I would help, but this is all yours." They started to walk down the long road that led to the ticket booth; it reminded him of his driveway at his old house. The trees on each side of them gave Florent chills, but at the same time, the scenery was lovely. "How's your wife?"

"She's good. Well, at least I think. She told me she wasn't feeling well this morning, and she won't tell me why. It has me very worried; I'm guessing she's just concerned about me and making sure everything with the park goes right."

"I hope she feels better soon."

"Thanks, me too."

A fountain, much like the one at his old home, sat in the center of the park. Florent hoped people would throw their pennies in it and make wishes. They approached the Ferris wheel, which had wooden carts with white paint. Florent looked at the top and had a memory of his father. He remembered getting stuck at the top to let people get on. He always got scared, but his father would remind him to look ahead of him to see the world that lay in front of his eyes. He did feel like he could see past the horizon, as if he could almost touch it.

Then they went over to the boat ride that went around in a simple circle though the woods. Florent remembered Althea mentioning how much she loved the cranes on the lake. Florent went up to the loading dock where the boats were lined in a row, ready for opening day. He went up to one of the crane boats and grazed his hands over the lettering. The name Althea was on the chest of the bird-shaped boat. He couldn't wait to give her a tour of the park and surprise her with the little details he had dedicated just to her. He then went over to the carousel, which had paintings of European cities on the inside, just like he remembered when he was a child. Pictures of Venice, Paris, Rome, London, Stockholm, and many more would go in a whimsical circle. He could hear the children's laughter and see their smiles when they held on to one of the gorgeously painted horses. Pink roses were painted all around the top of the carousel, which gave it an incomparable beauty.

Florent went to his most thrilling attraction, the wooden roller coaster, "The Wallop." It stretched through the woods and wound back and forth. Florent had always been too scared to ride on one, but his life had been about taking chances lately, so what's one more going to hurt, he thought. Lastly, he looked over the swing ride and the funhouse, which were the last of the attractions.

"Everything looks absolutely perfect, just what I was imagining." A tear started to roll down Florent's cheek.

Roger placed his hand on Florent's shoulder. "Everything all right?"

"It's just that it's weird when you see something you always imagined as a kid become real. I just can't believe this is happening."

"It's very much real, and it's all yours."

Florent heard footsteps and saw someone coming toward him in the distance. "Althea! You came!"

"I couldn't stay away. Do you mind if I have a tour?"

"No, I can show you everything right now."

"I'll leave you two alone. Here is the key to the front gates." Roger handed him the key and walked down the long road that led to the arch. Florent grabbed Althea's hand and started to walk toward the center of the park.

"Everything's ready to go; I was thinking we have the grand opening just two weeks from today."

"That sounds perfect."

"There's something I want to show you." Florent led Althea up the steps to the boat ride. "Notice anything on the boat?"

"It says my name! You remembered the night on the lake; I love it. I already know this is going to be my favorite part." After looking at the crane boats, they went over to the carousel. "This is gorgeous," Althea said. Florent took her hand and lifted her onto the carousel. They sat in the seat that looked like a coach from a fairytale. "All of this is unquestionably marvelous, Florent. It really goes to show how brilliant your imagination is; I think that's one of my favorite things about you."

Florent took her hands and kissed her passionately, and she returned it just as heavily, then pulled away.

"What's wrong?" Florent asked.

"Florent, there's something I need to tell you, and it's killing me the longer I put it off. I just don't want you to worry about anything, since you're so busy with this and I …"

Florent started to panic. "What is it? Are you sick? Are you in danger?"

Althea put her finger on Florent's mouth and smiled. "No, everything is fine."

"Then what is it?"

A moment of silence fell between them before Althea could finally get it out. "Well, I'm pregnant," she said as she let out a breath of air to release her nerves.

Florent released her hands slowly and looked to the floor in shock. "Oh … I … um."

"Florent?"

Althea began to worry as he just sat there completely mute. Then he turned toward her and hugged her, almost pushing her out of the cart.

"I'm just so happy; I don't know what to say. I mean, I couldn't be any more cheerful. We're going to have a child, a little person half me and half you. What else could I ask for?" He stumbled on his words and began to sweat.

"I'm thrilled too, but I'm scared, Florent."

"Of what?"

"I'm afraid I won't be a good enough mother."

"Althea, what are you talking about?"

"I couldn't even take care of my father, at least not well enough. If I just was a better caretaker, he would still be alive."

"That's not true; his time here had ended. There's nothing you could have done to prevent that."

"I know. I just felt I could have done better, that's all."

"You were only thirteen when you took on that responsibility. That's remarkably difficult. Besides, this time, you're not going to go through this alone. I'm here, forever and always, remember?" Althea had tears running down her cheeks as she nodded. She placed her hand and head on Florent's chest as he placed his arm around her. "I'm scared too, but we'll figure this out together, just like everything else we have encountered." Florent looked out and saw the moon glowing in the sky and the stars twinkling from every angle. It reminded him of the night when they were on the lake, just the two of them without a concern in the world. He remembered how stunning Althea looked in her wedding dress.

"Florent?"

"Yes?"

"You know what's missing?"

"What?"

"This place could use some more flowers. I can take care of that."

They sat and calmed themselves about what was to happen next in their lives. After they were finished, Florent gave Althea a tour of the rest of the park, but the sun started to fall behind the mountains, so he decided it was time to go back home. He couldn't believe he had spent all day here; the time seemed so short. Florent smiled and took her hand and headed toward the exit. He looked back at his dream once more before he left. The amusement park was small and simple, but it was his, and that was the best feeling he could ever ask for. He had created this little world out of his mind, and it was a beautiful sight. Florent then looked down at Althea and grinned. She looked back, returning the smile and hugged his arm tightly.

He glanced over to his right and could see a figure; it looked like a silhouette of a person, dressed in all black, staring at him. Suddenly, it turned the other direction and walked further into the darkness.

"What is it?" Althea asked.

"Nothing." Florent took Althea's hand, grabbing it tighter, and walking faster. He locked the gate and checked to make sure it was tightly locked. When they reached the road, they got into a taxi and were taken back to their house.

Florent awoke when a drop of water hit him in the face. He shot up and looked up at the ceiling. It was leaking, and a water spot was forming. He noticed Althea had already gotten up, and her side of the bed was completely soaked from the leakage. He walked to the living room, where Althea was knitting something white. "Good morning."

"Good morning!"

"What are you making?"

"A blanket for the baby. My mother taught me how to knit when I was very young, but I'm not exactly exceptional. I thought it would be worth a try. It's turning out better than I expected. Breakfast is on the table."

"Thank you." Florent was still in shock about the news. He didn't worry about Althea being a good mother; he knew she would be excellent. He did worry about himself, though. The only thing Florent knew to do was follow his father's ways. His father had patience and was always there for his family. He could never compare to his father, but he would try his best.

Florent devoured his breakfast, scarfing down the oatmeal and orange juice Althea had made. After putting his dishes in the sink, he joined Althea in the living room. "We need a better place," he said.

"What are you talking about? This place is perfect. We have made this house into a home."

"It's not what you deserve."

"Florent, I love it here. We have everything we need and, that is much more than I have ever had."

"I would like a place where I can sleep without waking up in a puddle of water."

"We could just get that fixed."

"Not only that. Where are we going to put the baby? It can't sleep with us forever."

"Florent, like you said, we'll figure this out. Don't worry about it."

Florent didn't say anything for about a minute until an idea came to his mind. "What if we lived at the amusement park?"

"What?"

"We could build a house right on the property. We could have everything we want in it."

"That will cost a lot of money; we just don't have it."

"Yes, but someday we may." Florent grabbed Althea's hand. "I promise to give you the life you deserve; you can count on that."

"I'm happy with what I have now; you have given me so much happiness. I don't think you understand that." Althea continued to knit the blanket. Florent put his robe over his pajamas to go to the mailbox. He walked out into the chilly air as the birds chirped outside. There was a single letter in the mailbox.

"What did we get?"

"Just this letter. I haven't looked it over." Florent was shocked to see his old address on top of the letter. "This is my mother's address." The front read, "To Florent Fayland." but it was not in his mother's handwriting.

"Who do you think it's from?" Althea asked.

"I don't know." Florent opened the letter, written in the same script as the envelope. He read the letter out loud to Althea. "Dear Mr. Fayland, This is your former butler, Steven Pierce; I hope I have the right address, and this letter finds you well. I found your new address in the local phone book. I wanted to inform you that your mother has not been doing well. Lately, she has seemed to have caught some sort of sickness. Her doctor is in the house several times a week, but he says that he doesn't know what she has. But he did say she's not contagious. She told me that she didn't want anyone to know, not even you. Your mother has been this way for as long as I have known her. She wants to appear strong, even in her weakest moments. I know she wouldn't want me to tell you this, but I think you should know before it's too late. Best wishes, Steven."

"You have to go see her right away."

"No, she wanted me gone, and that's where I'm going to stay."

"Florent, you have to go see her. She's your mother."

"No."

"Yes."

Florent started to walk back to the bedroom, but Althea jumped in front of him. "Althea, will you please let me through?" She wouldn't move, no matter which way Florent tried to escape her. "I'm not going, and that is my decision. Why would I want to visit the person who has disapproved of everything I have ever done?" Florent finally pushed past Althea.

"Florent, listen to me!"

Florent went to their bedroom and slammed the door, then sat on his damp bed. He placed his head in his hands and started to cry. He didn't even know why. Maybe he was worried about his mother, or perhaps he couldn't take all this pressure anymore. Althea calmly opened the door, peeking her head inside. Florent looked up, his face red and covered in tears.

"I would like to be alone, please."

"I just think that you better see her before you can never see her again; this sounds serious."

"Why?"

"You don't get it, do you?"

"Get what?"

"What it's like to have no family! I know you lost your father, but what if you lost both of your parents? Every day I wish I would have hugged my mother more and not had the stupid fights we would always have. How many times I wish I could have told my father I loved him. You can still do that with your mother; please see her. I know you feel that way about your father. Don't do the same with your mother while she is still here. You'll live in regret forever if you don't."

Florent stared at the floor and then finally got up. "I'm sorry for all this childish behavior." He hugged Althea and kissed her forehead. "I'll get dressed and head over as soon as possible. Could you please come with me?"

"Yes, definitely."

"I don't care if my mother wants you there or not. You are my wife. She's going to have to accept what I have chosen. For once in my life."

Florent held on to Althea's hand on the ride over to his childhood home. He was nervous; he didn't even know why. He couldn't control his feelings anymore. He found himself angry when there was no reason to be and scared when there was nothing to fear. He cried for unknown reasons. He and his mother had never really been close; the closest they had been was the night his mother had come to his room and comforted him. It just seemed that everyone he cared about was taken from him; the thought of this made him squeeze Althea's hand tighter.

"Are you okay?"

"Yes, I'm just nervous and worried about my mother." Althea hugged his arm. The taxi stopped in front of two black cast-iron gates. They were closed and locked for the night. The fog was halfway up the poles, almost hiding the estate from view. Florent had kept the key, just in case he ever did come back to his old house.

He got out of the car and unlocked the gates. After he got back in, the taxi driver headed slowly down the obscure driveway because of the intense fog. Florent started to breathe heavily and could feel the sweat dripping down his forehead. He was once again going down the path he had always hated.

They finally reached his house, and the sun was shining dimly over the mountains. The lampposts in front of the house were still on. The entire scene looked like a London morning. Stephen, the butler who had written to him, came outside. Florent assumed he must have seen him arrive.

"Mister Fayland, you came."

"Please, you don't have to call me that. Just call me Florent."

"As you wish." He noticed Althea get out of the car. "And how may I address this young woman?"

"Althea."

"My pleasure, Althea." He gave her a bow. Florent took Althea's hand and led her up the giant steps that led to the main entrance. He opened the door for Althea and led her inside. The house had an unsettling silence and seemed colder than usual. The entire house was dark; all the lights were turned off. Florent and Althea went up the large staircase that led to the second floor to his mother's room. Her door was shut, which was odd, and an unpleasantness filled the air. Althea sat on a love seat in the hallway and kissed Florent on the cheek. Florent slowly opened the door to a disturbing, dark room. He saw his mother lying in her massive bed. The gray comforter matching a canopy that hung above her.

"Mom?"

She coughed and tried to sit up. "Florent?" she said in a gravelly voice that sounded nothing like her own.

When he got closer, he could see how dreadful she really was. Her skin was as white as frost, and her hair looked like black spiderwebs just hanging off her scalp. Florent's shoulders slumped down, and a tear returned to his eye. She had always been so beautiful. To see her in this condition was more than Florent could bear. His mother held out her hand to motion him to come toward her. Her cheeks were hollowed, and dark circles formed underneath her eyes. Florent pulled a chair next to her bed so they could be at eye level. A tear was coming from his mother's eyes, just the same as his. She placed her hand on his cheek.

"I'm so sorry."

"For what, Mother?"

"For everything. I always had that image, an expectation of who you should be. I never stopped to realize all that is out of my control. You grew up to be such a handsome, brilliant young man. You were right about me, down to the last detail; I care too much about society's pressures. My whole life, people told me who I should be and what I should do; I was shaped by society. I grew up to society's standards, not my own. I never got to know who I truly was because everyone decided it for me. It's a shame that I just realized this on my deathbed. I was a fool for trying to do the same for you. Florent, you're wiser than I was. You always tried your best to do the opposite of what everyone wanted you to be. All my life, I never was brave enough to, well, to be myself and embrace who I was inside. By trying to have all the finer things in life. I lost sight of what was actually important, the people I loved. All the material things in the world can't replace the ones you love, no matter how much you try. I tried to replace your father with golden trinkets and diamond necklaces. What a fool I was. All my selfishness is how I lost you. Now my end is near, and I never had the chance to have any independence."

"Mother, don't talk that way. You still have so much life in you."

"Florent, you and I both know that's not true, I'm sorry to say. I don't really know how much time I have left, but I know it's not long."

Florent's tears fell, drop after drop, on his cheeks. "Mother, you don't have to be sorry for anything; just be at peace. I want you to rest."

"This girl you spoke of, are you still seeing her?"

"Yes, actually um … we're married."

She hesitated but gave a genuine smile. "Oh, congratulations. I'm very proud of you."

Florent couldn't believe he heard those words out of his mother's mouth. "She's here with me if you would like to meet her."

"Yes, that would be fine." Her voice was becoming weaker after each word she said.

Florent went out to get Althea from the hallway. "My mother would like to meet you."

Althea was taken by surprise. "Oh, um, okay."

Florent put his arm around her and led her into the room. Althea seemed nervous, but she always was shy when meeting someone new.

"Oh, Florent, she's gorgeous. How could I be so stubborn?" said his mother. She began to cough and coughed up blood onto a tissue that was on her lap.

Florent and Althea looked at each other with concerned faces. He took his mother's hand, which was icy to the touch. "We have some exciting news."

"What's that, dear?"

"We're expecting a child; you're going to be a grandmother."

Althea placed her hand on her stomach and smiled. His mother returned a smile.

"I hope I can see the day where I can hold my grandbaby. I can't believe all this is already happening. You two will make extraordinary parents, but you're still so young. Florent, you're not even nineteen yet."

"Yes, I know, but I couldn't be happier. We're going to be just fine." The more he said that, the more confident he became. His mother started to cough again, this time producing even more blood. "Well, I guess we better leave and let you rest. Is there anything else we can do for you?"

"This may sound fatuous, but could you read me that book over there?" She pointed to a book that was sitting on her vanity that had a very worn red cover.

"Of course." Florent sat back in the chair beside her bed. Althea went and sat on the vanity stool. The book had no title or author on the cover. Florent opened the book. *Clara* was written on the very first page in what looked like a child's handwriting. Clara was his mother's name; he assumed this was her book as a child. Florent opened it up and realized it was a book of short stories, tall tales, and fairytales. All his life, he never knew that his mother liked these kinds of stories. Maybe his mother and he had been more alike than he thought. He read three stories, which took about an hour before she fell asleep. Florent smiled as he shut the book and placed it on her nightstand. He took Althea's hand, and they walked out of the room together. Florent shut the door very gently so he would not wake his mother. "I thought we should stay here until my mother gets better."

"Absolutely. You need to be with her as long as possible."

"We can stay in my old bedroom for the time being."

Florent and Althea went to his bedroom and sat down on the bed. They remained in quiet for about twenty minutes. "My mother is only thirty-eight years old. How can this be happening? She still has so much to see."

"There is no answer to that question, but sometimes loved ones are taken too soon. Just like you said about my parents."

"I guess so. It just makes me feel that life may not be as long as I always thought. It can just end at any given second."

Althea put her hand on his shoulder. "That's why we must live in the moment; every day is a new chance and a new opportunity. If we regret the past and worry about the future, we miss what is most important, the present. One day, this will be the past, so we need to make what we have of it now, so we can look back and be happy with how we spent our time."

Florent turned around and kissed Althea then lifted her chin with his hand. "You always know what to say." He kissed her again and then kissed her stomach. "Have you thought of any names yet?" Florent asked, trying to get his mind off the negative thoughts.

"I was thinking if it's a boy, we name him Lawrence. It was my father's name."

"Of course. What if it's a girl?"

"I haven't picked one out yet."

"We still have plenty of time." Florent hugged her waist and put his head on her stomach. "Althea, you make all this pain go away." He squeezed her tight and tried his hardest to conceal his feelings. The tears still escaped.

Althea ran her hand through his hair. Florent stayed wrapped around her until the tears dried. It was painful to see her husband in so much agony.

The remainder of the day seemed to drag, but the sun at last started to fall behind the mountains surrounding the house. "Well, I guess I should begin getting ready for bed."

"Yes." Florent went to his closet to see if he had any sleepwear that he had left behind; he couldn't sleep in the suit he was wearing. He went over to the closet and turned on the light that hung over his head. He went to grab some folded pajamas that were on a shelf, and a box fell on the ground. The dusty box had a unique design; it almost looked like a small chest. *Florent* was written on the side. It was in a child's handwriting that looked so much like his mother's. The thought of this made him grin. He picked up the box and carried it back to his bed.

"What's that?" Althea asked.

"It's just a chest that I used to put my old stuff in." Florent changed into his pajamas and then went over to open the box. Fortunately, it was unlocked, because he hadn't seen the key in years. He opened the chest to reveal a massive number of papers. They were all drawings Florent had made. Althea picked one up.

"This is amazing, Florent! You were really an artist! How old were you when you drew these?"

"Probably around five to nine."

"These are very advanced for a child." Half the drawings were of himself standing in an amusement park in a green suit.

"I guess I've had this amusement park dream for quite some time now."

"Florent's park of wonders?"

"That's what I always called this imaginary place in my head." The title was on top of every drawing. Florent looked at these, and it made him light up from inside. He always pictured this place as a kid, now it was built just a few miles from his childhood home. And, greatest of all, he owned it. "*Wonder* is a word that you use to describe something unexpected, unbelievable, and beautiful, but most of all, it's a feeling you get. I guess that's why I called it that because that's how I felt when I drew this. When my dad died, my dream was the only thing that kept my mind off his death. It's a place that's filled with all those things, where you have to see it to believe it. Most of all, though, when you walk through the gates, reality doesn't exist, only fantasy. Fayland Park is very similar to these drawings. Granted there are no flying elephants, talking dogs, or floating automobiles, but the actual park is very close."

"That's a very fitting name; I can see you were just as intelligent and imaginative as a child."

"I guess."

Florent smiled and kissed Althea. "Good night, my love."

"Good night, dear."

Florent picked up all the drawings and put them in a drawer. He saw another paper hidden in the corner lid on top of the chest. He pulled it out to reveal much darker-themed drawings. The top one was still a drawing of him, but he was standing in the woods. Behind him was a silhouette of man. Florent didn't even remember drawing this. He looked at the picture behind it, which was his father, covered in blood. Florent shoved the papers back into the chest and shut it as quickly as he could. He turned around and noticed that Althea had already fallen asleep. She was breathing lightly, and he noticed her stomach, which was a small bump. Althea was right; it was time to start living in the moment. He was done being haunted by the demons of his past. Althea was his present, and their child was their future. He had always wished he could have kept that optimistic disposition.

Florent tried to sleep, but he couldn't get his mind to rest. He decided to get up and check on his mother. He walked down the dark hallway that led to her door. He went inside, and to his surprise, she was awake too. "Florent, is that you?"

"Yes, I just came to check on you. I couldn't sleep."

"Me either. While we're both awake, could you read me more of my book?"

"Sure." Florent picked up the worn, red book off her nightstand. Again, he read more short stories until his mother interrupted him.

"This book was my favorite as a child. Every time I read it, I imagined I was in the fantasy world in the stories; it was an escape from real life. Florent, you may have gotten your ambition and integrity from your father, but you did get something from me."

"What's that, Mother?"

"Your imagination," Florent looked down at the book, flipping to the first page, where he saw his mother's name. It looked just like his name in his chest of drawings. He already knew he had inherited his mother's imagination from opening the book the first time.

"I guess I did."

"Never let this world take it from you, okay?" Florent nodded and smiled.

"I want you to give my book to your child and read it to them often."

"Of course."

"You know, Florent, I'm actually not scared to die."

Florent took his mother's cold hands and soon fell asleep in the chair next to her bed.

Florent's mother didn't make it to the morning. He awoke to her breathless body, but she seemed to have passed calmly. He couldn't hold back his tears at his mother's death, but it brought him comfort knowing that they had made peace before she was gone, and he learned that they weren't so different after all. The funeral was attended by just Althea and him, along with their house's staff. It was a cloudy day, making the world look colorless. Althea held on to Florent's arm as he watched his mother's black, wooden casket be put into the ground. She was buried next to his father, inside the grand cemetery placed in the mountaintops specifically for his family. Althea placed black roses around her grave. To Althea, black roses meant new beginnings.

Florent felt the hot tears rolling down his cheeks. It was a quiet ride back to his mother's house, where they would collect her belongings and decide what should be kept and given away. He kept his mother's book inside his jacket during the funeral and was still carrying it with him. Althea was sitting beside Florent in the back seat of the taxi, still holding on to his arm. "Thank you."

"For what?" Althea asked.

"For encouraging me to reconcile with my mother. You were right; I would have led a life of regret if I hadn't spent her final hours with her."

" I'm just glad you got to see her before she left us."

The cab pulled into the gates at his mother's house, which technically belonged to him now. Florent had inherited all the fortune, including the land and home. He was a multimillionaire now, which did not matter to him, but he could now give Althea the life she deserved. He got out and looked up at the gray house, with its four giant marble pillars and large glass windows.

The steep steps that led to his home in the front entrance looked more massive than before. His butler, Steven, stood at the doors, ready to open them for him. "I send my apologies and condolences to you, Mister Fayland." He opened the doors to the grand lobby area, where the three crystal chandeliers sparkled from the light coming from the windows located on every corner. Florent had the house staff clean and organize everything, and he and Althea cleaned out the bedrooms. Florent opened the door to his mother's bedroom and stood in the doorway. He had cleaned almost everything out of the closet and drawers. He was going to donate her clothing but kept everything that she held dear. He looked into the dark room, which was only being illuminated by the sunlight through the sheer drapes.

"I guess this is our home now?" Althea asked.

He looked out to the hallway, then shut the door behind him. "No, there are too many painful memories here. I'm going to sell the land, along with the house. I don't think I could live here any longer." He took Althea's hand while searching for the book inside his jacket with his other hand. "I have everything I need."

That evening, Florent sat at the dining room table still in his mother's home. He looked around at the purple drapes that circled the room. He sipped tea that his mother's chef had made. He had promised the staff to find them new jobs within a week. He sat there, thinking about what was to happen next. His amusement park was opening in a week now. Althea sat in the chair next to him, drinking a glass of water. "Althea, what if we did build a house? I have been thinking more and more about living on the park's grounds. I think it is a wise decision. We could have everything we ever wanted in a home. We have the money now. I want to make it completely different than anything anyone's ever seen. I mean, that's how I do things, right? We could have a garden, like one you've always dreamed of. And we could have balconies in every room so that you could see the mountaintops, and long hallways that curve and wind in every direction."

Florent and Althea kept making suggestions to each other and were talking excitedly. "Think about it, we would always be there when we needed to be."

"I love the idea!" Althea blurted out.

"Most of all, it would be enormous, so that our child would have much to explore."

They had planned out all their plans for their future home. "My mother was friends with a very skilled architect who might be able to make this happen; I'll make an appointment immediately." Florent noticed Althea writing in a white lace book. "What are you writing?"

"It's just my diary. I write everything down in it, most of the things that are truly important in my life. You're in here quite frequently."

Florent smiled, but it slowly faded when he remembered something. He remembered seeing the pictures he had drawn as a child with the black silhouette of a man.

"Althea, there's something I need to tell you, something I have never told you before."

"What is it?" She placed her hand on his.

"Just a short time before my dad died, I started seeing a man, well I think it is a man. I remembered seeing his body's outline, and that's it. This thing would just stare at me through the darkness, especially when I was alone. I never told my parents because I didn't think they would believe me. For about a month, I didn't see him. Then, the night my father was shot, I saw him again. When my father was being taken out of the house, I remember looking over to the woods, and I saw him. After that, I've only seen him a few times. I have tried to push this memory of him to the back of my mind and forget the whole thing. Until the other night, when we were at the park, I saw him standing in the woods. I am going to ask Roger to make sure the park has extended security, especially at night."

"Do you think this man you keep seeing could be the person who killed your father? How do you know it's a man?"

"He's very tall and stout; it just doesn't look like a woman. That's all I know; I could never really tell what he looks like close up. And to answer your other question, yes I think he is my father's killer. If I ever get the chance to come face to face with him, I'll kill him myself." Florent felt a surge of anger as he said those words; it took him to the deep mental state he wanted to break free from all his life. Florent had had anger issues for a long time, especially when he thought about anything relating to his father's murder. When he had met Althea, he could control his emotions by thinking of her, and it all went away. He could feel the heat inside his cheeks, and he gritted his teeth in a fit of anger. Then he looked over to Althea to see her concerned, almost scared look. He saw her white-blonde hair illuminating from the sunlight and her diamond eyes looking back at him. Her scared look made Florent calm down right away. "I'm sorry, I just lost control there for a moment."

"I have never seen you have such a look of hatred. Are you sure you're okay?"

"Yes, with you, everything becomes okay."

Althea still looked worried, but she got up and hugged Florent, before leaving to organize more of the house. This time, she wore a blue floral dress that hung down to her ankles, which Florent had just bought her after inheriting the fortune. He also bought her a large selection of shoes, but for some reason, her feet still remained bare.

Chapter 8

OPENING DAY

June 1926

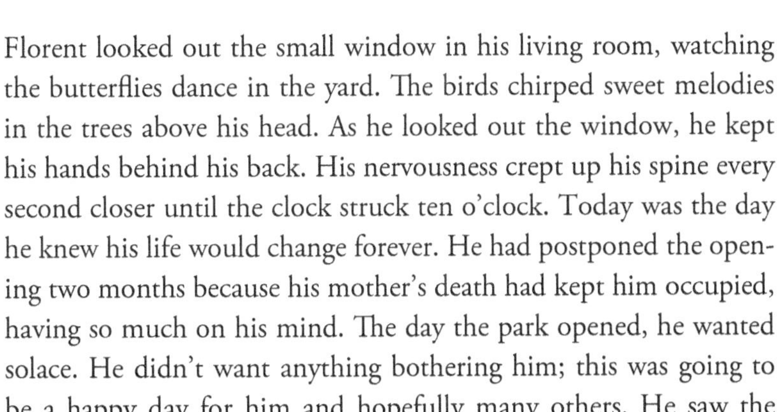

Florent looked out the small window in his living room, watching the butterflies dance in the yard. The birds chirped sweet melodies in the trees above his head. As he looked out the window, he kept his hands behind his back. His nervousness crept up his spine every second closer until the clock struck ten o'clock. Today was the day he knew his life would change forever. He had postponed the opening two months because his mother's death had kept him occupied, having so much on his mind. The day the park opened, he wanted solace. He didn't want anything bothering him; this was going to be a happy day for him and hopefully many others. He saw the advertisements throughout the town and the mention of the grand opening. "Well, darlin', how do I look?" Althea inquired.

Florent turned around and saw her standing in the entrance to the hallway. She wore a green dress that draped down to the bottom with a bow connecting the two sides. She had black, high-heeled, button-up shoes that made her appear taller than usual. A pearl necklace of his mother's hung around her neck. She had a matching green flower in her hair, which was put up very neatly. He could see her baby bump through the dress. Florent was not used to seeing her in such apparel. She usually appeared feminine and beautiful, but now she was astonishing and altogether sophisticated; she was a woman and a strong one at that. Florent stood there, with his jaw slightly opened. Althea walked toward him and closed it for him and kissed him deeply.

"You look stunning."

"Well, I don't usually dress up, but today is an extraordinary occasion," said Althea.

He was mesmerized by how she wore confidence around her neck, just like the necklace. When they met, she was timid, small, and insecure. Now he faced a girl who had transformed into a woman. It wasn't what she wore, but how she wore it that made her beautiful. Courage was the greatest asset a woman could have. He was proud of her, how she blossomed like the flowers she spent so many years growing. She was a flower, not his flower, but her own beautiful, strong rose that finally grew her thorns. He would still do anything in his power to keep anything from happening to her, but he knew that she had been carved into a fighter from her dark past, just as he had. "I got something for you," Althea said.

"What?" Florent asked, surprised.

"I had some extra money left over from what you gave me to get this outfit, and I thought you deserved something special to wear today, so I got you this." She pulled a clothing bag out of the hallway closet. Then, she opened up to reveal an exquisite suit. It was olive green, it was pressed down flawlessly, and it came with matching green leather gloves and a hat.

"Wow, this is magnificent; it's very refined." Florent went to change out of his usual black suit into his new apparel. He came out in the entire outfit and spun in a circle to model for Althea.

"It looks great on you!"

"I feel like a different person, but in a good way. Do you know what I mean?"

Althea looked down at her attire and smiled. "I know exactly what you mean."

"I love you," Florent said.

"I love you too." She gave him another kiss, the baby bump grazing Florent's stomach.

"Now, come on, let's go open an amusement park."

Althea smiled, and they both ran out of the house hand in hand.

When they arrived, Althea could tell Florent was nervous, so she squeezed his arm tightly. "Everything will be fine, I promise. This place has been your dream since you were very young. Today's a happy day. Don't let your nerves get the best of you.

Florent took Althea's hand, and they got out of the taxi together. He looked up at the white arch that guarded the entire park. The white wood, painted with bright-red lettering, spelled "Fayland Park." This brought a tear to Florent's eye. They walked down the long drive to the ticket booth to meet Roger, who had been here to make sure the employees were ready for opening day. Roger had hired all the staff and made sure every position was filled; Florent had never even met any of them. He could see the skeleton of a building being worked on that poked from behind the trees. It was Althea's and his new home. It would be done shortly. Roger hired his employees to build it much faster than what a house usually would take. When the home was done he could live in his dream world with his growing family. Roger came to greet them, giving both Florent and Althea a handshake.

"Everything is in order and ready to go. All the staff is trained and ready for the crowd."

"Do you think there will be a lot of people?" Florent asked.

"For sure, this is as much excitement this town has ever seen. This park is going to change many people's lives as well as the town as a whole. You should be proud of your accomplishments."

Florent smiled.

Several hours passed, which seemed to be a blur as Florent sat and waited in anticipation for the opening. When the time had come, he walked to the entrance, where a large red ribbon was tied from one tree across the road onto another tree. A large bow was in the middle, and Florent had the oversized scissors to cut it open. When he arrived, he was surprised at what he saw. Cars lined all the way back to the road; it was a greater turnout than he had expected. All the cars went and parked in the gravel parking lot, which was very small for the number of people there, with some parking in the grass. Florent stood in astonishment, unsure what to say or do; this was really happening for him. All the families gathered around the main entrance, where the ribbon was waiting to be cut. Roger gave an opening speech to the large group, welcoming them and explaining what the park offered. Everything went silent and still, as time had just stopped entirely. Florent turned around and cut the ribbon. At that moment, reality came back to him.

A roar of applause came from the crowd. Everyone came piling in as Florent, Althea, and Roger stood at the gates, welcoming them inside. Florent took a quick look at all the families coming in, and he saw something that took him by surprise—a boy riding on a man's shoulders. Around the age of five, the little boy smiled from ear to ear as his blond hair swung from side to side. It gave Florent a warm feeling inside. He knew exactly what the little boy was feeling.

When everyone was inside, Florent joined the crowd in the amusement park. He walked around with a smile on his face and his hands behind his back as families had fun. He watched a little girl skipping along the sidewalk with cotton candy in her hand as her parents tried to keep up with her from behind. He could smell the food aroma throughout the park, just as he did at the fair as a child. Walking through the park was like walking through a memory. He could not stop smiling, no matter how hard he tried. He heard the laughter of children, the small conversations of people walking by, and the excited screams each time the roller coaster raced down the hill. Florent looked over to Althea's flower stand, where she was selling flowers to many people. He ran over to her to check on her and see how business was coming along. "How's everything going?" Florent asked.

"Great! I have gotten so many compliments on these flowers."

Florent looked around the park to see all the flower beds and plants that Althea had been working on over several months, which really added a pop of color to the park. Althea had a large garden on the property where she grew all the flowers for her new flower cart. She was breathing hard and looked red in the face.

"If you need to take a break, you can anytime."

"No, I'm fine. It's just getting harder to breathe."

"I'll go get you a chair."

"I have one over there; I'll just take a short break."

Florent remained beside her and held her hand. "I was thinking later, we take a ride on the boats, sound good?"

"Yeah."

He noticed Althea was staring out in front of her with a smile. Florent smiled too. "What is it?"

"Look what you have done for so many people. It kind of just takes my breath away."

"What do you mean?"

"I have never seen so many people happy at once, but of course, I haven't been to many happy places in my life. I've never felt this way in my entire life, really."

Florent looked around the park with all the families and couples walking around having a spectacular time. He realized how it had changed the mood of the town. The sun seemed just a bit brighter in Fathorne that day, and the fog a little thinner. "This is everything that I have ever wanted." Fayland Park was small and simple, yet it held something mystical, and Florent could feel it. He had made a place where everyone could feel a little less sad when they needed it. He took one of the roses and clipped it down and put it into his jacket pocket. Althea smiled and placed her head on his chest. He stayed with her for the remainder of the day. Florent watched as the sun was setting behind the trees, which meant closing time was near.

It had been a perfect day; it was sad for it to end. "I better get back to the gates to tell everyone goodbye."

"Okay, I'll be here."

Florent bent down and kissed Althea before walking away. She took out her white diary from her bag and began to write something down.

Florent stood at the gates and watched all the families walk out with smiles on their faces. He shook everyone's hand and gave the kids balloons. A man who was accompanied by his wife and small son came up to Florent.

"All this was your idea?"

"Yes, but Roger Merriam took care of the construction and finances."

"Thank you for this; we had such a fun day. It brought me back to my childhood for a short time."

Florent felt his heart leap; he was so glad he could make people feel the way he had when he was a kid. The little boy hugged him, and Florent gave him a yellow balloon.

"Thanks for coming! Have a safe trip home."

The man nodded and then joined the rest of the crowd exiting the park. Florent locked everything up and made sure all was closed down for the night.

He returned to Althea, who was still writing in her diary. "Are you ready?" Florent asked.

"Yes." She put her diary into her purse and took off all her jewelry. She took down her hair from the neat hairstyle she had it in. Her blonde curls fell gracefully down over her shoulders, which made Florent's heart skip a beat. He took her hand and walked up the hill that led to the boat ride. He noticed she was breathing hard again, so he swooped her up into his arms and carried her up the hill. He swung her around, which made Althea laugh as she wrapped her arms around his neck. When they arrived, he gave the ride operator an extra wage for staying late so they could have one time around. Florent sat Althea down in the crane boat and placed his arm around her. The boat gave a small jolt, and they headed into the dark forest. The full moon was shining through the treetops. Fireflies were playing in dark spots, making the summer air fill with an illusion of glitter. Althea scooted closer to Florent and placed her head on his shoulder. "I hope things can stay like this forever."

Florent looked up at the stars and the moon once again just as he had all the other nights they had been together, and he heard the frogs croaking in the background. The stars seemed brighter and more populous the nights he was with her. He tilted his head back and took in a deep breath of the damp air.

"Me too." For the first time in his entire life, he felt what real happiness was. He had the love of his life under his arm, and he was expecting a child in only four months. It was as though the last piece had been placed into the puzzle his life had always been. The thought of this made a smile spread across his face as he looked up at the starry, black sky. He could see the top of their unfinished house peeking out over the trees. They passed a wooden board that was part of the ride's display that had a painting of a princess, a prince, and other majestic creatures.

Florent sat up and looked at the art as they slowly passed it. "My mother loved stories like those pictures on that wall."

Althea perked up as well. "I actually believed in those kinds of stories when I was young, until my mother died; that's when I found how truly cruel life can be. My favorite was about a princess who lived in a blue castle, and she loved to grow flowers. I guess that's why I became a florist. I always imagined living in a house just like that and having a garden as beautiful as hers. I know it sounds childish, but it's my dream home. At the end of the book, of course, she marries a prince; that's the part I didn't think would ever happen. As I told you the night we met, I didn't believe a man with prince-like qualities would fall for someone like me."

"I am far from a prince."

Althea smiled. "You're very much like a prince in my eyes. Now seeing your dream come true, I started to think the impossible is not so impossible."

"Maybe. I didn't believe in any of that nonsense either until I met you. Love at first sight was completely idiotic, and love itself was just a lie and a waste of time. But you proved me wrong. And you will always prove me wrong." Florent kissed the top of Althea's head, and she once again returned underneath his arm. They went all the way around the small circle and through the woods.

Florent took Althea's hand and helped her out of the boat. "Watch your step." They walked together down the murky path that led to the front arch. Florent happened to look out of the corner of his eye to reveal the man again. His black silhouette was standing in the darkness in between the trees.

Florent grabbed Althea's hand tighter and ran out of the gates onto the road, waiting anxiously for a taxi to arrive, but there was none in sight. "Did you see him again, the man?" Althea asked.

"Yes, he was in the woods. I asked Roger to increase the security, but it's not working. Maybe I'm just loosing my mind." Florent looked down the pitch-black highway in both directions to complete nothingness. The fog looked like gray smoke over the cracked pavement. Eventually, a pair of lights were shining through the mist. Florent opened the door for Althea, and they both got into the taxi together. As soon as the driver took off, Florent looked behind him to see the grand white arch disappearing into the fog.

Chapter 9
THE BLUE HOUSE
November 1926

The robin-egg-blue paint glistened in the sunlight. Florent and Althea's house had been built in such a short time with constant construction. The house looked more like a castle than someone's residence, but that's just how Florent had wanted it. He stared at its beautiful architecture, and he could see his future happen before his eyes. He had been coming once a week to check on the progress. He had done the same at the amusement park. Today was the first time Althea saw the house finished. A large garden beside the house held hardly any flowers, as winter took its place over the town. It looked like a painting filled with a splash of white, as all the snow lapped over each other. Althea stood in the middle of it all, camouflaging into the scenery like she could be a flower herself. She stood smiling as she smelled a pink rose. She had an atrium much like Florent's mother. In the glass room she could keep her garden year-round. Althea's giant baby bump was sticking out from her blue floral dress. It worried Florent when she was out of his sight; she was a week overdue.

The movers were almost done bringing everything into the house. "Would you like to go inside?" he asked.

"Yes." Althea grabbed his hand, and they walked together to the blue-covered mansion. "This place is beautiful, Florent; it's just what I imagined it would be like." She ran inside to the main entrance and stood in the center. Her mouth was wide open as she stared at the crystal chandeliers that hung from the glass dome. Gold was reflecting off the borders and windowpanes. She spun in a circle over and over again, breathing in the fresh air. The sunlight shone on her like a spotlight through the glass. It seemed to move with her as she walked, making her appear like she was the lead in a Broadway production. Her blue dress was twirling with her.

Florent stood in the doorway and leaned against it. He stood there and smiled at her astonishment as she took it all in. He then walked over to the side of the room, where a bouquet of pink roses sat on a marble table. He had taken these out of Althea's atrium earlier in the day when she wasn't around. He tied them up with white lace into a bow. "I believe these are for you."

"Oh, Florent, thank you!" She smelled the flowers just like she did with the one in the garden. She stopped and looked around until a single tear came down her cheek, ruining her blush.

Florent, confused, put his hand on her cheek. "What's wrong?"

"Nothing, I'm sorry for being so emotional. It's just that I never pictured I would ever live in a place like this, let alone own it."

"Life is just full of surprises, isn't it?" Florent said with a small smirk.

"I don't deserve all these exquisite things."

"Yes, you do." Florent bent down to kiss her. Before he could, he heard a knock on the door.

Roger peeked his head into the house. "Sorry, I don't mean to interrupt. Can I come in?"

"Of course, join us! Would you like a tour of the house?"

"That's all right, actually I came by to tell you some exciting news and drop off some housewarming gifts." Roger had a suitcase in his hand, which contained his gifts to Florent and Althea. He pulled out a sizable colorful quilt, which was pink and yellow. "This is for Althea; I had it custom made just for you."

"Why, thank you, I really appreciate this."

Then he pulled out a white teddy bear. "And this is for the little one when he or she arrives."

Althea put the quilt over her shoulder and held the bear to her stomach. "Thank you."

"And this is for Florent." He pulled out a gold pocket watch.

"This is incredible. Thank you."

"I want you to use this watch as a reminder that time is precious. It stops for no man, no matter who he is. Make sure you take time and use it to your advantage. Spend time with your wife and child, because no one ever promised you another day with them."

Florent looked up at Roger and nodded. "Of course, I will." Florent then took the watch out of the box and put it in his pocket.

"Lastly, another little something for Florent." He pulled out a full bottle of whiskey.

Florent's eyes widened when he saw the bottle. "How did you get this?"

Roger shrugged his shoulders. "I guess I just know the right people."

"It's not legal to drink. Where did you even get this?"

"I may know some of the right people. No, it's not legal but I won't tell. You've been working hard all these months; have some fun."

"I guess one bottle with the occasional sip won't hurt."

"Exactly."

Florent took the bottle from him; then Roger picked up his suitcase.

"You said you had some exciting news to share with us?" Althea asked.

"Yes. I'm taking a trip to Europe, and I don't plan on returning for a few years."

Florent and Althea looked at him in shock. "What do you mean?" Florent asked.

"I just have some business to take care of there, and I would like to explore the world more. This trip is mostly to collect myself and take a break."

"I don't know if I can run the park all by myself."

Roger put his hand on Florent's shoulder and looked into his eyes. "Yes, you can, I know you can." He then turned around, gave a wave, and then shut the doors.

Althea squeezed the gifts tighter to her and gave Florent a concerned look. "This is completely unexpected; why would he leave without any former warning before this?"

"I don't know, but it looks like we have a lot of work to do." They stood in silence for quite some time, trying to accept the fact their only friend was gone. "Well, I guess you should get to see the rest of the house."

"Yes."

Florent went to the kitchen and placed the whiskey bottle in the cabinet. He then took Althea's hand and led her up the grand staircase to the second level. He walked down the long hallway to two double oak doors. Althea gasped at what she saw.

A yellow glow illuminated the room along with blues and greens. The nursery did not hold back from the beauty of the rest of the house. The yellow wallpaper had jungle animals spread across the wall depicting tigers, elephants, monkeys, and snakes. A chandelier hung from the middle of the ceiling that twinkled when the sunlight hit it. Althea walked over to the corner, where a white lace bassinet sat. She put one hand on her stomach, and the other felt the white lace. Then she went over to a large window and stared outside. Florent joined her.

"It's beautiful," Althea said.

Their house sat on the edge of the woods by a mountain. Florent looked at the rolling green valleys that went as far as the eye could see and completely agreed with her. "It sure is." He put his arm around Althea as she put her head on his heart, as she did so many times before.

One perk of living in a town that sat on the mountaintops was the gorgeous view that one could always see from any angle. "Come on, I'll show you our bedroom." They walked together into the hallway.

Florent went to open the door until he realized Althea was not beside him anymore. "Althea?" He ran to turn the corner, and she was standing in the hallway, bent over, holding her stomach. She stood with a look of shock on her face. Florent ran toward her and noticed a wet spot on the floor.

She looked up at him. "Florent, I think it's time." He started to panic but tried to remain calm; it was a difficult task. He took her hand and led her to the bedroom. He had her lie down on the bed and propped the pillows up behind her.

"I'll be back." Florent then rushed out of the room.

The doctor finally came half an hour later, along with two midwives carrying his equipment. He noticed that some of that equipment had Fayland Medical on the side. He knew his mother had sold the business after his father died, but the company kept the name. "Dr. Wilson, thank you for coming on such sudden notice."

"I've been expecting a phone call; Althea was ready to go into labor at any moment."

"I'll take you to her; she's in the bedroom." Florent, along with the doctor and midwives, ran to the room as quickly as they could. Florent held the door open for them and started to follow them until the doctor placed his hand on him.

"I'm sorry, Mr. Fayland, but you're going to have to wait outside until the baby has arrived."

Florent hated this idea, not being able to help Althea through this, but he took a seat on the chair in the hallway. Florent kept checking his watch, but his child had not arrived yet.

The midwives updated him on how much Althea was dilating, but Florent wished he could be in the room with her, holding her hand. It had been nine hours in the hallway without any food or sleep. He did not care how much his stomach roared with hunger; he would not leave this spot. Each minute that passed was a strike of anxiety. After all the waiting, one of the midwives finally opened the door.

"Congratulations, Mr. Fayland, you have a healthy baby boy." Florent smiled and let out a sigh of relief and happiness. He got up as soon as he could and slowly walked into the room. Althea was lying in bed covered with sweat and had a glowing red face. Her hair was drenched from her sweat, and her face suggested she was exhausted, but even so, she was still elegant.

The baby was wrapped in the quilt that Roger had given her. Florent noticed a tear coming from his own eyes when he first saw his son's face. Althea looked up and wrinkled up her eyebrows and smiled, matching Florent's tears. Florent bent down and softly put his hand on the baby's head. Althea then placed the baby in Florent's arms. It scared him to be holding something so small and fragile, but that feeling quickly faded. He opened his large eyes to Florent. Though it was too early to tell, he had Florent's hazel eyes and facial features. His hair looked like the fuzz of a peach, and it was so blond it imitated the sun's glow. The white-blond hair was shining, even though the room was dimly lit. He had Althea's hair; there was no argument there.

No words came between Florent and Althea, but they knew they had shared the same feelings of pride, gratefulness, and love toward their son. "His name is Lawrence Alistair Fayland."

"It's perfect."

He looked down at the child and saw a beam of hope and glory in that little round face. He never imagined he would ever hold such a delicate thing, but here he held him as he took his first breaths.

After several hours, Florent took Lawrence's bassinet out of the nursery and placed it in their room. He felt he would be safer with them for the first few months. Althea had fallen asleep as Florent cradled Lawrence. He placed him in his bassinet then fell asleep himself with his arm wrapped around Althea.

The next morning arrived, and the sunlight danced on the floor and over Florent's head. Lawrence had only woken up once during the night with his small cry. Althea was still sound asleep; he understood why she needed her rest. He turned over to look over at his nightstand, which had a picture frame on it. The frame contained the picture of Althea and him in front of the flowered field by the inn. He finally received the picture after waiting a while. This picture was the first thing he wanted to see in the morning. He went over to the window and pulled the curtain back to look out at the new day. It was quite breathtaking; he had never noticed how simplistic yet exquisite Fathorne really was. Though it was built in the mountains, more magnificent mountains were the backdrop of the town. They were much larger than where the town was settled. It was a never-ending scene of silhouettes of the jagged shapes. He remembered his father telling him a story about the mountains when Florent asked him what the tallest mountain was. His father told him he didn't know, but never stop looking for it. Florent was confused by this remark, but now he understood it completely. His father was never talking about a mountain at all. Florent knew he had reached the peak of his life right now, but there was always a taller mountain waiting, more possibilities, and he couldn't stop trying until he found that tallest mountain.

He looked to the right and could see the Ferris wheel and some parts of the roller coaster. The park was closed for the winter season, and everything, including himself, was taking a break. The snow had covered the entire land, including the attractions, making it look like cotton covered the fields. In the glass reflection, he saw Althea waking up as she stretched her arms up to the ceiling. "Good morning, dear," Florent said.

"Good morning. Lawrence slept so soundly last night; I was expecting to be up with him so much more. I had an excellent sleep myself."

"I thought that maybe we should get some help," Florent said.

"What do you mean?"

"I mean, we should get a nanny to help you out; I had one when I was younger. Also, this house is much too large for just two of us to keep up on. I think we should hire some housekeepers as well."

"I don't think we need help; I can do this."

"This is all too much, Althea; you could use the help."

"I've been doing things by myself my entire life; I'll be fine. Now, I'm going to go make us some breakfast; then I'll come back up to feed Lawrence." As soon as Althea started to walk out the door, Lawrence began to cry. "I guess I'll feed him first, then make breakfast."

"I could make breakfast."

Althea picked up Lawrence and sat down with him. She looked shocked and said, "Okay, thanks."

Florent had never cooked in his life; he didn't even know where to start. He opened the large doors that led to the massive kitchen. He stood staring at the stove and around the room. "Who am I kidding? I don't know what the hell I'm doing," he said to himself. He looked in the cabinets to see what food they had left over from the old house. He found a loaf of bread in a container, so he decided to slice it up and put it in the toaster. He waited and waited until it was too late. The toast burned, but he placed it on the plates anyway. Then he took some strawberries out of the refrigerator and put them around the toast. He turned around and saw the whiskey that Roger had given him sitting on the counter. He couldn't imagine himself drinking any type of liquor; it didn't seem right. He placed the bottle in the cabinet away from everything else in the kitchen; perhaps he could save it for a special occasion.

Althea came into the kitchen, holding Lawrence, who was now back to sleep. She took her time and walked slowly into the room.

"That was fast."

"I know, poor dear, only ate for a few minutes before falling asleep again. So, what did you make?"

"Toast with strawberries."

"Yum! Sounds delicious!" Florent placed the plate in front of her with a look of worry on his face. "I'm so sorry; I wish I could help you more. I don't know how to do anything." Florent started to walk away with a sad face before he felt a tug on his pajama shirt.

"Florent, you did more than enough. You don't have to act as if you owe me something all the time. I'm going to eat this; it's not even that burnt. I am just so grateful for everything you do. Look around you, look what you've done. You have put a beautiful roof over our heads, and you make me feel loved each and every day. How many people can say that?" Althea handed Lawrence to Florent.

"Sit down, and I'll get you some juice." She came back to the breakfast table with two glasses of orange juice and took Lawrence back into her arms. Florent looked up at her as the sun reflected off her blonde hair, as it always did, and he couldn't help but smile.

Chapter 10

BACK INTO
THE DARKNESS

September 1996

I was back in Asher's truck, looking out the window at Fathorne's fog-covered atmosphere. "Are you sure you don't need me to take you to the hospital? You still look very pale."

"No, I'll be fine." The rain had started to come down hard. I watched the water droplets run down the window, as I always did on the train. "I told you, Asher, I have these visions all the time. Even my therapist and my mother thought I was crazy."

"Speaking of your mother, where is she? I've never seen her. Are you two on speaking terms?"

I looked out the windshield, then back down at my hands. I took a deep breath and started to twiddle my fingers. "She's dead."

"Oh, I'm sorry. I shouldn't have said anything."

"No, it's okay. About a year ago, she was in a car crash. It was raining like this, and she couldn't see the road. A car lost control from the wet pavement, and they crashed into each other. I have

122

been told by a witness on the road that it was no accident and the other driver deliberately hit her. But the road was very slick, so I don't know. A good indication that it was not an accident was that the other car was stolen and abandoned. The driver took off with what I am assuming were major injuries. The person was never identified. There was a paint rubbed on the side of my mother's vehicle, and the damage looked like it came from a head-on collision. That's how they knew someone hit her."

"I'm so sorry. What about your father? Is he still alive?"

"I don't know, I've never met him. He left my mom when she told him she was pregnant. She was only sixteen when she got pregnant with me. She still graduated high school and went through college to become a nurse. I am very proud to have had a mother like her. She raised me all by herself, though my grandparents helped out a lot. But, my dad, on the other hand, was nothing like her. So, I have no father in actuality; he's dead to me." Asher and I sat in silence for a while before I broke it.

"I have to go back."

Asher turned to me with a worried look. "What are you talking about? That place is dangerous, and we both know there's like a murderer that knows what both of us look like."

"Asher, I'm going back."

"Look, Kim, I can't tell you what to do, but are you really risking your life to get a job at some lousy newspaper place?"

"It's not just for the job; it's so much more."

"What do you mean?"

"I know this is going to sound weird, but I've always felt some connection to that place. I also saw a woman on the property, but she was different from the others. I was terrified because I didn't know what her intentions were. She didn't seem to have any negative energy, and I felt like I knew her from somewhere or like I did know her." Asher didn't say anything else, which made me think he thought I had lost it completely.

"I still think it's a bad idea, and you shouldn't go anywhere near that place."

"Okay, I won't go back."

It felt terrible to lie to Asher when he had done so much for me. I know he was just trying to keep me safe. I didn't know if I should listen to my instincts, but something told me to go back, there was still something left for me to discover. Asher pulled into the apartment's driveway, and we got out without saying another word. As soon as we got on the second level porch, Asher started to walk toward his apartment. "Hey, thanks for coming with me today."

"No problem, anytime." Asher went to unlock his door when I felt myself walking toward him. I grabbed his arm and gave him a quick kiss on the cheek.

"I'm sorry. This is probably a bad time, but I couldn't help myself."

He then returned to kiss on my mouth while his brown curls grazed my forehead.

He looked at me in awe right into his eyes. "There never has been a better time. Well, I guess I'll see you tomorrow," Asher said.

"Uh, yeah, sure." I was still lying to him; I felt so horrible. We broke off and went our separate ways. I went to sit on my bed and pulled out the picture of the couple. I lay back and extended the image in front of me. This picture was the real reason I wanted to go back; I seemed to have a relation with these people—all those mornings of seeing them dance in the fog; if it really was them. I put the picture in my backpack and fell asleep for the night.

I awoke the next morning, not even realizing that I had fallen asleep. I looked down to see I was wearing the same clothes as yesterday but had no time to change. My alarm clock read six o'clock a.m., and I wanted to leave as early as I could. I packed everything in my backpack that I would need, except for one thing. I quickly walked to the kitchen and put a knife into my bag along with everything else. I started to walk out the door before I noticed something strange. The rose petals in the trash had vanished. I wondered if that was all in my head, like everything else. I was starting to wonder if all these visions I had were truly there, since Asher saw the man in green as well. I suppose I would find out today when I went back to the place that always gave me nightmares, yet it also made me feel at home. I couldn't describe the feeling it gave me, but there was something there drawing me back.

I was finally going to confront the man in green, and nothing would stand in my way. It was time to face my fears and find out the truth. It was still dark outside, with the sunrise just coming over the horizon. I stepped outside into the chilly September air, which made me sink my face into my jacket. The fog was fiddling around my feet and moved along with me when I walked to Asher's door, contemplating if I should tell him. No, I told myself, I had to do this on my own. I brushed my hand on his door and then headed down the stairs into the unknown. I knew it was dangerous for me to be walking by myself in the dark, but my feet kept walking; nothing was stopping me. For once in my life, I felt valiant, like I was being called to my fate. The chill was making me shiver, and my hands, along with my feet, were going numb. I could hear the voices all around me, but it did not matter. I walked past the decrepit buildings of the town square and the fountain that was now turned off. I walked with my head held high and a stride of confidence.

It was a treacherous journey, but before I knew it, I looked up at the rotting white arch. The letters faded each day as time passed. I walked down the long path, where the forestry was overgrown. I heard a crunch of leaves, so I stopped right away. I quickly grabbed the knife and held it out in front of me, making a circle to check my surroundings. The wind had stopped blowing, and an eerie silence came over the woods.

I didn't hear anything else, so I kept walking farther and farther down the long path. Walking down this road felt like walking to the gates of hell. I knew I was getting closer when I saw the ticket booth and the pink roses getting more abundant in number. I stopped when I suddenly saw a figure standing in the distance. It was just a silhouette of man; he looked much different than the man in green. I didn't know if this was in my head or an actual person, but I ran as fast as possible. I finally got out of the shadow's sight and back up into a part of the park I had never seen before. This part of the woods was not affected by the fire; everything was untouched. I was taken by surprise when I looked down at an entire row of clementine trees.

Their fruit had not appeared yet, just budding white flowers. I recognized them because my grandmother used to have several in her yard. When my mother and I visited her house, she always had some in a bowl and gave me one. I touched the leaves and smiled; how I wish I could relive those days again. My grandmother, like the rest of my family, was dead. She passed away from cancer at the age of forty-seven. I never really thought about it, but other than Asher, I had no one.

Chapter 11
BAD DREAMS
July 1929

The sun was bearing down through the woods, making Fayland Park a hot, golden world. For the first time, the park was holding a Fourth of July celebration. Florent was walking through the park, watching over all the daily operations. He felt a small weight on his shoulders that was Lawrence. He was smiling and looking around him as the crowd went in every direction and watched the roller coaster drop. Business was booming as usual, and it was hard to move because of the large mass of people. Florent was drenched with sweat, but even on the hottest summer days, he wore the olive-green suit that Althea had given him when the park had first opened. He and Althea had become somewhat famous, known as one of America's most well-known business couples.

People had always known who Florent was locally, but he always felt like a fraud when people treated him like royalty because they only knew him by his father's achievements. Now, he was known across the nation and loved by all for operating a place that everyone adored. He was truly living his dream, and he always had the fear that someone would wake him from it. Florent had been invited on radio shows for interviews that spread across the country, and a massive number of newspaper articles claiming that Fayland Park was a huge success. It was also known nationally for its family-friendly activities and had become a hot spot for weekend getaways. The park doubled in size since its grand opening three short years ago. Florent had added ten new rides, along with various games and food stands. A new kids' area with children's rides had been added, where Florent and Lawrence spent most of their days. The park's biggest accomplishment was the new train tracks that led right into town, passing the arch. The train went by frequently, and people from all over could ride into Fathorne easily.

It seemed like every day, the park had more and more people pouring in. Florent took a deep breath of the smell of hot dogs and hamburgers filling the damp summer air. He looked up as he held on to Lawernce's legs. "Would you like a hot dog, kiddo?"

Lawrence looked down with a bright smile on his small face. "Yes, Daddy."

Florent sat Lawrence down and took his hand as they walked over the food stand. The steam from the stoves hit Florent in the face.

"Hey, Mr. Fayland! What can I get for you?

"Hi, Lance, can I get a hot dog for my son?"

"Sure, one hot dog coming right up! Anything for yourself?"

Florent felt the sweat rolling down his forehead. "Uh, just water, please." Florent gave him the money for the hot dog and water, then gave him a large tip. Father and son went hand in hand over to one of the picnic tables, so Lawrence could eat his dinner.

This day was one of the hottest in Fathorne history, but the guests didn't seem to mind as they went on having their fun, despite the heat. Lawrence stopped in mid-bite when he saw Althea coming toward them and gave his hot dog to Florent.

"Mommy!" He ran to her as she bent down with open arms, and

she scooped him up then kissed him on the cheek.

"Hi, sweetheart!" Lawrence placed his hands on her cheeks and smiled. Florent had never seen such a beautiful view as when the two people he loved most in the world were together. Althea came to kiss Florent. "Are you having fun with your father?" The boy nodded. "Well, I guess I'll be on my way. Just make sure you are back for the fireworks."

"Wouldn't miss it," Florent said, smiling. Lawrence waved goodbye as Florent waved back, then turned and disappeared into the crowd.

Florent said his hellos and shook hands with hundreds of guests. He was interrupted when someone stood out from the rest of the crowd. The man seemed to be the tallest individual in the large mass of people. He wore a black fedora and brown trench coat. "Roger?" Florent made his way through the crowd to the large figure. The man seemed to ignore him at first, then was taken by surprise.

"Oh, hello, my boy!" He shook his hand and then pulled him in for a hug.

"Why didn't you tell me you were back, or at least a phone call or a letter?"

"I thought I would give you a surprise visit. Besides, meeting in person is much more meaningful. Also, I would like you to meet someone."

Florent felt rude for not noticing before, but a small woman was holding on to his arm. "This is my fiancée, Winnie."

"Oh, nice to meet you." Florent held out his hand to shake hers as she lifted her head, and he could finally see her face from underneath her large hat. She had curly strawberry-blonde hair, pinned behind her head. Freckles spread across her face. Her petite hand returned with a handshake.

"Charmed, Florent, it's so nice to meet you finally. Roger has told me so much about his close friend from back here in the States." She spoke with an accent.

"If you don't mind me asking, where are you from?"

"All the way from Paris," she answered. Roger gave Winnie some money.

"Why don't you go get some cotton candy. I'll meet up with you later."

She walked off, and Roger turned back to Florent. "We have some catching up to do."

Florent smiled. "Yes, very much so."

"Let's start with you."

"Oh, okay. Well, I was blessed with a little boy who is already two years old; he is my entire world. Althea and I are still very much in love, and every day I wake up to see her beautiful smile makes me feel so undeserving. As you can tell, the park is doing very well. I couldn't ask for anything more. So, now you. How did you meet Winnie?"

"It's actually quite an interesting story. I would like to thank you for making it happen."

"What are you talking about?"

"The day I met Winnie was the single most incredible day of my life. It felt like something out one of those romance novels. I passed through France and happened to stop in Paris, and I'm not really sure what I was doing there. I was sitting at a small cafe at one of the outdoor tables in the pouring rain. I was soaking wet, but something told me to stay there and let the water go through my clothes. I saw a glow in the crowd; it was a woman whose grace made her stand out from everyone else. I remember you telling me how Althea made you feel, and I felt exactly what you described to me. I loved my first wife, Annette, the same way, but I guess it had been so long, I forgot how nauseous love could make you feel. A good nauseous, I suppose. She wore a string of white pearls and a glittery dress, like one you would see on a showgirl. I just stopped her and told her that she was the most gorgeous woman I have seen in the world and wanted to get to know her. I didn't even know if she spoke English. After I said that, I thought it was over. I knew I blew it; she probably thought I was the biggest creep she had ever seen. To my astonishment, she smiled and took a seat at my table. Luckily she did speak English. I know nothing in French. We talked and laughed for the entire day. That night, we kissed under the stars in front of the Eiffel Tower. Romantic, isn't it?"

Florent processed all the information that Roger told him in a short amount of time. "Yeah, very."

"The only issue, though, is she's so young; I can't hold her back from living her life with a man like me. She is twelve years younger than me. I loved her so much, though, I couldn't leave her behind. I knew she wouldn't leave her hometown for a man she had only known for a few weeks. So, I proposed to her and didn't believe that she would say yes, but she did. Her family actually knew who I was and my business. They were thrilled when I told them my intentions with Winnie. Her family is one of the wealthiest in France. Her mother owns a cosmetic company, and her father is a famous lawyer. Surprisingly, she was willing to come back to settle down with me."

Before they knew it, they had been so busy catching each other up on their lives that they noticed they were deeper out in the woods. "Is this still my property?"

"I believe so; we're not too far from the park."

Florent happened to look over and see the top of his house sticking up from the treetops. "Not far from my house, either. I guess this *is* my property. I just have never been in this area." Florent got distracted when he saw a small building in the distance built into the side of a small mound. It was painted a light blue, but most of the paint was chipping off. Florent walked toward it, kicking the tangled branches out of his way. A large door handle poked out from beneath all the overgrown vines that surrounded the small building. He pulled as hard as he could on the handle, but it would not give. Roger then followed and broke it open on the first try.

Florent went down a ladder and stepped inside to a small, dark room. Spider webs covered the entire ceiling, and green moss grew on the four walls surrounding him. The only light came from the sunshine that was coming in from the open door. "What is this place?" He noticed pictures surrounding the room with a woman and two small girls; some had a tall, skinny man. Florent opened a rusty metal cabinet to hordes of old, jarred foods. The smell almost knocked him over as he quickly shut the door and let out a cough of disgust. Newspaper articles were also spread on the walls, containing reports of the war and pictures of the battle.

"This is a bomb shelter, likely from the Great War; my guess is the person who built this built it out of fear. They probably wanted a place where their family could be protected if bombs were dropped," Roger explained.

"I wonder what happened to whoever owned this shelter," Florent said as he stroked the picture of the family with four members.

"I have no idea, but it's on your property, so technically, this is yours now. The family has probably moved on with their lives, leaving this behind along with their memories. So, you could tear it down or find another use for it. No reason to let it go to waste; it's very well built." Florent thought back to his old stick-built playhouse. He remembered how he turned it into many different things with his imagination, and how he and his father spent a great amount of time together in that old shack.

Florent turned to Roger. "I know exactly what to do with it."

For the remainder of the evening, Florent and Roger discussed more trivial topics. Roger updated Florent on everything he had seen in Europe, including some of the world's most famous and beloved landmarks. Florent told Roger of everything that had been happening in the park and what a success it had become. When they finished catching up on each other's lives, the sun was starting to go down.

Florent found Althea with Lawrence on her lap in the parking lot, where everyone else had gathered. The fireworks were going to be shot off far away from the woods, but the view should be clear. "Roger!"

"Hello, Althea."

"When did you return from Europe?"

"Just yesterday, actually. I thought it would be nice to see how things were going here, with my fiancée."

"Fiancée? Roger, when did this happen?"

"I guess I need to catch you up too. Florent is all up to date."

"I'll explain everything to you," Florent said as he sat down with Althea and Lawrence. "I see this is your son. I could tell by that bright-blond hair."

Roger bent down closer to get a better look at Lawrence. "And look at those hazel eyes, just like your father." Florent smiled, as did Lawrence, followed by a small giggle.

"Maybe someday I will have a child, and you could play together. Would you like that?"

Lawrence nodded. Everyone jumped with surprise when the fireworks exploded with many different colors in the sky. Blues, greens, reds, and every color imaginable filled the air. Althea lay against Florent as Lawrence pointed at each firework he found amusing. The fireworks lasted for about thirty minutes, which everyone found to be an impressive display.

After the show was over, Roger came back over with Winnie under his arm. She held out her small hand toward Althea. "Hi, nice to meet you; I'm Winnie. You truly are lovely and have such a kind smile."

"Oh, thank you," Althea said as her cheeks turned cherry red.

"We must have tea together sometime!"

"Yeah, okay, sounds good." After Althea and Winnie were introduced, they parted ways. Roger and Winnie left with the massive crowd. Florent and Althea stayed long after closing hours to make sure everything was in order for the next day. Lawrence had fallen asleep in Florent's arms, so he set him in the carriage-like seat on the carousel as Althea and he took a seat on a horse beside each other.

"Winnie seems very nice."

"Yes, she is."

"Strangely, he returned home without a single phone call or

letter to tell us in advance," Althea said. Florent told her the entire account of how Roger had met Winnie, and their incredible love story.

"That's astonishing," Althea said as she laid her head on the pole of the horse and followed with a faint smile.

"Roger has been married before."

"Wait, really?" Florent realized he never told Althea about the night Roger had given the tour of his house.

"Yes, he told me her name was Annette, but that's the only detail he gave me. That name, I've heard it somewhere before." Annette Merriam resonated in his head like a hazy recall. "I've spent so many hours with Roger building this amusement park and making plans that I guess I never got to know him much as a person. Besides you, he is the closest friend I have. I'm just glad he has Winnie to be there for him now," Florent said.

"Me too. He always seems so happy, but looking into his eyes, I can tell something is bothering him. Perhaps something is haunting him from long ago. Part of his life we never got to see." They both got off the horses, and Althea picked Lawrence up and headed for their car, which they had purchased not long ago. Florent felt strange, but he shook off the feeling of being watched as he shut the door and drove off.

Florent jolted up, his body covered in cold sweat. Althea had her hand on his shoulder. "Florent! What's wrong?" All he could do was look at her with frightened eyes and eventually relaxed and put his forehead on hers.

"I had another nightmare."

"What was it about?"

"I don't know if I'm strong enough to tell it."

"You don't have to say anything, but it's better not to let these things be bottled up."

"You're right," Florent sat up and stared at the wall in shock and horror. "It was night, and I was walking down some road. I had no idea where I was or where I was going. But I kept walking down this long path, much like the one to my old house. Suddenly, I came upon the park's archway, but the wood seemed to be rotting, and the letters had faded. I went inside and walked down yet another dark trail. When I reached the main entrance, there was something different. All the rides were decaying, and the forest was taking them over with black vines. I turned around to a circle of stakes, wooden poles. On those poles were you and Lawrence, hung up like some piece of meat." Florent curled himself up, having his legs meet his chest, and he put his head into his lap.

Tears rushed down his cheek in a fury as his eyes turned bright red. "My father and mother were there too. My father had a gun wrapped around his neck like a necklace, and my mother had blood spilling out of her mouth. In the center of it all was the tall, black figure. He just stood there in silence. And then I woke up." Florent stopped and sobbed, clenching Althea's nightgown as he buried his face in her chest. "I'm sorry you have to go through this and put up with me," Florent said with a muffled voice.

Althea lifted Florent's face up and then took her thumb to wipe away his tears. "Remember, dreams are dreams. They can't hurt you. Your nightmares truly concern me, though. I don't want to see you this way. Maybe you should see a doctor; it might be better to get some professional help. And I don't mind putting up with you. Your past may have brought you terror, but here in this moment, you are safe, and you are loved. I may not be able to provide much help, but I will always be here when you need it," Althea said with a small smile.

Florent smiled and kissed her before realizing he couldn't stop and continued by putting his hands on her waist. He felt himself naturally leaning her back on the bed while keeping his lips on hers.

They were soon interrupted when a small figure stood in the doorway. Lawrence stood there, wiping his eyes with one hand, and holding his white teddy bear with the other. Althea got out of bed and walked over to him. "What's wrong, sweetheart?"

"I had a bad dream. Can I sleep with you?"

"Of course, you can." Althea picked up Lawrence and brought him to bed.

"What's wrong with you, Daddy?" Lawrence had noticed Florent still had tears in his eyes.

"I had a bad dream too, kiddo."

"That's okay, Daddy; we can protect each other now." That made Florent feel at peace with himself, and both Lawrence and Florent went straight to sleep.

Florent had no more nightmares the previous night. Althea and Lawrence were still asleep next to him. He got out of bed to change into his green suit. He looked into the vanity mirror as he put on his green leather gloves and matching hat. He picked up Lawrence from the bed, along with his teddy bear. Then he kissed Althea on the head as she slept. He carried the little bundle and laid him on his bed in his own bedroom. "Wake up, buddy; I want to show you something." He sat up and rubbed his eyes.

"What is it?" he said excitedly.

"I can't tell you, or it won't be a surprise. Now, let's get you dressed." Florent helped Lawrence get dressed in a green patterned sweater and brown pants. As soon as he put his shoes on, Florent grabbed his hand and headed for the woods.

The bomb shelter was much closer to his house than he had thought. It still sat on the mound with its blue paint chipping away.

"Here it is."

"What is it?" Lawrence asked.

"It was a bomb shelter during the Great War, which ended eleven years ago. I was thinking about turning it into your own personal playhouse. What do you think?" Lawrence smiled and nodded in agreement. Florent forced the handle open once again, as rust had taken over most of it, making it hard to turn. They both walked into the little room and down the ladder into the bunker. "We're going to clean all this out and maybe paint the walls. What color do you want?"

Lawrence looked at Florent's green suit and smiled. "Green, like your outfit!"

"Okay, that will be done. We will have to do this another day, though; I have to make a phone call." Florent helped Lawrence back up the ladder and shut the door tightly.

When they went back to the house, Althea had made breakfast; he could smell her special pancakes. "What were you two up to?"

"I showed Lawrence an old bunker I found yesterday on our property that seems to have been abandoned many years ago. I told him I am going to renovate it so he can have a place to play. We can spend time there together, a little father-and-son time."

Florent sat Lawrence in his chair and pushed it to the table. "I'll be back; I'm going to try to see if I can find a number to a psychiatrist."

Althea placed her hand on his shoulder to tell him everything was going to be all right. Florent went to the phone and grabbed the phone book. His hand was shaking; he knew he needed it. But he had never spoken to anyone other than Althea about the horrors he had seen. It was only a short time before he got hold of the doctor advertised in the phone book. "Um, yes, my name is Florent Fayland, and I need to see someone about some issues I have been struggling with for quite some time." He listed his address for a home visit and a simple description of what he needed. The doctor would be able to make it in just a few hours. He didn't know how much longer he could take, trapped in his own mind. The demons of his past pushed down on him every second of every day.

Florent returned to the kitchen and put on a happy face. Althea placed the pancakes on the table, and Lawrence quickly shoved the pieces of his breakfast into his mouth, causing it to be sticky with syrup. As he looked at his family and realized that he had everything, something in him still felt hollow and cold. It was the feeling of an invisible, cold monster inside his body, trying to dig a hole to crawl out of, for it craved for a warm essence, longing for happiness.

Later in the day, the psychiatrist arrived just a little after noon.

Florent led him to his study, where a wooden desk with a large chair sat in front of the window. Next to the bookcases was a blue velvet sofa. He took the chair from behind the desk and offered the doctor the seat, which he accepted. Florent lay down on the couch, feeling nervous as to how this would go. The doctor started right away as he pulled his clipboard out of his bag and asked his first question. "So, tell me what is on your mind."

"I wanted to tell you about these recurring dreams that I've been having."

"Can you tell me what is in these dreams?"

Florent's heart started to pound in his chest. He hated having to relive what he saw, but he knew it was the only way to get help. "Well, the people in the dreams seem to be consistent. They are the people I love the most, my wife, my son, and my parents. And a shadow of a person, who I saw as a child standing outside my house. Actually, I still see him sometimes. This person, this thing always kills my family in my dreams."

"I know your story, Mr. Fayland. I know your father was shot inside your home, and I know you and your mother were in the house when it happened. It was all over the newspapers across the country; your father was very well known."

"Yes, but well liked, as far as I know. I don't know who would have so much hatred toward my father to go and shoot him." Florent continued to talk about his father and his nightmares, even telling the doctor things he had never even told Althea. The doctor wrote everything down on his clipboard.

"I think I may know what the problem is."

Florent perked up. "What?"

"You have suffered from trauma coming from the night of your father's death. It's what they call shell shock. It's much like when soldiers come back from war and have experienced horrible events. No child should have to experience something as tragic as that. Your living family members appear in these dreams because you fear the same will happen to them, and you feel that you don't do enough to keep them safe. Your parents are a constant reminder of what has happened, and you keep reliving it from the ordeal, for example, seeing your father repeatedly shot in your dreams. The shadow person you keep seeing, even when you're awake, is probably just an illusion. You fear that your father's shooter is still out there, and he will do to you and your family what he did to your father. I'm truly sorry that you have to live with all this, but there's nothing I can do to keep these dreams from happening except more therapy sessions." Florent sat up and was taken by complete surprise. All this made sense, and it made him understand himself much better. Yet, something was still not right inside of him; he felt that the doctor could do more to treat him. Florent could not come to tell him this, though.

"Thank you, Doctor. What you said really helped." Florent shook his hand and opened the door for him.

"You know, I brought my wife and two daughters to your amusement park last year, and we absolutely adored it. We plan on coming back sometime soon. I really appreciate you doing this for our worn-out town; it has made Fathorne a happy little place."

"Tell you what." Florent went to his desk and pulled out four tickets and handed them to the doctor. "This is on the house. Hope you can come to visit soon." His face turned red as he lit up in a smile.

"Oh, thank you. But I can't accept that. We have plenty of money to purchase tickets."

"Please, take them. It's my pleasure to do it. Can you find your way back out?"

"Yes, thank you."

As soon as the doctor left, Florent shut the door and walked back over to his desk. Everything that he said made complete sense, but he was wrong about one thing. The shadow he kept seeing was not an illusion; it was really there. Sometimes, Florent could even hear its low, shallow breathing. He pulled out a drawer, where he found a picture of his father. He had taken it from his mother's house and placed it in his pocket. He turned around to see the amusement park in the background, running its typical day. Maybe, he thought, he would always be trapped inside of his mind. But he had more important things in his life than to let his past ruin his future. At least for now.

Chapter 12

WATCHFUL EYES
OF THE NIGHT

September 1996

I was aghast as I looked around at all the trees that held white flowers. The leaves swayed with the wind, and the entire property sat in silence. I walked behind the trees and noticed an entire garden with a variety of flowers, fruit, and vegetables. Fayland Park had sat abandoned since the early sixties, but the garden looked well kept, as if someone had been taking care of it. I began to wonder if someone still lived on these grounds after all these years. I thought back to the neatly kept clothes in the closet and how some of the bedrooms had neatly made beds. Before, I feared ghosts and the supernatural that may wander this place, but now I fear I might run into someone still living, wanting to add me to the restless spirits.

I walked past the garden, farther into the black, ash-covered trees. It was strange that I could smell the burning of the wood pierce through my nose, but that wasn't the worst aroma. The stench of burnt flesh danced around my nostrils again, filling me with fear

141

and dread. It was the same smell that haunted me from my vision during the last visit. The beauty provided by the garden and clementine trees was starting to fade as more of the property turned into a destroyed world, ashes beneath my feet. I realized this was the part of the park that burned and couldn't be saved. These ashes meant I was standing where people had lost their lives trying to escape. I don't know the whole story; no one does. Though there were open woods everywhere for people to run and save themselves, the fire housed them in a fiery deathtrap. It made my stomach turn, thinking about the terror of that day. I looked around and realized that I had entered the other side of the woods, still surrounded by scorched trees. The grass under me was completely dead, just like the rest of this once-happy place. I stopped dead in my tracks when I came upon some sort of building.

The baby-blue structure was in a mound, and it had a single door. The strange color wasn't the most particular aspect of it, though. The door was cracked open just to reveal a small strip of light. I stood there for a moment before my curiosity took hold of me. "I've got to be the dumbest person alive," I said to myself out loud before I'd already taken my first couple of steps toward it. I gripped the knife tighter in my palm and prepared myself in case anyone was inside. I opened the rusted door, which made a loud sound of old metal scraping across the ground. I entered to find a ladder that led to a lower level.

I put my shaking legs on the ladder as it creaked and groaned—from age, I assume. I turned around to find something completely unexpected. I was filled with relief when no one was in the room with me. It was a single room that was painted olive green, the exact same color as the man in green's suit. Little animals were painted near the ceiling, circling the room. They were circus animals, which included elephants, lions, and tigers. A single cot sat in the corner, and a bookshelf contained more books than I could count. I noticed clippings of newspapers hanging around the room as well. Then I found the light source, which was coming from an oil lamp in the corner. I looked at the green-painted walls to find pictures, tons of them spread across the room in between the newspaper clippings.

The pictures were of a couple, a family photograph like I saw in the mansion, and just pictures of a single male figure. This certain person's face was scratched out, just like most of the other photos I have seen of him, but he had black hair, just like mine. The newspaper clippings were mostly about the fire, the death of those three teenage boys, and every other tragedy that has happened here. I didn't stay for long to look at the articles after I saw something gruesome. There was an article that was cut out of the newspapers about the murdered teenagers. Underneath, there were crime photos of the incident. The photographs contained the three young victims with blood smeared all over their bodies, and their faces completely pulverized. They were no longer three individual people; they had been chopped up so badly that they were just a pile of guts and gore. Their letterman jackets were buried beneath it all. I had no idea why anyone would keep or have these photos. I felt the bile coming up from up my stomach, and I had to look away, I had to leave.

I quickly ran up the ladder and jolted out of the bunker. I ran into the night without my flashlight and just a single knife. I couldn't believe that I had listened to my stupid head telling me to go here, even though I knew I would be in danger. I pulled out the flashlight from my bag, but it did no good. The fog was more intense than I remember, and the stillness was unsettling. I couldn't even hear traffic noise, not even the obnoxiously loud train close to the park's archway.

I gazed at a black world; the darkness was consuming me into a pit of emptiness. I flashed to the darkness and my surroundings until I finally saw a tree. The tree was blackened and lifeless, and leaves were all missing, not by the calling of autumn, but just like the park, it had been stripped of life for a very long time. Something strange caught my eye; many large birds sat on the branches, watching my every move in complete muteness.

They were vultures; their hollow eyes stared into mine. I looked away. I've never been fond of them but understood that their purpose is necessary. On the other hand, they reminded me of death. I kept walking deeper into the woods, for reasons I did not know. I smelled something that made my stomach churn with disgust and my nose burn. It was the same stench I smelled from the first time I came here and earlier, the smell of burning flesh and firewood. I knew the smell couldn't be here still, but then again, maybe it could. I kept walking until I tripped and landed face-first in the mud. I could not see what I fell over, so I quickly pointed my light at the source. I tried to hold it in, but I screamed bloody murder, letting anyone know that I was here. I couldn't even control my breathing; I grabbed my chest as a hot tear rolled down my cheek. I looked down into two dead eyes on a lifeless body, at least what was left of it. I could tell it was a young man around my age. I assumed the birds had been pecking at him and feasting on him.

Before I knew it, my feet were taking off as fast as they would take me. The fog intensified, as did the smell. I knew that man was not an original victim of the park's tragedy; his death must have been recent. The knife wounds in him were no accident; he was killed here or dragged from somewhere else. I ran and ran, even though my side was on fire with pain. I almost stepped into the water ride, the crane-like boats filled with algae, and something underneath made my heart almost jump out of my chest. I saw human remains and skeletons, floating in the filthy water. I saw the arch just around the corner, but as I turned, I hit something solid, knocking me to the damp, muddy ground once again. This time I didn't scream; I couldn't. Fear had paralyzed my body.

I looked up to the figure, but this was not a hallucination. As I looked up at him, his details were sharper, and he seemed more lifelike than I had ever seen him. I knew that I would look fear in the eyes this very night, and here I was doing just that. I did not cower; I sat up, looking at him with every ounce of courage I could get out of my small body. The man in green, standing in his usual attire, stretched out his hand to help me up. "Stay away from me!"

He walked closer to me as I scooted back.

"Don't be afraid."

I reached for the knife but could not find it.

"I'm not." I lied through my teeth. I finally stood up, wiping off the twigs and dirt on my legs and collecting what dignity I had. He got closer and closer as I stood my ground. He looked up, revealing his face that was hidden by the hat as he kept his head lowered.

I was in shock and almost sympathetic toward him. He still had the long, gruesome scar across his face, resulting in what appeared to be a blind eye. The rest of his skin was burned, looking like it would tear just from a gentle poke. He did not appear as malevolent as I had always believed him to be; his face suggested someone hurting. The face of loneliness, fear, and even kindness. I knew this look too well; most of the residents of Fathorne wore the same features. He placed his burned hand on my cheek to comfort me, but I jumped back in a state of confusion. His eyes grew wider, and his deformed mouth opened in surprise.

"Is it really you, my precious Ebony?" My heart sank. Ebony was my mother's name. I was completely dumbfounded and slightly angry. How did he know who my mother was?

I stood up and thought for a while; there could be another Ebony. But then I thought this was no coincidence since I have been told that I looked so much like my mother.

"No, Ebony is my mother. How do you know her?"

He turned away from me, and I saw a tear run down his face. He stood looking down the road until he turned back around to face me, looking me straight in the eyes. "She's my daughter."

Chapter 13
CLEMENTINE
October 1933

Florent sat slumped in a large armchair in front of the fireplace, giving a small amount of light to an enormous living room. His hand rested under his chin, for he couldn't even keep his own head up. The stubble of his face felt strange to him; he had never let himself go like this. He had been this way ever since the stock market crashed and he lost a decent amount of money. Most of his fortune he had inherited from his mother was kept safely in a vault; he just felt paranoid, leaving it outside of his keeping. The vault was hidden in the house. He would not spend that money unless it became absolutely necessary. He was glad he had decided to keep the fortune out of a bank and in his own home. He had returned to have a dim view on life; the world grew lifeless every day.

The park was closing for the season, which was a blithe occasion, because it was financially struggling. Families no longer had the extra money to spend on leisure activities, and fun seemed like a thing of the past. Florent had finally lived his dream, a fantasy that made people happy, and that made him happy. Now, even thinking about what had become of his achievement was a dismal affair. It was unpleasant to know that his cheerful and vibrant place could shut down at any time, but that day had not yet come.

"Dear, I have something to show you. Please come with me."

Althea had walked into the living room looking as beautiful as Florent had always seen her. She wore a red dress with yellow flowers that she had made herself. Real yellow flowers laid on top of her white-blonde hair.

Florent smiled. "I don't know. I'm pretty comfortable here; maybe you should join me."

Althea came beside the chair, pulling his arm, but she was not strong enough to get him to stand. Florent then grabbed her hand and pulled her on top of him. Althea couldn't hold her laughter as Florent tickled her. He stopped suddenly and looked into her eyes as she looked back into his. "How did I get so lucky?" Florent said before he kissed her and pulled her into a tight embrace.

"Come on, let's go!" Althea took his hand and ran out of the house. She was still always the antidote in his darkest of times. Florent never had to worry about a rainy day, when she was around to make everything better.

They came upon her garden, which was bursting with seasonal veggies, fruit, and flowers. A line of trees outlined the one side of the garden, which held nothing but green leaves, looking like something might be growing. "This is it; they are going to grow my favorite fruit very shortly."

"What kind of trees are they?"

"Clementine trees. I figured I would start growing more food in these uncertain times. Besides, my mother used to make a delicious clementine upside-down cake, and I think I still remember the recipe."

"That sounds delicious." Florent jumped when he heard a noise in the woods; he quickly put Althea behind him without hesitation.

"What was that?"

Lawrence jumped out behind one of the trees with two fake pistols and made shooting noises with his mouth.

"Lawrence! Don't do that! Do you understand?" He looked down sadly.

"Yes, Dad."

"It's okay, Florent; he was just playing. Lawrence, why are you already in your costume?" Althea questioned.

He stood in a sheriff's outfit like the ones in the Western movies he saw in the theaters. His blond hair, so much like Althea's, reflected the sunlight, and his hazel eyes looked up at her. "I really love this costume, Mom, and I just couldn't wait."

"Okay, just don't get it dirty before tonight." He ran to Althea and hugged her. "Now, how about you go back to the house, and I'll get some lunch ready for you here in a little bit, okay?" He nodded and ran away. Florent and Althea walked over to the clothesline and continued their discussion as she started to take down sheets and clothes.

"I love the kid, but sometimes he can be such a handful," Florent said as he leaned on the pole of the clothesline.

"Then I bet you wouldn't want to deal with another."

"Maybe someday, but I think we'd better wait until Lawrence is grown and on his own, or I'll be gray-headed by the time I'm thirty."

"I don't think that time is so far away."

"Why, am I already starting to show gray?"

Althea smiled. "No, the time for another child."

"I really think it's wise if we wait. I mean, I can barely keep up with just one."

Althea placed her finger on Florent's lip, just like she did seven years ago, and she looked up at him with her puppy dog eyes.

"Florent."

"Oh, wait, are you—when did you?"

Althea took his hands. "Yes, I'm expecting, and I'm sorry I didn't tell you sooner. I didn't think it would be so hard to tell you, but I was just as nervous as the first time. I actually think I'm pretty far along, but I didn't want to tell you with everything going on." Florent kissed the top of her head.

"There's nothing to be sorry about; I get to bring another life into the world with you." Florent pulled Althea into a hug, and he could feel her heart beating and her breathing unsteady.

"Hey, everything will be okay. You're the positive one between the two of us, and I know somewhere behind those worried eyes, there's always a beacon of hope," Florent said, pushing Althea's hair off her face. "This is good news to me; I want you to know that, and don't think that we can't get through this, because we have come this far. We can accomplish anything as long as we do it together. I woke up and was disgusted with the world, but since you shared this news, I feel a new spark of happiness. I hope this eases your mind."

"Yes, just a bit. I suppose we are very fortunate to have all the things we do have, luxuries that people have lost. This baby is just another gift we do not deserve."

"That's true."

Florent took her hand and started walking toward the house until Althea stopped and pulled him back. "There's something else I need to say to you."

"What's that, my love?"

"Thank you." She finally collapsed, and tears rolled down her face as she pulled Florent into another tight hug. He placed his hand on her head and looked down with a concerned look. "I know you always say that there's nothing to thank you for, but I don't think you realize what you have done for me. I know that I would have been dead from starvation or disease if you never invited me to dinner that extraordinary night. I would never have made it through this financial crisis without you. Florent, you saved my life."

Althea put her head on his chest, and Florent stroked her hair. He was at a loss for words. She was sobbing and taking deep breaths. "The things I have seen around town are unpleasant—children dressed in rags like I used to wear, while Lawrence wears fancy sweaters and leather shoes. People live in boxes with their skin hanging off their bones while we eat a four-course meal every night. Could we please donate money to shelters and food to soup kitchens? Those people need it."

"Of course." Florent was disgusted with himself; for nearly four years, since the country had been going through this crisis, he never once thought about anyone but himself, and he feared he was becoming like his mother. He wondered how they had gotten so fortunate to be living this way. He had always thought he had been generous and uncaring of wealth, but he never considered what it was like to live on the other side, even when he and Althea had nothing for a short period of time. But even then, they had more than most people had in a lifetime.

They walked to the house, and Althea's tears had dried, replaced with a faint smile as Florent tightly held her hand until they reached the front door. Lawrence was sitting at the table, waiting patiently while playing with small toy cars at the dining room table. Althea started to make their lunch, and Florent watched her from afar. "Are we going to tell Lawrence about the baby today?"

"I think we should," answered Althea.

"I think he will be happy to have someone to play with; he's been such a lonely child. We both know what it's like to be an only child; it's a lonely life." Florent looked out the window.

"Yeah, I had always wished to have a sibling."

"Me too." Althea set the table and placed sandwiches down, along with chicken noodle soup. When they sat down, Florent looked at Althea and nodded to tell Lawrence.

"Lawrence, why don't you say Grace, and then your father and I have something exciting to tell you."

Lawrence bowed his head, and they all shared a prayer. Florent grabbed Althea's hand, and they looked at Lawrence.

"Honey, you're going to have a baby brother or sister very soon." Lawrence said nothing but looked aggravated before he ran off.

"I'll take care of it," Florent said as he ran after him.

He found Lawrence face down in his bed, crying. He tried to talk, but his voice was muffled. "I don't want a brother or sister. I just want it to be you, Mommy, and me."

"What's so bad about having a sibling that you can play with and be friends with?"

"Because you won't love me as much and only pay attention to the baby."

Florent sat down on his bed beside him and placed his hand on his back. "Lawrence, it's true that babies require a lot of attention, but that certainly does not mean we will forget about you. We will love you two, just the same. You can even help take care of him or her; how does that sound?"

He turned around and sat up. He smiled and nodded in agreement.

"Your mother and I love you so much. That will never change, do you understand?"

He nodded again and hugged his father. Florent looked down at Lawrence's sheriff costume. "How about we go back and finish lunch, partner?"

Lawrence laughed. "Dad, that's what a cowboy says, not a sheriff."

Florent smiled. "Oh, my apologies." They then went back to the dining room, finishing their lunch.

When evening arrived, Florent put Lawrence's coat on him and was ready to go around the town of Fathorne to get some delicious treats. Trick-or-treating was a new event in Fathorne and still young in the nation. Florent had never been trick-or-treating since it didn't exist when he was a child. He thought it was odd for children to go around and knock on strangers' doors, asking for candy, all while being dressed up as something you're not, but he knew he would have enjoyed it as a child. Florent and Althea had decided not to pass out candy, since their house was in the woods, and it would be dangerous for children by themselves to be in this area at nighttime.

They got their coats on and were ready for a night of fun. As soon as Florent opened the door, he was startled. Winnie was standing there with a tea set in her hands. He noticed what he assumed to be her car parked in their driveway; he didn't even hear her pull up. "Oh, I'm sorry. Were you heading somewhere?"

"We were going trick-or-treating."

"Excuse me, what?"

"It's something for Halloween; it's a fairly new practice. Fathorne decided to join in on the festivities, and we're taking Lawrence out."

"I'm sorry. I had no idea. I just thought we could have some tea. I can come back some other time."

Althea placed herself in front of Florent. "That's all right, you went through all this trouble to get here and bring all this stuff. I'll stay. Florent, you go ahead. I wasn't really feeling up to it anyways. Also, I would like to get to know Winnie better."

"Oh, okay."

Althea bent down and kissed Lawrence on the cheek. "Mind your father, okay?"

"Yes, Momma."

Then she kissed Florent. "You behave too, mister."

Florent smiled. "Yes, ma'am." He took Lawrence's hand and went to their car. Lawrence got in the back seat and sat in anticipation. The town was dead silent, and the intense fog was just another recurring event in Fathorne. When they reached town, Lawrence went door to door, getting a large number of treats. Florent saw what Althea was talking about, the poverty that surrounded the town, and the sad faces and skinny figures.

They passed his and Althea's old townhouse, and it reminded him of the struggles they had gone through, but that was nothing compared to the conditions people were being put through now. Unemployment was at an all-time high, and many people lost their money. He wished he could help give people jobs, but it was no use. The park was closing for the season, and it just wasn't financially strong enough to support more employees. When the park opened and more people started to come, so did more businesses to fill the once-vacant business lots. Now the buildings were shut down once again.

Many people had gone to bed, so Florent led Lawrence back to the car with his bag of candy and treats. As soon as Florent started the vehicle, it began to rain hard. With the fog and rain together, Florent could hardly see. He put on the windshield wiper, but it was no use. He noticed he had finally reached their road when he saw the deep cracks in the worn-out pavement and the train tracks that ran right next to it. Something unfamiliar, yet so familiar caught to the corner of Florent's eye. He turned his head, and there was the shadow, just standing there, not making any movement. The wet road was causing the car to slide and pull to one side. Florent pushed the brakes to stop the vehicle from going out of control, but it went toward the woods. The car spun in several circles before it slammed into a tree, and that's when the world went black.

Florent awoke in a hospital bed with unimaginable pain in his left leg. He looked around, and his first thought was of Lawrence. What had happened to him? Where was Althea? His heartbeat increased with each agonizing question he asked himself. He felt dizzy, and his head was pounding. His drowsiness was intense, but he still tried to get out of the bed. A nurse rushed in and tried to get Florent to lie back down. He pushed her off. "Where's my son?"

"Your son is fine, Mr. Fayland. He was taken to the children's ward to get checked, but everything seems to be okay. Your wife is in the lobby; I will tell someone to get her and tell her that you're awake."

Florent was relieved Lawrence was okay. He looked down at his arms, which were covered with large bruises of blue and green. His memory was starting to come back to him as he remembered the night before. He had wrecked, and *it* was there.

He remembered seeing the tall figure standing in the woods; it seemed impossible, but he had caused this. At least, that's what Florent wanted to believe and that he didn't run off the road and put his son's life in danger. Althea appeared in the doorway, with her eyes drowning in tears.

She ran to Florent and grabbed his hand, which resulted in him yelping. "Oh, I'm sorry, dear." She sat in a chair beside the bed and gently put her hand on his arm. "I was so worried; they thought you might not wake up. I slept in the lobby, waiting for you to gain consciousness while the nurses at the children's ward kept me informed about Lawrence."

"How is he?" Florent said weakly, tasting blood.

"They said he only had a few scratches, but he hit his head really hard on the back seat. He keeps complaining about a headache; it has me really worried."

Florent started to cry. It hurt his chest from the bruises. "It's my fault."

"This is not your fault; this was an accident."

"No, I saw *him*. I kept my eyes locked on him too long, and I wasn't paying attention. That made me run off the road."

"The roads were very slick, your car slid, and there's nothing you could do."

"I thought getting a professional over these years would help me, but it hasn't done a single thing for me."

The doctor came in with a clipboard and paperwork. He explained the injuries and the severity of his leg. "Your left leg appears to be broken; you'll have to wear a cast for at least six to eight weeks until it is healed. I am going to have you stay here for a few more days just to make sure there aren't any other concerning symptoms. Any questions?"

"No. Thank you, doctor."

He then left the room, leaving Florent and Althea to themselves.

"Well, it looks like I'll be taking care of you for a while," Althea said.

"No, I'll do the best I can to care for myself. I couldn't ask to be dependent on you. You already do so much with Lawrence and the house. Besides, you need your rest."

"Florent, I love you, and I'll always do what I must."

Florent still didn't want her to take care of him regularly, but he knew he couldn't keep her from doing it; it just wasn't in her nature. Though it pained him to an insane degree to lift his bruised arm, he placed his hand on Althea's cheek. She grabbed it and put her hand on his. She kept it there as she started to cry.

"I hate to see you in any pain," Althea said.

Through the affliction, Florent wiped the tears off Althea's cheeks with his thumb.

He had always known they were in love, from the first time he had seen her, but this moment proved that he would always fall in love with her every time he saw her. She would never tire in his eyes or his heart. He couldn't express how grateful he was for everything she had done for him. Now he would lie in bed for several months, useless and unable to move while she did everything without asking anything in return. He looked into her diamond-blue eyes, and he finally truly understood what love really was.

February 1934

Florent sat out in the hall as his heart pounded; he felt all the nerves, just as he did the first time. Althea went into labor four hours ago, and he was waiting patiently for the arrival of their second child. It was a very stressful four months since the night of the wreck. His leg healed quickly, but not completely. He had a terrible limp in his left leg, and it was hard for him to move, but he wouldn't let it slow him down. Not now, anyway; he had to be there for Althea as much as he could.

These past months, he had watched Althea work herself to the bone caring for him and Lawrence, all while carrying a life inside her. She would go to bed late, and Florent watched as she threw herself on the bed and went straight to sleep. Her hair unkempt and her clothes wrinkled, it made Florent upset that he couldn't help her through these times. Even with her hardships, never once did she complain. She had done everything without a single request, except one. He had asked her to play her violin for him, which he knew would help her too. He remembered her telling him how it calmed her. Every day in the afternoon, she would pull up a chair and play one of her beautiful melodies. When she played, their concerns left, and for once, everything was at peace, just like when they danced together many years ago.

Florent was concerned about Lawrence, though, now sitting on his knee playing with a toy car. He was quieter now, and he would barely even look up. It seemed as if his childhood spirit had left. He acted strangely and spent most of the time in his playhouse, not asking anyone to play with him as he once did. Florent had always wanted him to be better behaved, but now he would do anything for him to act like a child again. It's like the wreck had changed who he was, but the doctors couldn't find anything wrong with him.

Althea decided to have another at-home birth because that's where she felt most comfortable and had more privacy. Soon a midwife opened the door and motioned Florent to come inside. He sat Lawrence down and took his hand, then went inside their room. All the memories were coming back to when Lawrence was born and the pride and happiness he felt. Althea sat in the bed with a small bundle, and Florent could see a tuft of white-blonde hair sticking up.

"It's a girl," Althea said softly. She handed her over to Florent as he held back tears.

"She's absolutely beautiful," Florent said. She looked just like Lawrence with her blonde hair and small, round face. He couldn't believe that he was holding his second child. The love for his two children was the most potent force he had ever felt. He looked over by the door to see Lawrence standing there with a worried expression. "It's all right, Lawrence, come meet your baby sister."

He slowly walked over to the bed and put his hand on the baby's head but then went back to playing with his toy car, uninterested. For the one split second, Florent could tell that Lawrence loved her too.

"Have you decided on a name for her yet?" Althea looked out the window and saw her garden with the clementine trees, and she smiled.

"How about Clementine?"

"It's perfect," Florent said through a smile and tears of joy.

Roger and Winnie came later in the week to offer their congratulations and give gifts to the baby. "May I hold her?" Winnie asked.

"Yes, certainly," Althea responded by getting up and handing Clementine to her.

"Oh, she is perfect. Her cheeks are as red as strawberries, and her hair looks like buttercream cake icing." Althea smiled. Everyone was gathered in the living room, having tea and snack cakes that Althea had made herself. Lawrence was nowhere to be found as his parents looked all over for him.

"We'll be back; we are going to see where Lawrence ran off to." Florent told their guests.

They searched every room and area in the house, but they could not find him. It took longer for Florent to get around their enormous house than it used to. He used to walk fast and steadily; now, his limp kept him behind. "Lawrence!" No response came. There was only one other place he could be. "Why don't you keep looking through the house and I will check the bunker," Althea commented.

"Good idea," Florent responded.

Althea walked into the woods and found the oddly shaped structure. She grabbed the lever-like door handle, pulled it back, and set her feet on the ladder. She tried her best, but she couldn't seem to get down it. "Lawrence, are you down here?" She heard crying and suddenly stopped when an answer followed her question.

"Yes."

"Could you help me down the ladder?"

Lawrence appeared and helped her reach the ground, then Althea held on to the wall for support. "Why are you down here? Roger and Winnie are here visiting."

"I'm down here because you lied to me." Althea maneuvered herself into the single olive-green room.

"About what?"

"You're giving the baby all the attention, and I feel alone. Dad and you used to come down here and play with me almost every day, especially when the amusement park is closed. Now that she's here, you don't even look at me."

Althea moved over to Lawrence as best she could and put her arm on his shoulder then bent down to meet him at eye level. "Lawrence, we told you that babies require a lot of attention. I will admit, though, I haven't been spending as much time with you as I should have. I need to let the excuse of being tired be pushed aside and get back to our old ways, and I promise from now on, I will. But I need you to know something." Althea pulled out the chair in the corner of the room and placed Lawrence in her lap. "Sometimes this world will leave you alone, and you may have no one, or so you may think. There will be times when loneliness will be your only companion, and sadness will be a recurring visitor. In these times, you'll feel isolated. You'll believe that no one really cares about you. You wonder if you left if anyone would even notice you were even gone. I felt that way most of my life until I met your father. You know why that is, Lawrence?"

He looked up at Althea with a curious look, and his eyes grew almost the size of his face.

"Because we shared something between us, love. What I'm trying to say is that you will always have people who love and care about you. And the love you share with others will always be your most powerful asset in a world that will always try to break you. There will be times when those people may not be around, but that certainly doesn't mean that they don't love you with all their hearts. Your sister will grow up, and she'll love you as much as you love her. You will always be her big brother that she will look up to for advice, comfort, and protection. Your father and I love you so much, Lawrence."

Lawrence hugged Althea tighter than he had ever hugged her. "I love you too, Mom."

Althea squeezed him into a tight embrace. "Now, let's get back up there."

Lawrence helped Althea up the ladder and followed her up.

Chapter 14
CLEMENTINE'S GIFT
August 1939

Fayland Park had a much bigger turnout on this very day than it had seen in a long time. The long lines for the rides were back to its earliest days. A little girl stood inside all the madness and took it all in with each passing second. Two white-blonde braids were pulled behind her head as she stood with an easel and paper. Her palette was on one hand as she filled a sheet of paper with a splash of color. Clementine moved with passion and determination with each stroke.

Florent came up behind her, but she never even noticed because she was so focused on her painting. "What are you painting, princess?"

Clementine turned around, and her pigtails swung around before falling back into place again. "The Ferris wheel, because it's my favorite ride. Do you like it, Daddy?"

Florent had seen Clementine's paintings before, but nothing like this. He stared at the picture for quite some time before Clementine interrupted his thoughts. "This is amazing, Clemmie!" Florent was taken by surprise by the amount of detail she had put in the drawing. The different-colored carts and even the people inside were remarkably enhanced for a five-year-old. "Do you mind if I frame this and hang it up in the house?"

"That would be amazing!" Clementine hugged her father.

"Have you seen your brother?"

"Last time I saw him, he was on the scrambler ride with a girl."

"Okay, I'm going to go look for him. You better get back to the house. It's almost closing time."

"Yes, Daddy."

Florent walked through the park, joyful as he looked around. He had missed the park's busy days. He didn't like being in crowds, but it brought him joy that other people were having the time of their lives. People still hadn't entirely recovered from this depression, but things seemed to be lightening up. Florent searched all over the park for Lawrence's blond hair. He looked through the entire crowd, which was heading toward the exit for closing hours. He checked every ride and every building on the property but could not find him. He finally spotted him behind one of the food stands, talking to the girl Clementine must have seen. Florent rolled his eyes but couldn't help but smile, watching his son flirt for the first time. He could not believe how much Lawrence had grown; he would already be thirteen in just three short months. Lawrence finally noticed his father watching him.

"Dad, that's really not okay of you to spy on me like that."

"I wasn't spying on you; I was just waiting for you to get done talking to that girl."

"Okay, Dad, whatever you say."

"Who was she?"

"Does it matter?"

"No, I was just curious; you seem to really like her."

"You seem to know a lot for not spying. Anyways, her name is Ruth, but she's from out of town."

"I see."

"At least we had fun, even if it was just for today."

"I'm glad you are making friends with people from all over the country and possibly even the world."

"I guess I have met people from all over."

They reached the house and went straight into the dining room, where Althea had everything placed out for dinner. They didn't use the dining room all that often, but since it was the last day of summer vacation, Althea wanted to make a special meal and eat as a family at the dining room table. The dining hall was one of the most impressive rooms in the house, with light-brown walls and velvet curtains draped on each window. A chandelier hung from the ceiling right above the table, sparkling like a giant diamond. Lawrence sat down beside Clementine and waited until Althea was done with the cooking. Florent went to the kitchen to check up on Althea and show her Clementine's painting, which he was still holding in his hand.

"Oh, hey, dear, I'm almost done."

Florent handed the painting to Althea, and she stared at it, amazed. "This is really good. Did a fan of the park paint this for you?"

"No, it's Clementine's painting."

"This is incredible." Althea wrapped her arms around Florent. "She has her father's talent."

"This is beyond what I could do at her age."

"She certainly has a gift. She's signed up to take art classes at school; I hope she sticks with it."

"I'm going to frame this and hang it up somewhere in the house where everyone can see it."

Florent walked into one of the spare bedrooms where they kept most of their extra items. He went to the closet and pulled out a box of unused frames, pulling out a frame that looked like it would fit the painting. He placed it in the frame, and it all came together for a beautiful piece of art. Florent hung it above the fireplace in the dining room. Clementine smiled when she saw the painting up there, filled with a sense of pride.

Florent sat down at the table, joining the rest of his family. Althea made a casserole with just about everything one could imagine. They all said Grace and started to eat their food. When Althea finished eating, she got up from her seat and rushed to the kitchen. After a few minutes, she brought out was her clementine upside-down cake. It was Clementine's favorite dessert too, and she was ecstatic that this sweet fruit was what she was named after. Althea placed the orange cake in the center of the table and began to cut it into even slices as the white powdered sugar fell off like snow onto the table. She gave a piece to each of them, then a bit for herself.

The beginning of the next day was chaotic as Florent and Althea got their children ready for their first day of school. Althea sat in Clementine's room, brushing her hair. She sang a song as Clementine played with a doll. She placed a large black bow in the back of her hair, then dusted off her black dress and made sure everything was perfect, from her Mary Jane shoes to the top of her head. Althea bent down and placed her hands on Clementine's shoulders. "You look so pretty, and you're so smart. You're going to be just fine, I know it." Althea started to cry, even though she tried to hide it.

"Why are you crying, Mommy? Are you sad?"

"Oh, sweetie, I'm not sad. I'm just so overwhelmed by how fast you and your brother are growing up. It seemed like just yesterday I was holding both of you in my arms."

"I'll always be here when you need me, Mommy."

"And I'll always be here for you. I told your father to let go of the past and live in the moment. So, that's what I need to do. Though I hope time goes slowly. I want to see the woman you become. I get to watch you and your brother grow up, and that is an amazing gift."

"Are you girls almost ready?" Florent asked.

"Yes, dear." Althea looked over to Clementine again, making sure nothing was out of place. Lawrence was standing behind Florent in his school uniform, looking neat as usual.

Althea came out and noticed some syrup on Lawrence's cheek. "Wait, hold on." She pulled out a white cloth she kept in the pocket of her dress and wiped his cheek.

"Stop, Mom."

"No, your face is a mess. There we go, now you're ready."

Lawrence and Clementine grabbed their schoolbooks and walked toward the arch, where the bus would stop. Florent and Althea watched their children get on the bus, and then it quickly drove off. They waved to the departing bus.

"It gets harder and harder every year to let them go because I know each year they are getting older," Florent said.

"I had a similar conversation with Clementine, but we must remember to live in the moment." Florent stood in silence for a short period of time, while Althea placed her head on his chest.

"Live in the moment," Florent whispered.

After a long school day, Lawrence and Clementine entered the house, where their parents waited for them. Clementine was sobbing, with tears running down her face, and she quickly ran to them. "What's wrong with her?" Florent said in a panic.

Lawrence shrugged his shoulders. "I don't know. I asked her, but she won't tell me."

Althea pushed Clementine's hair out of her face, which was sticking to it from the tears. "Honey, what's wrong?"

She just buried her head into Althea's dress then ran to her room, still sobbing loudly. Althea started to run after her until Florent put a hand on her shoulder.

"I got it."

Althea nodded and led Lawrence into the kitchen to talk to him.

Florent slowly walked up the stairs, still with a limp, which he tried to hide as best he could. "Clemmie?" Florent walked to her bed and sat down beside her, placing a hand on her back. "Can you tell me what's wrong?"

"I'm never going to paint again."

"What are you talking about? You're very talented."

"I told my art teacher that I wanted to be an artist when I grew up, and he laughed."

"What do you mean, he laughed?"

"He told me that I would not be successful. He told me my paintings were uninspired and there was nothing interesting about what I painted. He said that I would never truly make it as an artist.

Florent's face was red, and he could feel the heat coming off his cheeks.

"Clemmie, look at me. You can be whatever you want to be. It's true. Never let anyone tell you what you can and cannot do in your life. Not a teacher, not a boyfriend, not a husband, not even me. If you want to be an artist, you're an artist, and you'll be amazing. The only person who can tell what to do with your life is you. You're smart, and I know you will make good decisions that will make your mother and me proud. Never let anything stop you from getting inspired, and never stop your creative mind. When I was young, I had dreams of building an amusement park, and of course, people told me that would never happen. They told me it was foolish because they wanted me to live the life they thought I should live. Now, look around you. I built my dream. Did I do it alone? Of course not. I had the people who supported me the most by my side. In your life, people will tell you can't do something because you are a woman, but prove them wrong. To tell you the truth, I hope people doubt you, because that can motivate you to work harder to prove all of them wrong. Carry yourself with pride and flaunt everything they told you you would never have. Now promise you'll keep on painting, won't you, princess?"

"Yes, Daddy."

"Paint everything. Paint everything that makes you feel something. Paint life's happiest moments and the sad ones too. But most importantly, paint whatever you want, and find the happiness and purpose that most people search their whole lives for."

Clementine hugged her father, and Florent hoped that what he said had changed her perspective. After they finished their dinner, they talked about the rest of her school day for the remainder of the evening. He saw so much of himself in her; she would speak of the things she was passionate about for hours as her eyes twinkled with excitement.

When night came, Florent went to grab his mother's fairytale book. He read the stories to her as she lay in her bed. The top of her head was barely visible as she was snuggled into her large comforter and surrounded with many pillows and dolls. Althea came in to listen as well. After a while, she interrupted his reading.

"Florent." He looked over and saw that Clementine was fast asleep. They both kissed the top of her head and then left holding hands as they shut the door.

Several hours later, Clementine awoke to hear soft music playing. It sounded like some type of slow waltz music, which she thought was beautiful. She got out of bed to see where the sweet melodies were. She walked down the hallway, where the music was increasingly louder each step she took. She started to run as her long, blonde hair swung behind her, and her nightgown bounced above her ankles. She peeked into her father's study, where her mother and father were. She knew what they were doing; they were dancing. Clementine smiled.

They reminded her of the princesses and princes in the book her father read to her at night. It made her sad that her father couldn't really dance well with his limp, but her mother held him up, and they danced as best they could. She realized she never wanted a prince when she grew up. She wanted a love like her parents' because that was a love of the purest kind. She quietly turned around to go back to bed and danced down the hallway as she listened to the echo of the music.

She stopped suddenly when she noticed a black figure standing close to her doorway at the end of the hallway. It stood there without any movement, and it did not speak. Clementine had never known a stranger and always wanted to meet everyone she could. She waved to this mysterious being, but it did not in return.

"Hello, I'm Clementine. What's your name?" There was no response. "There's no need to be afraid; I won't hurt you." Clementine reached out her hand to touch the figure, but when she got close, it vanished. She stepped back, aghast at what had just happened. She ran into her room and shut the door as quickly as she could and went to bed, confused by what she just saw.

Chapter 15

THE MAN IN GREEN

September 1996

I could hardly stand and slowly backed into a tree. "I'm sorry, but I think you are mistaken. My grandparents, the parents of my mother, go by different names, and have different appearances."

"You mean your grandmother Nancy and grandfather Fred?"

"Yes," I said nervously.

"I'm afraid they lied to you, which is what I told them to do."

"Your grandmother is not your grandmother at all; she is your great aunt. And Nancy is not her name; it's Clementine." As much evidence as he was throwing at me, I didn't want to believe him. The fruits in her kitchen were clementines, like the trees planted on the grounds, and I remember the paintings throughout her home, just like the ones I saw in the blue house. I felt foolish for not realizing it sooner. All my childhood memories were coming back to me, which seemed like another lifetime when things were simple. I wondered if this man, or perhaps spirit, had been stalking me and learning about my past just to lure me in to kill me.

I wondered if that was the fate of the person I tripped over in the woods. "I don't believe you." He stepped closer to me, and I flinched when he made a movement. He took off his green hat that usually would just show a small amount of his face, that sad, lonely face. I couldn't deny anything he had just told me. I looked at him with the utmost shock. It was like I was looking into a reflection. I fully saw the scar spread across his face and the terrible burns that I could only partially see. His good eye was of a blue diamond color just like mine, and he had long, black hair pulled into a small ponytail. Some gray strands stuck up from the jet-black hair. I could tell behind the tragedies that had scarred his face, he was once very handsome, and he couldn't be over sixty.

"Now do you believe me?" That's all he had to do to earn my trust and faith in him. He was undeniably my relation.

"You're Vincent Fayland?" I could tell from the newspaper articles. I saw so much of my mother in his face, so much of me in his face. "I'm perplexed and have so many questions. I guess my first question is why I had seen you in my nightmares and my mind when you were never really there. Are you actually dead?"

"Technically, no, I am alive, but I haven't actually felt alive for a long time. I have an answer to why you have been seeing me through dreams and hallucinations, but it's not exactly straightforward, and I'm not sure I understand it fully. Let's go inside the house. I can answer that question and all the other questions you have."

As we walked, my head was throbbing. The questions I had to ask were about to burst out of my brain. "I recognized your face from newspaper articles I saw in the library, along with your siblings. It said you were dead."

He changed his tone and turned toward me. "All those articles were supposed to be burned! How were they there?" It scared me the way he looked at me.

"I was just doing some research, and they belonged to the

librarian. She said she was the mother of one of the teenage boys who were murdered here."

His facial expression changed into disgust.

"She thought it was you, but I don't believe that now."

He looked down at the ground, then straight ahead, this time without a single expression. "She's right."

My heart skipped a beat, and I could feel it try to escape my chest. "What?" I stopped and could feel tears starting to form. "You really are a murderer, someone I don't want any part of!"

I started to run, but he grabbed my arm. I screamed and kicked to free myself, but I couldn't escape his grasp. He grabbed my shoulder and pulled me near his face.

"Please, I am not the monster you think I am. I have done things I am certainly not proud of. They haunt me to this day, things that are hard to live with, but I need you to trust me. I promise I am not going to hurt you."

"You killed that man in the woods too and left him to rot!" I spit in his face, and he finally let me go.

"Please, don't go. I can't lose you like I lost your mother all those years ago." I looked into his eyes, one dead and gray and the other blue just like mine.

"Fine, but only because I need my questions answered. I want to trust you, but I'm still skeptical."

"I killed that man because he was vandalizing my property. He was trespassing and wrecking my home. He's not the first, and I'm sure he certainly isn't the last."

It was no excuse to kill someone, but I still followed him into the large blue house that Asher and I ran out of the day prior.

"It's best to find somewhere where no one can see us when the sun fully comes up." I looked up at the large decrypted building that was once a beautiful home to what I assumed was once a broken family. I had to make sure I stepped over all the pink roses and avoided their thorns, unlike my first visit here. We walked into the debris that was once a magnificent mansion. The sunlight was shining in from the broken glass dome over our heads. The cracked marble floor underneath had broken glass, which crunched underneath my feet when I walked. He led me up the grand staircase to the study that held the paintings I had found.

He sat on a velvet sofa facing the window, and I sat in the large armchair adjacent.

"So, you've been living here all these years?"

"Yes, I'm letting time do what it does best, destroy what you love until it finally crumbles into nothingness. Also, I want it to look like no one lives here for my protection." I did not know what he meant by this, but I let it be and did not say anything. "I haven't seen the outside world for I don't how long. I haven't walked past that pathetic, decaying arch for all this time. I keep myself alive by tending my mother's garden." He pulled a cigarette box out of his coat pocket and then placed a cigarette in his mouth as he pulled out an old match and struck it on the side, igniting into a single flame. He lit up the cigarette and took a puff of it. "I have a man go into town to get these for me. But he won't say a word about me or this place." He pulled out a knife from his jacket. It made me squirm, and I did not ask how he knew this man, so I decided to change the topic.

"Those paintings on the desk there, I'm guessing were my grandmother's? I mean, my aunt's?" It still seemed strange to me, like I had been living a false truth.

"Yes, those were my favorites that she painted." He got up and grabbed the paintings from the desk and brought them over, setting them on the small, round coffee table in between us. He only brought three over, the three that had featured people.

"Do you mind explaining these to me?"

He picked up the first one with his face on it, back when he was very young. I was guessing he was a teenager. "This one is me, but you could probably guess that." He then pulled up the one with the girl in the swing. "This is one she sent to me in the mail eight years after she left. The little girl is your mother; this is the only painting of her she sent me. However, she did send me a lot of photographs every year as your mother grew up."

He got up again and went to the bookshelf to pull out a photo album, which he handed to me. I opened it, and I could not fight back my tears. There were at least one hundred pictures of just my mother. Pictures of her as a baby in the bathtub, birthday parties, first days of school, her first car, then after her high school graduation pictures, there were no more. There were many pictures of my mother smiling and the happiest that I have ever seen her. Even though I was sobbing, I couldn't help but smile back at her.

"Not long after your mother graduated high school, Clementine frequently got sick. She fought so hard, and she told me that she had recovered, then one day, I stopped getting her letters. I assumed whatever she had been battling with had won."

I looked up with sad eyes and let out a sigh. "It was cancer." I could see the pain in his face when I said this.

"What about your uncle?"

"He died a few days after her, the doctors assumed from grief."

"Your uncle's real name was Finnick. He worked here at the park, ran the Ferris wheel, which happened to be Clementine's favorite ride. They fell madly in love and got married in such a short time. It's such a shame what happened to her. My sister was the only person, other than my wife, who ever treated me with kindness. Everyone looked at me like I was a freak; maybe after all this time I really am. Your mother was eighteen in that picture, and that was the last picture that I ever saw of her. That's why I assumed she was here; you look just like her. I thought you were the shadow I kept seeing. Though I could see only a shadowy silhouette of you, sometimes I got close enough to see part of your face. Being trapped here, I guess I have lost track of time. I don't know how many years have passed."

"My aunt didn't die until I was five, though. Why didn't she tell you my mother was pregnant or that I was born?"

"I'm not sure, but her frequent sickness and assuming her

chemotherapy, I didn't expect her to write to me anymore. I wanted her to live her life and spend her last days focusing on herself. And lastly, this was my wife, your grandmother." He handed me the painting I saw yesterday, and I looked at the woman's beautiful face and strawberry-blonde hair. I didn't tell him that I saw her in the small cemetery outside the house. I didn't ask him how she died either because I could tell it hurt him having to relive these memories. I could see so much of my mother in her as well.

"The newspaper articles I read said that your brother, your sister, and you died in the fire."

"Everyone assumed that the people who did not escape were dead. My sister and I went into hiding to protect me. As for my brother, I never knew what happened to him. His body was never found; I believe he is still alive. After the fire, they left the place to rot as I sat inside on this desolate land and did the same."

I decided to finally ask the question that had puzzled me ever since I heard the story of this place. "Who started the fire? What happened to this once-happy place?"

"Before I tell you, I need you to do something for me." He bent down on his knees and took my hands. "Could you call your mother and ask her to come here? I want to see the beautiful woman she has become and tell her the truth about both of your pasts."

I sat in silence for a moment before I gave him a sad look.

"What's wrong?"

"I guess I never got the chance to say it, or perhaps I didn't want to tell you. My mother is dead; she's been dead for almost a year now. She was killed in a car crash. It is still a mystery if it was an accident or done on purpose."

He gave me a look of horror and frustration. He released my hands and slowly stood up before grabbing his chest. Tears poured from eyes all the way down his green suit.

"All these years … all these years, I stayed alive, hoping I would be reunited with my daughter one day. Even though deep down, I knew that would never happen. I wanted her to live a life without me. She had a better future with my sister. Clementine was a better parent than I could ever be. And as soon as my face was seen in public, I would be sent to jail. I would be tried for every death that has happened here. It would be partly a lie, and I would likely be killed for it. I could not face a life of sitting in prison and people believing that I killed all those guests and my very own family. My daughter was my reason to keep living, and now I'll never get to see her again. It is too much to take."

I was crying too. We both shared the same grief, and we didn't know how to comfort each other. I took his hand, trying to console him as best I could, knowing that it probably wouldn't do any good. "I guess you're the only family I have left, and I'm yours." He smiled, even though it looked hard for him to do with the scar and burns on his face. What kind of life must he have had to not be able to smile even when he wanted to?

"Yes. So, I guess it's time you hear the truth and know who you truly are. The ending of this place started at my beginning."

PART TWO

Chapter 16
BÉATITUDE ÉTERNELLE
May 1940

The fog made Fayland Park look like a blurry memory. A small amount of sunlight glared in the sky, giving some light to a dreary morning. The safety inspectors walked around the park, checking that all the rides were ready to go for opening day of the season. Workers were preparing the food in the stands, and employees were cleaning everything up. "Good morning," Florent said to a few of them.

"Good morning, Mr. Fayland," they replied. He wore his green suit, just like he did every year on opening day.

Clementine was following him around, watching his every move. She held on to his hand as she licked a giant lollipop. "Daddy, when they finish with the carousel, may I ride it?"

"Actually, it looks like they're done now. You'll be the first rider of the year."

That statement made her smile, and she handed her lollipop to Florent and ran to the ride. The ride operator greeted her and helped her on her favorite horse. Florent came and stood behind the gate that circled the ride to watch her. The carousel started to go around in its circular motion as the beautifully colored horses went up and down.

Clementine rode the horse with a yellow mane and tail, which had pink flowers and blue ribbons. She smiled and laughed the entire course of the ride and would wave to Florent every time she came around. It warmed his heart that his children were now experiencing what he had felt as a child. Not only his children but thousands of others had the same experiences. The park was successful and made a considerable amount of money, but that's not what Florent cared about; he had never cared about money.

It was the smiles on children's faces and the laughter that filled the park and the memories they made with their families. Florent saw Althea and Lawrence walking toward him; they were both dressed up for this occasion, which was important for their family and the town. Althea wore a blue dress that went off her shoulders, with a black bow tied in the back with flowers. Lawrence was smiling for once, as he wore a brown tweed suit with brown shorts and his hair pulled neatly back.

"Wow, you look gorgeous." He took her hands and pulled her in for a kiss. Lawrence rolled his eyes and stuck out his tongue in disgust at their display.

"Are you ready?" Florent asked Althea.

"Yes," she replied.

"Clemmie! Time to go!"

"Okay, Daddy!" The carousel stopped, and Clementine jumped off.

Florent picked her up and put her on his shoulders. They all walked to the front gate, where cars were lined up all the way down the road. Florent gave a thumbs-up to the people at the gate, their signal to open. He then joined his family on a platform on which they stood to greet their guests. Opening day was one of the busiest days of the year, as people finally got out of their houses and had a little fun. The park had returned to its glory days back when it had opened, except now it was much larger and more popular than ever. The Faylands were known nationally for this simple yet amusing park that had caught the attention of millions. It was a place where people could step out of reality and forget the rest of the world even existed. Florent and his family waved and greeted everyone who came into the park; every one of them was unique and appreciated by Florent. The summer air and sunshine made today nearly perfect. As Florent gazed at the crowd, something caught his attention.

Roger and Winnie were in the middle of the large crowd. Roger's towering figure and black suit, along with Winnie's bright-red dress, were easy to spot. Florent waved at them, and they waved back excitedly. Florent got off the platform to go and greet them. "Let's meet up after a while; what do you say?" Florent nearly yelled.

"Definitely, see you then!" After that, a family came up and asked for all their autographs, which ultimately took Florent by surprise, but he did not mind.

Althea leaned over and whispered in Florent's ear. "Wow, this really is something."

Florent looked out to the crowd. All the families who were coming in were smiling brightly. "It truly is."

Roger and Florent walked the park just like back in the day, even when it was being constructed. Florent had to dodge people left and right; he almost ran into a girl who was blowing bubbles and not paying attention. "Have you been downtown recently?" Roger asked.

"No, I'm afraid I've been busy. Why?"

"The town is growing like I've never seen before. Businesses are opening up, ones I never knew existed. And it's all because of you and this place. I knew this was a terrific idea, something to wake up our dying little town. You're the first person here I have ever met with any sense of purpose or hope."

"Well, I'm just glad my dream is helping other people. To help bring some light to the darkness, as Althea would say."

Florent noticed the large wedding band on his finger. He and Winnie had married five years ago, and the wedding was exquisite and cheerful. Florent was honored to be his best man and happy to be at one of Roger's happiest moments. "I assume you and Winnie are getting along fine?"

"Oh, yes, I'm very fortunate to have her. Listen, I know this is sort of short notice, but could Winnie and I join you for tea tonight?"

"Of course. You're always welcome in our home, anytime."

"Thank you; I very much appreciate that. Well, I'm going to find her and perhaps ride a few rides. I'll catch up with you later."

"All right, see you then."

They departed in opposite directions as Florent went toward the back of the park. He stopped at a large white building, recently built, which was a funhouse. The inside twisted and curved with mazes, ball pits, and crazy mirrors. The outside was something completely different, though. Colors of red, yellow, and blue swirled together to make a festive entrance. Painted on the sides were the words, "House of the Bizarre." The words were spread across the top in red, much like the lettering on the entrance arch. Shapes of all kinds filled the front of the building, mostly stars, clowns, and spirals.

No one would ever guess that this paint job was done by a six-year-old. It still amazed Florent just how talented Clementine was. He got lost in the colors and watching the long line of people entering the opening, he hadn't realized that he lost focus until jumping when he heard his name. "There you are. I have been looking all over for you. It gets harder and harder, the larger the crowds get." Althea came up and grabbed his hands. "Come on; I need you to do something for me."

"Anything, what is it?"

"It's a surprise." She took out a piece of cloth from the pocket on her stunning dress and blindfolded Florent with it.

"What is going …?" Before he could finish his sentence, he felt Althea's lips on his. He melted into her and felt her hand take his. She led him into the more crowded area of the park; he could tell from the increasing sound of people's voices and the shoulders bumping against his.

They stopped suddenly, and Althea removed the blindfold. He was standing in line for the roller coaster, and Lawrence stood there smiling at him, a mischievous smile. When he realized what was going on, he tried to escape, but more people surrounded him; he could not move. "Hey, now wait a minute!"

"Mom and I thought it was about time you faced your fears and rode this thing. I have been riding since I was eight years old. I'm sure you can handle it."

Florent turned to Althea, standing on the other side of the fence that separated the waiting line and the open space.

"Have fun," was all she said before she walked off.

"You and your mother should really stop spending so much time together; you always mastermind all these evil plans." They stood in line for nearly forty-five minutes before they came upon the loading dock. As they waited for the train to come back, Lawrence noticed Florent shaking. It was strange to see his father so scared, but everyone has their fears, he supposed.

"Dad, really, it will be fine; actually, it will be fun. Besides, you know all the drops and turns. You helped build this."

"I do know about those. That's why I don't want to ride it."

As soon as he finished his sentence, the train came to a stop right in front of them. The blue carts sat and shimmered from the sunlight coming in from the wooden building's open sides. Lawrence got in first, and Florent sat beside him. It was a tight squeeze, but it wasn't unbearable. They both put on their safety straps across their waist, Florent pulled his as tight as he could get it. Two employees walked down both sides, ensuring that all the straps were safe and put on correctly. "This is the most popular ride here, Mr. Fayland! I'm glad you're finally riding it."

"Well, I'm not." Florent grabbed onto the bar as tightly as he could when he felt a jolt underneath him as they started moving. When they exited the platform, the sun hit him in the face right before they went around a sharp turn. They were quickly escalating up the first hill. The clicking metal made Florent uneasy, and he happened to look over the edge to see the trees getting farther away from them. Florent grabbed on tighter to the bar, the closer they got to the top, and he shut his eyes until the drop. He opened them as soon as they were hanging down, ready to be shot down the hill. Florent screamed as he felt his stomach lurch forward, and the air hit his face. Next thing he knew, they were going over hills like the waves in the ocean as the steel and wood cracked underneath them. It was only a two-minute ride, but it felt like a lifetime.

As they pulled back into the loading area, Florent's hair looked like a small tornado went through it, sticking up in all directions, and he had the look of horror on his face. Lawrence looked at him and laughed. "Nice hair, Dad." He quickly put his hair back to normal and looked embarrassed.

Althea was waiting on them at the exit with a grin on her face. "Well, how was it?"

"You're just lucky I love you."

She let out a small laugh as she took his hand and placed her head on his shoulder. "I love you too. I knew how scared you were to ride it, but sometimes you must take chances. If you never face your fears, you'll never know how to be brave." Althea was right; she was always right. He hated every second of that experience, but a part of him felt freed. She gave Florent the courage to do the possible when it seemed impossible. She healed his wounds, whether literally or figuratively. But most importantly, she was a comfort in a time of pain.

Evening had come, and the skyline looked like one of Clementine's paintings. It was as if God had taken a paintbrush of purple, pink, and yellow to the sky as he forcefully stroked each color to the once baby-blue sky. The fireplace in the living room was crackling in the distance, bringing a small amount of light to the room. The flames danced from each note that came out of the record player. Althea had entered the room after putting Clementine and Lawrence to bed.

She had changed into something much more elegant, a white satin gown that accented her figure. A diamond necklace hung around her neck, and her hair curled just underneath her neck. Florent stood up and looked her up and down. How many times in their lifetime would she make him stand paralyzed with astonishment?

Winnie sat on the small sofa, sipping tea out of her floral teacup, with Roger right beside her. Althea poured herself some tea from the tea set sitting on the coffee table. "Thank you for this, Winnie; you always have the best tea and lemon bars."

"No problem, glad you like it." As soon as Althea sat down, Winnie raised her teacup in the air for a toast, and the rest of them followed.

"This toast is to *béatitude éternelle*! It means may we forever live in eternal bliss. My family used to say it; basically, it means to live life to the fullest and be happy with what you have."

"Well, Winnie, are you going to tell them?" Roger asked.

"Althea, Florent, we have some exciting news. We waited four years engaged, waiting to get married, and now we decided to stop waiting and go another step further. I'm pregnant!"

Florent smiled and couldn't hide his excitement. "That's incredible. Congratulations!" He looked over to Althea to see her expression, but instead of happiness, she looked perturbed about something.

"What is it?" Florent asked.

Althea smiled and looked at Winnie. "Me too."

Florent smiled and then realized what she just said. He looked at her with his mouth open; he didn't know why he was so surprised every time this occurred. "Sorry, Florent, I was going to tell you next week, but I thought it would be appropriate now."

Florent grabbed hold of her and hugged her, then kissed her forehead. Winnie got up and hugged her too.

"Oh, this is wonderful! They are going to be best friends. I just know it!"

"Yes, this really is a blessing." All four of them got up and hugged one another.

After a short time of talking about gossip and each other's lives, Winnie seemed to sit up, and her eyes grew wide. She noticed a violin sitting in the corner of the room. "Does someone here play the violin? It has always been one of my favorite instruments."

Althea gave an embarrassed smile. "I do," she said quietly.

"Oh, you must play for us!"

"I don't know; I'm not very good."

"She lies. She plays the violin as I have never heard before," Florent said.

"Well, all right," Althea said, getting up.

She grabbed the small wooden violin while turning off the record player and began to play. The melody she played made everyone get tears in their eyes; it was a gorgeous piece. She played each note with a delicateness that only added to her beauty. Florent sat and watched her and fell in love with her more than he thought was possible. They all clapped when she was done, and that brought a smile to her face.

"I told you she was good," Florent said with a smirk.

Althea turned the record player back on and returned to her seat on the couch next to Florent. The fireplace glowing in the background with the soft, elegant music made their shared happiness a beautiful memory. It was a night to remember.

Chapter 17

THE DEATH
OF FLOWERS

December 1940

It was like the time before and the time before that. Althea was in labor, and soon Florent would meet his third child. He sat in the same hallway in their home and waited as the midwives and doctor delivered the baby. He couldn't wait to look into another pair of innocent eyes and feel the baby's soft hair. He and Althea would bring another life into this world, and that was a terrifying but incomparable experience.

One of the many Christmas trees in their home sat at the end of the hallway. It looked like a bunch of stars in the night sky. Althea had made the house look like a winter wonderland. Christmas had come and gone before they knew it, just five days ago, and it was incredible. They never got the chance to take down the decorations. Clementine was asleep on his shoulder, and Lawrence sat beside him, twiddling his thumbs. Florent could tell he was nervous about his mother. "Hey, you ready to be a big brother again?" He looked at Clementine, and he smiled.

"Yeah, I guess I am."

Florent smiled back at him and put his free arm around him and squeezed him into a small hug. It was taking longer than usual, which made Florent begin to worry.

Florent perked up and smiled when the midwife finally came out from the bedroom. It was time, another incredible moment in every father's life, to hold his newborn baby for the first time in his arms. His smile quickly faded when the midwife looked troubled.

"Mr. Fayland, come in, it's urgent."

He got up quickly, and Clementine jolted awake.

"Lawrence, stay with your sister."

"What's going on?" Lawrence asked.

"I don't know. Just wait here until further notice."

He walked into the bedroom and nearly fainted. Althea was sitting in tears and sweat as blood soaked the bed. Florent rushed to the side of the bed and pulled a chair next to it; this brought back a memory he did not want to relive. "What is happening?"

She was almost screaming as she pushed as hard as she could. The midwife just looked at him with the utmost sympathy.

"She is losing a lot of blood; we don't know if she will make it. I'm so sorry."

Florent took Althea's hand, and she squeezed his hand very tightly. Suddenly, he heard crying; their baby had arrived.

The doctor turned to him while holding the baby in his hands. "It's a boy; he seems perfectly healthy." He handed the baby to the midwives for him to get cleaned up. Althea sighed, and her head fell back. She then turned her head slowly to Florent, not even looking worried, but brave just like she always did. She put her hand on Florent's cheek, and he took it into his hands and squeezed it. The doctor stood behind Florent and put his hand on his shoulder. As soon as the midwives cleaned up the baby, they brought him over in a white blanket and placed him in Florent's arms.

Althea smiled. "He's beautiful. Let me look at him before I depart."

"Depart? What do you mean? You're going to live, Althea."

"Florent, they did everything they could, but they couldn't stop the bleeding." Florent could feel himself shaking and trembling as hot tears poured down his face. She took her hands out of his and placed them on the baby's cheek.

"I want to name him after a name I heard once. I don't know where or when. It just echoes in my head like a faint mirage. The name of someone I know but never met in a place I have never been before."

"What's that, dear?"

"Vincent."

Florent looked down at the baby and knew the name was perfect. "I love it."

Each word Althea said was a struggle, for they were her last breaths, and each of Florent's words was a battle through his weeping. She placed her hand back on Florent's cheek.

"Oh, my love, you were my reason to live. You gave me hope in a hopeless world, and you were the light in my darkest times. You gave me three beautiful children, and even though I will not see Vincent grow up, I know he will make me proud, just like his siblings. Tell Clementine never to stop painting her wonderful art, and tell Lawrence to never stop being courageous. Mostly tell them how much I loved them and always will, even after I leave this world. Just remember, Florent, you have given me a life that I never deserved or ever thought I would have. You have filled me with happiness I could never imagine, and you made my life full. Remember, this is not the end; there are no endings, just new beginnings. This baby proves just that," she said as she caressed the baby's cheek and gave a smile. Her words were becoming fainter and fainter, like the melody of a sweet bird flying away into the distance.

Althea was crying now too, and as much as Florent told himself she would make it through this, he knew it was a lie to himself. Althea reached out and wiped his tears from his face. "Don't cry for me. Thank you for everything."

Florent couldn't see through his tears. He sucked in the air, fast with each word that came out of his mouth. She had nothing to thank him for, but two words came out of his mouth. "Of course."

Althea gained as much strength as she had to say her final words. "I love you." Those last three words were like a whisper from a different world; it was like an angel had touched his ears.

"I love you too."

After Florent finished saying his last words to her, her body slowly relaxed into a lifeless state until he was the only one crying. He looked into her diamond eyes one last time, wiped the last tear she would ever shed, extended his arm, and shut her eyes forever. He didn't get to tell her everything he wanted to tell her. She looked so peaceful.

She was taken too soon, just like everyone else he had lost in his life. He looked down at his son, who was still in his arms. He took his first breaths as his mother took her last. It sent a shiver down his spine when he noticed that the baby looked much different from his siblings. He looked just like Florent, with thick, black hair, but his eyes were different. Although unlike most babies, it was almost impossible to tell their eye color until later on. It was obvious Vincent was going to have his mother's eyes, which would be a constant reminder of what he had lost. He got up and walked out of the room to tell his children that they had lost their mother; it was the hardest thing he had ever done and ever would do.

Lawrence rushed in and looked at his mother before throwing himself by her side. He buried his face into the blankets and silently cried. Florent had always known that Lawrence was much closer to his mother than he had ever been to him. Clementine said nothing and kept her distance by standing at the edge of the bed as tears rolled down her face. Florent had felt anger in his chest starting to ignite, a feeling he had not had in a long time. He couldn't control it; Althea had always been there to calm him in the past. He gave Vincent to Clementine and ran out of the room.

The doctor and midwives were just outside the door, packing up their things, looking defeated. The doctor looked up at Florent. "I'm truly sorry about your loss." Florent could feel the veins in his head and neck popping out, and he gritted his teeth. "Sometimes this happens, mothers don't survive childbirth. It's a harsh reality, but it happens, and it's a blessing that the baby is healthy."

"You could have saved her."

"I'm sorry, Mr. Fayland, but her blood loss was too significant, and she suffered from complications. We did all we could."

"Well, you didn't do enough." The rage overtook Florent as he grabbed the doctor by the collar of his coat and slammed him against the wall, holding him there. Florent's saliva was hanging out of his mouth, and his eyes gushed tears, like a wild beast.

The doctor cowered in fear and looked like he was afraid he would be killed. Florent, realizing what he had done, let him go. "I'm so sorry." The doctor grabbed his suitcase and equipment, and the midwives looked at Florent with fear like he was a monster. The doctor straightened out his coat and recollected himself.

"Goodbye, Mr. Fayland." He quickly walked out, and the midwives followed.

Florent went back into his bedroom, where his children stood looking at their deceased mother. She was an angel in a blood-soaked bed. Florent took Vincent in his arms and joined his children. They had lost a parent, and Florent knew exactly what they were feeling. He stood there and stared at her, realizing that all beautiful things would fade away eventually, leaving only their memories.

The world was once again filled with gray mist, and the sun hid behind the clouds like it was too sad to come out. The entire town seemed to mourn the loss of Althea, and its heart ached with pain. Florent stood out in his yard, looking at Althea's garden. All the plants and flowers were dead. It was a strange phenomenon, but it made sense to him. Everything that Althea had put so much love and time into had quickly tattered away, himself included. He had ordered black roses to bury her with, just like she had done with his mother. Her burial was in thirty minutes. He decided to spend that time looking at what she had created, but even that was now gone. He began to cry; he couldn't control his emotions. Most of his days were spent locked away in his room, just letting himself drown in his tears and misery. Snow started to fall on his head, and his tears were mixed in with it.

Snowflakes landed on the tip of his nose and tickled his eyelashes. He had picked a beautiful spot on his land to have her buried; it was right by the house and close to the woods. The sun hit the place just right, making the one plot of land gleam even in the Fathorne fog. He turned around to see Lawrence and Clementine walking down the back stairs all in black to mourn their mother. Clementine wore her hair down for once in a long time instead of her long braids. Lawrence looked much more lavish than usual. His hair was neatly put back, but his eyes were red and swollen and his face extremely pale. Clementine took Florent's hand, and Lawrence joined his side, and the three of them stood staring at the once-colorful garden, which was now lifeless and dull.

Winnie came out of the house carrying Vincent, Florent was very grateful that she and Roger had helped with all the planning of Althea's funeral. Winnie handed Vincent to Florent, who was wrapped up in a blanket and a black outfit. Her stomach seemed like it would burst at any moment as Roger and she waited for their child's arrival. After the half hour was up, everyone shifted to her gravestone, where her casket was sitting, still opened for everyone to see her face one last time. Many people of Fathorne came to her funeral because they remembered her gorgeous flowers. She lay there in her yellow floral dress, the same one she wore when Florent saw her the first time. She was wearing it when he fell in love with her. A bouquet of pink flowers was placed in her hands.

Florent stood there, staring at her, and didn't know how to respond. He was looking at the one person in the entire world who had made him feel like someone. He took his finger and stroked her face, feeling her soft skin against his one last time. The snow started to fall harder, and Florent shielded Vincent's face from the cold. He almost jumped when Roger came behind him and placed his arm around him. He knew it was his way of sending his condolences, and Florent cherished it very much. He looked over to Winnie, who was crying. The pastor began talking, and he knew that the end was near. The lid was shut on her casket, locked away from Florent forever. Soon her casket was lowered into the ground, and black rose petals were gracefully thrown in with her. Snow dusted her gravestone, which had an angel on the side. This was his last goodbye.

When the snow had ceased and the ground was covered in white, it was already dark outside. This day had been the most devastating of Florent's life. He sat by Althea's grave long after everyone had left and his children had gone to bed. He already hired a nanny; he felt like he could not care for them the way they deserved. He was afraid of himself, fearful that his anger would get the best of him and hurt them. He could never let them, no more pain on the ones he loved. His children were the only family he had left now, and the only way to protect them was to keep his distance. Without Althea, he was just an endless pit of hatred and fury, and the little bit of light that was left in him was gone.

Florent finally had enough strength to get himself up. He walked into the house and searched for anything that would numb his pain. He still had a bad limp, and it was hard to get around in the shadowy house, but he stumbled to the kitchen regardless. He opened all the cabinets and drawers, not even sure what he was looking for, until he came across the whiskey bottle that Roger had given him all those years ago. He didn't know the shelf life of liquor, and he didn't care. He popped the lid of the bottle and started to drink it. He had only had two drinks in his life for special occasions and just a glass at a time. He kept drinking the bitter liquid until he reached the bottom, then threw the bottle back into the cabinet. He stumbled out of the kitchen, knocking items off shelves and running into the side of walls.

He finally reached his bedroom and slammed the door, slowly

sitting on the floor in front of the door. He let out a small scream of agony as his tears ran into his mouth. Looking around his room, he knew this would become his forever prison. He wanted to lock himself from the world for all eternity. He got up and looked into the vanity mirror and was disgusted with what he saw as he stood there, staring into red eyes and a drunken face. He went to the closet and pulled out one of Althea's old floral dresses from when they first met and put it up to his face. It still had her scent; she smelled like vanilla and flowers.

He cried into it as he lay on the floor in his misery. Eventually, he looked up and saw the black figure standing right by his head. It didn't talk or move; it just stood there motionless. Florent looked up and quietly asked, "What do you want from me? Why do you keep following me?" Again there was no answer. "Leave me alone, you son of a bitch! Can't you see how the world has taken everything from me? If you want something from me, everything is gone. Do you want some money? Just take it and let me be!"

The next thing Florent knew, his vision was getting blurrier, and he looked up into a familiar face, but he could not recognize it through his tears. Then the room became darker and darker as he was staring at this shadowy figure, and the room faded into nothingness.

Chapter 18
THE SCAR
March 1947

Vincent sat on his bed, looking out the frosted window. Spring was coming soon, but the cold weather still occupied the mornings in Fathorne. His bedroom faced his mother's white gravestone. How he wished he could have met her. His sister had always told him how captivating she was, that not even the flowers their father planted for her were as beautiful as her face. She also told him how kind she was and that she made you feel protected from all the evil things in the world. One day, Clementine gave him a painting of their mother, of what she had remembered of her when she was still alive. Vincent had put in a frame on his nightstand so that she would be the first thing he saw every morning. The only person he ever really knew close to a parent was Darlene, their nanny. She was kind and fair, but he knew that she would never be his actual mother. He only saw his father at some meals and occasionally in the garden. He took the picture from his nightstand and headed outside.

When he reached the back porch, he saw his father planting his usual pink flowers. Vincent didn't know why he did this, but they were stunning. He planted many every day, covering the entire garden, making it look like a cotton candy–covered field. A white fence surrounded the garden, and the roses were gracefully climbing up the railings. The flowers were starting to overtake the land. Florent looked up, and it scared Vincent, making him try to hide on the porch.

"Vincent, what are you doing?"

Vincent slowly popped his head back up and walked down the porch's stairs. He knew he shouldn't be scared; this was his father, but something made him timid. "I was looking for Clementine." Vincent then hid the painting in his jacket. He started to walk away, which would have been the smart thing to do, but his curiosity took hold of him. "Dad, why do you plant all these roses? What are they for?"

Florent stopped what he was doing and just stared at the ground.

Vincent already regretted saying something.

Without ever looking at Vincent, Florent answered his question. "They are for your mother. Pink roses were her favorite flower, so I plant them for her." Another moment of silence fell between them before Florent continued. "It's one of the only things about her that I still have. Every year, they will grow and remind the world of her. That way, her spirit never dies. She was a rose in her own wonderful way." Florent just stood there and stared at nothing.

Vincent didn't really understand what he meant by his last phrase and did not ask. This conversation was one of the only times in his entire life when Vincent heard his father say more than just a few words. "Leave me be, please."

Vincent obeyed his wish and continued trying to find Clementine. His father always acted strangely, like he was in a different place. Perhaps it was something that adults felt that he didn't understand yet.

He walked onto the park's grounds, where a silence swept over the land. He couldn't believe that his father had created this place; he just didn't seem lively enough. Vincent walked past the funhouse, the carousel, the food stands, and the roller coaster, but there seemed to be no sign of his sister.

"Hey, Vincent!"

He jumped and turned the sound. Clementine was over by the Ferris wheel in paint-covered overalls with her long white-blonde hair pulled into a ponytail.

"What are you painting?" He noticed that the Ferris wheel no longer had the plain white carts it once had but had images. She had one painted with flowers and cherubs on the back; it was a classy upgrade.

"Just giving the Ferris wheel a new paint job."

Vincent sat down in the grass and watched his sister paint the cart. He pulled out the painting from his jacket. "Clementine?"

Yes?"

"Could you tell me more about Mother?"

She never stopped painting as she spoke and kept her focus. "I've already told you everything I know about her. Why do you want to know so much about her?"

"Everyone tells me how beautiful and kind she was. I just want to know who she was. Also, everyone at school has their mothers, and I watch them hug them and kiss them. I never got to experience what a mother's touch felt like."

"I'm sorry, Vincent, but I told you everything I knew about her. I wish you could have met her too. Remember, I was only six when she died, and my memory of her is slowly fading. It's sad, but it's true. Every day my mind forgets more and more of her. Her face is becoming blank to me. I try to cling to the memories, but they are slowly leaving my mind."

"There's really no more you can tell me?"

"Well, I do remember that she loved flowers. She worked in her garden all the time. I have never seen someone grow flowers as beautiful as she did. I remember her upside-down clementine cakes she would always make for me. I haven't had one since she passed. I also know that Father and she were very much in love, a romance that I would love just to have a part of for myself."

"Dad doesn't seem to love much of anything."

"Oh, but he loved Mom. I remember them dancing."

"Dad danced?"

Clementine smiled. "He wasn't the greatest at it with his limp, but he managed. I also remember sneaking out of bed many nights that I saw something wonderful."

Clementine stopped painting and stared at nothing as she spoke with a huge smile. "Father sat on the couch as Mother played her violin for him, it was beautiful. Sometimes I would stand at the doorway just to listen to her."

"Wow, I never knew that about her."

Clementine soon changed the subject, which made Vincent aggravated; he loved hearing about his mother.

"How are you doing at school?" she asked.

"My grades are excellent, straight As, but not so much on making friends."

"I don't understand; you're a very kind person."

"Thanks, but apparently that doesn't make friends. I don't really talk that much and spend most of my time reading. Many people make fun of me for being such a big egghead."

"I don't think you're an egghead; you're intelligent and shouldn't be criticized."

"Thanks, Clem."

"No problem, just remember that just because I'm your sister, doesn't mean that I can't be your friend." She stood up and extended her hand. "Friends for life?"

Vincent took her hand. "Friends for life." They shook hands, and it made a commitment to Vincent, which he found very dear.

Vincent, like many days, spent his time walking in the woods that surrounded his family's park. The evenings were the most magnificent part of the days in Fathorne. There was no fog and this particular day, no rain, just the sunshine and the birds that flew above his head, singing a cheerful tune. The woods were his one place to think and escape the chaos that he felt in his mind. Perhaps he was much too young to feel feelings of pain and loneliness, but no one should ever be alone. Out here, he was more isolated than anywhere in the world, but all the lonely feelings melted away when he entered these woods. He walked and watched the naked tree, not yet graced with spring, sway in the wind. It was a lovely sight, he thought, not really knowing why, but it was peaceful and somehow soothing. The sun shone above, letting in small patches of light, making a pattern of streaks through the woods.

He kept walking until he reached a building of some sort. He remembered his brother talking about an abandoned bunker that their father had turned into his playroom and his own personal hangout. He stopped coming here years ago, leaving everything behind. The grass and weeds were overtaking the front, and the blue paint was chipping away, revealing the stone walls while the algae covered the rest.

Lawrence was away at college, majoring in business and learning as much information as possible. Florent had told Lawrence, being the oldest child, that he would be the heir. Vincent saw this as unfair, but his father still believed in older practices. Florent told Lawrence to receive an education in business so one day he could run the park and carry on the family business. Lawrence had the qualities and the responsibility of a leader. Someday, Clementine would go off somewhere too, leaving him behind in this prison. She would marry and have children of her own, while Vincent would be stuck in his brother's shadow and always being the lesser of the two. Vincent knew he himself was smart, but he was diffident and couldn't run a business. Not only that, but his brother was also the eldest, much more handsome, and even more intelligent. They never had a good relationship anyway. Lawrence pushed Vincent aside and never spoke to him; he always seemed angry at him and never even smiled at him. Perhaps he had done something wrong without ever knowing it.

Vincent pushed on the metal door as hard as he could. Fortunately, it opened. He went down the ladder, running into a few spider webs, into a single dark room. He stood in the web-covered room with its olive-green paint. Little animals circled the room, and Vincent smiled. Toys were scattered across the floor as dust collected on them. A bookshelf sat in the corner with a few children's books. It was evident that Lawrence hadn't been down since his childhood. He looked through old boxes and a discarded toy chest to see what he could find. He found an old, white, tattered teddy bear sitting all alone on the floor. Vincent decided this would now be his hideout, a place where he could go to be alone with his thoughts and away from people's criticism.

When Vincent arrived back at the house, darkness had claimed the land. He must have been gone longer than he had thought. As he came out of the woods, he noticed an elegant car parked in his driveway, its brown exterior gleaming off the porch lights. He knew the vehicle belonged to Roger and Winnie, his father's friends. It had been several years since Vincent had seen them, since they went back to France to visit Winnie's family. They had a daughter who was a month younger than Vincent, and they had only met once when they were around four years old. He couldn't even remember what she looked like, only that she wore a pink dress and shared the same color hair as her mother. He opened the large glass entrance doors to his house to a dark interior. A small amount of light gleamed from the living room, and he could hear voices coming from inside. He peeked around the corner to see his father out of his room, socializing. This was a rare occasion for him. He seemed as though he was enjoying himself but drinking as usual with a whiskey bottle in his hand. Clementine sat on a sofa away from the adults' conversation, next to a strawberry-blonde girl in a pink dress, just like Vincent remembered her, except taller and more mature looking.

"Vincent!" his father yelled, almost falling over. "Don't just stand there; we have guests." Florent had spotted Vincent sneaking from behind the doorframe. "Vincent, I don't know if you remember, but this is Roger and his wife, Winnie. They are longtime friends of mine, and Roger helped build and fund the amusement park."

Vincent was uncomfortable; he did not enjoy social interaction with people he barely knew, so he simply nodded.

"And this is Marie, their daughter."

Vincent turned to see the girl coming toward him in her frilly pink-and-white lace dress and her reddish ringlets bouncing as she walked. Something inside him felt strange, but in a good way. His stomach felt like it had dropped, and his heartbeat sped up. What were these feelings he felt?

Marie came up to him and extended her hand. "Hi, it's very nice to meet you!" she said as her pearly white teeth were displayed.

"Nice to meet you too," Vincent said, almost under his breath. He could feel his cheeks turning red as he felt the heat on his skin. "I'm Vincent."

He walked over with his sister to the sofa she was formerly sitting on, and Marie joined. Clementine pulled the easel from behind one of the bookshelves and placed a piece of paper out along with paint. "You know, your sister is an excellent painter. I asked her to paint a portrait of me."

"Yeah, she really is a good painter." That's all Vincent could say for the rest of the night. He felt nervous around Marie. He didn't want to say or do anything stupid around her, and he had a habit of making things awkward. After only a short time, Clementine gave Marie the painting, and she smiled, revealing her white teeth again.

"Thank you so much. I love it!"

Clementine blushed, as she did every time someone complimented her paintings.

"Come on, Marie, time to go!" Winnie called out.

"See you later," Clementine said as Marie hugged her.

"It was very nice to meet you; I hope we see each other soon!" Marie said to Vincent, hugging him tightly as well. Vincent tensed up; he couldn't even remember a time when someone hugged him, if ever. He liked the feeling, though, as he felt the softness of Marie's hair and the warmth that she gave him. He finally relaxed and placed his arms around her as well.

"Yeah," was all he could manage to say back to her. She then skipped to her mother and grabbed her hand, waving at Clementine and Vincent. His heart was still beating, and for the first time he felt something—a feeling he couldn't describe.

The house was once again silent as Clementine went to bed, and his father had left the room. Vincent sneaked passed the nanny and started to walk toward his father's room. He saw his father go toward the back door, likely to the garden to plant more roses for his mother. Even though Vincent was young, he understood his father's condition when he started to act a certain way. Clementine explained to him that their father was usually drunk. He drank whiskey day in and day out, causing him to stumble around the house and have redness in his eyes. The worst part of it all was that his father became aggressive and violent, and that's when he would lock himself in his room. He pulled out the painting of his mother once more and looked into her delicate eyes, identical to his own. He remembered that earlier Clementine had told him about their mother's violin, with which she had once made music.

Perhaps he could learn how to play it and play for his mother at her grave; the thought made him happy. He hoped his mother could hear him from heaven and be proud that he had followed in her footsteps. Soon he was standing at the double doors that led into his father's room; he had never been in there before. He pulled down on the doorknob, and the door creaked as he slowly opened it. What he saw inside sent a shiver down his spine. Wallpaper on the walls was cut by what appeared to be a knife or some type of glass. Papers were spread across the floor, all with the same three words on top. "My dearest Althea," was written with nothing afterward. Some had more writing but were scratched out. One paper stood on the vanity, and it actually had some writing on it. Vincent assumed it was the most recently written. It read, "My dearest Althea, Before I met you, there was no happiness in this world. I only saw darkness around every corner; the waves of the ocean were violent inside my mind. My mind took me down a dark path I never wanted to follow. You were right about this dark, cold place, but someone will be there to light the way. That's what you were, the brightest light in the darkest abyss. Now that you're gone, I rot away in the house we made into a home. I no longer see the same man in the mirror I had once seen. I plant roses for you every day to remind myself that your presence is always near. They vine up your gravestone like art; I feel that even the earth itself misses your sweet touch to such a harsh society."

This letter to his mother that she would never be able to read made him understand his father. An understanding that he never really could find before. He turned around to the room, which was a mess; it looked like a wild animal had gone through, destroying everything in its path. It was the display of sadness that had turned into madness. Vincent saw a white lace book that sat on one of the nightstands, that he assumed was his mother's side. He opened the book, and words were splashed on every page; it was like looking at a beautiful, chaotic mess. He didn't have time to read when he saw the violin sitting in the corner of the room, displayed magnificently as if it were waiting for someone to play it. He placed the diary back where he found it and rushed over to the pretty little instrument. The black wood was very nicely crafted, and it was in perfect condition. He picked it up as if he had been doing this all his life, like it was his destiny. He took the bow and glided it across the strings, making a horrific noise. It made him squirm, but he kept playing. He could learn how to do this; all he had to do was ask his father if he could.

He suddenly looked up to see his father, leaning on the doorframe with a whiskey bottle in his hand. It took him only a second to notice Vincent, and he rushed toward him. "Vincent, what are you doing here? Get out!" His father's face looked inhuman, and the redness in his eyes was intense. "Stay away from that!" Vincent didn't know why he didn't obey his father's wishes, but he stood there as his legs failed him. He supposed it was fear keeping him nailed to the ground. Florent took the bottle and slammed it against the wall, creating a loud crash, which made Vincent jump. "Never come in here again, and never touch your mother's things."

"Father, I was only trying to ..." Florent looked at him with his bloodshot eyes, and Vincent could see the anger in them. He approached him in a fit of rage, limping badly. He took the top of the bottle that was now a large shard of glass and struck Vincent across the face. Vincent screamed out in pain as he felt the flesh on his face be torn. The glass's pressure had caused a large scratch across his face, along with his eye, which became blind. He could feel the wet, sticky blood pouring down his face; he put his hands over it to try to stop it. Pieces of glass were stuck in his skin, and parts of his flesh were now hanging.

Florent stared at him in fear and quickly came to his aid. Though the blood was going into his eyes and he could only see out of one eye, he could tell his father was scared. Florent placed his hand on his back and pulled out a cloth from his pocket in panic, trying to soak up as much blood as possible. "Vincent, I'm so... what have I done?" His father was now crying and couldn't finish a sentence.

Darlene came rushing in and almost screamed at the sight of Vincent. "What happened? I heard screaming."

Florent looked down at the ground.

"I, um, tripped and cut my face." Vincent lied. Florent looked like he was about to say something but passed out, sprawled across the floor in the mess he had created. Darlene helped Vincent out of the room and kept the cloth on his face.

Clementine eventually came to and was terrified at what she saw. She left with Darlene to take Vincent to the hospital. The blood and glass remained scattered around Florent as he lay unconscious on the floor.

When Florent woke up, he could only remember half of what had happened just hours ago. He quickly got up to look at the clock, which read two ten. He assumed it was early morning, since it was still dark outside. He looked back at the broken glass and blood that spread across the floor; his own son's blood stained his hands along with his clothes. He was disgusted with himself; how did he ever become this monstrosity? He had finally allowed his anger and foolishness to hurt someone he loved. He was so selfish, and Vincent lied for him, even though his actions were inexcusable. Why would his son try to cover up the person who hurt him? His son's blue eyes were like daggers into his heart, and all the pain of losing Althea had come back to him, a pain he believed would never heal. It was not Vincent's fault, and he knew that he was only trying to find out more about his mother.

He got up and ran to the hall as his head pounded. He turned every corner and opened every door in the house, but Vincent, along with Darlene and Clementine, were nowhere to be found. He threw himself on a wall and slowly lowered himself down and began to sob into his hands. His memory failed him after a certain point in time. All he could remember was striking Vincent and his terrible scream, which made Florent sick in the stomach.

He jumped when the phone rang in his study. He limped into the room as fast as he could to answer it. Darlene was on the line, and she seemed to have a calm voice that relieved Florent. He knew when he hired her to take care of his children that she really cared about them. She had never once called out Florent for being a lousy father, even though he knew she should. "Mr. Fayland, I'm so glad you answered! I took Vincent to the hospital, and they said he is going to be okay. He had to have stitches across his face. They don't know if he will ever have sight in his one eye ever again." That made Florent's heart sink, and he was again sickened with himself.

"That must have been a really nasty fall," she said in a suspicious tone. Florent knew that she really knew what happened; it wasn't the first time he had lashed out, but he had never physically hurt anyone in his family. Florent knew he was vile when he responded with, "Yeah, it was." He also knew his children would be taken away from him for abuse if they ever found out that he had damaged

Vincent's face. He didn't want to lose his children when he had lost so much already, even though he thought perhaps they deserved better. He never told the truth about that gruesome night, and it would haunt him forever.

Vincent came back from the hospital after a few days. He got out of Darlene's car with bandages wrapped around his face. Clementine helped guide him out of the vehicle now that he had impaired vision. Florent watched from a window that looked out to the driveway and saw the mess he had made. His little boy now looked like a science experiment with stitches across his face and one gray eye; the other eye was just like his mother's. Florent vowed to himself that he would keep away from his children even more than before; he couldn't endure looking at Vincent. It killed him inside, knowing that he would not be there for his children, but they were safer and in better hands when they were with Darlene. As much as he had always tried to conceal his anger, it never worked.

Althea seemed to be the only thing that could calm his behavior, but now she was gone. He still depended on alcohol to get him through each day, even though he had seen the damage it had caused. It was the only thing that would ever numb this pain. He wanted to be with his children and move on from loss as he did in the past, but something dark lingered with him. He could not escape.

Vincent came into the house and noticed that his father was nowhere to be found. He had sworn he saw him staring out the window. Vincent was scared of his father now and didn't know how to forgive him. But Vincent understood that he shouldn't have been meddling in his mother's things. They were the only belongings his father had left of her. He was a fool for thinking that it was wise to mess with such valuable items.

Florent had finally come out of the secrecy of the living room and confronted him. His father couldn't even meet his gaze. He was holding on to Althea's violin. "Here, take it. What I did was unforgivable, and I ..." Before he finished his sentence, Vincent stopped him.

"It's my fault. I shouldn't have been messing around with things that don't belong to me."

His father bent down to meet his eye level, and for the first time, Vincent could see his father's eyes, his real eyes. The same color that Clementine and Lawrence shared. They were not the red, hatred-filled eyes disguised with sadness.

"I know that you are curious about the person your mother was. Her violin was one of the most significant parts about her. The way she played sounded like something from a music box. It brought peace to my mind, just like she did. I may not have your mother anymore, but I have you and your siblings. Through all of you, I see her. The same way I see her through the pink roses that bloom. I was hoping you could learn how to play this and bring back her beautiful melodies." He pulled out a book that had all the notes and instructions to get started. "I know she would have wanted to share this with you."

Florent then got up and walked away, Vincent assumed back to his bedroom. It was not just a room; it was hell. But just like his mind, he could not escape it, no matter how hard he tried. Vincent picked up the violin and book that was left for him on the ground. He then went to his mother's grave to play for her as well as he could.

Chapter 19
CALLING OF THE HEART
April 1959

Vincent sat in the old green, painted bunker, thinking about simple thoughts and complex ones too. He often thought about life and the meaning of being alive. What was his purpose, or did he even have one? He sat in an old armchair that he placed in the corner. He had made quite a space for himself. He put all his favorite books, and there were many, on a bookshelf that sat in another corner. He had a desk with an office chair where he had spent many days completing homework and writing poems, short stories, and nonsense. Writing was his solace, just as painting was Clementine's. He never planned to have them published; they were more for his own eyes. He had hung many of Clementine's paintings on the wall, making it look almost like an art museum.

She had gone and completed college, getting a degree in fine art. It was now her career, and she made good money doing it and was semi-famous for her painting. Although she could go anywhere in life, she chose to come back home and work. She often kept up with the park's painting jobs. All the rides and buildings were like nothing else, as each thing she touched turned to art. She even repainted all the paintings on the ceiling of their house. They looked better than the originals. Vincent looked down at a picture that was taken of his siblings and him. It was taken in front of the garden after one of Lawrence's breaks from college. He looked at his scarred face and was disgusted by it each time. He also felt outraged by looking at Lawrence.

He despised his brother, and he knew he shouldn't, but he did. All his life, Lawrence hated him right back for no reason, so Vincent felt he would treat him the same. He had locked him in this bunker when he was a kid several times as a joke. Their nanny would have to find him later, but she would no longer be able to rescue him. When Vincent reached the age of thirteen, his father had let her go. Lawrence made Vincent's life miserable. He called him names and degraded him every chance he had. Vincent even had a few bones broken by him. His brother was over thirty years old, but he still acted like an immature teenager, like the ones at Vincent's high school.

Vincent still lacked any friends, except his sister; she had kept her promise. He had suffered being the weird one before and after he was given this scar, but now people never missed the chance to mock him and his flaws. He would graduate in one short month, and he couldn't wait to leave the constant torture. He loved learning, but he couldn't help but fear every time he entered the school building. He was disturbed with humanity; he didn't believe there was one decent being anywhere. He placed the picture back in the drawer and headed up the ladder.

The morning sun hit him in the face as he exited the bunker into the open world, back to reality. He looked around at the world that he had always hated. He no longer saw beauty in anything, not even in these woods he once thought looked like something out of a fairytale. Their cook was most likely serving up lunch, and Vincent did not want to be late. He noticed Roger's car was parked in front of the house again. It was probably just another visit that he made every so often to talk business with his father. Vincent assumed they spoke about the park and what was happening in their lives. Florent hid the sadness and chaos that he usually displayed when no one was around. Roger had no idea what really went on inside of those walls. Vincent tried to sneak into the kitchen, but it did not work. Everyone stared at him as he entered the room; he got that a lot. No matter how many times Roger or even his own family saw the scar, they couldn't help but stare at his mangled face and gray eye.

He was caught by surprise when Roger wasn't their only visitor. Winnie was there too. And someone was hanging on to Lawrence's arm, a girl in a pink dress. Vincent's heart sank when he realized who it was. Marie had changed so much since he had seen her last. The last time was that one night when they were six years old, just children. Winnie homeschooled Marie. She had spent most of her childhood and teenage years working on her studies. She also went back and forth between her home here and France to her mother's family. There was no time to visit, with her busy schedule. Marie noticed Vincent and smiled along with a wave; she remembered him.

Her smile quickly faded when she got a better look at Vincent's face. She approached him, and Vincent almost stumbled backward on a vase. "What happened?"

Florent looked at Vincent with a nervous stare. "I tripped and broke a mirror, landing on the glass face first. One of the pieces made a diagonal slash across my face." Vincent lied once again, but he had been covering up his father's story all these years; today was no different.

"That's terrible; I'm so sorry." Vincent could tell she was legitimately sorry for him. She was very enchanting. Her teeth were still as white as the snow-capped mountains that surrounded their property. Her hair was a strawberry-blonde perfection. Her pink dress swayed below her knees when she walked, and she had a small pink bow on her head.

He felt sick but didn't know why. She went back to Lawrence and took his hand. Vincent could feel the hatred for his conceited brother. Were they a couple? When did this happen? Vincent sat down as the maid placed a plate of food in front of him. He suddenly wasn't hungry. His appetite had seemed to vanish in the last ten minutes.

At the far end of the table, Roger stood up and raised his glass for a toast. "I would like to make a toast to two very special people we have here tonight—the joining of Lawrence Fayland, the son of my longtime friend, and my daughter, Marie. I could not picture my daughter with anyone else. Lawrence, being the heir to a percentage of the Fayland fortune and Fayland Park, it seemed to be perfect. I could not ask my daughter to marry into any more of a perfect family. Just two weeks ago, I introduced Marie to Lawrence at my house, and they hit it off right away. So, with that being said, I would like to say cheers to new love!"

"To new love!" everyone at the table repeated, except Vincent.

He had been so busy watching Lawrence and Marie, he didn't notice how many other people were in the room. They must have parked somewhere on the park's lot. Marie kissed Lawrence on the cheek, and Vincent clenched his fists. He should have been happy for his brother, but he felt nothing close to that. He didn't know that arranged marriages even existed anymore. He noticed other people at the table he had never seen before; he thought perhaps it was Roger's friends. Men in black suits stood around the dining room, which seemed strange. Vincent couldn't believe he hadn't seen them sooner.

Everyone at the table talked with excitement and seemed to be catching up on each other's lives, which Vincent saw as uninteresting and meaningless. Everyone's plate was almost empty, except Vincent's. He got up to take his plate with half-eaten food to the kitchen, just to escape the torture inside that room. The conversations and talk of politics and social standings were everything Vincent hated. Besides, no one had the decency to talk to him anyway.

They knew he was there, but they avoided him at all costs. They were too afraid to say anything about his face since he was Florent Fayland's son. He sometimes forgot that the broken man he always knew his father to be was actually very successful and wealthy. But this proved to him that success and money aren't always the path to happiness; his father was everything but happy.

Vincent scraped the food into the trash and placed the plate into the sink. He jumped as he noticed that Clementine had followed him. She held a glass of white wine in her hands and seemed celebratory, just like everyone else. "Isn't it amazing? Marie is going to be my sister-in-law. I have always thought she was such a lovely girl. I've always wanted a sister; now I guess I'm going to have one. I never thought Lawrence would ever get married. He had never even seemed interested." She almost choked over her words because she was talking so fast.

"Yeah, it's great. I'm happy for them," Vincent said in an unenthusiastic tone.

"Hey, what's wrong?"

"Nothing, I just feel a little sick, that's all."

"Oh no, do you need anything? Can I do anything for you?"

"No, Clem. I'm just going to go lie down."

She looked at him sorrowfully. "Oh, um, all right."

Vincent knew she could tell he was lying. There was something deeper down below the surface. Something that he couldn't even understand himself.

The next morning, Vincent got up early, just as he had done for some time now. It was still dark outside, as the sun hadn't come up yet. He changed into a blue-and-gray sweater along with gray pants. He also put on a jacket, since April mornings still had a bit of a chill in the air. After he changed, he grabbed his mother's violin and headed out the door. He pulled the jacket closer to his face as the cold air swept across him. He passed the rose-covered garden. His father's planting was getting out of control. The roses were now climbing up the porch and other places outside of the garden, though it did look gorgeous. The roses were also growing around his mother's grave; they vined around it gracefully. He began to play the best he could. His playing had significantly improved over all these years of practice; he started to sound like a real musician.

He was quick to stop when he heard footsteps behind him and prepared to fight whatever was coming his way. It was Marie; she was in a pink lace nightgown. Even in the moonlight, her face beamed with grace and kindness. She had stayed the night in their guest room. The room faced the gravestone; he must have woken her. "Oh, hello, Marie. I'm sorry if I woke you up."

"You did, but that's okay. I usually get up around this time anyway. I just heard beautiful music, and I had to see where it was coming from. Where did you learn to play like that?"

"I taught myself. It was my mother's violin. I play for her every morning."

"That's so sweet! I'm really sorry about your mother. I am sad that I never got to meet her. My parents said she was one of the sweetest people they had ever met."

"That's what everyone tells me. I never got to meet her either. She died at childbirth."

"That's what my parents said; that's so tragic."

Vincent turned to his mother's grave. "Yeah, it truly is."

"Do you mind if I stand here and listen?"

Vincent felt utterly embarrassed but couldn't deny her request.

"Of course not." He noticed her covering her arms and shivering; she must have forgotten a jacket. Vincent took his off and covered her shoulders without hesitation.

"That's so generous, thank you."

Vincent just gave her a small smile, and they stared at each other for a few seconds before they realized they were doing it. He went back to the violin and continued playing. It made his heart flop, knowing she was behind him, listening to every note he played. He was starting to understand what he was feeling. He was falling in love with her, or perhaps he had always been in love with her. But this was forbidden and never could happen. She loved his brother, and there was nothing he could do about that. As long as she was happy, that's all he wanted, even if it made him suffer.

Chapter **20**

FATE AT THE FERRIS WHEEL

April 1959

Clementine awoke to birds chirping outside her window; it was a pleasant tune. She got out of bed and pulled the large curtains to allow the sunlight to light up her room. She let out a happy sigh. She had a busy schedule ahead, as many of the rides needed their yearly touch-up. The first on her agenda was the Ferris wheel, her favorite ride. She used to prefer the carousel. Now she loved the Ferris wheel because she could see for miles. Miles of trees, mountains, and the natural beauty of Fathorne. Many people thought that this town was just a boring, fog-filled place, but Clementine saw so much more in her home. That's what life was all about, she thought. Life is what we choose to see. We can either stand in the fog or dance in it. And just like her parents once were, she was the dancing type. She put on her old painting overalls and tied her hair up in a high ponytail out of her face. Lastly, she grabbed her painting supplies and headed out toward the amusement park. It was a beautiful day; everything seemed perfect.

The sunshine and warm air grazed Clementine's face. She walked down the driveway, then down the long road to the park. When she arrived at the Ferris wheel, she set all her stuff down and started to prepare the colors. She opened up a can of white paint, lifting it to put her paintbrush inside. Someone came from out behind the Ferris wheel, causing Clementine to scream. She threw her paint, which spilled on her overalls as well as the other person. Shaken, she held out the paintbrush as if it were a weapon. It was a man who, at first, just stared at Clementine in awe. "Calm down; I'm just fixing up the carousel. I didn't mean to scare you." She lowered her paintbrush and collected herself.

"Oh, I'm sorry. I didn't think the staff had arrived yet."

"Hey, wait a second, you're Clementine Fayland, *the* Clementine Fayland." He looked completely starstruck like Clementine was a celebrity. He had a thin figure, and freckles were splattered across his face. The wind blew his soft brown hair in all directions.

"Um, yes, what's so special about me?"

He stood there and looked at Clementine like she asked a stupid question. "What are you talking about? You're one of the greatest artists of all time. I'm such a fan of your paintings; they're gorgeous."

"Thank you. I didn't know that I had any fans." She let out a small laugh.

"Are you kidding me? You painted one of the most exquisite paintings I have ever seen."

"This is some kind of joke, isn't it? You're being sarcastic!"

He came closer to her; his hands and face were dirty. His overalls were stained just like Clementine's. "Why would I joke about this? You are famous. I'm not sure if I ever met someone that was famous and didn't know it."

"I mean, I knew people liked my work locally. But outside of Fathorne, I'm just an average artist. I have never seen you here before. How long have you worked here?"

"This is my first week. I just arrived in Fathorne about a month ago."

"Where are you originally from?"

"Nowhere exactly."

"What does that mean?"

"Well, I've been about everywhere in my thirty years of life."

"You're thirty?" Clementine stood in shock.

"Yes, is that a problem?"

"No, it's just you don't look a day over twenty."

"I get that a lot. I get it from my family, I suppose, whoever they are."

"So, what made you come to Fathorne?"

"That's a long story."

Clementine looked down at her clothes, dripping with white paint, along with her arms. "Actually, why don't you take a break and come with me to get some more paint. You could tell me your story and perhaps, something to drink?"

"Talented, generous, and may I add beautiful all in one."

Clementine felt a tugging in her chest when he said that, but all she could do was smile and roll her eyes.

They walked to the house together, which only took around five minutes before they walked down her driveway. "Wow, you live in a castle."

"It is big, but it somehow feels small." It did feel small ever since her mother died; something felt like it was missing. She didn't want to mention her pain or personal stories with a stranger.

"Why are there so many roses?"

Well, so much for not bringing Mother up, Clementine thought.

"My father plants them for my mother; she passed away when I was still a child."

"Oh, I'm sorry."

"It's all right. I miss what I remember of her; it's a shame I didn't get to know her all that well."

"I never knew my mother either, well neither of my parents, actually."

Clementine gave him a look of sympathy and looked down at

the ground. "I've been so rude! I never asked for your name."

"Finnick."

When they arrived at the kitchen, Clementine guided Finnick to the small breakfast table that sat by the large windows. She poured iced tea for the two of them and then joined him. "So, what brought you here?"

"Well, I suppose I should start from the very beginning. I was found in an alleyway as an infant, abandoned and left to die. I don't know if my parents died or just left me to defend for myself, but all I knew was they were gone. A woman found me who ran an orphanage not too far from where I was found. My orphanage was overcrowded, and the food was scarce. I spent my childhood in starvation. As soon as I came of age, I ran away from the only city and the only life that I had ever known. With no money, I became a thief to steal what I had to survive. I wasn't proud of it, but I had to do what was necessary. Ever since I was a boy, I could fix almost anything, so I got odd jobs fixing different types of machinery, but it wasn't stable enough to get me enough money to put food on the table or a place to live. One day, fate led me to a mansion, just as exquisite as this one. The owner had passed away, so all his belongings were going up for auction. I knew there had to be something there worth taking; this man had riches beyond belief. There were gold trinkets and treasures that I had only read about in books. One swipe of any of his rare artifacts, and I could live like a king for the rest of my days.

"As I went to grab his diamond-encrusted watch, I noticed something much more magnificent. It was a painting, not just a painting, a masterpiece. The artistry that this one painting had was beyond compare to anything that I had ever seen before. The detail and craftsmanship. I turned it over to reveal the artist's name and, in cursive handwriting, read, Clementine Fayland.

"It wasn't just the artwork that I found astounding; it was the girl in the painting. She took my breath away; I had never seen someone so mesmerizing. I grabbed the art and darted out of the house. Fortunately, with my years of stealing skills, I escaped with no issues. I had to find this artist, so I could ask her who the girl in the painting was. This girl was going to be the love of my life.

"It took five years of traveling on trains with the small amounts of money I collected from jobs in towns where I would temporarily stay. Then about a month ago, I was taking a train that was intended to go to a different destination. The train was having problems, so it stopped at the nearest train station to get help. I considered myself a mechanic, but that was out of my skill range. It stopped at this small town of Fathorne, which I had never heard of before. I just decided to get off here and try to see what jobs I could find.

"Job postings were set up outside the train station, and I saw that the local amusement park needed a mechanic; I was up to the task. It was the only qualified job for me. I almost passed out when I read the name of the park. I didn't know if it was a strange coincidence or if maybe they were related to the artist. Later, I found out this place was sort of famous, as was the family who owned it. I read about how Florent Fayland had just vanished, completely disappeared from the public's view. I learned how this park changed this town forever and became an iconic tourist attraction. Something about this place was almost magical, and inside its gates lies a disconnection to the rest of reality. Lawrence, I'm assuming your brother, gave me the job. With nowhere to stay, I just sleep on the benches in the middle of the park. When I saw you with the paint and supplies, I knew it was you. And, not only that, you are the girl in the painting."

"I remember I sold that self-portrait to an elderly man who seemed to have come from wealth. Sometimes I sell them in a booth when the park is open, and I remember the day he bought it. I never thought it would have such significance to someone. Where is the painting now?"

He pulled out a medium canvas that had no wooden frame and folded in half. He unfolded it to reveal Clementine's teenage face. "I was sixteen when I painted this; it seemed like yesterday." Finnick put his hand over Clementine's.

"Don't you see? All this brought us together; it is our calling."

Clementine pulled her hand away and quickly got up from the table. "I'm sorry. I need time to think about this." Clementine thought about everything that he had just told her. In her twenty-five years of life, she had never felt love for any man. She did feel something for Finnick. The painting, the broken-down train, his job were just coincidences, but then again maybe not. For five years, he had searched for her, just because of a painting. No one had ever been so committed to being with her. Maybe this was fate, something she didn't even know if she believed in. "I think we should get back to our jobs."

"Yes, I suppose we should."

Back at the park, now working on the carousel, they both worked in silence. Finnick felt stupid and embarrassed for pouring his heart out. He felt rude trying to have a girl he had just met fall in love with him. He couldn't fight the feelings he had for her. The painting had always pulled at his heartstrings. He would stare for minutes at a time at her white-blonde hair and hazel eyes. The picture was nothing compared to her in person, though; her movements were graceful with each stroke of a paintbrush. Her dirty overalls and messy ponytail somehow made her glow even more. As soon as he finished checking to make sure everything was up to date on the carousel, he walked over to the other side.

"Hey, I'm sorry if I made you uncomfortable earlier. It's just nothing ever as exciting or assuring has ever happened in my life. I thought that you were the one thing that would forever change everything for me. But I understand you not wanting to be with someone you just met. A dirty thief like me wanting to be with a lady like you is absurd. And also, me talking about some crazy destiny I thought I had to fulfill."

Clementine stopped painting the horse she was working on and stood up to face him. She stepped off the carousel and walked to him. "Actually, I think you were right about fate bringing us together. I mean, all the men I have been with have been such scum and just wanted one thing from me. You're not like that, not one bit. You traveled the country just because of some painting I painted of myself nine years ago. You never stopped until you found what you were looking for after all this time. And I'm starting to believe that you can find anything if you never stop looking. I have never met someone so determined to go to such great lengths just for love. It's so pure and kind; I don't think I'll ever find anyone like you in my lifetime."

"Really, you think so?"

"I know so." Clementine took his hands in hers and pulled him closer. Their eyes met until it was like she could see into his soul, and he could see in hers. Without hesitation, she gave a quick peck on the lips, and he did the same.

"Whoa. That was everything I imagined it to be," Finnick said.

Clementine smiled, matching his blushing. Both of their faces were bright red, but not out of embarrassment. It was exhilarating, and Clementine had never felt so alive.

The two spent the rest of their day together. They talked about their lives and hopes for the future as she painted and he inspected the rides. "So, why did your father disappear out of the public eye?"

"Well, ever since my mother died, he has never really been himself. He used to be kind and caring; I had never seen such love in one person. But, like everyone, he has a hidden side. A part of ourselves that we sometimes cannot control. It took the tragedy of my mother for it to reveal itself. My grandfather, Horace Fayland, was shot dead when my father was only eight years old, and he has had to deal with that tragedy as well after all these years. His mother died young as well, from some type of illness. But my mother was there to heal his wounds and ease his mind; he always said that her embrace was the best medicine and her kiss was the best therapy. She allowed the broken parts of him to be hidden away underneath his true self. He was loving and the best father I could ever want. But when my mother was taken from him, something inside him snapped, and the dark parts of him took him once again, destroying the man I once knew.

That horrible day, I lost both of my parents, really. Though my father is still here, the real him died alongside my mother. As she was buried, my father's heart went with her. What was left was a broken man filled with nothing but the gloom he had tried so desperately to hide. Now he locks himself away in his bedroom, keeping himself away from us and drinking liquor to escape the truth of what had happened." Clementine felt tears starting to form in her eyes. She had always tried to act like everything was fine and nothing tragic was happening inside the walls of her home, but she was lying to herself that she wished to go back to when her mother was alive and their family was whole. Then again, if Vincent were never born, she would not have her best friend, her little brother she loved so much.

"Oh no, I'm so sorry. I shouldn't have said anything."

"No, it's okay. It's good that I got that off my chest. I have always wondered what it would be like if things were different, if my mother was still alive, but she's not. I guess I just have to accept the fact that everything happens for a reason."

"Yeah, that's true."

"My brother Lawrence, the person who hired you, basically runs Fayland Park now. I'm lucky to see my father even once a month. He locks himself up in his personal prison, away from the rest of the world."

Nighttime fell over Fathorne as Clementine and Finnick finished up their daily tasks. Fayland Park was restored to its colorful self, and the rides were ready to thrill riders for another year. In just a month, the park would open up for another season, and people from all over would come to enjoy everything it had to offer. A place filled with so much happiness was also the place of immense sadness. Finnick, now covered with oil and dirt, appeared from the bumper cars. "Well, that's the last one. I guess I'll see you tomorrow." He started to walk off before Clementine ran after him.

"Wait, Finnick! You can't stay out here; it's too cold. My brother's girlfriend is staying in our guest room, but you could stay on the sofa in our living room. There's a fireplace in there to keep you warm and plenty of food to eat instead of old gas station food."

"That's so kind, but I don't want to get in your family's way."

"Well, they're just going to have to deal with it. You're my guest. We never treat our guests with disrespect."

"Wow, thank you so much."

Clementine put her arm around his and guided him up to the house.

Finnick was even more amazed as he saw the inside of the house. His mouth remained open until they reached the large living room. The giant chandelier glistened on the ceiling, and the fireplace was already lit. "This house is like nothing I've seen before. I mean, I've seen extraordinary mansions, but this place is unique. The paintings, the marble flooring, and the blue exterior. It's like something out of a fairytale."

"That's what my mother intended. When my father was having this place built, he made sure everything was to my mother's image."

"Well, she had good taste."

Clementine smiled as she got a throw blanket and a pillow from the closet. She made him a bed on the large blue sofa that sat in front of the fireplace.

"I guess I'll head up to my room. I'll tell the head maid you're here, so they don't try to throw you out." She kissed him on the cheek and walked off with a little skip in her step.

She climbed the grand staircase to the bedrooms on the second floor before someone came out of the dark and grabbed her arm, pulling her into the darkness. She let out a small scream. "Lawrence, you almost gave me a heart attack!"

"I saw you bring that employee in the house. What in hell are you thinking, bringing him into our home?"

"What, are you spying on me now, brother? I am twenty-five years old, which means I'm a grown woman. I don't need you watching my every move!"

His grip tightened around her arm. "Maybe you do, bringing

dirty riff-raff in here. I only hired him because we needed a mechanic and he proved he is a good one. But I know of his history, and he needs to stay away from our house and you."

"He is perfectly fine. I am a great judge of character. Yes, he is a thief when he needs to survive. He is a gentleman, something that you will never be. I don't know what Marie sees in you. You're envious, selfish, and ignorant. And you let your jealousy drive you to great measures. You do everything to keep Vincent and me from taking your precious future fortune. I don't even want it, and neither does Vincent. Now that Father has left you responsible for running the park, you have let that power go to your head. And you will never be able to control my actions or this family!"

"Why don't you go doodle or something?"

"Lawrence, let go of my arm! What the hell is wrong with you?"

"You think all those things about me simply because I won't let you bring a stranger in the house?"

"No, I've thought about these things for a long time. I just now got around to saying something. Now let me go!"

Lawrence finally let her go and gave her a chilling stare before turning away and going back into the dark hallway. She feared her brother, and she always had. Something was off about him; he would act normal one moment then strange the next. He would be social, then completely go mute. He had always been cruel to her and Vincent for no apparent reason. He had been this way for as long as she could remember. Clementine reached to open her bedroom door before she was caught off guard by something. Soft music was playing from somewhere, the same type of music her parents would dance to together. She slowly pulled her hand away from her door and walked toward the music.

It was coming from her father's room. The door was cracked open, just enough for her to see inside. Her father was slowly swaying to the same elegant piece of music that he and her mother had danced to all those years ago. He had his arms in a position like her mother was still in them. He limped badly, but that did not stop him. He took each step in the dance slowly and did everything he could not to fall. It was haunting to see him in this condition as he danced solo to a medley that once was the tune of his love. But mostly, it was sad to see him so broken, so lonely as the moonlight hit his face through the large window. His hair was now graying on the side, a reminder that time stops for no one. The once-handsome and loving person she had once known was truly gone. Clementine never realized how much she missed her real father until she told Finnick of his tragedy.

Fear built inside of her as he suddenly stopped, and he looked at her. "Come here, Clementine." She felt her stomach twist as she pushed the door the rest of the way open. She couldn't even look up to meet her father's face. He walked toward her with his limp slowing him down. He put her hands on her face, which made Clementine jump. Her breathing was getting heavier, and she could feel sweat forming on her forehead. She could tell he was drunk as she looked into his bloodshot eyes and could smell the strong liquor on his breath. Scratch marks covered the walls, papers were all crumpled on the floor, and Vincent's blood still stained the carpet. Clementine knew how her father was when he was drunk—abrasive and aggressive.

She knew the truth of what happened to Vincent; it was no accident. He was still holding on to her face, but not suggesting that he wanted to hurt her. It was soft, it was kind, something she had not felt from him since she was six. The music still echoed in the background from the record player in the corner. A tear rolled down from his red eyes, showing a small feature of humanity. "You look so much like her." Clementine stared at her father and felt sympathy for him. To love someone so much that losing them can drive a person to complete madness. She looked over to see a framed picture of her mother and father on the bedside table. All these years, the memory of her mother had faded. Florent had taken down all the pictures of her throughout the house to help him cope, but it did no good. He left this one picture, though, the one where they had nothing. Her mother stood in a ragged yellow floral dress, and her father's face barely looked over fifteen, even though he was a few years older. They had joy on their faces, but still, they shared so much pain. But at least they had each other.

He released Clementine's face and went over to the window without saying another word. She stood there, staring as her father turned away from her until she slowly left the room. That was the first thing her father had said to her in months, and she wished she would have said something back. But it wouldn't have mattered. He was drunk and stuck in his own world. It was nice just to have that one moment of gentleness, and she was always glad that he had said those six gentle words.

Chapter **21**

THE CONFESSION

May 1959

Vincent awoke earlier than usual, but then again, he didn't get much sleep these days. Every night when he went to sleep and every morning when he awoke, he had one thing on his mind. It was Marie, every passing hour, and it was agonizing. For a month, Marie had been going back and forth between her own house and his. Every other week, she would stay in their guest bedroom for a whole week and spend the rest of her time with Lawrence. Except at dawn, when the sun came up above the mountains to shed light on their murky world.

When he played violin for his mother, that was their time. Marie sat out by his mother's grave every morning to listen to him play. At times, they didn't even talk, but even in silence, he enjoyed her company. She was the only person who looked at Vincent like he was a normal human being and didn't see the nasty scar that protruded across his face. Even his own sister was sometimes caught staring at his scarred face. Though he could only see out of one eye and his vision was hazy, Marie was radiant.

Vincent lay in his bed for hours, staring at the ceiling, imagining a life with Marie, a future that would never happen. At least he could picture his perfect life in his head. He imagined living far away from his home, somewhere by the ocean. They would have a simple house, nothing too fancy. Every morning they could sit on the back porch and listen as the ocean's waves hit up against the current. All his fantasies vanished as he was startled by a knock on the door.

Vincent got up quickly to open it, and the person on the other side shocked him. "Dad?"

He was holding a bag, which looked like it had a suit in it. "Do you mind if I come in?"

"No, come in."

"I hope I didn't wake you."

"Actually, I've been up for a while now." For the first time, he was seeing his father sober. His eyes were not bloodshot, and he couldn't smell the whiskey that usually scented his breath.

"I want to give you this." He unzipped the bag to reveal an olive-green suit that had a matching hat and leather gloves. "I haven't worn it since your mother died. I would wear it to every opening day. I loved this suit, but I think it's time to pass it down."

"Shouldn't Lawrence get this? I mean, he is the heir to everything anyways. And he runs the park; I figure you would want him to have it."

"You are more deserving of this; I think it's more appropriate for you."

Vincent did not understand why he was more deserving of it, but he did not ask questions. Vincent happened to look up, noticing Marie walking past the doorway and gave a smile and a wave.

"Thank you."

"Of course. Why don't you wear it today, since today is opening day."

"Absolutely." Vincent didn't know why, but he had a burning question to ask his father. "Dad?"

"Yes?"

"How did you know you were in love with Mom?" Florent turned around, and Vincent could see the surprise in his face from his question. He looked down at the ground, trying not to make contact with his father. Perhaps this was a bad idea and would bring out the rage in him. To Vincent's surprise, he looked up and talked gently.

"I just did. I guess it was the first time that I ever saw her, and my heart ached for her. She was my only thought each and every moment. But my love for her happened before I actually ever saw her. It was her voice, that sweet melody that I now only hear in my dreams. I know that sounds strange, but when I first heard her talk, life seemed to have meaning. It gave life an undertone that I had not known since I was eight years old. It was comforting. When I saw her face, something inside me changed for the better.

"She brought out the best in me; the best anyone could ever get from a mess like me. I fell in love with everything about her except her looks. Oh, she looked breathtaking, but I fell in love with her big heart and kind soul. Those are things that will never age and rarely ever change. I remember laying my head on her chest when I had night terrors, and I could feel her heart beating. It was music to my ears. I never felt something so fragile and pure as her heartbeat. When it stopped beating, I wanted time to do the same. But that's just not how life works. I have been trying my best to get better, lay off the alcohol and compulsive behaviors, because your mother would have wanted me to be happy. There was no thinking or contemplating that I loved her; I just knew. So, what I'm trying to say is there are no symptoms to reveal that a person is in love; they just know. Your mother and I went through a lot of hardships and uncertainty. So, you know what we did?"

"What?"

"We danced through the night. I would put on some music, and I would hold her body close to mine. And our bodies became one with the melody, and the worries faded away."

"Clementine told me about that."

Florent gave a faint laugh. "Yes, sometimes we knew she was there, but we didn't bother her. We wanted her to know that we were very much in love, and someday she could find that same feeling."

Without another word, his father left, leaving the suit on Vincent's bed and quietly shutting the door. Vincent pulled the suit out of the bag and could tell that it was expensive. He put it on, and it fit him perfectly. He placed the gloves and hat on to finish the look, and he had to take a second look in the mirror. He had seen pictures of his father wearing this suit, and it was almost chilling how much he looked like him. Looking into the mirror was like looking at his father, except for his diamond-blue eyes. Looking at the clock, he realized that it was time to head outside. He kept the suit on and grabbed his mother's violin.

He walked past the garden, staring at the pink roses that were everywhere. He stopped in his tracks when he saw the back of Marie's head, sitting on the stone where she usually sat. Her strawberry-blonde curls were picked up by the wind. As usual, she wore a pink dress with a ruffled bottom. She held one of the roses in her hand, and she was humming to herself. The fog moved slowly near the ground around her feet. Vincent smiled the best he could. His scar made his smile awkward, and it wasn't the easiest thing to do. Not that Vincent had much to smile about until now. Marie must have heard him walking toward her, as she quickly turned around startled.

"Oh, hello, Vincent. I couldn't sleep very well, so I came out here earlier this morning and waited."

"I couldn't sleep very well this morning either."

"Wow, you're looking quite dapper this morning."

"Thanks, my father gave me his old suit."

"Well, it looks terrific on you."

Vincent felt himself blushing. Marie smelled the rose in her hand. "These roses are stunning, and they just happen to be my favorite color. I love pink, if you did not notice." She let out a small laugh and motioned to her dress.

"Yes, I noticed. Why do you like pink so much?"

"I don't really know. Pink is such a happy color, I guess. It reminds me of summer night kisses, cotton candy, and the summer breeze of my grandparents' terrace in France. It reminds me of all the delicate details in life. Mostly it's such a feminine color; it reminds me of strength."

"Pink roses were my mother's favorite flower. One decent thing my father does is plant them for her, which makes him feel that she is always near him. I agree with him; I feel her presence somehow when I walk through the garden."

"In a way, people are a lot like roses."

"How so?"

"In the beginning, they bloom beautifully, but if their petals are stripped from them, all that is left is the thorns." Vincent stood in silence until he nodded and smiled.

Vincent held up the violin, ready to play before Marie interrupted him. "Can I ask you something?"

"Yeah, what is it?"

"Lawrence wants me to be with all of you when the opening ceremony begins, but after that, he has to go around the park the entire day and oversee everything. This is my first time really spending the day in the park, and I want to have fun, not just walk around and examine things. What I wanted to ask is if I could spend the day with you."

Vincent's heart started to pick up speed again; this was a dream come true. A day to spend with Marie. To hear her voice and see her pleasant smile.

"Oh yeah, definitely."

"Oh, thank you so much!"

"It's no problem. We can ride all the rides, get some food from the stands, and play some games."

"That sounds perfect! I really do appreciate it." She stood up and hugged him. Vincent's entire body tensed up, just like it did when they shared a hug when they were children, but he finally relaxed and pulled her into a tight embrace.

"Am I interrupting something?" Lawrence said as he walked around the garden to where they were. "Come on, Marie, breakfast is prepared." Marie joined him, and he put his arm around her. "You should come too, Vincent."

Vincent picked up the violin and headed up toward the house behind his brother and Marie, who were holding hands. He did his very best not to show any signs of jealousy.

Vincent sat down to a plate ready for him that included eggs, bacon, and hash browns. The house staff was working extremely hard, making sure that the house was spotless as usual. Lawrence and Marie sat across from Vincent. As soon as they were done with their meal, they started kissing right in front of him. Clementine sat further down at the table, holding Finnick's hand. Ever since she began to date Finnick, she had become a stranger to Vincent. He used to know everything about Clementine; she was his best friend.

"Wait a minute, isn't that Dad's suit?" Lawrence asked with an angry expression.

"Yes, he gave it to me."

"You lie. You stole it, didn't you?"

"No, he gave it to me this morning before breakfast."

Lawrence was about to get up, but Marie put her hand on his arm. "It's true. I happened to be up this morning and saw your father give it to him."

Vincent mouthed *thank you* to Marie. She smiled and mouthed *no problem* back to him.

Vincent finished his breakfast. When he happened to look up across the table again, he saw Marie and Lawrence kissing again. He quickly got up from the table and ran as fast as he could to the park.

He kicked the rocks and clumps of dirt beneath his feet as he walked at a fast pace. His fists were in his pockets, clenched and ready to punch someone or something. The thought of Marie kissing his brother made him angrier than he had ever been. Also, the sight of Clementine and Finnick holding hands made him furious for reasons he did not know. Maybe he was selfish; he just wanted Clementine to spend time with him like they used to. But she was happy now, and he always knew someday she would find someone and leave. He always knew loneliness would greet him eventually.

Employees were everywhere in the park, trying to get everything in order before Lawrence opened the front gates. Vincent looked up at the cloudy morning sky in between a circle of trees. Birds were flying overhead, chirping without a care in the world. Light carnival music was playing on the speakers throughout the park; it was almost peaceful. The rides were doing their final test runs before they held riders. Even though he had lived on these grounds ever since he was born, the beauty of Fayland Park had never ceased to amaze him. His father must have once had such a beautiful mind to create something so spectacular. Flower beds sat empty throughout the park, which must have been taken care of by his mother. But the trees and natural beauty created a world of whimsy and joy. Vincent understood why so many people loved this fantastic amusement park.

"Vincent!"

He turned around to see Clementine running toward him.

"Are you okay? You stormed out of the dining room. I was worried."

"I'm fine; I just needed some fresh air."

"Okay, but if something is bothering you, you can always tell me."

"Yeah, I know. Thank you."

"Alright. Never hesitate to come to me for anything." She then left to go get dressed for the ceremony, which was now only in half an hour.

Vincent spent the rest of the remaining time sitting on a bench, staring at his surroundings. He caught himself daydreaming again when he imagined all the rides he and Marie could ride. This was going to be the best day of his life so far; he could feel it. After the thirty minutes were up, his family came to get him. They had all changed into formal attire, and they all looked like they just came from a ball. Clementine wore a green dress that swung by her knees and a diamond necklace. The necklace was their mother's, as was the dress. He saw her wearing them in a painting that Clementine had done of her. He assumed that his father's green suit wasn't the only thing that he had passed down and let go. Finnick stood in a green plaid suit that made him look like a completely different person. Vincent was used to seeing him in an oil- and gas-stained outfit with sweat dripping from his hair. Lawrence wore a red suit, which looked like typical carnival apparel. The suit itself was red, and the shirt underneath had red and cream stripes, finished off with a bow tie.

Vincent felt chills go through his body when Marie come from behind his brother. As usual, she wore her pink attire, but the dress made her look like a fantasy. Two small pearl necklaces grazed her neck. The pink dress had ruffles from top to bottom, with a pink bow in the back. A matching bow sat on the top of her head, and spotless white gloves covered her delicate hands.

Lawrence caught him staring at Marie, which resulted in him giving Vincent a stern look. "Are you ready?"

"Yes."

"All right, everyone get behind Marie and me. And everyone, please try to look presentable and not act like children. Vincent, try to hide your face the best you can. There are children here. I wouldn't even have you come, but Father instructed me he wanted all of us to be at the opening ceremony since it's tradition," Lawrence said with a smirk.

Vincent felt the anger burning inside him; all he wanted to do was punch him in his smug face. Marie hit Lawrence on the shoulder and told him something that Vincent couldn't hear.

They all walked onto the platform and spread out to a large crowd waiting for the gates to open. These people had already paid and parked near the main arch. They now waited to be let into the main area. Vincent stood at the far left beside his sister. Every step he took, he could feel the stares of the crowd. Every year he had to go through the torture of people whispering and looking at his deformed face. Lawrence stepped up to the microphone that sat near the front of the platform. "Welcome, everyone, to the opening ceremony of another year of family fun at Fayland Park. This year we celebrate thirty-three years of the amusement park that changed my family's life forever. What you witnessed today was just drawings in my father's notebooks as a child. His imagination and determination are what made this place come to life. Also, today we have my father's business partner, Roger Merriam, and his wife, Winnie Merriam."

Roger and Winnie came up the stairs from behind. "He made all this possible as well; there would be no Fayland Park without this man." Roger gave a faint smile and wave. "My father has retired from running the park and has given me the honor of operating such a spectacular place. I have help from my little sister Clementine and little brother Vincent." They both smiled and waved to the unsuspecting crowd. They deceived everyone, making them think they were a perfect and happy family, which was so far from the truth, Vincent thought. "Now, enough of my talking. Let's open the gates!" Two employees on both sides opened the gates, and the people started pouring in. "Welcome to Fayland Park!"

As soon as the guests started to come in, his family blended in with the crowd. He got on his tiptoes to try to find Marie, but he had no success. Eventually, he found her talking to her parents. She broke off from them and saw Vincent. She ran toward him. "So, what do you have planned for us first?"

"Well, I was going to start with the carousel or something small and work our way up to the more thrilling rides."

"Okay, sounds good to me. I want to do everything!"

Seeing her so excited about everything made Vincent love her more. When she smiled, dimples formed around her mouth that made him melt.

They got in a reasonably long line for the carousel, but Vincent didn't mind wasting time with Marie. They stood in silence before

Vincent asked a question. "So, what does Lawrence think about you spending the day with me?"

"Actually, I never told him. He doesn't have to know everything I do."

"That's true."

"I am a grown woman. I don't need a chaperone or someone to permit me to spend a day with my friend."

"I agree. You should be able to make your own choices and think for yourself. You should never have to ask for permission."

Marie smiled at Vincent. "I like the way you think."

Before he could say any more, they were next in line. They entered the ride's gated area and picked out their favorite horses.

"Oh, I like this one." Marie jumped up on the horse, putting her petite body on the fake saddle. Vincent sat on a simpler horse with a brown frame and black mane.

"That horse was always my sister's favorite."

The horse had a white body, a blond mane, and blue and pink flowers were freshly renovated.

"Is it true that your sister painted this entire carousel?"

"Yes, she made it look better than the original paint job."

Marie looked around, amazed. "It's remarkable."

Vincent turned to see his face in the mirrors that were located in the center of the carousel. He really did look like the freak everyone made him out to be, like a creature out of a horror story. The diagonal scar slashed across his face and his eyes of different shades. His mouth partially opened on one side from the stitches that once held it together.

The man who did this to him was supposed to be his hero and the man he most admired. In a way, he did feel all those things toward his father, especially when he gave him his suit, but was this just some cheap apology for ruining all his chances of being ordinary? He also felt hatred for him, but he still forgave him all those years ago without a single apology from him. He looked at Marie and her delicate, gorgeous face, and he lost all hope. He was happy to be spending the day with her and to be in her presence. But that's all they would ever have. He would never reject her friendship, but just being her friend made him live in misery.

The carousel gave a lurch, and they started to move up and down. Vincent looked over at Marie, who was smiling and taking in everything she could. The wind was swirling her red-tinted hair all around her face, and Vincent's stomach felt a sharp pain. He really was in love with her; there was no denying it now. They went around several times before Vincent saw his brother standing in the distance, talking to some guests. Vincent tried to duck down behind the horse's head. When they came back around, he was gone, and he gave a sigh of relief. The ride came to a stop, and Vincent took Marie's hand to help her off the horse. "Thank you, my kind prince!"

They both exited the ride as Marie still had the expression of excitement on her face. "I haven't ridden a carousel since I was, well I'm not sure when. It's been a long time since I had any real fun. "What's next?"

"Maybe the scrambler?"

"Yeah, sounds good!"

They walked toward the ride until Vincent saw something that upset him. A small boy was standing near the line to the scrambler, crying. He ran up to him to see what was wrong. Maybe it was none of his business, but he felt that he needed to help if he could. The boy's mother was there as well, but she couldn't seem to comfort him. "Hey, bud, what's wrong?"

His mother stood up from her crouching position to meet Vincent at eye level. She was hesitant to speak to Vincent and just stared at his scar. "He wants to ride this, but he is too scared."

The child's crying got louder, and more tears started to flow out of his eyes. Vincent put his finger over his own lips to try to silence him.

"Everything will be okay. There's nothing to fear. Tell you what, my friend and I were about to go on here, and you could ride with us if you would like." He stopped crying and gave a small nod. "Is that okay?" Vincent asked the boy's mother.

She couldn't help but stare before saying, "Yeah, sure."

Vincent took one of the boy's hands, and Marie took the other. Marie couldn't help but smile at Vincent's kind gesture.

"So, what's your name?"

"William."

"That's a nice name," Marie said. They walked up onto the ride and chose a vibrant yellow cart with blue stars spread across it. The boy sat between the two of them, being securely squeezed in. The boy looked at Marie in amazement.

"You're really pretty." Marie smiled once again.

"Well, thank you."

Then he turned to Vincent, "You're really lucky, mister."

Vincent quickly responded as he felt a little embarrassed. "Actually, we're just friends, but I am fortunate to be spending the day with her."

The ride operator came around and put the bar down, having them all tightly smashed together. They all put their hands on the bar right before the ride started. It got faster and faster before they began turning sharp corners, looking as though they would hit the cart beside them. They got thrown into each other, which made them all laugh.

Vincent looked down at the boy, who was smiling and having fun. This must have been what his father had always intended when he built this place. To see a child smile and laugh was one of the purest joys. Having the ability to make a child happy and have unforgettable memories to last a lifetime was an honor. When the ride stopped, the boy thanked Vincent and Marie. "That was so much fun! I'm not afraid anymore!"

They began walking to the next ride, until Vincent noticed Marie was limping. "What's wrong?"

"These heels are killing my feet. But I'll be fine." Vincent bent down and started to take off his shoes.

"What are you doing?" Marie asked, coming behind him.

"Here you can wear my shoes. They might be a bit big for you, but they're better than walking in those feet killers."

"What are you going to wear?"

"I'll just go barefooted. It's not like I've never done it before. I actually prefer it."

"Oh, well, okay." She slipped her feet into Vincent's shoes, who were not much bigger than her own. They moved up and down, but not drastically.

"Ow! I must have a blister or two; it still hurts to walk."

Vincent swept Marie up and held her in his arms, proving to himself he was much stronger than he appeared.

Marie let out a small scream and then laughed. "You don't have to do this; I can fight through the pain."

"I want you to have a perfect day, and I will do anything to make sure that happens. You can't enjoy yourself if you are in distress."

Marie wrapped her arms around his neck, making it easier for him to carry her. She stared at him, but not at his flaws and deformities. She was staring into his eyes.

Vincent looked back at her, looking into her eyes as well. He didn't know how long they stayed like that, but what a feeling it was.

Vincent and Marie spent the rest of their day enjoying the park. Vincent had never laughed or smiled as much as he did that day. Marie made everything fun, even standing in line, waiting for an hour just to get on a ride. At the balloon-dart game, Marie was fascinated by a white stuffed toy tiger. Vincent had one good eye, and his aim had never been great. When he stepped up to the opening, he held the dart and focused as best he could. Out of chance, he threw it. To his surprise, he hit two balloons at once and won the small stuffed animal. Vincent handed it to Marie, who wore a face of gratitude. "Thank you so much!" It was getting darker, and the wind was starting to pick up.

"There is one last ride we haven't ridden. I saved it for last because there is nothing as glorious as the sunset."

"Oh, okay."

Once on the Ferris wheel, Marie seemed very tense and nervous about something.

"Are you okay?"

Her words shook as she spoke, and Vincent could see the sweat on her forehead. She held the toy tiger closer and closer to her chest when they started to move. Marie suddenly grabbed Vincent's hand, but quickly took it back when she realized what she had done. "I'm sorry."

"That's okay."

"I guess I should have told you I'm sort of afraid of heights." When they almost reached the top, she covered her eyes and buried her head in Vincent's shoulder. Vincent looked straight ahead to the mountains and the blue sky that was turning pink and orange. They finally stopped at the very top to let people on at the bottom.

"It's okay; you can look. Don't be afraid."

She lifted her head and looked out to the mountains, just as Vincent had. The sun was just peeking through two mountaintops.

"Wow, it's amazing. It's not as scary as I had thought. Actually, it's not scary at all. It looks like one of your sister's paintings. I guess you helped two people conquer their fears today."

"I guess so. Sometimes all you have to do is tell fear that you are not afraid and face whatever scares you most."

Marie was still looking out at the scenery with a look of wonder on her face. But Vincent thought the sight of Marie was much more breathtaking than any view of the mountains. She turned to look at him, remaining silent. She started to lean in and closed her eyes. Vincent began to panic inside and wondered if she was going to kiss him. His mind was racing with an enormous number of questions. Was she really going to kiss him? Could he do this to his brother? How could she love someone like him? All these questions faded as he started to lean in for her as well. He didn't care about what anyone thought about him now; all he wanted was her. He could feel her breath, and he tilted his head until they both tore away from each other. A loud bang went off in the distance—the fireworks from the town square. They had become a tradition for every opening day and Fourth of July now. The opening of Fayland Park was no longer just a celebration for staff and guests inside the park; the whole town celebrated.

The Ferris wheel started to turn again. It eventually stopped, and they got off, smiling at the view of the fireworks and mountaintops that surrounded them. Neither of them mentioned what almost happened between them, though. "I could use another snack before closing time."

"Me too."

Marie ordered an elephant ear and a soda. "This is huge! Maybe we should share it?"

"Okay." Marie took her first bite, and her eyes grew much larger. "This is so delicious."

"Have you never had one of these before?" Vincent asked.

"Are you kidding? No, my mother makes me eat all the healthy stuff that she likes. This is a treat to me."

After they finished their food, a man announced over the speaker that the park was closing in ten minutes. "Well, I guess it's time to go. Lawrence told me that he would wait for me in the parking lot and drive me home."

"Okay."

"I had a lot of fun today. You know what?"

"Yeah?"

"I was thinking of taking a bike ride tomorrow, just to get out of the house. Do you want to join me?"

"Yeah, absolutely."

"Great! I guess I'll see you tomorrow, let's say at ten o'clock?"

"That works for me. Wait, I don't own a bike."

"That's all right. I have an extra you can borrow."

"Okay, thanks." Vincent started to walk toward his house, while Marie went the other way before she came running after him.

"Vincent! I just wanted to say thanks for letting me be a kid again."

Vincent looked at the ground then back to her with a smile. "You're welcome."

She turned around and went with the crowd toward the gate. Vincent gave a wave that she never even saw.

Vincent took the long way to his house, the path through the woods. The rain had started to fall on him, but that did not matter to him now. He couldn't count the number of times he had walked through these woods, despising life. Now he walked with his head held high, as he had one small ounce of hope. He never really knew what hope looked or felt like, but now he could see it clearly. Hope wore pink, and strawberry-blonde curls. The thought made him feel giddy inside. Usually, he would tire of things after a while; he could not see the joy in much. But with her, he couldn't get enough. He looked up to the tree line where the moon was taking the sun's place in the sky. He couldn't help but let the rain splash on him and run down his face. The face that people had always feared, just because it was different. The face that didn't bother Marie, as she stared at him with compassion and not fear. She would never know how much that meant to him.

He eventually came out of the woods and made his way down their long driveway. He must have taken longer on the path than he had thought; he saw Lawrence's car parked in front of the house. He must have already dropped Marie off and was back home. Vincent opened the door as quietly as he could. Luckily, no one was in the main entryway. He tried to sneak up to his bedroom without letting anyone know he was there.

"Vincent?"

Vincent jumped and grabbed his chest like he had a heart attack from fright.

Clementine got off the sofa in the hallway and came toward him. "Sorry, I was just up reading a book."

Vincent needed to get what he was feeling off his chest, and he trusted Clementine. "Clem, remember that you said I could tell you anything if something was bothering me?"

"Yes, what's wrong?"

"Can we go to my bedroom? I need to talk to you in private."

"Sure."

They reached his bedroom without running into Lawrence or Florent.

"Okay, what is it, are you okay?"

"There is something I need to get off my chest that I can't hold in anymore. I mean, you're basically my closest friend, so I trust you as the one I should tell." Vincent stood there with the words on the tip of his tongue, but he couldn't say it.

"Well?"

He looked down at the book Clementine was holding and decided to come up with a lie. "I'm writing a book."

"Oh, that's great! What's it about?"

"Uh, I haven't decided."

"When you do, I would love to hear it, and you better let me be the first person to read it. Well, it's getting late. I better go to bed. Good night!"

"Good night." Vincent threw himself on the bed and let out a sigh. Was love supposed to be this hard? He sank into sadness once again.

He thought he must be kidding himself about believing Marie actually liked him back. It was in his head, what had happened on the Ferris wheel. His mind would be the only place where they would be together. He looked into the mirror once again. His large scar was across what may have been a handsome face, one that Marie could love. He took a cologne bottle, which happened to be the closest object, and threw it at the mirror. Both shattered, so he would no longer have to see himself. He changed out of the suit, feeling unwanted. The suit was just not him; he was more comfortable in his usual attire. He placed it in the suit bag and put it toward the back of the closet. After putting on his pajamas, he lay down on the bed and stared at the ceiling as tears rolled down his cheeks.

The next morning Vincent woke up feeling dreadful from such a small amount of sleep. He looked at the clock and realized that

Marie would be there in half an hour. He quickly got dressed, putting on a cardigan sweater and tan pants. He brushed his black hair out of his face and tried to look presentable. He no longer had a mirror to see if he looked at least decent, but he refused to look at himself. Fortunately, Lawrence was busy at the park, and Clementine was spending the day with Finnick out of town. Florent was spending a day with Roger to talk about future park renovations, which was still one duty he did. Lawrence watched over the park, and Florent did everything behind the scenes. With his family members away, he could sneak out of the house without being asked where he was going.

He walked out onto the porch and looked down the driveway; there was no sign of Marie yet. He sat on the porch swing and waited in anticipation for her arrival. It was only ten minutes before he saw a car quickly coming toward the house, a pink Cadillac, the shade of everything else she owned. She had a white scarf tied around her head, with matching cat-eye sunglasses on her face. She looked like she just walked out of a movie scene. She pulled around to the front of the house and waved while driving. "Hello!" Marie yelled.

Vincent came down the steps and stared at her along with her car. "Wow, I love your car."

"Thank you! I couldn't imagine any other car than this for myself." She was distracted, getting the bikes off the back, and she somehow managed to get onto the small back of the car.

Unsurprisingly, her bike was hot pink with a white basket on the front. The one she brought for Vincent was plain blue with black trim. "All right, shall we start our adventure?"

"Sure."

"Is it okay if I leave my car parked here?"

"Yes, as long as we are back before one. That's when our dads are supposed to be back."

"We will be. I'm not actually supposed to be out of the house anyway. My mother sleeps in late, so I knew I could sneak past her."

"I don't want you to get in trouble."

"It's all right; I sneak out of the house all the time. I'm a professional at it now," Marie said with a mischievous smile. "Now, let's get going!"

Marie jumped on her bike and started to dash down the driveway while Vincent was walking with his. He had failed to tell her that he had never actually ridden a bike before. Marie looked back and stopped. "Well, aren't you going to get on?"

He got on and started to pedal just as she was, but the bicycle came crashing down with him. "Um, I don't really know how to ride a bike." Vincent was preparing for her to look at him like he was stupid and laugh.

"That's okay; I can teach you." She turned around and came back toward him. She picked up the bike and swept the dirt off his clothes.

"Okay, the first thing is to obviously get on." Vincent obeyed her and got on while she held on to the bike. "The main thing is balance; as soon as you have that, you're already there, for the most part." She let go of the bike and let Vincent try to balance. He failed the first few times, falling face first into the dirt. On the third try, he started to pedal, and he was staying up without any help. "You're doing it!" Marie clapped and bounced up and down for him like he was her child. She quickly got on her bike and joined riding beside him.

"So, where are we going?"

"There's a path I like to take, just follow me." They swerved in and out from each other and giggled. Vincent was surprised at how fast he had learned to ride a bike. "You're doing great!" Marie yelled.

"Thanks, I didn't know I was such a quick learner."

They rode through the bright sunshine as the wind kept hitting their faces. They were riding on a curvy road that led up a hillside, much smaller than the mountains surrounding Fathorne. As soon as they reached the top, Marie led them to a field with rolling green grass and flowers beyond what the eye could see. Vincent looked out to the green scenery and thought to himself that his mother would have loved this. They parked their bikes in the grass and went over to a large willow tree swaying with the wind. The sun beat down, but the shade from underneath the tree was cool and blocked out the light.

Marie carried a plaid quilt and picnic basket from the basket on her bike. She laid it out and placed the picnic basket on top, opening it to reveal a large quantity of food. She then sat down to take all the food out, and Vincent joined her. "I'm sorry, I should have asked what you would like. I just bought potato salad, grilled cheese, and water."

"That's perfect, thank you. I didn't know we were having lunch."

"I sometimes come up here to get out of my house and away from my parents."

"Do you not like your parents?"

"I love my parents, of course. I just feel so suffocated and trapped."

Vincent looked at her with a confused expression.

"My whole life, my mother constantly had me learning lessons, because she wanted me to be smart. And then, on top of that, my mother had a lady come to teach me. The lady taught me all my manners and how to be proper. My father is not home that much since he has his business and helps your father. Even when he is home, he doesn't want to be bothered. He has his assistants, or whatever they are, take me out and lock me in my room when I try to go into his study. And he always kind of made my life choices for me. All these rules and restrictions are completely old-fashioned to me. I never really had a childhood or any kind of life growing up. That's why yesterday was so special to me because I could finally be young and live life. So, now when I get even the smallest chance to have freedom, I take it."

"My childhood wasn't so great either. I spent my childhood, even now, alone. You and my sister are the only friends I really have. And I have never really had a parent, expect our old nanny. My father has kept himself inside his room for my entire life; it's like he's not even there."

Marie looked at him with a puzzling look like he gave her. "Lawrence and my father told me that about Florent but never exactly why; it seems selfish to me."

"I don't think he is only grieving and thinking about himself. As my sister always said, part of my father died along with my mother. When her heart stopped beating, his heart shattered. He was already on edge with everything that he has seen in his life. But I still see light inside of him."

"Vincent?"

"Yes?"

"You didn't really get that scar from falling, did you?"

Vincent looked down at the ground and sat in silence before finally admitting the truth. "No."

Marie put her hand on his cheek, right over the scar. Vincent flinched, not being used to people touching him.

"That's what I thought. It's a shame that happened to your father, but I don't agree with what he did to you."

"He may have did this to me, but I don't hate him."

"How can you not be at least a little resentful?"

"I do hate what he did to me, but I believe anyone could be so broken that they do the unthinkable."

"My parents did tell me about your mother and father's love. They told me they had never seen a love so magical and unreal. They told me how your father has never been the same after her death. My father said he couldn't explain what he saw in them, but it inspired him to find the same for himself. I wish I could find something so special to share with someone."

Vincent swallowed the piece of food he was chewing and turned to her, confused. "What about my brother?"

"I don't love Lawrence. I guess I just wanted to make my father happy and do what he wants me to, as always. I don't even know why he wants me to marry him; I guess because your father and mine are friends and he wants me to marry into your family. I really think it's all about money, though. That's why he wants me to marry

Lawrence, the heir. That way, his precious little girl is provided for her entire life, and so is he. Also, Fayland Park is a gold mine and, though he helped build it, he wants it in his family name too. Again, with his old ways of arranged marriages. Besides, I think I'm in love with someone else."

Vincent felt sadness overcome him once again. At least when she was with Lawrence, he could see her. "Who was this other man, and when did this happen?" Before Vincent could ask for the man's name, he felt her hand slip into his. He quickly pulled his hand away. He didn't know why, since this is what he had wanted since he had known her. "I'm sorry," Vincent said through shaky words as he stood up. "You can't possibly mean me?" he quickly noted after his apology.

She stood up to meet his eyes. "But I do."

"Why? What do you see in someone like me?"

"Vincent, you're everything that is missing in humanity. Kindness, selflessness, and decency. The traits that I thought no longer existed."

"But my face. It's deformed and unattractive. Someone as beautiful as you could never want someone as disastrous looking as me."

"You are so handsome, with or without the scar. And those eyes? Well, those eyes are to die for. But that doesn't matter to me anyway. Anyone could put on some rouge and lipstick, but inner beauty is something that very few can have, and it's hard to accomplish. I love *you*, Vincent Fayland."

Vincent turned the other way. "I don't believe you."

Marie came around and placed her lips on his while her body melted into his embrace.

"Do you believe me now?"

Vincent was shaking, and the thought came over him of what had just happened. He smiled as best he could. "I guess I have to after that. It's just that I don't really know how to love."

Marie smiled to match his own. "Does anyone? It's just something that naturally happens, and when it does, it's unbelievable. I think about you all the time and how I want to spend every moment of every day with you."

"I feel the same way about you." Vincent said with a blush.

Marie kissed him over and over until they both fell over into the tall grass and laughed. They remained there for a short time while staring at the clouds and holding hands. Marie put her arms around Vincent's neck as she laid her head on his chest. "I guess we're just going to have to figure out this love thing together, huh?"

Vincent looked down at her. "Yeah, I guess we are."

Chapter 22

VINCENT'S RESCUER

May 1959

Vincent felt hope rise in him once again as he and Marie were riding back to his house. Looking at her was looking at love. A feeling so strange and unknown, yet it felt so usual and familiar, like he had loved her his entire life.

They went back a different way, headed straight for town. Vincent hadn't been to town for as long as he could remember. Businesses and shops lined all the way down the streets, and shoppers were everywhere. The train station was packed full of tourists and sightseers. Marie quickly stopped and stared at one of the shop windows in awe. She jumped off her bike and ran toward it. Vincent pushed on the handle to stop himself and run after her. He came up beside her to notice she was staring at a necklace in the window.

"Isn't it stunning?"

Vincent wasn't really interested in jewelry and didn't have the fascination that she had with this piece of jewelry, but the look on her face made him smile. "Yeah."

"This store has had this necklace ever since I was a little girl. I guess no one has ever loved it as I have." The gold was bouncing in their faces from the sunlight, and the pink-coated pearls glistened. She turned around and started to head toward her bike. "Vincent, are you coming?"

He stood there staring at it, and he had no other choice but to go in there right away and purchase that necklace for his love. He remembered Clementine telling him of the time she went into their mother's closet. She found flapper dresses and exquisite things from when she was very young. She said their mother told her that their father had bought all those things for her from saved-up money he had for years. Vincent stopped himself when he realized he had no money, at least not enough to buy something like that. He turned around and grabbed his bike. They left the main town square and were back on the lonely road that led to his house. As Vincent stopped, Marie followed. "One day I'm going to buy you that necklace, you can count on that."

"Oh, Vincent, no! I couldn't ask you to do that." Before Vincent could open his mouth to tell her that he would do anything for her happiness, he felt a massive blow to his head.

He was knocked to the ground, causing blood to come from his nose. "I didn't know they let the freaks leave the amusement park." He looked up to see a classmate of his, Dean Welsh. Vincent spit the blood that was running into his mouth into Dean's face.

"What were you doing? Watching me in the woods?" Vincent asked.

"I happened to be taking a stroll through the woods and saw you, I couldn't miss the opportunity to bash that ugly face of yours in. And I saw you holding this pretty little thing hostage."

"Leave him alone!"

"Don't worry, sweetie, I'll save you from the hideous creature."

"I don't need saving, but you might."

"What are you going to do? Kick me with those scrawny legs or spray perfume in my eyes?" He leaned in to try to kiss her, but

Vincent punched him in the face. He grabbed his jaw, which was now covered in blood, just as Vincent's was.

"Okay, that did it." He was coming near Vincent at full force until Marie wrapped her arm around Dean's neck. She knocked him to the ground and placed her shoe on his neck.

"Don't let a pretty face fool you. Just a tiny amount of pressure, and I could kill you in an instant. But I'm feeling nice today. So, you can have your freedom if you apologize to the man I love." Marie looked up and winked at Vincent, making his heart skip a few beats again.

Dean let out a small laugh. "The man you love? Are you kidding? Darling, with a body like that, you could get any man you wanted."

She put more pressure on his neck as he let out a cry of agony. "Trust me, I know. And never call me darling. Now apologize!"

He hesitated, but through tears and blood, he finally told Vincent he was sorry. Marie let her foot off his neck, and he jumped back on his feet as fast as he could. She then took the scarf around her head and pulled it around his neck, drawing him close to her face. "Now get the hell out of my sight. And if I ever see you bother Vincent again, I won't be so kind as to let you go free."

Dean gave Marie and Vincent a horrified look before running down the road.

"What a coward," Marie said as she pulled some napkins out of her bicycle basket. Vincent stood with his mouth open, in complete shock.

"Where did you learn to fight like that?"

She placed the napkins under Vincent's nose and held them there to stop the bleeding. "My father. I have seen him do some pretty violent stuff over the years."

"That doesn't seem like Roger at all."

"He just doesn't let anyone take advantage of him."

Vincent was confused when she talked about Roger being violent. He had always known him to be mild mannered, but he guessed he didn't know Roger as well as he thought. Marie removed the napkins and kissed him. Her soft lips made the pain go away.

"Now, let's get back before he uses some of our tactics on us."

"Hey, Marie?"

"Yes?"

"Thanks."

"Don't mention it. I'd do anything for you."

As soon as they arrived back at the house, Marie had to leave. Before she got into her car, she took Vincent's hands in her own. "I'm going to break it off with Lawrence tomorrow. Then we can truly be together." She got on her tiptoes and kissed Vincent. He placed his hand on the small of her back and pulled her into a tight hug, and he never wanted to let go.

"There's a diner uptown that has delicious milkshakes, and I wondered if you want to come with me next weekend?"

"More than anything."

"You could say it's like our first date."

"Yeah. I like that idea." She kissed him for the last time before she got in her pink car and drove down the driveway. It made him feel like a piece of him left with her, and he missed her already. He wouldn't see her until next weekend, which made him feel glum.

He dragged himself up the steps and opened the door to his boring, dark, quiet house. It felt like he just woke up, and the day he had spent with Marie was an incredible delusion. Clementine appeared out of the dining area, looking worried. "Vincent, where have you been? I was worried something had happened. I couldn't find you anywhere."

"Clementine, I'm eighteen years old. I can go places by myself without someone holding my hand. I thought you and Finnick were going to be gone all day, so I went to the bunker to read."

"But I checked, and you weren't in there." She got closer to him and started to smell him.

Vincent jumped back in confusion. "Clem, what are you doing?"

"You smell like perfume, a familiar perfume."

"I don't know what you're talking about."

Then she noticed something on his face that made her gasp. "And you have lipstick smeared on your mouth!"

Vincent quickly wiped it off. Again, he hated lying to his sister, but he was not ready to tell her about Marie.

"It's not lipstick. It's um … well … all right, it's lipstick."

"Vincent Fayland, are you telling me you have a special someone?"

Vincent blushed as a grin spread across his face. "Maybe," he said with a shy smile.

She squealed and almost knocked him over with a hug. "That's so great! So, what's her name?"

"I can't say."

"Oh, come on, Vincent, just tell me."

"I'll tell you when I'm ready to tell you." He started to walk up the stairs when he felt a tug on his sleeve.

"Vincent, we used to tell each other everything."

"I know, but I can't tell you. I'm sorry." He couldn't believe that she had not noticed all the signs pointing out that it was Marie he was talking about. The perfume, the pink lipstick, the secrecy were all givens, but he was glad she had not realized this yet. He quickly walked to his room and shut the door behind him. He threw himself on his bed, but not out of anger or sadness. This time he had a smile on his face and the recurring butterflies in his stomach.

He knew he must have fallen asleep when he awoke to someone knocking on his door. He looked over to his clock and realized he must have been asleep for several hours. He went to open the door and was surprised to see his father standing there once again. "Hey, Vincent, can we go somewhere and talk?"

"Uh, yeah, sure." They went to the back porch and sat on the chairs that faced the garden and his mother's grave.

"It's pretty, isn't it?" Florent asked.

"Yes, the roses have almost taken over the entire backyard."

Vincent felt tense and nervous, talking to his father in a regular conversation. The only other time they had done this was when he gave him his suit. He looked at his father, who seemed in pain, not physically, but like something was troubling him from inside. He could see his eyes watering up. He opened his mouth as he was about to say something then stopped. "That was it, I just wanted to show you these beautiful flowers that remind me so much of your mother."

"Oh, okay."

"You can go back into the house."

Vincent knew there was something else that his father wanted to tell him, but he just couldn't do it. When Vincent got to the porch, he looked back to see his father in the garden. The pink roses were overtaking the land, as he planted a significant number each day. Who knew that chaos could be disguised as something so delicate and so beautiful.

Chapter 23

LOVER'S SECRECY

May 1959

The week had dragged on, feeling like an eternity. Vincent was once again sitting in the bunker he had turned into somewhat of a study, finishing up his weekend homework before his date with Marie. He stared down at the numbers and instructions repeatedly but still could not focus. He was usually good at mathematics, but not when he was filled with a very nervous feeling. He knew that Marie loved him, but he felt that he would mess it all up. He put the papers and textbook back into his school bag, deciding that he would just do it later. He looked at his watch and realized it was time to go anyway. He gathered all the courage that he could round up and left with his head full or worry and doubt.

He walked through the same foggy woods on the trail that led to their house, but it seemed quicker than usual. His nerves made him walk extra fast, just as fast as his thoughts were in his mind. Marie had broken it off with Lawrence, and as expected, he did not take it well. He stormed through the house and was angrier than ever. Of course, she didn't tell him Vincent was the reason that she no longer wanted to be with him but told him there was someone else she was in love with. Lawrence told her if he ever found out who this other man was, he would kill him. The look in his eyes suggested that he was not lying, and if he ever found out it was Vincent, he would kill him in a heartbeat. Just because Vincent was his brother meant nothing; he would have no mercy. Lawrence had no sympathy or regard for others; he only cared about what he wanted for himself. Vincent thought this was the worst trait in a person.

When he reached the driveway, he got into Clementine's mint-green Chevy Bel Air and quickly drove down the driveway. He had to lie to her and tell her he was going to the library. He had trouble driving as he looked down at the address Marie had told him over the phone. He turned into the woods, past the park, and stopped at the exit. After a few wrong turns and a lot of confusion, he finally found the diner. The entire building was covered in chrome; it was almost blinding. The neon sign that hung on the side of the building was almost as showy as the building itself. The sign read, Glen's Burger Shack, with a woman in a red polka-dot dress holding a tray of burgers.

"Hey there, good lookin!'"

He turned around to see Marie, but it didn't look like Marie. Instead of her usual feminine, pink-tinted dresses and pearls, her attire was something completely different. She wore a bright-pink leather jacket along with matching leather pants. Above all, she traded her pearls for studs and her scarf for a pink wraparound head-band. He couldn't even believe it was her.

"Wow, you look great."

"Thanks." She kissed him, and then he knew for sure it was her. "C'mon, let's go, I'm starving!"

She grabbed his hand, which made him blush and quickly follow her along into the diner. Vincent was dumbfounded when they stepped inside the chrome world. It was just like in the movies and television shows he watched. Music blared from the speakers, and a dance floor was set toward the back of the restaurant. "Table for two, please."

"All right, this way, ma'am." They followed the waitress in a white dress and a matching apron to the back of the restaurant.

On their way to the table, people stared at them. Vincent knew it was because of his gruesome facial features, but Marie was just breathtaking. He felt jealousy filling him when guys almost snapped their necks trying to look at her, making their girlfriends jealous. They were seated near the back of the restaurant at a green-and-silver booth. Everything around him was overwhelming.

"Somebody will be with you to get your drinks," the waitress said.

"Okay, thank you. Vincent, are you okay? You seem distracted."

"Oh, no, it's just I've never been to any kind of restaurant before."

"Wait, really?"

Vincent never really thought about it, but he had never been outside his family's grounds much. He had only ever been to school and, occasionally, the library. He always tried to stay out of the public eye, being too embarrassed to show his face since people always stared and whispered. But with Marie, he felt much more self-assured; he felt like he could go anywhere. "Yeah, I'm not much of a people person, but you're starting to change my mind."

Marie smiled and grabbed his hand as she looked at her menu. "Well, since you've never been here before, I can give you some suggestions, if you would like."

"That would be great."

"I would get a cheeseburger with everything on it, and then finish off with a large cherry shake that we should share."

"Sounds good!"

"Okay, then it's settled." The waitress came over with her small pad of paper. "We'll take Glen's burger platter and two red cream sodas. Oh, and a large cherry shake with two straws."

"All right, dear, I'll get that in, and it will be out shortly."

"Thank you." They handed the waitress the menus and waited for their food to come out.

"So, how is Lawrence taking things?" Marie asked.

"Well, he hasn't talked to my sister or me since you broke up with him. He seems really irate. Usually, he takes his anger out on us. It's terrifying because he hasn't done anything."

"He threatened me when I told him I didn't want to be with him, but I told him if he ever laid a hand on me, it would be the last thing he would ever do. He restrained himself, but his fists were clenched, and his face was red. I got out of his room as soon as I could."

"He threatened you?" Vincent could feel anger crawling up inside of him.

"Yes, but he doesn't scare me, but what does scare me is that he will hurt you. I already told you he would kill the man I was in love with, and we both know he would do it without a second thought. He acts so strangely, and his moods change constantly; he is not to be trusted. I even caught him talking to himself one night when I was at your house."

"I thought everyone did that occasionally."

"This was different, though; it was an entire conversation. It was like whispering, it was weird, and it creeped me out. Even if I didn't want to be with you, I think I would have broken up with him regardless."

"Do you think there is actually something wrong with my brother?"

"I do."

"I think as long as he doesn't find out, we will be safe."

"He isn't the only person we have to keep us hidden from."

"What? Who else cannot know?"

"When I told my father that I didn't want to marry Lawrence, he freaked out. I thought he would be mad, but he was furious. His demeanor changed, and his eyes went cold. He looked almost as bitter as Lawrence. I thought for the first time in my life he was going to strike me. But he just said that I ruined his plan."

"Plan? What plan?"

"I don't know, but it was bizarre. I guess he meant that …" She was interrupted by the waitress, who brought their food and drinks.

"I think he just meant that he wanted me to marry the heir; like I said, it's all about money with him sometimes. Let's just keep our relationship a secret for safe measure."

"You must really love me to go through all this trouble."

"Damn right, I do. Being with you just feels right, like it was meant to be. I just feel safe and cherished when I'm with you. I just feel less …"

"Lonely," the two of them said together.

"Yeah. Let's not worry about a thing right now," Marie said as she reached across the table and grabbed Vincent's hand again. They stopped talking about their concerns and enjoyed their meals. They finished off by sharing their milkshake. Vincent could hardly breathe after all the food he ate. Marie got up out of her seat and pulled Vincent up. "C'mon, let's go dance!"

"I don't dance, at least not in public."

"Well, you do now."

It was puzzling to Vincent how Marie could just get him to do things that he would have never done before. And she could do it before he even knew what was happening.

Marie ran to the dance floor, where she started to kick her legs and shake her shoulders, matching everyone else. Vincent stood in the distance, not letting himself be seen. He stood and stared at Marie, giving a quick grin before she grabbed his arm and pulled him onto the dance floor beside her. Vincent felt out of place, not knowing any of the dances everyone else seemed to know by heart. He just stood there feeling embarrassed, and Marie must have noticed. "It's okay; just follow my lead."

Her body was moving too fast to tell what she was doing, but Vincent tried to follow her steps as best as he could. She grabbed Vincent's hands and put them on her waist, and before he knew, he was matching everyone else on the dance floor. He had never felt so alive and energetic. He felt each beat with each spin and step. For the second time in his life, he had real fun, the first being the day he had spent with Marie at the park. He learned the dances to at least five songs, and he didn't want to stop. He held Marie's hand as he waited for the next song, but a waiter came over the speakers telling them the dance session was over until this evening.

"Well, I still have some time to spare. What should we do now?"

"I know this is risky, but we could just go back to my house. Lawrence is working in the park, so we won't have to worry about him. We can get in my sister's car, and I can drop you back off later."

"All right, let's go!" She grabbed her purse and took Vincent's hand as they ran out of the restaurant.

As they headed down the road, Marie rolled down the window and laid her head on the window and let her arm hang out.

"Are you okay?" he asked.

"I'm better than okay. There's nothing like the wind going through your hair and letting all your troubles get swept away. I feel so scared all the time and unsure of the future."

Vincent put his hand on hers. "What's going on?"

"Not only do I feel the stress of keeping our relationship a secret for fear of being hurt by our own families, but there is more. My mother and father fight all the time about the smallest things any-more." Marie burst into tears. "He even hit my mother last week and left a mark."

"Oh, Marie, I'm so sorry."

"My mother told me she may end up divorcing him and moving back to France. They always seemed so happy together when I was growing up. These days, I only see my father about once a week. He is always at his factory with his assistants, which I think is why they started fighting. The men in black suits that follow my father around, I call his assistants, but I'm not really sure what purpose they serve. They even block my mother from seeing my father when he doesn't want to be bothered. Being with you in this car and feeling the fresh air hit my face and messing up my hair is a paradise. Every time I'm with you, I feel released from the unpleasantness."

Vincent smiled, knowing that she made him feel the same way.

They arrived at Vincent's house and quickly got out of the car to avoid anyone seeing them. "I think Clementine may be home, but she won't see us if we hurry up to my room." They ran up the porch stairs, though the glass doors, and up the grand stairway until they finally reached Vincent's room. He slammed the door and felt a rush of relief as he and Marie let out a sigh.

"So, this is your room? I never had the pleasure of coming in here before. It's very spacious, and I love the wallpaper." She touched the green-and-blue-striped wallpaper Vincent had since he was a child and always found ugly. She sat down on the bed, and Vincent joined her by her side. "Is that your mother?"

"Yes, Clementine painted that of her out of memory."

"She was stunning. Those eyes look like someone else I know." She stared at Vincent before scooching closer to him and kissing him one time and then another until Vincent lost count. All he knew was he wanted more of her and kissed her back like he couldn't get enough. He laid her down until all he could see was her face directly in front of his, and he could feel her breath. He began to kiss her neck and made his way to her mouth. Their private moment was interrupted when someone burst through the door.

"Vincent, I have some exciting news!" Clementine said, smiling with an almost scream. When she noticed the two of them, she gasped and backed up, hitting her back on the door. "Wait, what? How … when … I'm confused."

Vincent quickly got up and shut the door, locking it this time like he should have done before. "Remember when you asked me if I had a special someone and I said yes, but couldn't tell you their name? Well, this is why. It's Marie."

"I mean, this is great; I just don't know what to say. How long has this been going on?"

"Since last weekend," Marie answered. "I am madly in love with your younger brother. I started to fall for him the morning I discovered him playing for your mother. We also spent opening day in the park together and took a bike ride. That's when I confessed that I loved him. He is so affectionate and everything decent. How could I not fall for a guy that actually treats me kindly?"

"So, is this why you broke up with Lawrence?"

"Well, there were multiple reasons, but that was the main one, yes."

"Please promise to not say anything to Lawrence. If he found out, who knows what he will do," Vincent said.

"Of course, I won't."

"We didn't want to tell anyone, not even you."

"Vincent, you know you can trust me."

"Yes, I know."

"So, are you just going to keep this a secret for the rest of your life? How is this going to work? How will you get married or ever have children? You can't keep that a secret."

"Whoa, slow down, Clementine. We haven't thought that far ahead."

"We can figure that out when we get there," said Marie.

Vincent looked at Marie and took her hands. "What if we do get married, like in the next week?"

"Vincent, I love you, but we have only been dating for a week. I don't think that is such a good idea."

"Why not? I love you, and you love me, I think?"

"Well, yes, but …"

"Then what's holding us back? If we get married, then no one can split us up, and I know you are the person I want to spend the rest of my life with."

"Our parents got engaged within less than a week of knowing each other, and they turned out okay," Clementine said.

Marie hesitated while she sat and thought about this drastic life decision. "Okay, let's do it!"

Vincent kissed Marie and held her in his arms.

"Yay! I'm so happy for you two!" She joined in on their hug before Vincent noticed something shiny on her finger.

"Hey, wait a minute, what's this?"

"Oh, right! Before I noticed you two, I came in here to tell you Finnick and I are engaged, so that makes two of us, I guess."

"Congratulations!" Marie and Vincent said together. They stayed in each other's embrace for what seemed like half an hour.

"Finnick and I are waiting about a month before we get married, and we hope you'll both come. Finnick and I will, for sure, be at yours."

"Clem, we don't want Finnick to know either."

"It's okay, he doesn't like Lawrence at all; he won't tell him. All Lawrence does is boss him around."

Marie perked up. "So, tell us how he proposed."

"Well, he called the house from one of the phones down at the park and told me to come to him. I walked to the park to find him standing at the Ferris wheel. I asked him what he wanted, and he pulled out a small box from his overalls pocket. He got down on one knee and asked me to marry him."

"How romantic! Let me have a good look at the ring." Marie took Clementine's hand and let the ring twinkle in the light. "This is stunning."

"I know he has saved almost all his money from working at the park. I'm very proud of him. Well, I'll let you two have your alone time back."

As soon as Marie shut the door, Vincent quickly grabbed Marie's hands. "So, when should we do it?"

"Oh, what the hell, let's do it tomorrow!" she said, getting up and swinging her hands in the air. She walked over to the window and looked at the mountains and scenery. Vincent came up behind her and hugged her from behind. She smiled and put her hands on his, which were wrapped around her waist. "You know, I just remembered something."

"What's that?"

"I remember a poem from a poetry book I used to read. I loved it so much growing up that I memorized the first two stanzas. That was only a small portion of it, but they gave me guidance to our love. The poem went like this.

"Lovers, oh, lovers
What a beautiful path
Two hearts beat as one
Two pieces never split into half
When the soul aches, something has begun
Lovers, oh, lovers
Reach for a twinkling star
And underneath it share midnight kisses
If passion burns you into char
Let it burn inside, for the heart never misses."

Chapter 24
THE PHOTOGRAPH
September 1959

Vincent and Marie were married the day after they were engaged. The air was humid and the sun glaring, but they did not mind. The hot weather reminded Vincent of their own romance burning inside of them, just like the poem Marie had shared with him. They married in a small church in the country. Vincent had graduated from high school, still lived at home, and began photographing wildlife on their property. He took pictures of nature at Fayland Park and sold them at a booth to make a profit. Vincent feared getting an actual job at a business for the fear that people would stare and ridicule him. He was saving up his money so that he and Marie could get a house of their own.

Clementine's painting booth was right beside his photography booth. She was recognized more by the minute for her paintings and was given opportunities to travel the world making art. She decided she would stay at home and do what she had always done. She married Finnick a month after Vincent and Marie were married, as she said. They were building a house on the property to have their own privacy but still be close to family. Lawrence went on running the operations of the park as their father locked himself away in his room.

Lawrence never spoke to Vincent, or anyone for that matter. He just gave him glower looks and had a continuing look of hatred. Vincent finally realized that Lawrence really did love Marie too. It was like he was no longer a part of their family. Although they lived in the same household, it was as if they were from different planets that happened to orbit past each other now and then.

Vincent was now in the woods with his new camera that Marie had bought for him, to capture some pictures of wildlife on their land. He looked up to see a squirrel looking down at him with a mischievous look. Vincent snapped his camera as the squirrel ran further up the tree as the flash went off. Over the next hour, Vincent took many pictures throughout the woods of wildlife and different flowers. After getting everything he wanted to be captured in a photo, he walked back to the house. As he was walking, something felt off. A feeling of being watched filled him with dread. It was like someone was walking right beside him, but both sides of him were vacant. He ran faster and faster until he reached his porch and got up to his bedroom.

He opened the door to his bedroom and saw Marie sitting in his armchair facing the window. "Marie, are you all right?

She looked up at him with tears in her eyes, then ran to him and hugged him.

"Marie, honey, what's wrong?"

"My mother left my father. She is going back to France without giving me much notice. She brought a letter here earlier today. After a week of our marriage, I told my mother about us. I told her that I chose love over social status and chose what made me happy. She was understanding and promised not to tell Dad. That's how she knew to deliver the letter here, after telling her I was coming here today. She asked me to go with her, but I couldn't. I told her that I couldn't leave with you here, and I'm also not going to drag you to another country, asking you to leave everything behind. Not only that, I would rather stay here. This is my home." Vincent placed his hand on the back of her head as she rested it on his chest. "That's not the only thing; there is something much more concerning."

"What's that, sweetheart?"

She looked up with her glossy, sad eyes. "I'm pregnant."

Vincent felt as if everything had stopped. It took a moment before he even realized what she said. His heart picked up speed, and he struggled to find words. "Oh, are you sure?"

"Yes, I am certain. I have all the symptoms. There is no other reasonable explanation. Vincent, we are having a baby. We can't keep this secret anymore. If Lawrence finds out, he'll kill you. I can't let anything happen to you! I love you so much. If only our circumstances were different." Marie covered her mouth to conceal her sobbing.

"Lawrence doesn't need to know."

"What about my father? I think after a while, he'll notice."

Marie buried her head in Vincent's chest as tears rolled down her cheeks.

"I was told there is always one thing you can do when you're unsure about everything else."

"What's that?"

"Dance."

"Vincent, it's really no time for dancing."

"It's always time for dancing, at least if I'm with you. Just trust me." Vincent took a deep breath and held Marie's hand, guiding her out of his room.

"Vincent, what if we get caught?"

"It's okay, Lawrence is still at the park."

"All right."

Vincent led her to the living room and dusted off the record player his parents had used for many worrisome nights or just to have fun. He put on the newest record they had in their collection, and it started to play a slow melody. He took her hand and pulled her in. He placed his hand on her back, and she released her tension. They relaxed into each other so they could feel each other's heartbeats until it sounded as if it was coming from the same chest.

"Two hearts beat as one," Marie whispered.

"When the soul aches, something has begun," Vincent replied. "It's strange that dancing is the only thing that can slow down time and speed it up all at once."

"I guess it is," Marie responded with a smile. "Oh, Vincent, for as long as I live, I will never forget this moment we shared. And the way you made me feel."

Vincent kissed the top of her head. He happened to look up at the doorframe to see a figure.

It was his father staring in at them. He smiled then walked away without saying a word.

"What is it?"

"Nothing." Vincent was scared; his father knew about the two of them. He feared his father would be furious at how Vincent could have betrayed his brother. But that smile that he gave was one of kindness. Perhaps, Vincent thought, the dance reminded him of his mother. It might have been like looking at memory of all the love he shared with her in the same room.

After about an hour, they finally stopped dancing. "Do you feel better?"

"Very much so, thank you." Marie had left her car at the diner again, and Vincent picked her up and took her to his house every time she would come over. If her car was seen at his house all the time, people would grow suspicious, and Lawrence might see.

"I think it's time to take you back to your car."

"Yes, unfortunately."

They broke their embrace and walked with a gloomy demeanor to Clementine's car. When they entered the vehicle, she began to cry again. Vincent grabbed her shoulder. "Everything is going to work out okay. I promise it will." He wiped the tears off her face and kissed her forehead. She nodded, never letting her eyes leave the ground.

Vincent started down the driveway. "You know what, I'm going to tell my dad about the baby. He doesn't have to know who the father is. And he is just going to have to deal with it. I am a grown woman, and I should be able to make my own choices."

"Whatever you decide to do, I'll know it will be right."

"Thank you."

He pulled into the diner's parking lot and parked beside her pink car. He kissed her. "Thank you for making me feel better, like always. I love you so much."

"I love you too."

"I'll call your house when I get the chance to tell you how my father responds. Also, we can plan when we want to see each other again. Oh, I don't know how much more I can take of this."

"Of what?"

"This whole secret relationship thing. I mean, you're my husband, and I only get to see you once a week if I'm lucky." She placed her hand on his cheek. "You should be the first thing I see every single morning and the last every single night. I want to share a home with you and raise our child without any of this worry."

He took her hands in his. "When I raise enough money, we'll run away somewhere far. We will buy a house near the ocean and spend the rest of our lives listening to the waves crash against the rocks and feel the warm breeze on our porch. And when that day comes, we will no longer have to worry about our past and the lives that we spent here."

"That sounds lovely." She kissed him one final time and got out of the car, getting into her own. She waved and pulled out of the parking lot, leaving Vincent there by himself. After he saw the pink car disappear down the road, he headed back to his house.

A week had passed since Vincent had seen Marie, and he was getting more worried the longer time went on. She said she would call, and he expected it to be within a night. He had not heard from her at all, not even a single letter. He was waiting for her to tell him that her father had accepted what she had chosen. He sat in his sister's car as it poured outside, in front of the drugstore to get his pictures developed from the past week. He waited until the rain slowed down before he finally got out of the car. He walked into the store with eyes staring at him; he was used to it.

He walked over to the photography section of the store, where a lady in a blue dress wrote something down on a piece of paper. "May I help you?"

"Uh, yes, I'm here to pick up some pictures I had developed under Fayland, Vincent."

"Oh okay, just a minute, I'll get them for you." She went to the back room and came back out with a large envelope.

"Thank you."

"I just wanted to say that my family loves your park. You are the youngest Fayland boy, correct?"

"Yes, I am."

"Well, it's really a great place. We'll be there in a few weeks."

"Great, I hope I'll see you there. Or you may see my brother, Lawrence, or my sister, Clementine." Vincent took his pictures and headed for the door.

He looked down at the envelope to count the pictures and make sure they were all there. When he looked up, he saw something that disgusted him. Though he didn't like to think he had enemies, his worst foes were all he could think to call them. They were vandalizing his sister's car. "Hey! What are you doing?" He met face-to-face with three men he went to high school with, Jack Darcin, Bobby May, and Dean Welsh. They had scratched all the paint off the side of the car and threw down the keys they were using and advanced on him.

"Well, look here, it's the freak and the loser, Vincent Fayland."

"I'm the loser? I'm married and living an extremely comfortable life. While you're still wearing your letter jackets, hanging out together, and vandalizing property like in high school. Hey, news flash, high school is over. But I guess being popular in high school was your peak. And Dean here got his ass kicked by my wife."

"Shut up! That never happened!" Dean spat back at him. Bobby, the largest of the three, came up to Vincent and put his hand on his neck. He threw him into the car, leaving a significant dent and cracked the window. Dean fired a spitball in his face, and Jack kicked him in the head. "Never talk back to us again, do you understand?" Bobby gave him another blow. Dean got right into his face and tilted his head. "Or we will splatter your guts all over the sidewalk. This is your final warning."

Vincent coughed up blood and doubled over in pain. Soon the drugstore owner came out to see what the commotion was outside his store. All three of them jumped into Dean's car, a red Thunderbird. They sped down the road, leaving behind nothing but dust. Vincent saw their car, and he sought revenge. He never believed in revenge until this very moment. He had done nothing to them; they tortured him in high school and probably would keep doing it. "Are you all right, dear boy?"

"Yeah, I'm fine."

The man ran back inside and gave him a free pack of bandages to heal the cuts on his skin.

"Here you are, put this on when you get home."

"Thank you, I appreciate it." He got into the mangled car and opened the envelope to look at the pictures. They were all stunning, as they captured images of nature's beauty. The film held small images, but they were all very clear. He placed the pictures back into the envelope and started the car. Luckily it still ran all right; it was just the exterior that looked dreadful.

He pulled into the driveway, and Clementine happened to be sitting on the porch reading a book, as usual. She quickly reacted to the scrapes on her car. She ran down the steps, almost tripping over her own feet. "What happened?" she said, aghast.

"Those damn guys I went to high school with. I guess they

thought this was my car, since they have seen me driving it. They happened to be at the drugstore when I was."

"They got you too, didn't they?"

"Yes," he said with his head down.

"I don't care about my car, but I do care about you. Let's get you fixed up."

She pulled him into the living room and took the bandages that Vincent had received. She wrapped the bandage around the hand that had been cut from the shattered glass. Following that, she took a rag and cleaned the blood from his face. "Thank you so much. You really didn't have to go through all this trouble for me."

"Yes, I did. That's what big sisters are for."

Vincent gave her a smile. "So, how is your house coming along?"

"It's almost finished. Finnick and I can't wait to finally have our own place. We plan on moving in there in just one short month. How are you and Marie doing?"

"I'm actually kind of worried about her. We haven't talked in about a week."

"Why?"

"I don't know. She was supposed to call me after she told her father about …" Vincent stopped. He didn't want to tell anyone about the baby until later, when they had everything figured out.

"About what?"

"Well, I guess it's all right to tell you. Marie is pregnant."

Clementine gave out a small squeal and jumped to hug Vincent. "That's wonderful!"

"Ow!"

"Oh, sorry. I'm just really excited! My baby brother is growing up! And I'm going to be an aunt! But how are you going to keep this a secret?"

"That's just it, we don't know."

Their butler came into the living room not long after and requested Vincent.

"A woman calls for you at the door."

"Oh, okay, I'll head there now. Thank you." Vincent jumped up as quickly as he could. Marie's absence and silence over the past week had scared him. But if it was her, how had their butler not recognized her? He opened the door to find Marie disguised in a black wig and a yellow jumpsuit of some sort.

"Marie?"

"Yes."

She was crying, and her mascara was running down her face from tears and the rain. The rest of her was soaked. She had a large suitcase and another bag in her hands.

"What is going on?"

She forcefully hugged Vincent. "Can we talk somewhere in private, please?"

"Yes, I know a place." He took his cardigan off and put it over her shoulders and then took the bags.

"Thank you."

"Just follow me." They walked in the pouring rain into the woods until he found the bunker.

"What is this place?"

"An old bomb shelter that my father turned into a playhouse of sorts when Lawrence was small. When he outgrew it, I claimed it as my own secret hideout." Vincent climbed down the ladder and helped Marie down as well. He sat the bags in the corner and guided Marie to the chair. She ripped off the wig and cried into her hands, sobbing without breathing.

Vincent took her hands. "Hey, slow down. What is going on?"

"My father, he kicked me out of the house. I told him I was pregnant, and he slapped me across the face. He told me that I should be ashamed of what I have done and called me a whore. I didn't tell him about us, I couldn't. He told me once again that I should have married Lawrence and that I ruined him. He told me to get out of his house, or he would have his men remove me themselves. Vincent, I have never seen this behavior in my father before, except these past few months. My mother warned me that he was not the man he says he is, in the letter she sent me. She pleaded with me to come with her, but I just couldn't leave you here for months at a time. I barely get to see you as it is. Now I'm scared and have nowhere to live."

"But you do. As long as my house is still standing, you will have a place to live."

"I can't live here. Lawrence will find out about us, and so will your father. I can't risk that. I know what your brother said, and I know he would shoot you dead if he found out we are married and that you're the father of my child."

Vincent sat and thought for a while before coming up with a plan he couldn't believe he hadn't considered before. "How about this—you live here. I could bring you food and whatever you needed from the house. When everyone else has fallen asleep at night, I can sneak you in, and you can sleep in my room. You can't stay here; it can get really chilly or really hot here at night. Besides, I want you in my arms."

"That sounds complicated, and I don't know if I can stay here all the time. I spent my entire life feeling like a prisoner. But I do love you, and there are just some sacrifices I can and will make. What about when the baby arrives? It will make noise."

"My house is huge. You can't really hear anything outside of the room you're in. Lawrence and Dad's rooms are in another wing. It will be fine. I know this isn't easy on you, but the main thing is we will be together, and you'll be safe."

"I just don't know about anything anymore. The father I once knew isn't really who I thought. Everything I once knew is gone. My parents are split, my father is now a brute, and I have to keep my husband a secret, just so his brother or my father won't kill him. I still don't understand why my father wanted me to marry Lawrence so severely, but like I said, I guess it was all about money. How selfish to think about wealth over the happiness of his only child."

"I agree, it's very ridiculous."

"And now I'm going to have this baby, and I don't know the first thing about being a parent."

"It's okay, I don't either. It's just something new parents have to work together to figure out. I know life is chaotic right now, but at least we have each other. I try to think about the things I have, compared to the things I don't."

"You're right." Marie got up and hugged Vincent as her tears soaked into his shirt.

They spent the rest of the evening together talking about the future and their plans. Vincent looked at the clock he had placed on the wall; it was getting late. "It should be dark outside, and everyone will be in bed by now. We should be getting back to the house."

"All right, just let me grab my pajamas out of my bag." She grabbed a pink striped pajama set and left the bunker with Vincent. Outside was pitch black, and the fog was intense. Vincent tightened his grip on Marie's hand. The wind picked up as they walked through the woods. At night, these woods seemed thicker, the fog more intense. They could hardly see, but they heard the shuffling in the woods, most likely animals running away.

After what seemed like an hour, they finally reached Clementine's wrecked car. "I forgot my photographs; let me grab them real quick." Vincent reached for the white envelope though the broken window. He took Marie's hand once again, and they quietly sneaked into the house.

They entered his bedroom without anyone noticing them. Vincent pulled out the photographs he had taken in the woods while Marie put on her sleepwear. "Wow, these turned out better than I expected." He looked down at photos of rabbits, birds, and the scenery of the forest. One picture almost made his heart leap from his chest, and he let out a gasp. The photo fell to the ground when he jumped back.

"What is it?"

"There is something in this picture. I can't make it out." It was supposed to be an ordinary picture of a deer eating, but something haunting occupied the background. A black silhouette stood behind the deer, facing the camera.

Marie came up behind him. "I'm not sure, but it's very creepy. I feel like I have seen that figure somewhere before. I just can't remember when."

"Maybe I should ask my sister or father if they've ever seen it."

"Yes, you should, but let's not worry about it right now and go to bed."

Vincent put all the pictures back into the envelope and set them on his dresser. They both got into bed, and for the first time, he got to wrap his arms around the love of his life in their very own bed. It was a much better situation than the back of a car or somewhere secret. Her strawberry-blonde curls sat in front of his face, and he could smell the sweet floral scent of them. It was the most excellent feeling to feel her body next to his in his own bed. It made him smile to know she would be the first thing he would see in the morning.

He awoke the next morning with Marie still in his arms. She awoke just a few minutes after he did. He looked over her shoulder to see her face. She turned over to face him and smiled. "Good morning."

"Good morning." He kissed her and placed his head on her shoulder.

"This is just what I wanted. Maybe being kicked out wasn't such a bad thing after all."

"I'll be back, I'm just going to go down and get some breakfast. I'll bring you some when I'm finished."

"All right. I'm hungry, so don't take too long," Marie said with a smile.

"I'll try not to." He grabbed the picture with the figure in it and headed down to the dining room.

Clementine was coming out of her bedroom as Vincent was walking down the hallway. "Clem, I need to show you something."

"Okay, what is it?"

Vincent showed her the picture. "Have you seen this thing before? It looks like a shadow of someone."

"Actually, I have, when I was a little girl before you were born. I have only ever seen it one time. It was late at night, and I was heading back to my bedroom, and there it was, standing about where you are now. It scared me beyond belief. I never knew what it was. After a while, though, I just didn't think about it anymore."

"It's just so strange. It's like it's looking at me, watching my every move."

"I really wouldn't think any more into it. Like I said, I have only seen it one time, and that was it."

Vincent didn't want to just ignore it, but maybe it was for the best.

He walked down to the dining room, where Lawrence was already eating his breakfast, sipping his coffee, and reading a newspaper. Vincent's plate was sitting in his usual spot at the table, but he grabbed it and went into the kitchen to get the extras for Marie. He got another plate, and the cook placed eggs and bacon on it.

"Hungry, are we? And just where do you think you are going?" Lawrence asked, peeping over his newspaper.

"Um, I have a lot of work to get to. And all the work is really working up an appetite."

"All right, then."

Vincent could feel himself relax after Lawrence bought his lie, even though he did seem suspicious. It was strange that Lawrence was actually talking to him once again. He went back up to his room, his hands burning from the hot plates. "Here you are."

"Looks good, thank you."

"My sister said she has seen that figure in the picture, once when she was a little girl. It was in our house."

"I know I have seen it somewhere. I was always alone, and I felt like it was watching me."

"She told me not to worry about it, so I won't."

As soon as they were finished eating, Vincent took their plates. He went back to the kitchen to ensure that Lawrence had gone to the park. He then took Marie back to the bunker without anyone noticing. It was like locking away his treasure, and he felt disgusted having to hide away his beautiful jewel. But for their safety and to keep her from being taken away, it had to be done. For the remainder of the morning, he played the violin for his mother at her grave. As he played, the fog eventually lifted, and the sun had come out from behind the clouds.

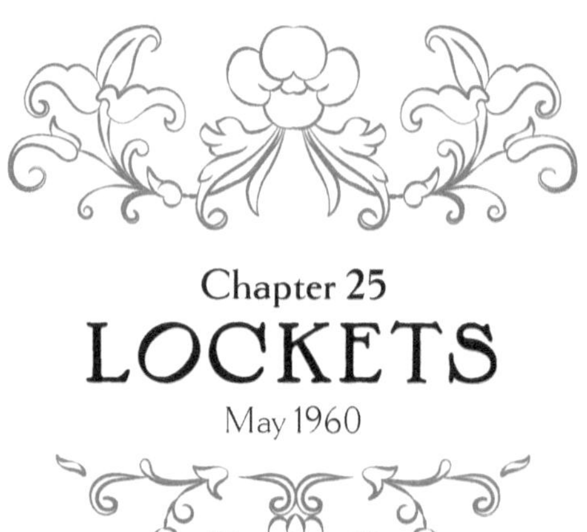

Chapter **25**
LOCKETS
May 1960

The happiest day of Vincent's life came on a sunny spring day. Everything was perfect, from the sun hitting his back as he sat on a concrete bench to the birds above singing their morning melodies. It had been a long time since Clementine and he had time together to just sit and talk. When they were younger, they would talk about their dreams and plans for hours on end. The older they got, the more complicated things became, and they never got to spend as much time together as they once had. They sat in front of Clementine's house, which was now finished. It was a decent-sized home with three bedrooms and two bathrooms. It was not fancy, just an ordinary home, but it was everything Clementine had always wanted.

Vincent was grateful for everything in his life right now.

"Marie is getting really big. I bet she will have the baby in the next week," Clementine said.

"Yeah, I want the baby to be here, but I can wait. I'm just so nervous about being a father. I never really had one of my own, and it's terrifying."

"You'll be great at it."

"Thanks, Clem, you have always seemed to see more confidence in me than I see for myself."

"You're a great person, Vincent, and if anyone deserves to raise a child, it's you."

"I'm not so sure about that."

Clementine stared out at her house, looking at the window of an empty bedroom. Then she began to cry, bringing her knees to her face and sitting in a crouch.

Vincent quickly put his hand on her shoulder. "What's wrong?" It scared him; he thought she was hurt.

"I wasn't going to say anything, because we don't really know what's going on. But over the last couple of months, Finnick and I have been trying to start a family. We've done everything the doctors have told us to do, but nothing has worked." She sat silently while the tears poured down her face before she finally started to speak again.

"I actually got pregnant once, but not long after, I suffered a miscarriage. I did my best to try to hide my grief from all of you. It was almost too much to take, and I can't go through that pain again. Nothing has happened since. I just don't think we were meant to have children."

"I'm so sorry." Vincent didn't really know what to say to her, but he sat there and shared in her pain. He couldn't imagine having to go through something so harsh. "But there's always a chance. I wouldn't give up."

"Vincent, you know I have always been a pretty optimistic person, but I just don't think it's going to happen."

They sat in silence for a while, since Vincent still had nothing to say. Her tears finally dried, and she became her happy self once again. "I was thinking of painting our family, at least Finnick, Marie, and you. Would you and Marie be willing to pose for some paintings?"

"I'm all in, of course. I'll have to ask Marie."

"If I've learned one thing in my entire life, it's that nothing is permanent, and I want to capture something that will be a lasting memory."

Vincent could hear people's voices through the trees, which meant the park was open. He also listened to the clinks and clanks of the rides firing up. All this meant that Lawrence was most likely at the park, and he could bring Marie in the house for Clementine's painting. "I can go get her now, if you would like."

"Yes, that would be great. Just have her meet me in the living room."

"Okay, I'll see you there."

Vincent walked the short path to the bunker and heard faint music coming from inside. He climbed down the ladder to see Marie sitting on the office chair. Her feet were kicked up on the desk as she read the latest issue of a fashion magazine.

"Oh, hello dear, I wasn't expecting you until later."

"Clementine wants us to pose for some paintings."

"Why?"

"She just wants some paintings of the family."

"Well, all right. But what if Lawrence sees us?"

"The park is open right now; he should be there."

"Okay." She put the magazine down and took Vincent's hand. She wore a short, puffy pink dress, and her stomach was almost hidden by all the layers, but not entirely.

When they got to the living room, Clementine was already prepared with her paint and canvas. "Thanks for doing this, Marie."

"Oh, no problem."

"Just sit on the sofa, and I will begin." Marie sat up straight as Clementine started to paint her face. Vincent sat in an armchair on the other side of the living room. All of them jumped when they heard a voice.

"Marie?" Lawrence said from the hallway out of shock. Vincent could feel himself tremble.

Clementine stopped painting and quickly responded. "Lawrence, I thought you were supposed to be at the park."

"I was just changing into some cooler clothing. Marie, what are you doing here?"

"Clementine wanted to paint a portrait of me." He came around the sofa, and his eyes grew wide.

"You're, um, with child?"

"Yes."

"This other man you said you loved, I assume, is the father."

"Yes, now please stop asking me questions. I told you I never wanted to talk about it. Clementine is my friend and I can be here if I please."

He changed his demeanor and got in Marie's face. "Don't you dare come to my house shouting commands at me! I say what happens in this household." Vincent jumped out of the chair and yanked Lawrence back.

"What do you have to do with this? Mind your own business!" Lawrence yelled and, without hesitation, raised his hand to slap Vincent across the face before Clementine got involved. Clementine kicked him in the chest, and he fell into the coffee table. Lawrence's abuse brought back horrible childhood memories for Vincent.

"This isn't your house, Lawrence! As long as Father is still alive, this is still his house," Clementine shouted.

"Don't be an idiot. That man locks himself away, and we never see him. This might as well be my house." Lawrence got up and left the room in a fit of anger.

"He needs to fix his anger issues," Marie said. She didn't even flinch when Lawrence got in her face.

It took only two hours for Clementine to finish the small painting of Marie. It looked like a photograph, not a painting, with all its details. "This is absolutely marvelous, Clementine!"

"Thank you. I gave it a title on the back." Marie flipped it over, and her eyes filled with tears.

"Sisterhood," Marie said in a soft tone.

"You're the closest thing I ever had to a sister, and I am very thankful for it." Marie stood up and hugged Clementine.

"I feel the same way about you."

"All right, Vincent, your turn!" Clementine shouted out. Vincent came and sat on the sofa next to Marie. After another two hours of waiting, posing, and sitting, she finished his portrait as well. Clementine took the painting off the easel and handed it to Vincent. He looked down at his deformed face and his mismatched eyes. The back said, "My brother."

"So, what do you think?"

"It's excellent."

"I'm going to put these in my special collection in my room at home. I'll be back."

Vincent was left alone again with Marie, and he counted each minute as a blessing.

"Vincent, I have something for you."

She slipped her hand into his. "I was going to wait until tonight to give it to you, but I'm just too excited. Since it's our first anniversary, I thought I would get you something special. She pulled out a wooden box from one of the hidden pockets in her dress, opening it to reveal two gold pieces of jewelry. She put one on her neck, which was heart-shaped with a vibrant design, and the other around his neck, which was more of a dog tag style. "Okay, on three, let's open them together. One … two … three!"

They opened them to reveal a picture of them, one side Marie and the other Vincent.

"Marie, I love it! Thank you so much." He hugged her, and he could almost feel the tears coming.

"I'm never taking this off," Vincent said as Marie smiled.

"I'm glad you like it."

"That's not all, though!" She pulled out another white box.

"You got me something else? You shouldn't have gone through this trouble."

"It's nothing, now open it."

Vincent opened the small box to find a decent-sized pocketknife.

"You never know when it might come in handy. I get worried about you walking in the woods at night alone."

"Thank you." He hugged Marie. "Now, I didn't forget about this very special occasion. I bought you a little special something too." Vincent gave her a quick kiss and ran off to his room. He had been waiting two months to give her this gift. As soon as he had enough money, he went to the store right away.

He grabbed the small bag with pink gift tissue paper sticking out from all sides. His heart was thumping, and he couldn't wait to see the look on Marie's face. He came back into the living room as she waited patiently. "Okay, here it is."

He handed her the bag, and she pulled out the tissue paper, throwing it around like confetti. She pulled out an oval-shaped gray box. She smiled, and once again, tears came from her eyes. "Oh, Vincent, you didn't! I never imagined I would ever hold this necklace in my hands." She got up and hugged Vincent tightly. "Thank you! Thank you! Thank you!" She looked at the necklace again. "How did you afford this?"

"I have been saving money from birthdays and Christmases for a long time. My father did the same for my mother when they were struggling; at least that's one of the stories Clementine told me. And my photographs are selling reasonably well at the park."

"Vincent, I know you love me, but I am not worth all this. That's your hard-earned money you should have spent on yourself."

"Are you kidding me? No riches in the world could compare to seeing your beautiful smile."

She kept crying, and her makeup was getting smeary. She hugged Vincent once again before he pulled the necklace out of the box.

"Come here." She followed him over to a large mirror placed on one side of the room. Vincent put the necklace around her neck, on top of the heart-shaped locket. She put her hands up to her mouth and let out a small gasp.

"It's just as stunning as I had always hoped." The pink jewels sparkled when she moved from side to side. "It's so …" She let out a small scream and grabbed on to her stomach. "Vincent, something is wrong. I think I may be in labor."

"Oh, uh, all right." He placed his coat around her shoulders. They had nothing prepared; they weren't expecting the baby to come for another couple of weeks. He put his arm around her and guided her out of the living room. Clementine was standing just outside, coming back from her house.

"What's going on?"

"The baby is coming!"

"Oh, my goodness! I'll drive."

"Okay."

They ran out to the car as fast as their feet could take them. Clementine's car had been repaired of the damage. Vincent still would get them back someday for what they had done to his sister's car. He had other matters to attend to at the moment. Vincent climbed into the back with Marie, holding her hand tightly. "Everything is going to be all right. Just keep holding my hand and breathe."

Her face was red, and her eyes were drowning in her tears. "Vincent, I can't do this!"

Vincent put his hand on her cheek. "Yes, you can, I know you can."

"No, I can't."

"Yes, you can, you got this."

Clementine pulled into the hospital and let them out at the entrance. As Vincent entered, everyone stared at him, and people cowered. Everywhere he went in the building, he could feel the eyes of everyone around him looking at his face.

They checked in, and two nurses guided Marie to a room. Vincent took a seat beside her bed and kissed her hand. "You're going to be just fine."

"With you, I know I will be."

Ebony Althea Fayland was born after fourteen hours and was perfectly healthy. Vincent lay on the bed beside Marie while he had his arm around her. The baby had thick black hair that covered her entire head. She barely made any noise, and when she did, it was almost like a whimper. "Isn't she lovely?" Marie said.

"Yes," Vincent answered as a smile stretched across his face, the most enormous smile his face would allow.

"Thank you for helping me bring this precious little girl into the world."

"No, thank you." Vincent leaned over and kissed Marie. "I never imagined I would ever get married because of how I look. Now I have the most beautiful wife and the most beautiful daughter in the world. Funny how life works."

Marie grinned and opened her mouth to say something before Clementine came walking through the door.

"There she is!" She walked over to the bed to get a better look at Ebony as Finnick followed her. "Oh, Vincent, she is just as stunning as you described her on the phone. Way to go, you two!" They both blushed and smiled at each other.

"May I?"

"Yeah, absolutely."

Clementine extended her arms and cradled Ebony in them. "Hi, sweetie, I'm your aunt Clementine, and this is your uncle Finnick." She turned Ebony toward Finnick, and he gave a little wave. She carried Ebony to the small sofa by the window in their hospital room. She and Finnick looked so content, staring at her and hearing her coo. Vincent was pleased to see his sister so happy. Finnick had his hand rested under Ebony's head while Clementine kept her in her arms. They would have made wonderful parents.

"You know there will probably be times when Marie and I will be exhausted and may need a break to spend time as a couple. What I'm trying to ask is if you could babysit Ebony if we ever needed it." Vincent knew that Clementine would not only be happy to do it, but she would also want to.

"Definitely! You trust me with something so fragile?"

"You're the most trustworthy person I know."

Clementine looked up and gave a smile. Vincent had never really felt like he had a complete family until they were sitting in the hospital room together. His wife, daughter, sister, and brother-in-law were the only family he ever needed.

They spent about an hour sitting on the sofa and gazing at Ebony as she lay perfectly quietly. "Well, Finnick and I are going to head back home. I'll see you tomorrow when you leave the hospital."

"All right, drive safe," Vincent said.

"Thanks for coming!" Marie said, sighing as Ebony was back in her arms. "I just can't get over how adorable she is, and she looks just like her father." Vincent had seen pictures of himself as a baby, and his daughter did look just like him. Vincent joined Marie by her side and kissed her shoulder before he laid his head on it. He had his whole world in this small hospital room.

Eventually, Marie fell asleep, and Ebony did as well. They both had a long, hard day. He gently lifted Ebony and placed her in the hospital bassinet and made sure the blanket was snug around her. He wondered if his father had ever held him the same way, and it was hard to imagine himself being so small and delicate or his father being so gentle. He went over to Marie, covered her up with a blanket, and kissed the top of her head, then went over to a chair in the corner and laid his head back. He felt a small lump under his shirt, the locket that Marie had gotten for him. He opened it up and looked at the happy couple inside. He couldn't believe it was him with the beautiful Marie Merriam that he had always adored, even as children. He looked up and noticed that the necklace was placed around her neck as well. She hadn't taken it off since she went into labor and arrived here; neither had he. He slowly closed the locket, kissed it, and then fell asleep.

The next week they were allowed to go home. Vincent had been spending his days with Marie and returning home at night. Clementine and Finnick helped them move all their belongings to the car and drove them home. They pulled into the driveway, and Ebony started crying. Marie got Ebony out of the car and began to rock her. "What's wrong, sweetheart, are you hungry? It has been a while since she has eaten. I'll go get everything set up in the bunker. Vincent, could you take her up to the room and place her bassinet until everything is ready? I'll be up shortly to make her a bottle."

"I can do it."

"Oh, okay, I'll meet you up there when I'm finished." Vincent took Ebony from Marie and picked up the diaper bag. She then headed off toward the woods behind the house. Clementine headed toward the woods too, on a path they had paved up to their house.

"Clem and Finnick, thank you for helping us through this. Getting all the supplies we still needed and driving us back and forth. It really means a lot to us."

"No problem. That's what big sisters are for, remember?" They shared a smile and then went their separate ways.

Vincent looked around, almost looking like he was breaking into his own house, to make sure there was no sign of Lawrence. He placed a pacifier in Ebony's mouth so she would stop crying until he got her bottle. Fortunately, there was no one around as he quickly walked up the stairway. He tried blocking the sun from the skylight from Ebony's face. He walked down the hallway and around the corner. As he turned the corner, he came face to face with his brother, inches from running into him. Vincent froze and stared at him, not knowing what to do. Lawrence was stupefied.

"Whose baby is this?"

"Marie's." He had to quickly think of a lie. "I, um, am babysitting for her. She had to go run some errands, and no one else could watch her."

"I'm not really sure why she would trust you, but all right." Lawrence then walked past him and down the hallway. Vincent could feel the sweat dripping off his forehead. How many lies could he get away with until the truth finally came out?

He opened the door to the hue of pink bouncing around his room. Marie had moved most of her belongings into his room, including most of her pink bedroom set. Ebony's white lace bassinet, which Clementine had bought, sat beside the bed,. He gently placed her inside, and she began to squirm. "I'll be right back, sweetie. I'm going to the kitchen to make your bottle."

He shut the door and started to walk down the hallway. As he was walking down the steps, he heard a door open once again. He first thought it could have been his father, but he decided to go check. He walked past his father's door, and it was locked, meaning he was likely still inside. He turned the corner to find his door standing wide open.

When he came in, Lawrence was standing with Ebony in his arms. "Lawrence! Put her down!" He actually listened to him and put her back but then started slowly walking toward him.

"She is yours, isn't she?" He said in a quiet and menacing manner.

"What? No."

"Liar! I know she is your daughter. She has your eyes. She has Mother's eyes. This room is filled with Marie's things. You're the other man, the one Marie loved, aren't you?" Before Vincent could answer, Lawrence pinned him to the wall. Vincent struggled but could not get free. "How could you betray me like that? Sneaking around with the love of my life and then convincing her to leave me? Did you threaten her or something?"

"No! We share the same feelings for each other. We love each other. She is not the love of *your* life."

Lawrence lifted his fist and was ready to punch Vincent when Marie came into the room.

"Lawrence!" Marie took his arm and turned him around to face her.

"Marie, tell him you never loved him. What did he do to you? Did he force you into this?" Lawrence said as he grabbed her shoulders.

"Absolutely not!" She stepped in between Lawrence and Vincent.

"I'm sorry, but I really do love Vincent. I couldn't be with you while I was in love with your brother."

"How could you love this ugly monstrosity over me? You could have had all the fortune and this house if you married me."

"That just proves you don't know me at all. I don't want any of that. I've always had feelings for your brother, ever since we were children, even when I was too young to understand what those feelings were. I just can't believe it took me this long to figure out that I had loved him all these years."

Vincent couldn't believe that she had loved him since childhood, just as he had her. "So, you've been dating behind my back this entire time?"

"Actually, we're married."

Lawrence looked like his head was about to explode, and it was turning to a bright shade of red.

"But it doesn't have to be this way. You could find a wife and move on, then we could all be friends. Like with Clementine and Finnick. We just can't be together; you have to move on."

"But what about all those nights we had together laughing and kissing? You seemed to like me then."

Marie took Lawrence's hands. "I do like you, just not in a romantic way. I just wanted to make my father happy and fulfill his wishes. But when I listened to my heart, I knew I couldn't stay with you."

"Marie, I love you. You are the love of my life. I have lived each day in agony without you, wanting to ruin the man who took you from me. Vincent isn't right in the head; he'll hurt you. I know it, there is something not right about him."

Vincent hated Lawrence for trying to convince Marie that Vincent was degenerate when he was really the manipulative one.

Marie pulled her hands away. "There is nothing wrong with Vincent! I don't want to hurt you, but I don't love you, and that is that. I'm sorry."

Lawrence looked down at the ground. "*Sorry* won't fix all the pain I had to endure for an entire year. I'll get you back, Vincent, you just wait and see!" That threat and the look Lawrence gave him made Vincent's spine tingle.

"No, you won't. If you ever hurt Vincent, I'll do something terrible to you. And it will be something you will never recover from."

Lawrence stormed out of the room.

"Marie, we have to get out of here. I don't want to fear Lawrence, but I know he will do something, and not just to you or me. He may do something to Ebony."

"That's why I can't stay in this house. And the bunker is just too small for Ebony and me. I have considered living with your sister. I just don't want to put any more burdens on her, since she has already done so much. They built that house to have some privacy; they're adults and need to be by themselves."

"I would feel guilty asking them too, but it may be our only choice. But then again, we can't risk Clementine getting hurt trying to hide us."

Marie then changed her mind. "You know what? I'm tired of hiding and all this secrecy. I say we just live our lives, and when we get enough money, we can move out of this place. You said you have some saved up already, right?"

"Actually, I spent a lot on your necklace, and it cost everything I had saved. I knew it was an unwise decision, but I just had to see the look on your face."

"I'll get a job. I should have done it a long time ago. You could go to the park every day and try to sell your photographs and get another job as well. And we could ask Clementine to babysit."

"Yes, that sounds like a good plan."

"I don't see why Lawrence can't move out. He is thirty-two years old for crying out loud."

"He said it's because he is running the park and is the heir to the house, so I guess he'll never leave."

"That's a poor excuse."

"I'll start looking for jobs in the morning."

"Me too. We will get out of here as soon as possible. We will leave all this nonsense behind."

They sat on Vincent's bed, and Marie placed her head on his

shoulder. "Thank you for saving me from Lawrence. If it wasn't for you and Clementine always saving me, I would have been dead a long time ago."

Marie laughed. "No problem. Lawrence still scares me, though. I'm afraid he will try to hurt or kill you. There is something deranged about him."

"I know. I have been enduring his torture for years."

"Well, whatever he is, I won't let him do anything to you. I'm going to make Ebony's bottle now." Marie kissed Vincent and left the room.

Vincent looked into the bassinet to such an innocent face. Ebony knew nothing of this cruel world, and it sickened Vincent that she would one day have to face it.

Chapter 26
THE APOLOGY
May 1960

Vincent awoke in his bed, still in his day clothes. Marie was asleep beside him, and Ebony was as well, in her bassinet. He must have fallen asleep earlier without knowing it. He rubbed his eyes and got out of bed, knowing that he wouldn't be able to fall back asleep. He needed some fresh air and just some time to think. It was too dark to walk in the woods to the bunker, so he thought he would go out to the porch swing and think for a while. He put on his jacket and left his room. On the way, he looked back at least every five seconds to make sure Lawrence wasn't waiting for him with a weapon to kill him on the spot. He took every turn with caution and kept a lookout for him. He was relieved to pull the doorknob of the large glass doors that led to the back porch.

The porch light was already on, and Vincent nearly screamed when he saw someone sitting on the swing. "Oh, hey, Vincent. What are you doing up out of bed?" Clementine said in a tired voice.

"I was getting ready to ask you the same. Why aren't you home?"

"Growing up, this was my place to get my thoughts together. Every time something was bothering me, I would come out here. It was especially peaceful on summer nights like this when I can hear the frogs and see the fireflies. Just me and the stars."

Vincent sat down beside her on the swing. "Is there something bothering you right now?"

"It's Dad."

"What about him?"

"I mean, I've been worried about him ever since Mother died, being locked away in his room and his compulsive behavior with the roses and the alcohol. But now I worry about his health. Our family has a long history of dying young, either from health issues or unfortunate incidents. Before I moved out, I could hear him coughing constantly. I noticed his limp has gotten worse, and he just looks ill. I don't know how much longer we have with him." Clementine started to sob and couldn't control her tears. "Vincent, I've told you a lot about Mom, but not Dad."

"How was he before Mom died?"

"He was kind and gentle. He was my hero. I looked at Fayland Park and was so proud that he had made a place where families could be happy and have fun. We actually used to be very close. Before you came along, I considered him to be my best friend. He took me to the carousel almost every morning, and we had tea parties together. I guess I'll never have those days back."

Clementine looked into the darkness toward the garden, and at first, he thought she was staring at nothing. But when he got a closer look, he could see his father in the pitch black. Florent was planting more roses; they were now growing up on the porch, and rose bushes were taking over the house's back side like never before. He was struggling to get around with his bad leg, but it didn't stop him.

"No one ever told me how he got that limp."

"It happened before I was even born, but Father told me about it when I asked him many years ago. He told me that one night he had run off the road with Lawrence in the car. Father got a broken leg that didn't seem to heal right, and Lawrence hit his head really hard."

Vincent perked up and could hear his heart pounding. "Do you think that's why Lawrence is the way he is?"

"Perhaps, but I believe it was Mother's death that messed him up too. I think it's just that he has a hard time dealing with his grief. In that sense, he and Father are just alike. When he fell in love with Marie, I believe he felt something again."

Vincent felt terrible that he may have caused Lawrence to fall into a deeper pit of despair.

"It's not your fault. Marie loves you, and that's just the way things are."

"Even though Lawrence and I have despised each other our entire lives, I hope he does find someone and is happy. Everyone deserves to be."

Vincent and Clementine just sat and stared at the starry sky, thinking about how their lives had changed so quickly. "I better go home. I told Finnick I would only be gone for an hour."

"Are you sure you will be okay? It's not safe to walk in the woods at night."

"I'll be fine. I've done it plenty of times before."

"Okay, just be careful."

"Good night."

"Good night." Clementine walked down the steps and headed toward the path that led to her home.

Vincent could see his father better as he got closer to the house. He thought about what Clementine said about not knowing how much longer their father would be with them. At that moment, Vincent decided to tell his father the truth about everything. He walked down the steps and finally decided to confront him.

"Vincent, is that you?"

"Yes, I need to tell you something."

"Okay, what might that be?" Florent was no longer planting the roses but standing in the garden, staring at the pink-covered land.

"I want to let you know that you have a granddaughter."

He perked up, and some life came into his eyes. "What are you talking about?"

"You have probably heard that Marie decided not to marry Lawrence."

"Yes, Roger had told me."

"The reason for that was because she loves me. And I love her. We married last fall, and she got pregnant a few months later. It was unexpected, but we couldn't be happier. She gave birth last week to a beautiful, healthy little girl." Florent didn't show much emotion, but Vincent could see that he was astonished by all this.

"May I ask her name?"

"Ebony Fayland. Ebony *Althea* Fayland."

Florent couldn't hold his smile or his tears when he heard her name. "That's wonderful, son. I'm very happy for you. I suspected you and Marie were together. I seen you two together a few times. But why didn't you tell me until now?"

"We didn't know how you would react. I knew you wanted Lawrence to marry Marie, since he is the eldest and the heir."

"I don't care who my children marry, as long as they marry for love. My mother tried to force me into marrying girls I felt nothing for. Marie marrying Lawrence was Roger's idea. Speaking of Roger, he told me Winnie had left him. We haven't spoken since. Does Marie know anything about him?"

"No, she lives here. He kicked her out when she told him she was pregnant."

"Well, you did a great job of keeping all this from me. I had no idea that Marie or a baby were in the house. What made you tell me all of a sudden?"

"Clementine and I were talking about how you aren't in the best of health, and she is worried about you. I was afraid that if I didn't tell you, I would never get the chance to."

"I'm fine. Clementine worries too much. I love that about her, though, just like your mother. But she has a point. People can be taken from us at any time, so it's best to tell them how you feel. Let's go up to the porch." Vincent followed him up the steps to a little white table with two chairs.

"Go ahead and sit down." He never made eye contact with Vincent, but he could feel every word. "There is something that I need to tell you too. It's something I should have done a long time ago. The night I gave you that scar was the night I thoroughly despised myself forever. For such a long time, a part of me blamed you for your mother's death. That was a thought I wish I never had. I had always had an anger problem, and the alcohol didn't help. I let all my selfish ways take control of me. I want you to know that the person I am today is not who your father really is. That man has been trapped for a long time. I hope to become the man again that I once knew, that young and naive kid who had dreams and felt hope, even in the darkest times, even though it was your mother that kept me sane. I was always thought dreams were something you achieved, a place you went, or a job title. I realized that's not necessarily true when I met your mother. I never knew that a dream could be a person. I had everything I have always wanted when I opened the park, but when your mother died, I didn't care about what I once loved. What's the point of living your dreams if you can't do it with the person who helped you achieve them? She always believed in me and made me out to be a better person than I actually was. And the problem was I started to believe her." He perked up, and his eyes grew wider. "And that is the essence of loving someone."

"What is?"

"When somebody makes you feel like a better person and brings out the best in you, even when you can't see it yourself. She brought out the brightest side of myself. A part that had been hiding since I was eight. If you ever get that, don't let go of it. It may be rare, but it's not impossible."

Vincent smiled when he thought about Marie.

"Vincent, I understand if you don't forgive me, and an apology can never make up for what I did to you. But I want to say that I am so very sorry for hurting you. I guess that's why I never did apologize, because I'm pathetic. I felt that no apology in the world could make up for what I did to you. I don't deserve a son like you. I'm sorry for having you lie for me all these years."

Florent was crying at this point, and Vincent could feel himself doing the same. "I have forgiven you long before now."

"Why?"

"Ever since that night, I have always resented what had happened. I was furious at what you had done to me. I always thought you were the reason I have lived a life of ridicule. But I knew that you loved me, even if you have never really shown it. And I knew you must have been in real pain to hurt someone you truly love." Vincent could fully see his father under the bright overhead porch light. Florent's hair was now starting to get grayer, and he had stubble on his chin. Vincent never noticed how quickly his father was aging.

"After what Clementine had told you, I had to apologize, because she's right. I lost my love early and suddenly. They always say that love makes you do crazy things, but they never said that losing it will make you absolutely insane. I always thought that I would lose your mother violently and quickly, like I had lost other people in my life, and I would do anything in my power to protect her from that happening. But I lost her slowly and quietly like a whisper, and I couldn't do anything about it, and she was gone before I knew it. One day, I may lose you, or you may lose me, and I couldn't bear to never give you the apology you deserve."

Florent stood up, and Vincent followed. Florent hugged him, and it felt strange. Vincent had never experienced any sort of affection from his father. "I'm also sorry that I have never been any kind of father to you. I have tried so many times to tell you these words, ever since you were that small six-year-old boy. I had placed an ugly scar on my own child, and I feel like a monster."

Vincent wanted to tell his father that everything really was forgiven, and he no longer felt resentment toward him, but all he could get was a single tear to roll down his cheek while he hugged his father as tightly as he could.

Chapter 27
REVENGE
June 1960

Vincent held Marie's hand as they spent a day in Fayland Park together. The crowd was just as large as usual. It was a slightly cloudy day, unlike most of Fathorne's blazing summer evenings. Marie pushed the stroller with Ebony with her other hand. Ebony still barely fussed, and she was mostly smiling. Every time she would share one of her broad smiles, Vincent felt something glowing inside of him. They walked past one of the food stands that sold as many sweets as one could think of and saw the fluffy, pink, sugary snack that had always been one of his favorites. "Shall we share some cotton candy?"

"Yes, that sounds yummy!" was Marie's reply.

"One cotton candy, please, pink, preferably."

"Okay, coming right up, Vincent." He watched as they took a large white cone and stuck it into the swirling machine. The vendor handed it to him, and he could feel the warmth coming off the cloudlike treat.

Vincent could not hold his happiness back, and just like Ebony, he couldn't help but smile. Today was the first day that he and Marie had off at the same time. Marie was now a waitress at the diner where they had their first date, and Vincent was a cashier at the local drugstore. They looked through the crowd and all the occupied picnic tables surrounding the area. Finally, after ten minutes of searching, they found one unoccupied and sat down as fast as possible. Marie pulled Ebony to the side of the table so she could keep an eye on her. Vincent looked at Marie and grinned. Every day she made him feel like he was the luckiest person on Earth. Lawrence still had not done anything or even said anything, so Vincent had forgotten all about his threat.

Vincent held up the cotton candy, which was as large as his head. "Shall we?"

"We shall." They both bit into the cotton candy, and Marie held on to the cone while she kept her hand over Vincent's. Eventually, their mouths met in the center. Marie laughed and licked the sugar off her lips. They then went in for another quick kiss. People around stared at them in disgust, but neither of them cared. When they were together, no one else mattered.

Something about his father's amusement park made every emotion feel exaggerated. Perhaps it was because he had his first alone time here with Marie, but when they spent their time together in the park, it seemed whimsical. "Well, it's nearly eight o'clock, and the park will be closing soon. Besides, I would like to get to the drive-in early so we can get a good spot," Marie said, getting up from the table.

"That's a good idea. I told Clementine that we would drop Ebony off around eight thirty."

Marie grabbed the stroller and diaper bag as they headed toward Clementine's house.

Clementine was already waiting on them when they walked up to her door. "Hey!"

Marie pulled Ebony out of the stroller and gently handed her to Clementine. Finnick came out of the kitchen, wiping off a large ladle, suggesting that he had been washing the dishes.

"I thought I heard you come in," Clementine said.

"All right, here is her diaper bag. Everything should be in there. I packed extra diapers and formula just in case. I know she's in good hands."

"We should get going, Marie."

"Yes, I know. It's just that this is the first time I'm leaving Ebony all night."

"She'll be all right."

"I know, but it's hard." Marie placed her hand on Ebony's head and kissed her cheek. She finally joined Vincent, ready to depart for the evening.

"We'll be fine. Also, I put a full tank of gas in the car," Clementine said.

They turned around and opened the door to leave. "Try not to have too much fun, you two," Finnick said.

"No promises," Marie and Vincent said together. They got into Clementine's car and started to head toward the drive-in. Vincent rolled the windows down as Marie and he felt the wind blow through their hair. The radio was blasting, and everything about this night seemed perfect.

"Man, do I miss my car."

"Someday, I'll get my own car, and we can go wherever our hearts desire whenever we want."

They got to the drive-in just in time to get a great spot near the middle. They had their radio placed near the car, and everything was in place for the movie to start. No more than ten minutes later, the sky was pitch black, and the large screen was filled with moving pictures. Marie snuggled up to Vincent and laid her head on him. "I'm so glad we finally got a night to spend together. Just you and me, forgetting all our problems."

Vincent kissed the top of her head and felt the same. All that changed when he happened to look up at the car parked vertically, about two rows in front of them. A bright-red car containing three men Vincent despised. Dean, Jack, and Bobby were all sitting in the vehicle while a car with three girls sat beside them. The girls got out and joined the guys. Vincent assumed they were their girlfriends.

"What are you looking at?" Marie asked.

"Nothing."

The first movie out of the two showings for the night had ended after nearly two hours. Advertisements were now back on the screen. Many people were going to the bathroom and concession stands during the intermission. Marie had fallen asleep on Vincent's shoulder. He looked back up to the car and noticed the girls had left entirely, and the guys had left their car as well. Vincent knew that if he didn't do something now, he might never have the chance. It was stupid to seek revenge, but after what they did to Clementine's car, he felt the rage pouring out of him. He laid Marie down on the seat and pulled the keys out of the ignition. He walked as fast as he could so he would not be seen. He was standing right in front of the attractive vehicle, and he began to grow nervous, but he was going to do it. He looked around, and none of the guys was in sight, so he put the key to the red exterior. He let all the anger inside him go through the key and let the red paint peel away. He slashed every single side of the car until it looked frightful.

"Hey!"

Vincent jumped and ran as hard as he could. He saw all three of them coming toward him at a fast pace. He jumped, ran in front of cars, and almost tripped multiple times. "Marie, we have to leave right now!"

She quickly sat up and rubbed her eyes, not sure what was happening. "What's going on?"

"I'll explain later." Vincent pulled out of their parking spot as fast as he could. Marie was thrown into the side of the car, not having her seatbelt on. He wheeled it out onto the road and started to drive to his house as fast as possible. He looked back to make sure they were not being followed; fortunately, they were not anywhere in sight. He felt safe once again as he pulled into the park's entrance and then down the rocky road through the woods that led to his house.

"Vincent, what was all of that?" Marie asked, breathing hard through panic.

"Remember the guy you nearly killed when you saved me?"

"Yes."

"Well, he and his friends never liked me in high school and were constantly torturing me. When they vandalized Clementine's car, it made me want to do the same to them. I got the opportunity when I saw their car parked so close to ours. So, when you were asleep, and they left their car unattended, I made my move. I completely destroyed the paint on their car. It was foolish of me to do, but I couldn't stand that they had done the same to my sister. No one ever messes with the ones I love."

Marie wrapped herself around his arm and placed her head on his shoulder. "And I love you for that. I don't blame you for what you did. Those punks deserved it."

Vincent looked back to no longer see the bright headlights that had been trailing them back on the road. They must have lost them when Vincent quickly turned the car on the grounds.

"I have a feeling they won't let this go, though, and they'll be back. They know where I live and who I am. They know that my father owns the park."

"Don't worry about it, Vincent. I'm exhausted. I couldn't even stay awake to see the movie. Your sister planned on watching Ebony overnight anyway, so we can pick her up in the morning."

Vincent listened to Marie, and they went to his bedroom. Marie changed into a nightgown and covered herself up with her pink lace comforter. She quickly fell asleep while Vincent stayed up, staring out the window from the living room. He watched the driveway for nearly an hour to make sure no one was there. No one ever came up that driveway, only the dim lampposts and fireflies filling the darkness. Vincent hated to admit that he was scared of his former classmates, and they were much more dangerous than just high school bullies. They had the same hatred in their faces toward him as his brother. If they had the chance, they would kill him. He never understood why people had always hated him so much. Perhaps it was because he was living a better life. Or because they possibly saw him as just a freak and a coward, too vulnerable and quiet to say anything.

He went back to his room to a sleeping Marie, who looked so peaceful. Vincent still did not understand how such a miracle as she would ever love a scar-faced boy as himself. Men like him never got the girl in the stories that he had read as a child, but somehow, he did. He drew the curtains closed, making the room pitch black. He climbed into bed beside Marie and took her in his arms. When they were close, his fears seemed to just vanish, even if it was only for a little while.

Chapter 28
TRAGEDY UNFOLDS
June 1960

Florent awoke in a strange place, at least he thought so at first. He was back on his parents' property. He could smell the honeysuckle bushes surrounding his body as he lay in the overgrown grass. He started to get more details as to where he was. He was in the neighboring field that sat on his parents' property, where his playhouse used to be. The empty field was now where the town's train ran through, bringing mostly people from out of town to the park. What surprised him most was when he felt something warm in his left hand. It was a small, delicate hand that he knew all too well.

It was Althea's hand, and she was lying beside him. He identified her from her cheeks of bright red and vibrant pink lips. How he had missed her white-blonde hair that shimmered in the sunlight. She was laughing, her sweet melody of laughter. It was a sound that Florent had shamefully almost forgotten, and hearing it brought back so many memories. She quickly got up and pulled Florent up with her. He was so shocked that he couldn't even ask questions about what was happening. Had his life all been a dream? Had he just fallen asleep in that field, and his mind had made up a false future for himself?

"Come on, let's go!" Althea raced ahead of him into the woods. He chased after her, not wanting to lose her. She kept running farther into the woods.

The trees were much taller and more haunting looking than he had always remembered. Althea turned into what appeared to be a cave, which was covered by a curtain of vines. Without hesitation, Florent followed her into the cavelike structure. He pulled back the vines, and what was behind them was completely unexpected. It was almost like another world. It was his park, except everything seemed grander and had more of a dreamy quality. The park looked more like what he had always pictured in his mind as a child and what he turned into drawings. He looked for Althea until he saw a little girl, which as first he thought was Clementine when she was a child. There was something different about this girl. It wasn't Clementine at all; it was Althea as her child self. He could tell by a small freckle above her one eyebrow, which still remained as an adult. He had also seen one picture of her as a child that she kept.

Florent looked down at his hands and noticed they were much smaller than usual. He passed the boat ride and could see his reflection in the water. He too was a much younger version of himself. "Come on, Florent, catch me!"

Althea laughed and ran around the park, waiting for Florent to catch her. He could hear himself laughing along with her, sounding like he did when he was just a kid.

Florent eventually caught up to her and took her hand. When he grabbed it, everything went pitch black. Florent stumbled around, trying to see what had happened. When he got his vision back, the scenery had changed completely. He was back as his adult self, and the park was deteriorating. The flags that once flapped in the wind with pride on the roller coaster were ripped to shreds. The Ferris wheel was leaning sideways, and most of the carts were detached.

The sky was filled with dark clouds, and the trees were all blackened as well. Something terrible had happened to his amusement park. A screeching sound could be heard in the distance, an eerie wail that made Florent shiver. He stopped looking around when he heard a woman's scream, which sounded much like Althea's. He panicked and began to run but couldn't get anywhere; he stayed in the same spot. He was eventually let free from his trap and ran toward the scream. He yelled out when he saw Althea's body strung out on the ground. She was lying in a puddle of blood, and her white hair was turning red. Two pink roses were pierced into both of her hands. Pink rose petals laid around her like at her funeral.

Florent could hardly breathe, as he could hear himself sobbing and desperately sucking in air. Hot liquid ran down his face that he was too familiar with. As he got closer, more bodies started to reappear. His father, his mother, Lawrence, Clementine, and Vincent were all laid in a row with blood soaking their bodies. Even Ebony's little lifeless body lay in her own blood. There was no sign of Marie, which confused him. He cared about Marie as well, the daughter of his best friend, his goddaughter, and now his daughter-in-law. She was nowhere to be found among his other loved ones. Then again, there was no Roger or Winnie either. Florent tried to make sense of what he was seeing. He looked up and saw the black figure standing in front of him with a gun to his head. Before Florent could react, he could feel the bullet penetrate through his skull, and he hit the ground, joining the rest of his family.

Florent, like so many times before, woke up in his own cold sweat. He quickly turned around to put his arm on Althea to comfort him like she had always done, but then reality caught up with him once again. There was no one there, just like there hadn't been for nearly nineteen years. He still couldn't believe it had been that long since he had last felt her presence. He couldn't get back to sleep after his nightmare, so he decided to get out of bed and get a glass of water from the kitchen.

As he was walking down the hallway, something caught his eye.

At the end of the hall was a sitting area with a few chairs and a coffee table along with something peculiar. He could see the top of someone's head with strawberry blonde hair; after seeing the color, he knew exactly who she was. "Marie?"

She jumped, startled by Florent's sudden appearance. "Mr. Fayland, I wasn't expecting you to be out of your room. You startled me."

"I apologize. Is everything all right?"

Marie looked at Florent with a distrustful look. She had never really spoken to Florent that much, and in a way, he frightened her.

"Yes, I woke up and couldn't go back to sleep. Vincent was asleep, and I didn't want to wake him, so I came out here to be alone with my thoughts. Vincent told me he told you the truth about everything."

Florent felt awkward around her and wanted to talk to her, but he couldn't think of how to start. "How's Ebony?"

"She's great. She is with Clementine for the night. She's grown so much over the past month, and she sure isn't going to stop. I never realized how much your children grow in such a short period of time."

"I know exactly how that is." Florent was starting to feel more comfortable as their conversation became more casual. "Do you mind if I sit here?"

"Not at all."

Florent sat in the chair next to hers. "Vincent told me your father kicked you out. That doesn't sound like him at all."

Marie looked down as if she was about to cry. "I know. He used to be so different when I was a little girl. He told me that I had ruined his plan when I denied Lawrence my hand and that he never wanted to see me again. My mother told me my father was a different person than she thought, and I suppose that's true."

"Well, he hasn't been here for months, and he used to visit at least once every month. There must be something going on."

Marie decided to change the subject from her father. "Vincent and I have been saving our money to move into a home of our own. But we plan on visiting as much as we can."

"You are adults now, and I hate to see you leave, but I knew it would come one day. I have never been very good at letting people go."

Marie smiled with a face of sympathy; she knew he was talking about Vincent's mother.

"I'm truly sorry about what happened to Althea. I know she passed away before I was born, and I would have loved to have met her. Clementine has told me all the wonderful things about her. Vincent has a small painting of her at his bedside. She was very beautiful. But the person I learned most about her from was Lawrence. The way he talked about her was lovely. He wasn't much on emotions, but when it came to his mother, he talked so eloquently about her."

Florent smiled. "Lawrence and I were never really that close. I am his father, and he is my son, that's about it. But Althea and Lawrence were connected at the heart. When he was little, he followed her everywhere. When he was troubled with something, it was Althea that he turned to. There were times when we shared our moments, but I never came close to sharing the relationship between him and Althea. He was also the most affected by her death out of his siblings. At times, Althea was the only one that could truly understand him. Vincent is fortunate to have you, I'm glad you two got together."

Marie blushed and smiled. "Me too."

"He is a good kid." Florent looked down as if he was suffering. "You know, I'm the one who gave him that scar. Not a day goes by that I don't regret it."

"I know, but he has forgiven you for everything. And I have too." Marie had always despised Florent for what he had done, but if Vincent could forgive him, so could she. Marie noticed the sun was starting to shine through the windows. "It was nice talking to you, Mr. Fayland. I better go pick up Ebony."

"Oh, okay."

Marie left Florent sitting in the chair as she went to grab her coat.

She entered Vincent's room after about twenty minutes with Ebony cradled in her arms. Vincent was awake and sitting up in bed. "Good morning, Vincent!"

Vincent rubbed his eyes and sat up, still groggy from the night before.

"Clem said that she barely fussed all night, but we have a problem."

"What's that?"

"She had a little incident and accidentally knocked the diaper bag on the floor from a high shelf, causing all her bottles, except one, to shatter. I'll have to go into town sometime this evening and buy some new ones. I get off work at seven; the grocery store should still be open by the time I get off. She also needs some new formula and clothes."

"I would go ahead and grab them for you, but I have to work until seven as well. Actually, I better start to get ready soon."

"Me too, but I'm going to try to get Ebony to sleep."

Vincent watched as the sunshine came through the window and hit her perfectly. Her skin and hair were shining in the light as she rocked Ebony. She had a faint smile as she looked down at their daughter.

Eventually, Ebony fell asleep and was put in her bassinet. They both stared down at her as she sweetly slept in her little bed. Vincent put his arm around Marie and then went to sit on the bed to put on his shoes. He looked at the painting of his mother and could see his own reflection in the glass of the frame. He did look like her in the face, but his hair and body looked much like his father. He cringed when he saw the gruesome scar spread across his face and his mismatched eyes. There was no escaping it, no matter how hard he tried. Marie was undressing to get into her waitress outfit, and Vincent got into his uniform as well.

"Marie, may I ask you something?"

"Yes, what is it, dear?"

"Is it true that you have loved me since we were children?"

"What?"

"That's what you told Lawrence."

"Of course, I loved you, but I never actually fell in love with you until that one morning I found you playing your violin for your mother. Then when you helped that little boy overcome his fears. And carried me when I wore those painful shoes. When you gave me a day that I never could forget, that's when I fell in love with you. But I guess I always knew we were meant to be."

She sat down beside Vincent and placed her hand on his cheek, the one with the scar going down to his jawline. And she kissed him, but it was different from all the times before. This was much more passionate and forceful, like it would be their last kiss forever.

"What was that for?"

"I know you still are insecure about our relationship, but trust me, I love you with all my heart, and I never want to be with anyone else. Never forget that."

"Are you kidding me? I never could." They hugged until they had lost track of the time.

She looked at the clock and quickly got up. "I have to go. The train leaves soon. I'll see you this evening." She kissed his cheek and was out the door. He would have to leave soon as well, but he decided to spend the hour he had left with Ebony, who was still peacefully asleep.

Clementine came to their house earlier than expected to watch Ebony, as Vincent finished getting ready for work. He still had thirty minutes left until he actually had to leave. "Thank you for doing this, Clementine. It means the world to Marie and me."

"It's no problem at all."

"I mean you, watched her all last night and now all day."

"Really, Vincent, it's okay. I love watching her. It's no burden."

Vincent thought about what he could do with his spare time and looked at the violin in the corner. He had been so busy with everything else in his life that he had not played for his mother in a long time.

"I'll be outside."

"Okay."

Vincent grabbed the violin and headed to the garden, where his mother's grave was. He looked around at all the rose bushes overtaking the land. Roses tangled up her gravestone like they never wanted to let go. Vincent began to play, and all the familiarity of the instrument and notes went through him. He became part of the violin when he played, and he could almost feel his mother's presence. Each note was like a memory of his mother that he never even had, a false sense of nostalgia. After playing for his spare thirty minutes, he looked back at the house and could see a curtain being drawn back. His father stood at a second-floor window. It was dark, and Vincent could barely see his father's aging face, but he could see the grief and the gratitude he had. It didn't just help Vincent share time with his mother that he never got in this lifetime, but it brought back memories for his father that may have started to fade.

The music that came through this violin was something they could share to remind them of something they had lost. Vincent smiled back at his father while they both shed a tear. Vincent ran back into the house and up the stairs to the second floor. He found the window his father was standing at, but it was vacant. He placed the violin back in his room and walked out of the house to go to work.

The workday for Vincent dragged on as usual. He watched the old clock that hung on the floral-wallpapered walls. Every time he stepped in this tired drugstore, time itself seemed to go exceptionally slow. It was a typical day of bagging customers' groceries and medications. People stared at his face like it was a picture of revulsion. Vincent laid his head into his hand and leaned over the counter and waited for another customer to check out. He almost fell asleep until he was awakened by a phone ringing. The pharmacist picked it up, and Vincent assumed it was just someone asking a question about their medicine, but he called Vincent over and said the call was for him. Surprised, he got up and took the phone from the pharmacist.

"Hello?"

"Hi, honey!"

"Oh, hello, Marie. Is everything all right?"

"Everything is just fine. I just want to tell you something exciting. Debra, my friend, who is also a waitress here at the diner, is having a dinner party tonight. She wants to meet you, and I want you to meet her. This could be a great way to make some new friends and be able to unwind. I told her that we would be a few hours late, but she said that would be okay, and she'll save us some food."

"That sounds great." Vincent didn't care much for social gatherings, but it seemed to excite Marie, and he would do anything for her.

"All right, so on my lunch break, I'll go get the white satin gown that I love so much and change after work. I'll run to the store before I get home to get Ebony's things. After that, I'll meet you at home. Vincent, could I ask you a favor?"

"What's that?"

"Could you wear your green suit? It just looks so good on you and so sophisticated."

"Yeah, sure."

"Oh no, I forgot about Clementine watching Ebony. She did it all last night and today. I couldn't ask her to do it again."

"She loves watching Ebony, and I'll give her extra money for doing this for us. I know she will be willing to."

"Okay, then I guess everything is in order. I'll see you tonight at the house. I love you!"

"Love you too."

Vincent smiled because any night that he got to spend with Marie was a blessing. The rest of his workday seemed even slower than before. He was looking forward to his night out with Marie. He was also happy that she was making friends, since she had such a lonely childhood. Vincent had always felt sorry for himself, having a loner past, but at least he had his sister. Marie spent her days locked away in her room as her parents made her study along with her governess, who was strict and demanding. She spent much of her young life between countries without a single friend in the world.

After many hours, Vincent had finally reached the end of the work-day, and he now sat in his bedroom. He got out his green suit from the closet and slowly unzipped the sizable white bag it resided in. Once the bag was open, he could see the striking olive-green color and the matching hat and green leather gloves. It was rather strange and out of fashion, but something about it screamed elegance, and the man wearing it knew about class. He put it on, and the material shaped him well. His father and he must have been the same size. Even after a year without wearing it, it still fit perfectly. He turned around to look into what once was a mirror above his dresser. It was still shattered from his fit of rage. He looked at the mirrors in the hallway and saw his flawed reflection, just as he had always seen it, but now he wore it with confidence.

Marie proved to him that love doesn't come from someone's appearance, but what they hold inside. Beauty can be appreciated and admired, but it can never express love. People can fall for some-one's enticing looks, but eventually, that all fades because that's just not love. Lust is often mistaken for love every day, which many believe to be synonymous with each other, when they couldn't be any more different. Vincent knew this was true because Marie's love for him was the proof. He decided to believe her view of him, instead of everyone else's crude remarks about who he was. It only took one person to show him kindness to completely change his perspective on himself.

He straightened his tie and left the mirror. He was on his way to the park entrance to meet Marie there. It was already getting dark, and he did not like Marie walking in the woods alone at night. She walked all the way from the train station to the house, a fifteen-minute walk. The weather couldn't have been any more perfect. Summer nights were always his favorite compared to the rest of the year.

He walked through the woods, and he could hear frogs croaking in the distance at a nearby creek. Vincent was happy, and he didn't really even know why he just felt joy inside himself. All that stopped when he heard someone following him, not just the sound but the feeling that he was being watched. He often felt like this in these woods, probably just being paranoid, but tonight it felt more real. He tried to shake off the feeling, but it was unsettling walking through the park. It closed at only eight o'clock on weekdays, compared to the long weekend hours. During the day, it was one of the happiest places to be. There was fun around every corner, but at night, all that disappeared. The nonmoving rides, the vacant stands, the slow-moving water at the river ride—all this was unnerving, and the trees swaying in the wind surrounded the park like a wooded trap.

Vincent waited at the large white arch, which had become an icon of the town. The red paint looked like it could use a touch-up, as Fayland and Park were beginning to fade away. He looked at his watch and then back down at the long, dark, twisted road. The fog was again terrible and made it almost impossible to see.

After thirty minutes of waiting by the arch, along with a darkening sky, a figure appeared out of the fog. Marie walked up in a white satin gown, accompanied by an open pink trench coat. She carried a cardboard box with all the things she had bought for Ebony. Vincent smiled as he went to the operator's box to open the gates and let her in. He closed it right away after she entered the property. "So, how do I look?" Marie asked as Vincent exited the small booth.

"Like always."

"What's that supposed to mean?"

"You look perfect, like always." Vincent knew it was a banal compliment, but he still managed to make Marie blush. She kissed his cheek. They walked through the fog together, and Vincent took the box for her as she grabbed tightly onto his arm. "Vincent, I know I always act really tough and that nothing bothers me, but I really am scared of the dark. It almost scares me as much as heights. I'm glad you always come and meet me at the arch when I get off work."

"I'm scared of the dark too, to be honest. I used to walk these grounds all the time, but nighttime is a different world."

They kept walking, trying to keep a fast pace to get to the house as soon as possible. They both stopped when they heard footsteps. "What was that?" Marie said, breathing hard.

"I don't know, I heard it earlier. I'm sure it's nothing, probably a deer." The footsteps got louder until they sounded like they were coming from three different directions.

"Vincent, what is going on?" The fog was so thick, they couldn't see what was happening around them. The footsteps got louder and louder until they suddenly just stopped. Vincent and Marie stood in silence and confusion. "I think it's gone, let's keep going," Marie said. Vincent took a step forward, but he was quickly pulled back, leaving Marie. The sudden jolt caused Vincent to drop the box, and all the baby bottles shattered on the concrete path underneath them. Marie screamed and was dragged in front of Vincent until they were facing each other, both with a hand on their mouths. They looked at each other in fear, unable to see who was doing this to them.

The fog thinned, and Vincent could finally see his surroundings. Jack Darcin was holding on to Marie, and from what Vincent could tell, Bobby May was holding on to him. Dean stood near them with a knife in his hand.

"Well, what a pleasant surprise," Dean said with a mischievous smile. Marie couldn't even move, though she tried. Bobby and Jack were much larger and more robust than Dean.

"I didn't like the new paint job you decided to give to my car, so I thought I'd pay you a visit."

"You did the same to my sister's car, and I was just returning the favor." Vincent was proud of his remarks. He had always been too scared to say anything before, but since Marie had saved him, he felt that they could be defeated. "Not to mention all the hell you put me through during high school. Slamming me into lockers, spitting in my face, beating me until I bled," Vincent said quickly after his first statement. He then spat in Dean's face. The spit landed right in his eye, and Dean removed it with his sleeve.

Dean quickly reacted and held the knife to Vincent's neck. "You better shut that ugly mouth before I give you another scar. And as for you, his pretty little wife. There never was a dinner party. Debra is my girlfriend, and she was all about getting you back after what your husband did. I also told her about how you attacked me."

Marie opened her mouth as if she was about to say something, but Dean held the knife to her throat. Vincent kicked and stumbled to get out of Bobby's grip. "I knew that you two would be together sometime tonight to get ready to go to the fake dinner party, so we waited in the woods for you all evening. You really should get better security. We got in here without any problem." Dean looked at the ground and gave another sinister smile. "Oh, this will work perfectly. I was just going to use my knife, but I think a shard of glass will be much better." Dean put the shard of glass on Marie's cheek. "Glass will give her more of an uneven cut. Vincent, I think your wife could use a scar just like yours, so you'll be exactly alike." He started to cut her cheek, and she let out a cry of pain.

Vincent elbowed Bobby in the stomach and ran toward Dean, but it did no good as Bobby yanked him back with his strong arms. "Bob, keep him under control! Or I will." Dean gave the shard of glass to Jack, and he held it to Marie's neck. Dean then pulled his knife out again and placed the blade under Vincent's chin. "It looks like I'm just going to have to make you more of a damn abnormality than you already are."

Marie shouted and struggled to get free, "No! Don't touch him!" she desperately cried out. Vincent was panicking and focusing on the knife when he happened to look over at Marie. She kicked, spit, scratched, and did everything she could, and Jack kept his grip along with the glass under her neck.

Eventually, she kicked Jack in the groin, and he quickly moved his arm, causing the glass to be shoved into her neck. Dean turned around in a state of horror. "Shit!" Jack himself looked like he was going to vomit and on the verge of crying.

"I … didn't mean … she kicked me and caused me to …"

"I don't care what you did! Let's get the hell out of here!" Bobby released his grip on Vincent, and he fell to the ground.

All three of them took off into the woods. Vincent scurried over to Marie, and he couldn't breathe as grief made his chest and neck feel inflated. He could hear himself crying and could taste salty tears rolling into his mouth. He screamed out in pain, and his body shook all over. Marie lay face down on the ground with a puddle of blood underneath her. Vincent turned her around and let out another scream of agony as he looked at her beautiful face. Her neck was split open, and the blood poured out all over her body.

"Marie!" She had her eyes still halfway open, and she was barely breathing. She put her hand on Vincent's face, over the cheek with the scar and gave a weak smile. She then closed her eyes, and her body went limp in his arms.

He pulled her body to his face, burying it by her chest. He looked out to the woods where the three men ran like cowards. They murdered her, and Vincent would get them back once again, and this time would be the last. This wasn't a vandalized car or just mean words said to his face. They killed the one thing that made him happy for the first time in his life. The person who never thought of him as an abnormality. The only person who made him care about the person he was on the inside. And he didn't care if it was an accident or not, this was their fault, and they would pay dearly. He had been stripped of his last petal.

Chapter 29
THE DOWNFALL
June 1960

Vincent ran toward the woods as fast as could, his legs moving faster than he ever imagined. Tears and mucus ran down into his mouth. He didn't know he had such speed underneath him, but he was proving himself wrong. He saw three figures running through the woods, and Vincent had an advantage over them because he knew these woods like the back of his hand. He had no sympathy in his mind or any morals. He just wanted to end the madness, even if he did it with more chaos. He couldn't believe that he caught up to them, but he did. Bobby, though the tallest and most buff, was the slowest. Vincent came up behind him and pulled out his knife from his jacket pocket, the one he carried with him everywhere, ever since Marie had got it for him.

He stabbed Bobby in the lower back, and with a scream, he hit the ground, lying in his own blood. Vincent left him lying there as he ran after the other two. Jack was next, and he wasn't hard to catch up with either. Vincent grabbed him from behind and turned him around and put the knife to his neck. "Let me go!"

"No, I don't think I'm going to do that. But I will do this." Vincent pushed the knife as hard as he could into Jack's neck. The blood splattered out and hit Vincent in the face, even getting into his mouth. His green suit had been spotted red, completely ruined, but that was the least of Vincent's concerns. Dean was the last, and he was the one responsible for this entire mishap he had planned. If it wasn't for him, Marie would still be alive. Dean was much faster than the other two, and Vincent couldn't catch up with him. Dean had almost reached the entrance to the park. Vincent threw his knife and hoped for the best. Dean let out a yelp as the blade landed right in the back of his head. It must have hit him in the brainstem, as he died instantly. Vincent pulled the knife out of Dean. He stood in the hot, sticky blood of the three men he despised. He walked around and saw the three bodies.

Guilt started to rise up in Vincent as he realized what he had done. Perhaps it was his fault that Marie had died. If he hadn't sought revenge and destroyed Dean's car, none of this would have happened. He stood breathing hard and felt sick. As soon as they were discovered, Vincent feared people would know he had done it, and he would be thrown in jail. His brother would do everything to prove him guilty. Maybe he should turn himself in, but he thought about Ebony and how she would have neither of her parents. She should at least have her father in her life. Vincent reacted quickly and decided to bury the bodies near the bunker, where no one could find them. He dragged each body by a large tree one at a time without anyone noticing.

He looked down at their smug faces, and the anger filled up inside him once again and turned back to the cryptic place he had been only ten minutes ago. He started to stab them nonstop until they were nearly unrecognizable. More blood splattered on Vincent, including his face and hair. He stopped when he heard footsteps again. There was no time to take them any farther, so he ran, leaving the bodies by the large tree. He almost stepped in the water for the boat ride and finally realized where he was on the property. He ran just as fast as he did before and ran back to find Marie's body. He found her not too far from where he had come from. She lay like a fallen angel in the fog, which was getting sparser. He picked up her lifeless body and looked down at the large cut that spread across her neck. "I'm so sorry, Marie, this is my fault." He began to cry once again, but he couldn't stay in one spot for long. He carried Marie though the woods, trying to get her back to the house. She died so suddenly that he didn't even have the chance to say how much she meant to him. She meant *everything* to him.

His entire front was covered with blood, including his green leather gloves. The hot, red liquid was also mixed with dirt and his own tears. He was miserable and scared as he walked through the pitch black. He saw someone in the distance, two people actually. It was hard to tell who they were, but Vincent was relieved when he recognized the two figures as his sister and brother-in-law. When Clementine saw him, she began to run toward him. When she got close enough to see his red-stained clothes and a dead body in his arms, she screamed. Finnick's eyes grew in terror as well, and he looked like he could pass out at any moment. They must have been on a walk and were the noise Vincent had heard by the tree. "Oh my God, what happened?" Clementine said, panicked.

Vincent failed to get words out through his sobbing. "They killed her."

"What, who killed her?"

"Those guys from my high school. They took a glass shard to her neck, and as she struggled to get away, it sliced her neck."

"I don't know what to say." Clementine began to sob and placed her hand on Marie's head. "I'm so sorry. And I promise those men will pay for what they did to Marie. I'll make sure that they rot in jail for what they have done. I don't care if it was an accident. They will be punished." Clementine said nothing more, but Vincent could tell he had her sympathy. Vincent noticed there was no sign of Ebony; he was so caught up with everything happening, he had not noticed.

"Where's Ebony?"

"I visited Father before Finnick and I went out for a walk. He agreed to watch her, so we could have our evening stroll."

"Oh, good."

She placed a hand on his shoulder as they walked, and they both shared tears. Vincent watched his tears hit Marie's face, and somehow, her makeup and hair remained beautifully untouched. Vincent really meant what he said to her; she always had a near-perfect appearance. He hated knowing that her face would fade in his memory, just as Clementine had with their mother. But her love and kindness would forever be a memory. It was the way she made him feel that would impact him forever. The memories in our hearts are always stronger than the ones in our minds. The heart has a special way of letting love never be forgotten.

One week had passed since Marie's death, and Vincent could feel the emptiness inside of him more and more every day. He tried his best to at least look optimistic. He tried each day to put on a brave face. Most of all, he decided to get out of the house as much as possible to get fresh air. He wanted to go on with life, even though he felt dead inside. He knew how grief almost drove his father to madness. But this morning, he locked himself in his room. He put on a new black suit he had recently purchased and hid the green one away at the far end of his closet. The closet still held all the pink wardrobe that Marie had always loved so much. He sat on her pink lace comforter. He could still smell her perfume floating around the room. Ebony, in her bassinet, started to fuss. She was oblivious to what was happening and what had happened to her mother.

Vincent picked her up and placed her head on his shoulder. He patted her back and kissed her cheek. She was still a newborn, and tragedy had not struck her yet, but it only took a month of her short life to face the harsh reality.

There was a knock on the door as Vincent put Ebony back in her bassinet. He opened it to find Clementine standing there. "Hey,

Vincent. Do you mind if I come in?"

"Not at all."

Clementine came in and sat herself on the bed. "How are you holding up?"

"Not great, but I'm trying my best."

Clementine then stood up and hugged him. "I truly am sorry you have to go through this. I can't believe those bastards are missing. They probably ran off like the cowards they are. There hasn't been any word from the police, has there?"

Clementine told the police that Vincent witnessed them murder Marie, but Vincent knew they would never find them, at least not alive. He was forced to tell the police himself what he had seen, even though it was all false accounts. The only truth he told the police was that Marie had been murdered.

"No, I haven't heard anything."

"They probably fled town or something to get out of what they did. It's truly disgusting."

Ebony began to cry again.

"I think she's hungry; it's time for her bottle." Vincent started to bend down to pick her up, but Clementine stopped him.

"It's okay, you go ahead outside. I'll take care of Ebony for today. You already have so much on your mind."

"Thanks." Even though his thanks were light and hardly spoken, he meant it with all his heart. He appreciated everything his sister had done for him.

He walked out to the garden, where the pink roses still bloomed. Marie's casket was open and sitting on a bed of flowers. The casket was white with gold trim, Vincent paid for it with all his savings. There would be no use for all his earnings anymore. He looked down at his wife, who wore her favorite pink dress and the pink diamond necklace he had bought for her. He took her locket and kept it in a box with some of her other belongings. He was currently wearing his around his neck. He felt the tears come again as he looked down at her motionless body. She lay gracefully in her casket. Death had taken her life, but not her beauty. Death had also stopped her heart, but not her spirit.

A few chairs were placed outside for the family. Roger was never told about any of this. He had kicked her out of his life, and Vincent believed it should stay that way. He never cared for Roger much anyway; there was just something about him that was troubling. Vincent had found the note from Winnie to Marie, stating that she was leaving. It had an address on it to where Winnie was staying. He had written a letter telling her about Marie's passing. There never was a response, and a seat sat empty that was reserved for Winnie. Only his siblings and father attended her funeral. They had closed the park for the day so they could all mourn together. Lawrence came down the stairs of the porch in his best suit, his hair combed to the side. He joined Vincent's side and looked down at Marie with just as much sadness as Vincent's eyes. He began to cry as well and bent down by her coffin. He wailed out to her. "Marie, you are the only woman I ever really loved. I can't believe you are gone."

Lawrence got up and looked Vincent straight in the eyes. "You couldn't keep her safe! This is your fault! You watched her get murdered and didn't do a damn thing."

"I couldn't stop them. They held me down. I loved her too, and I did try to save her."

Before Lawrence could say any more, Florent, along with Clementine and Finnick, joined them. They all took their seats as the minister opened up with a prayer.

The entire service only lasted around thirty minutes. A place in the ground by his mother's grave was open for Marie's casket. As it was lowered, Vincent played his violin, just as he would every morning, not only for his mother but for Marie as well. When her casket was in the ground, Vincent stopped playing and felt an arm wrap around him.

It was his father, and he knew that he had been through the same pain he was experiencing right now. It was then that they shared the same grief. Never had he related to his father as much as he did at this moment. "She is now a star looking down upon us. She is alongside your mother. When the darkness approaches, they'll be there. That way, it's never truly dark because they will be your light. And that way, we are never truly alone. Your mother told me this about the stars, and I wish I had realized this sooner." Vincent said nothing, but he gave his father a smile of gratitude for such uplifting words.

The day after Marie's funeral, Vincent spent the day in the park. He understood why his father had stopped coming here and gave Lawrence the responsibility of running it. This was once a place of happiness for both of them, a place to escape the pain. But it was here they shared those happy memories with someone they loved. Now it was just an ordinary amusement park, left with decaying joy. He pushed Ebony in her stroller, who was sound asleep.

People moved around them like they didn't even exist, smiling happily and going on with their days. Vincent didn't even pay attention to their laughter and excitement. He just kept walking toward the park, seeing the moving rides from the corner of his eye. He sat down at a picnic table and decided to take a break. He looked up to the sky, which was a bright shade of blue. The large white clouds moved faster across the sky, and the sun peeked out from beneath them. He went into a trancelike state, looking up at the sky, and he just stared. He wanted to get his mind off everything that happened in the last week, which made him feel numb. He must have completely zoned out when he heard his name being called out to him, but only faintly. The longer he stared at the sky, the louder it became. He jolted up when someone shoved his shoulder. It was Clementine, who was drenched in sweat and her face full of worry. "Vincent!"

"What's wrong?"

"It's those guys that killed Marie. Lawrence discovered their bodies hidden behind a large tree. It's over by the water ride. People complained to Lawrence about a smell, thinking it was a dead animal or the water. I'm completely freaked out. You have to come see for yourself." She was on the verge of tears, and her face was cherry red.

Vincent grabbed the stroller and followed her toward the back of the park. As they were walking to the crime scene, Clementine remained silent and kept her head down. She then said something, and it sounded as if she felt guilty saying it. "You don't think?"

"Don't think what?"

"That Lawrence killed them, do you?"

Vincent could feel his heart start to race and panic rising inside him. "What makes you think that?"

"Well, Lawrence has always been quick to get irritated and have strange behavior. He loved Marie too, at least I think, and maybe he wanted to get revenge on them for killing her."

"I really don't think it was him."

Vincent could just say that it was Lawrence, and he would get off free, but his conscience told him otherwise. Lawrence was still his brother.

"Yes, but it makes perfect sense, in a way."

"It wasn't him, okay!"

Clementine jumped when he said this. He had never snapped at his sister. Maybe he was crazy, a monster like the rest of the men in his family had been.

"I'm sorry, I'm just tense."

Clementine glared at him with a worried look. "That's all right, I understand, with everything you've been through. I would be the same way."

Vincent walked over to the large tree where he had left three bloody bodies to rot away. He told Clementine to stay back out of the crime scene and take the stroller. Lawrence stood in front of the bodies in complete shock and terror. "These are the men, are they not? The men that killed my sweet Marie."

"Yes, this is them," Vincent said, shuddering after what he called Marie, when she was not his.

"But if they killed Marie, then who killed them?"

"I don't know," Vincent said without making eye contact. The police who were not examining the bodies were taking notes on everything. Photographers from the newspaper flashed their cameras, taking pictures of the massacre.

Lawrence pulled Vincent out from the crowd of reporters and police officers to have their own private conversation. "Perhaps, dear brother, you're not telling the whole truth."

"What are you saying?"

"I'm *saying* that you killed all of them, even Marie." Vincent felt his heart leap.

"I always had the theory that you drew her in with your little mind games because you were jealous of me. When you seduced her and married her, even going far enough to have a child together, then you killed her off just so I can never see her again. Then you craved more blood; it was not enough for you. So, you went after your high school bullies and killed them off too."

"You're insane if you think I would ever harm Marie."

"What about these guys?"

Vincent said nothing. He didn't want to lie, but he couldn't confess the truth, even though it was the right thing to do.

"This is going to completely destroy the park's reputation for being safe, and we could lose business drastically. If you did this, I might just kill you myself. You could destroy everything Father and I had ever worked for." Vincent spat in Lawrence's eye, and he yelled out.

As Vincent started to walk off, Lawrence yelled out at him. "You'll regret everything," Lawrence said darkly.

Vincent did not care anymore. All of this felt like a nightmare that he would never wake from. He lived each day in mourning and guilt. Ever since that night that changed his life, he had cried for what he had done. He could not change the past. Vincent took Ebony from Clementine, and he went back to the house.

He placed Ebony in her bassinet, then quickly slammed the door, locking himself away from what was really happening in his life. He threw himself on his bed and sobbed until he became too numb to feel anything. When his eyes dried, he looked out the window to the two gravestones that sat in his back yard. He then touched the scar on his face and thought to himself, *When did it all go wrong?* Vincent kept himself locked in his room, trying to calm himself and collect his thoughts on everything that had happened in his life. The good and bad parts all played like a movie in his head.

The next day he could no longer produce any more tears, and he felt strange. He couldn't shake off the odd feeling he felt, so he continued his usual morning routine. He started by getting dressed and making a bottle for Ebony. He looked back at the blank space on his vanity where a mirror used to be. He looked at the photographs on his nightstand, and he could see the portrait he had taken with his siblings so many years ago.

He was disgusted by his face, just as he was disgusted with himself. He took the knife out of his pocket, which had been cleaned of all the blood. He pressed as hard as he could on all the pictures he could find of himself and erased his face. He kept scratching his face off every picture until it was just a white blob. He didn't want to see his disturbing face ever again, because it would only bring him pain. It would remind him of the terrible things he had done, which he could never forgive himself for. The locket pictures remained untouched. In that small, golden trinket lay the only place Marie and he could be together forever. He aggressively threw all the pictures in the drawer, leaving them there to be forgotten forever. The only picture that remained on his nightstand was the one portrait of his mother. That portrait would stay there until the end of his days.

Vincent picked up Ebony and left his room to get breakfast and coffee. He walked down the hallways and down the grand staircase to get to the kitchen. Their chef had prepared waffles, fruit, and scrambled eggs. Vincent didn't feel like eating, now that he looked at the vast quantities of food. His appetite had rapidly declined over the past week. He got some coffee and headed to the living room. He wanted to be alone, just him and his daughter. Any alone time gave him time to just think, even if it was made-up scenarios, which were much better realities than the one he was actually in. Someone sitting in the large armchair, facing the window. It was his father, who was now out of his room more than ever before.

Florent turned around to see who had made the wooden floor creak, which had given him a jump. "Hello, Vincent. You startled me. I didn't know you were awake."

"I'm sorry. I just came down to get my coffee."

Florent looked back at Vincent and noticed he was holding Ebony. "If you don't mind, I could hold her while you drink your coffee."

"Oh, not at all. That would be great." Vincent handed Ebony to Florent.

He cradled her head and smiled, then quickly went back to a frown. He stared out the window, something that Vincent himself did when he was upset.

"What's wrong?"

"I was just thinking about those bodies found on my park's property. The men who killed Marie have been murdered themselves. Are you sure you didn't see anyone else in the woods after they let you go and run off?"

Vincent could feel the guilt rise up inside of him again, and he grew nervous. "No, there was no one else around."

"Fayland Park was a place to go to feel safe and secure, no matter how crazy the world was outside. Lawrence gave me the attendance number this morning, and it is much lower than usual. It scares me still that a murderer is running around here in Fathorne. I guess my main questions are, why did their killer kill them, and did this person see them kill Marie? There are many unanswered questions about all of this, and the police are still looking for answers."

Florent dropped the subject and moved on. Vincent knew it was hard for his father to talk about such a tragedy at his park. Vincent felt very culpable for everything. He should have buried the bodies and not left them to be found so easily. Maybe he should have just let them go and had them arrested for Marie's murder. But that was not enough. Every time he thought about how they just ran away after killing Marie, it made his blood boil, and the hatred took over him. Florent looked down at Ebony and gave another smile. "She looks just like you did as a baby. I can hardly tell you apart. Sadly, I never took care of you much when you were her age. The nanny did most of the work. How selfish I was. I couldn't even pick my head up, and here you are being so strong after you had experienced losing the love of your life."

"I'm not as strong as you think, Dad. I can't even stand to see my own face after what has happened. I've done things I'm not proud of," Vincent said, looking up with teary, bloodshot eyes.

Before Florent could respond, they both turned when they heard someone running down the hall. Clementine burst into the room. Her hair was sticking to her as sweat dripped down her red face. She came in out of breath, looking like she was on the verge of tears again. Florent quickly stood up. "Clementine, what is it?"

"I was taking my morning stroll through the woods when I noticed that I wasn't alone. Roger was walking just outside the park's grounds. He had a large pistol in his hand, and he looked angry. I don't know his intentions, but they don't look good. I don't think he noticed me. I just ran as fast as I could to get up here and warn someone."

"I'll go check it out. I'm sure it's nothing, but it does sound out of character for Roger." Florent gave Ebony to Clementine.

"Stay here and keep out of sight until I know what is going on." Vincent went with his father out of curiosity, as a million questions turned over in his mind. Was Roger here to kill him? Roger knew nothing of Marie's death or that Marie and he had married. But then he thought of one person who was likely to tell Roger everything.

Florent ran, even with his limp, out of the house as quickly as he could with Vincent right behind him. They ran through the woods, looking in every direction to see if they could spot Roger, but they had no luck. When they got closer to the park and could hear the rides and the crowd, they heard a voice. "Ah, Vincent Fayland. Just the man I was looking for." Vincent recognized the low, intimidating voice. He turned around quickly to find Roger behind him with the pistol that Clementine had described. Florent began to approach him like he wasn't a threat.

"Roger, what is the meaning of this? We haven't talked or seen each other in months, and you show up here unannounced and ask for my son?"

"That son of a bitch killed my daughter, and no one even had the decency to tell me that she died!"

Vincent felt his heart leap.

"What are you talking about? Vincent didn't kill your daughter. He loved her. He would never cause her any harm."

"He didn't love her! Lawrence told me the truth about what happened. He married her, then when he got what he wanted, he killed her."

Vincent stepped forward with rage on his face. Lawrence did say that he would get his revenge. "Lawrence is such a liar! Marie and I fell in love. I couldn't steal something away that never belonged to him in the first place. You kicked Marie out of the house, so you basically kicked her out of your life. That's why no one told you about her death. She was murdered by some former classmates of mine who had always hated me. I got revenge by destroying their car after they did the same to my sister, and they tricked us and attacked us." He could tell that he had infuriated Roger by what he said.

"I don't care what the truth is anymore, to be honest. The point is my daughter is dead, and you ruined everything for me. I should have been spying on you instead of your father."

Florent perked up and gave a stunned look. "Spied on me, what do you mean spied on me?"

Roger gave a fiendish smile. "Florent, do you know that shadow figure that had tortured you your entire life?"

"What are you getting at?"

"That was me. You see, my family possesses a special ability. It skips every couple of generations or so. There is no origin story, and it's a mystery to how or why we have it, but we do. It's some sort of mix of telepathy and teleportation. I can enter people's minds, and I can see where they are without actually being there, and I can watch from afar. It's like I'm actually there with you, but I see everything in my mind. I can focus my eyes and subconsciously go somewhere else. I can see you, and you can only see a blurry silhouette because it's not really me. I can shift into a shadowlike creature, and my mind can go anywhere I please. It's almost unexplainable, and I can barely understand it myself. When I was little, I was able to do things with my mind that no one else could. I could see other members of my family in my room doing what they were doing in other parts of the house."

"If this is true, why have you spied on me since I was a child?"

"So I could get you when you were most vulnerable. That's how I knew you were at that bed and breakfast all those years ago. When you left the protection of your mother's house and had nothing, that's when I decided to make my introduction."

"Why? What do you have against me?"

"Nothing, it's your father that I had the problem with. I saw how much time he spent with you and that you were the most important thing in his life."

"I thought you liked my father and saw him as a hero. My father was a good man. What made you turn against him?"

"He couldn't save my wife, Annette." Florent's memory came back to him and why the name sounded so familiar. Roger lowered his gun, and a tear came from one of his eyes.

"We were very young and fairly poor when we got married. It wasn't two months later when she started to get very sick. We discovered she had heart problems and that she needed a very complicated surgery. I heard of this surgeon by the name of Dr. Fayland. I had heard he was almost a miracle worker. He was only a few towns over from where we were currently living, so we made our journey. Your father told us that he could save her, but the surgery would be very costly. I worked day in and day out to get the money I needed to pay for it. The day finally came, and I kissed her forehead as she was taken into the hospital. I watched her lay on her bed and was wheeled into the operating room. Then I was given the horrific news that she didn't make it. I ran into the emergency room and went after Horace Fayland. He told me that he could save my wife; he was my only hope. I ran into the operating room while my wife laid in the hospital bed dead. Your father didn't even act like he cared that the surgery was unsuccessful, probably because I was not as important or as wealthy as his other patients, so he just pushed her aside without even trying to save her life. He tried to push past me and told me he had another surgery to perform without even looking me in the eyes. I yelled and screamed until I eventually lunged at him but was taken out by security."

"My father tried very hard. I remember him talking about her. He said that he would do everything he could to save her. I remember him mentioning an Annette now."

"That's bullshit! She meant nothing to him. He had done surgeries on some of the most famous and richest in the world. My Annette was dirt under his shoes. I paid him every penny that I made, and he just let it go to waste."

Roger was now red-faced and sobbing through his story. "He told me that he could save her, told me that he *would* save her. But he didn't even attempt. That night, I cleaned off my old gun case and pulled out the large pistol that I'm holding now and went to pay your father a visit. I got past your house staff and broke into your parents' room. I was very skilled at shooting a gun. I've done since I was young. But I had no use for it, so I just let it sit under my bed to collect dust until that night. I hadn't lost my touch, though. I shot him with one pull of the trigger, and he was dead."

Florent started to move his chest faster in a fit of rage. "It was you! You're my father's killer! And to think I let you into my home and let you share my dream and let you near my children! If you wanted me dead, why didn't you just kill me the first time you met me?"

Roger looked at Vincent's scar. "I believe you have always been more of a threat to your children than I could ever be. The reason I didn't kill you right away was because you were still that naive eight-year-old boy, standing in the doorway of your house. I knew you were your father's pride and joy, and I was going to destroy everything your father ever loved. I saw you standing there, just a small child in his pajamas, so innocent, but I despised you. I did more research on who your father was and who his child was so that I could take everything from him, just as he did me. An eye for eye, if you will. I couldn't get to you, since your mother had upped security. The only thing I could do was watch you. Besides, the longer you crave something, the better it tastes when you finally get it. After my wife died, I got into the moonshine business and got a few followers along the way. These men remained loyal to me ever since and did all my bidding just because I gave them free liquor and a large sum of cash. If I wanted a man dead, they would do it. But you were more personal, and I would kill you myself.

"I never ran any factories; that was all a cover-up. Even after the Prohibition, I sold liquor illegally and made big bucks from it. So, after I became wealthy, I would do anything to help your dreams come true whatever they may be. When you left your mother's protection and had nothing, I could offer you everything. I thought that wanting to own an amusement park was a little far-fetched, but I knew it would become a success in this little monotonous town. I would watch it grow and watch you build your own wealth and empire, then I would shoot you dead just like your father and take everything you owned. I had to be wise and stealthy, or I would be caught. I waited for the perfect time to make it look like you died in an accident. So, one night I decided to watch you from afar, and my mind took me to that road. I told Winnie, who was innocent to all of this, to get to know Althea better that night and take some tea. I would kill Althea later, making it look a suicide, like she couldn't deal with the grief. But that wreck didn't kill you or Lawrence as I had planned. Now I had to wait and think of something else.

"My plans were delayed, but I thought it would be worth the wait. As soon as Marie was born, everything fell into place. When she turned eighteen, I would have her marry Lawrence, the heir to the park. As soon as they married, I would kill Lawrence and then you. After both of you were dead, I would have my men come in and kill the rest of your family off. I would be the only tie with the family and the park, so I would get everything you ever worked for. Then I would have finally had my vengeance, and my mind would be at peace. But things didn't turn out that way. My wife left me after I told her this truth, and my daughter is dead. The person who really screwed up everything was the youngest of your offspring."

He pointed the gun at Vincent so quickly that he didn't have time to react. Vincent heard the gunshot go off, and he braced himself to be hit with the bullet. He stood as his muscles tensed and looked away, but he never felt anything. He opened his eyes to see his father lying on the ground in front of him and his blood pouring from underneath him. "Dad!" Vincent picked up his head and looked into his eyes. Tears rolled out from both of them.

"I can't express how sorry I truly am. You were the last gift Althea ever gave me. I love you, Vincent, my dear son."

"I love you too, Dad."

Florent closed his eyes and let out his last breath, dying in Vincent's arms as tears raced down his scar. In just the past week, he had two loved ones die in his arms and both of them were to save his life. Roger approached Vincent quickly and pistol-whipped him in the head.

Vincent fell to the ground, but it didn't kill him like Roger had hoped it would. He could feel the pain throb in the front part of his head, though. Vincent didn't move, so Roger would think otherwise. He thought about what Roger had said about one shot. He realized Roger had only brought one bullet, since he was the only person he had planned on killing for the day until his men came and killed the rest of his family. From the blow, Vincent's knife fell out of his pocket. Roger walked over to the side of him and picked it up. Vincent didn't know what he wanted with his knife, but he carried it off. He heard something make a scratching sound, and he opened his eyes far enough to see where Roger was. Roger had a box of matches, and he lit one. He dropped the match onto the ground, where dry grass surrounded the area. The fire started to eat up everything in its path since everything was so dry, and the day was sweltering.

Vincent could hear the fire eat up the grass and make its way to the surrounding trees. Roger walked a few more steps and flipped open Vincent's knife, holding it to his own throat, and just like that, he hit the ground, lying only a few feet from his father. Vincent never understood why he so suddenly decided to take his life; perhaps it was because he had nothing else to live for. Maybe revenge was not what he hoped it would be.

His vision got hazier by the second. Though the blow to his head did not cause him any serious issues, the pain was unbearable, and he seemed a little disoriented.

He lay with two dead bodies, one his father and the other his father's killer. Black smoke was filling the air, and the fire was tearing down trees like a beast. From his good eye, he saw someone moving. The figure became more apparent as it got closer, and he noticed white-blond hair. He was relieved when he thought it to be Clementine. But this woman looked like a teenager, much younger than Clementine, and her facial features were slightly different. Her blue eyes were like looking into a reflection of his own. She wore a yellow floral dress and no shoes on her feet. Then Vincent could see someone else coming from the other side of the woods. A young man emerged from behind the trees, ignoring the flames that bounced all around him like they weren't even there. He just smiled and kept walking toward the open area where Vincent was lying, as did the woman.

He carried a pink rose in his hands. Vincent could recognize the face, so much like his own as well. The woman stretched out her hand, and the man took it as she took the rose in return. They both turned to Vincent and just gave him a smile, which he knew meant something so much more than just a facial expression. Then they began to walk away, toward the woods, hand in hand. They walked into the burning forest, disappearing behind the smoldering trees. The destruction around them didn't faze them; they just seemed happy to be with each other again. He looked over to his father's dead body, still lying beside him. He knew that he had just seen his parents but as their younger selves, looking as they did when they first fell in love. Their smile gave him the motivation to get up and find his sister and daughter before it was too late.

He slowly got up off the ground and rubbed his eyes. His gait was a bit clumsy, but he eventually got to walking normally. When he could walk again, he began to run as fast as he could. Trees were falling all around him, and he dodged all that he could. He could feel the heat brush his back, and the smell of smoke took over his lungs. When he got closer to the park, he could feel his heart sink. He heard screaming, but not out of joy. He saw a tree topple over some of the food stands, and the flames ate other buildings like it was nothing. The scent of burning flesh singed his nostrils. But he kept running and heading for his house to get Clementine and Ebony. He turned a corner, where a family of four were running for their lives to escape the surrounding fire. A tree fell swiftly, landing on them without any chance to escape.

Vincent winced and wanted to cry for their deaths, but he had to keep going. He ran through the chaos while everyone did the same around him. He turned again, this time down their driveway. He looked back at the destruction until he ran into something solid. He lost his balance slightly but did not fall.

There was his brother's face right in front of his. Once again, he felt the fury inside of him. He pushed Lawrence to the ground as hard as he could. "You told Roger that I killed Marie? How could you just lie about me like that?" He picked himself back up.

"Oh, Vincent, did I not warn you that you would regret everything?"

"Father is dead, as is Roger. Your little lie caused more devastation than me killing those guys and ruining your reputation along with the park's."

"So, you admit it, you did kill those three men! You know, I think I'll tell the cops about that."

"Go ahead, at least that won't be a lie. I will face my crimes."

"I'm not finished. And I will tell them as well that you murdered Marie, Roger, and Dad. I'll tell them you killed all these innocent guests by setting the woods on fire. To top it off, since she always took your side and were such buddies, I'll tell them Clementine helped. After that, you'll be finished, and both of you will sit in prison for the rest of your lives."

"I don't care about what you do to me, but leave Clementine out of this. She's your sister too. What do you have against me, anyway? You hated me before you found out about Marie and I."

Lawrence grabbed Vincent by the neck and got up in his face. Lawrence did not have an irate expression, but a sad one. Tears began to fall from his eyes, just as Roger had done.

"Don't you get it? You killed my mother. The one person who truly cared about me."

"I'm sorry about what happened to our mother, but she was my mother too. I think sometimes you forget that we share so much, including blood. I never got to know Mother, and I envy you for that, but the point is we both lost her. All we can do now is keep our memory of her and hope that one day we can be with her once again."

"You are right. All I have are the memories. You don't understand the absolute hell that I went through. You always thought that you were the hated and neglected child, but you weren't the only one affected by Father's negligence and abrasiveness. You have no idea how Father treated me when no one else was around. You and Clementine were always so close and I felt distant. I had no one to turn to. I was the oldest, so it was expected of me to look out for both of you and everyone wanted too much from me. Everyone acted as though I didn't have feelings because I was older or as if I wasn't allowed to. Marie made me feel human again. She made me feel the way Mother made me feel. It was warm, it was soft, it was *kind.* The time I had with Marie was the happiest time I could remember since Mother had passed away. I wanted so desperately to shoot you after I found out about you and Marie. But every time I look at you, I see Mother. Your eyes pierce right through me as I see her in you. Every time I saw your daughter lying in her bassinet, I just wanted to strangle her, because she is supposed to be mine. But then she opens her big blue eyes, and the same feeling takes over me. It was my command that Roger set this place ablaze. The good and bad memories both haunt me. I want to watch all of them burn."

Lawrence released Vincent and just stared at him. "I am going to ruin you for every single thing you have done that has caused me pain. I will destroy the thing you love most." Lawrence said, and then he ran past Vincent toward the burning park, never to see his brother again. *Ebony,* Vincent thought. Vincent ran toward the house at full force and saw Clementine coming toward him with Ebony in her arms.

"Vincent!"

"Oh, thank God you're all right!"

"I was standing on the porch waiting to see what Roger was doing with that pistol. I saw smoke coming from the treetops and called the fire department immediately, and they are on their way. What happened?"

"There is no time to explain." Vincent had to save his sister from Lawrence. He took Clementine by the shoulders. "I need you to do something for me."

"Anything."

"I want you to leave this place and never come back. Change your name if you must; make it look like you died here. Find all the records or any evidence of the park and our family and destroy them. Lawrence has threatened to turn us both in for the murders that have happened. I have to save you."

"Where is Father?"

"Dead."

Clementine looked up to Vincent with the saddest expression.

"I will explain everything to you later. Write to me and deliver it here to tell me that you did what I asked and also so I know you're alive."

"What about you, are you not coming with me?"

"No, my face is too recognizable. Everyone will know it is me, even if I did try to hide and change my identity. I will stay here and hide in the bunker for a couple of days until all of this has passed, so it looks like I died here as well. Everything we once knew is burning as we speak. Let this place be forgotten. Let us be forgotten and live new lives. I have one more thing I need you to do."

Vincent stood and felt his chest tighten as he had to make the hardest decision of his life. "Take Ebony with you and raise her as your own. Send me pictures of her growing up and her accomplishments, so I can see what she becomes." Vincent placed his hand on Ebony's head and kissed her forehead. She squirmed a little but remained happy lying in Clementine's arm. She was happiest there and always would be. "Your father loves you very much, Ebony. Maybe someday our paths will cross again." Clementine hugged her brother one last time, her face wetted by her tears.

"Promise you'll stay alive for me," Clementine said as she buried her face into Vincent's chest.

"I promise." Clementine released Vincent and started to walk away backward. "Oh, and Clementine, your little brother loves you very much. Friends forever?" Now Vincent's tears matched his sister, who was growing farther from him with each word they said.

"Friends forever," Clementine said quietly, but loud enough for Vincent to hear.

Finnick came out of the woods and hugged Clementine. Vincent assumed he had been searching for her. They ran off together down the long driveway, which was now covered with fallen, scorched trees. He got one last glimpse of his sister and daughter before they were gone from his life forever. Vincent turned toward the woods and ran as fast as he could. Trees were falling more quickly than his steps. He could feel the scorching heat on the back of his neck. He felt himself choking up, getting ready to cry once again, but he had no time to feel anything. He saw the bunker, just a few feet away. A smile spread across his lips, and he ran faster than his legs could take him, but something grazed his back. A large limb had fallen, landing on him, which caused his clothing to start on fire. Just like the trees and buildings, the flames spread quickly. He screamed out and hit the ground. He rolled around vigorously, trying to extinguish the flames from his body. Eventually, by rolling around quickly, the flames extinguished. Even though it was less than a minute that the flames touched his skin, it was almost unbearable.

His arms looked like melted plastic as he saw his skin mixed with blood and char. It had reached him up to his neck, then down his entire body. He limped and basically crawled to the bunker that sat only a few feet in front of him. He grabbed the door handle, pulling himself up. Fortunately, he still had enough strength to open the stubborn latch. He got inside, but before he shut the door to the world for a few days, he stared out into the burning woods. He could even see the heat waves surrounding him and could smell burnt flesh, which made him feel sick. He glanced out at the ignited woods, then at his own body. All the scars, cuts, and burns on Vincent's body were permanent reminders of a dark and painful past. He looked down at the wrinkled, burnt flesh, and then once again, he looked out as his father's childhood dream turned into a nightmare.

Chapter 30

ROOM OF EVOCATION

June 1960

Vincent awoke to another day hidden in his bunker. Marie's flowery perfume still lingered in the decaying concrete walls. He awoke in the middle of several nights, feeling like she was there with him. He even thought he had heard her voice, though it was distorted and soft. She told him everything was going to be okay, and that was all he could hear, but that was all he needed. Vincent wondered if his father had ever felt the same delusions and misleadings after his mother passed away. He wanted to believe it was real, but perhaps it was in his head. Only true love could drive one completely mad; no other force in the world could quite possibly have the same effect. It had been three days since he had watched the only world he had ever known burn and collapse.

He could hardly breathe through the dust and musty air that was trapped inside the small room. The wallpaper with circus animals was starting to peel off the walls, decaying like everything else.

He thought it had been enough time since the fire, it would be safe to venture out and see what was left of Fayland Park. It scared him still that Lawrence would be waiting for him. His burns were healing, but they still looked gruesome. Hunger was taking over, as he had not eaten since he had gone underground. His entire body cried in pain as he tried to climb the ladder, but it wasn't half the challenge as climbing down. When he opened the large rusty door, the sunlight hit him directly in his face; he had not realized how much he missed the sun. He looked out to the woods, a place he knew all too well, destroyed. Some of the trees still stood tall as if nothing had happened, while others lay on the ground.

It was the same with the park. Most of the attractions had vanished entirely as they lay in ashes. Vincent could feel himself getting choked up. He knew that people had lost their lives in the tragedy. He looked around and saw the Ferris wheel still standing tall, not even touched by a single flame. Clementine's paintings on the carts still glistened. The little crane boats still floated in the water, docked and waiting for the next riders. That's what they would all do. They all waited for another round, waiting for passengers to get on, but instead, they would rot and decay as time did its job. Or perhaps they would hold on to hope, knowing it was useless, believing maybe someday fate would be kinder than it had been. A place that was meant to create fantasy had turned into a place of devastation. His father tried to create a place that could escape whatever tragedies happened outside of its borders. It didn't work, though. Even a place of happiness could not escape the harshness of the outside world.

The smell of death filled the air, and Vincent could almost feel the victims watching him through the slits of the trees. He walked through the sad little amusement park and headed toward his house. He did not know if it had been affected or not, but he wanted to find out. To his luck, he saw the large blue mansion standing and looking as whimsical as ever. The part of the forest the house sat on did not look touched. The pink roses were vining up the porch and all over the land, just as before. Vincent did not know if this was normal behavior for roses, but he thought it looked beautiful nevertheless, and he would never remove them. His father had spent nearly nineteen years planting them in the memory of his mother, and now they became his memory of both his parents and a time he never really knew.

He pushed open the large glass door, causing a loud squeaking noise. Vincent was used to the house being quiet. The only sound that ever came over the house was Clementine's brushstrokes, an occasional cough, or footsteps. But this was something entirely different. It was a strange silence, not necessarily bad or good. Vincent grazed the furniture with his hands; it had never felt so good on his skin. The marble flooring under his feet sounded like a melody with each step. He walked up to his own bedroom, opening it to the pink glare. Everything was still tidy, just as Vincent left it. He walked over to Ebony's bassinet that sat empty and felt the white lace that hung on it. He already missed her thick, black hair, soft skin, and precious little face.

How could he live the rest of his life without his daughter? She was with Clementine, and as far as he knew, she would grow up believing that she and Finnick were her parents. Vincent could have run too, changed his name, but as he told his sister, his face was too recognizable. He could not have his daughter know that her father was a criminal or that terrible events transpired in her grandfather's amusement park. Vincent knew there were alternatives where he could be with his daughter and live their lives together, but it was best she was with Clementine, and he didn't exist, as far as she knew. He wanted the best for his daughter, even if it meant never getting to see her again. If he was here, he would be forgotten like Fayland Park. Here he could live his life without destroying anyone else's.

He walked out of his room and quietly shut the door behind him. He started for the steps, but his curiosity had taken hold of him. Before he knew it, he walked toward his parents' bedroom, like the night he was given his scar. He opened the large wooden doors to the mess that his father left behind. Papers were scattered on the floor, his mother's gowns laid out upon the bed, and furniture was out of place. He walked over his blood that was still stained on the carpet. Once again, he noticed a white lace book sitting on the nightstands. Vincent found his mother's diary. Even after all these years, there wasn't a single speck of dust on the book. He grazed his hand over the beautiful handwriting.

He began to read the stories of his father and mother's love. It was almost poetical. She wrote the most exciting events but also the simple ones too. He was crying as he read it but couldn't help but smile. Their romance was so similar to his and Marie's. He expected empty pages after the date of his mother's death but was surprised to find something much different. Different handwriting was placed on the pages, which was a little more sloppy, his father's. He had finished the pages in the diary, talking about how much he missed her. It was like he was writing to her as if she was still alive. It talked about his guilt at what he had done to Vincent and how he felt like a despicable human being to scar his own child's face. He spoke of the pain in his heart and his mind. But mostly, he talked about the fear he felt each day of losing another loved one, and he was scared that would be the reason. Vincent realized the man he had always feared had feared himself.

Vincent wiped his face of the tears. He mostly felt lost inside. Everyone he had once loved was gone and out of his life forever. He placed the white-laced book inside one of the nightstand drawers. What a tragedy it would never see its writers ever again, but its pages were filled with words of love. Vincent picked himself off his parents' bed and went to the mailbox as fast as possible. Each step was painful, but also with each step, he began to gain more strength. He walked out of the house and avoided the thorns of the roses that were wrapping around the entrance. Remnants of a madman who so desperately wanted his love back and to be loved. Vincent went to the mailbox to see if Clementine had left him anything. She was to deliver it herself. A letter in a large envelope rested inside the mailbox, as well as a newspaper. Vincent grabbed the letter as quickly as he could. He ripped it open, and he tried to read it faster than his own brain would allow. The letter read:

My dearest brother,

I write to tell you that Finnick, Ebony, and I are safe. I hope you are the same. I've been terribly worried about you since we have parted ways. The fire killed over two hundred people in the park, and the attendance was about three hundred. I saw people on fire and families separated, things that haunt me at night. I know at the right time you will tell me what happened. I don't understand your plan, you're innocent. It would have not mattered if Lawrence had reported us. They would find no evidence of us killing those people. I sent you this newsletter to read about the fire and the deaths that occurred at Fayland Park. They think that we are all dead. I don't know if Lawrence is actually dead or not as the paper states, but his body was not found. All records have been destroyed, and all that is left of father's park is in people's distant memories. Finnick and I are staying in a hotel in town, at least until we can find a place to live. Our house was destroyed, and so were all our belongings. I miss you, and I love you. Please write back as soon as you can so that I know you're okay. I will return to this mailbox in a few days with updates and check for a letter from you.

With love,

Clementine

Vincent placed the letter in his sweater pocket and took out the newspaper. The Fayland Park burning was all that was on the front page. He looked down at his face and his two siblings', never realizing how much he looked like his brother and sister. He had his father's hair and his mother's eyes, whereas his siblings had the opposite features. But they all shared the same smile, their father's smile. He looked at pictures of the remains of his home. Everything he had once known was destroyed by one flick of a match.

Chapter 31
A FINAL FAREWELL
September 1996

I listened to every word that my grandfather had told me, and I felt pressure in my chest. My brain was throbbing. He looked out the window with misty eyes; it made him look more vulnerable than ever. I sat in silence as I stared at the back of him while he stood without saying a word. Finally, he turned around but never made eye contact with me.

"I sent a letter back to Clementine that very evening, and she picked it up from my mailbox a few days later. I eventually told her that I killed those three men. She was horrified but forgave and understood what I had done. Truth is, I've never forgiven myself. I turned to nasty habits, just as my father did. I began to drink from dawn to dusk and smoke. I still don't know if Lawrence survived the fire, and it is for that reason I never really left. I told Clementine that perhaps I was spineless for not facing the truth and not turning myself in. I just wanted to be forgotten and left behind with my childhood home, and I got my wish.

"Clementine said that as soon as the park was left abandoned, the town completely dried up. The damage was too expensive to fix, and no one really knew the truth of what had happened here. With a murder scene and many guests' deaths, there was no hope for its future. Everyone believed that my whole family died. With no rightful owner or heir, they left it abandoned. It was the mystery that scared so many people, and the rumors of this place. I don't know where our family's fortune is or who even holds the deed to this land. I believe Lawrence is alive and took it all himself; that is what he wanted. After all, he was the heir, and if he survived, the only known living person in our family. I had Clementine and I appear as if we died so that Lawrence would never torture us again. I had Clementine destroy the records because I knew that it would never be the same. It would shut down anyway, and I didn't want my father to see that happen, even after his death."

I sat and remained in silence, feeling myself tensing up. "I still have one question."

"What is that?"

"How come I have been seeing you all these years?"

"Actually, we never really saw each other in person. You have Roger's gift. When I saw you, all I saw was a shadow, a blurry vision of what appeared to look a lot like you. You can travel wherever you please, and your mind often thinks about this place. My guess is that you don't know how to use it, and your mind would take you here when you thought about it. Sometimes the mind knows where we should be looking before we do. I don't understand anything about the telepathic powers that you possess. I tried to quiet you and catch you, but it was no use. I didn't mean to frighten you all these years."

I understood then why he had always held his fingers up to his lips, and I saw roses. He was only trying to calm me. It is very confusing to me too.

"He said it skipped every so many generations, and I thought your mother got it and that it was her that I was seeing. But it looks like you were the one."

"So, the shadow figure you see is where I am looking in the perspective of my mind?"

"Yes, that's what I understand about it. It's a rip in physical existence. A person isn't supposed to be in two places at once. It's almost as if your brain teleports to where you are thinking of. But it doesn't quite get all the momentum it needs to move your matter. So, what other people see of you is almost a hologram; it's you, but not entirely."

"I'm just average. There isn't anything special about me."

"I wouldn't believe that. You're everything but average."

"I'm sorry, I still don't quite understand the whole telepathy thing."

"I don't either. Perhaps we should leave some things a mystery, huh?"

I smiled, thinking about my fascination with the unknown. "Yes, perhaps we should."

For our entire conversation, I thought I was in some kind of illusion. "So, what now?"

"It's time to finish what Roger started."

"What do you mean?"

"I have told you everything you need to know about this place and what it once was. I only really stayed around to watch your mother grow. Though I never actually got to see your mother face to face, through these pictures, I got to see her grow up. And I know now that I have a wonderful granddaughter." I didn't know how to respond, but before I knew it, I was hugging him. My tears streamed down my face as I held on to him; he was the only family I had left. I looked up to see his teary eyes as well. His hair in a short, messy ponytail and his eyes gleaming. The man I had always known existed was no longer a villain to me, but a victim.

"I want you to take that photo album with you and my mother's diary and Clementine's paintings."

"Won't you miss them?"

"Yes, but I think it's time for me to move on. There is nothing here left for me. Besides, I'm ready to see your grandmother again," he said with a smile.

"Wait, you can't possibly mean that. You're the only person I have left."

"I want you to go live your life and not have me to worry about."

I started to sob, knowing that I would have no one, just as I haven't since my mother's death. "I am only twenty years old. I should have my family and loved ones, but they're all dead. You really are the only person I have."

"You are right, you are only twenty, and I know life has not treated you fairly; it doesn't anyone really. But I want you to go and live a life you're proud of and that you can say that you really lived it. And before you go, I want you to have one more thing. With this, we will always be together." He pulled a locket out of his jacket pocket. He put it on me with a giant, sad smile. His locket still remained around his neck. "I give you a final farewell."

I clenched the locket in my hand and held the other heirlooms tightly, and I smiled. I hated that he had made this decision, but that was the way it had to be, I guess. I took my time leaving, I started to smell smoke and see flames. It didn't seem to bother me. I walked out of the large living room and out of the deteriorating house altogether. I started to walk down the long driveway when I began to hear music play behind me and crackling of some sort and felt heat behind me. I turned around to see the large blue mansion in flames. The roses ignited as the beautiful building behind it started to crumble. My grandfather stood in the window of one of the upstairs bedrooms with his violin in his hands. He gave me a wave and a smile. There was no fear in his face. He then continued to play his haunting melody and then slowly backed up, disappearing in the smoke. That was the last time I ever saw him.

Chapter 32
RESOLUTION
November 1996

My last moments with my grandfather were much like the other deaths of my family. I barely had time to say goodbye, and they were gone so quickly. I wish my grandfather hadn't chosen to die with the remaining debris. I didn't agree with his choice of murder, but I didn't see him as a monster like everyone made him out to be, and I was going to tell some of his story. I sat in my living room with a coffee cup in one hand and looked down at a mess of papers. I had my unfinished work all over my floor and tried to put together all the pieces I could. I had decided to forget the newspaper job altogether. The story of Fayland Park was too massive and too special to me to just be a little article in the newspaper.

I began writing down everything that my grandfather told me about the amusement park. There was nothing left of it now, not even a single wooden plank from a ride, just ashes. I wanted to preserve the memory of this place, even if not all the memories were pleasant. Everyone's story deserves to be told, even places. I even told the truth about the murders and the Fayland family's hidden side. I did not want to put fear in people's hearts like rumors or tall tales everyone told about Fayland Park. There were dark parts to the story, but also beautiful parts. I simply told the truth about love, loss, and tragedy.

I read my great-grandmother's diary to know the story before my grandfather. I smiled, cried, and laughed. She was just an innocent young woman, so in love, and she told the story of her life. I decided to become a writer, the one thing I really wanted to be. I had already written several fiction stories just for fun. My work was beginning to get recognition, and my life had changed entirely.

I started to understand the powers that I possessed, but I never really used them all that much. I never told Asher that I had telepathic traits; I didn't know how he would respond. I had a date with him in just half an hour at a little diner downtown, one of the few remaining businesses in Fathorne. I placed the coffee mug into the sink and laid the newspaper on the counter. Asher was still at work, but I wanted to get there early to request our favorite table. It sat in the very back with a large window. As I walked to the train station, which wasn't far from my apartment, I no longer heard voices or a violin being played. It was dead silent, and now it was the silence that made me uneasy.

I reached the train station in just ten short minutes. Luckily, there weren't many people boarding at the time. I claimed a stained seat near the front of the train car and placed my oversized backpack in my lap. The train gave a lurch, and I was on my way. I looked around at the same dull faces that I was used to, all looking almost motionless. I was no longer part of that crowd. I seemed to understand myself better than before, which brought a smile to my face every time. I grabbed the locket around my neck and held the shiny gold heart in my hands. I opened it to reveal my grandparents, Vincent and Marie Fayland. He looked so young in the photograph, with dimples and neat black hair, the same shade as mine. The scar that ran down his face did not detract from his appearance. I'll never understand why people mocked him for it, perhaps because he had one thing that was different from them and he was ridiculed for it.

When I looked up, we passed the old Fayland Park grounds. A large dirt plot was in the place where the arch used to stand. I remember how it mesmerized me with the rotting wood and red, fading letters. All that surrounded the area was burnt trees. Then, not long after, the train passed that large open field, which still held the same grass and wildflowers, but it was missing one thing. I never saw the dancing couple anymore; they vanished with the park too, I suppose. For such a long time, I had watched them gracefully dance across that dust-covered field in each other's arms. There were times when I could almost hear the music. And after all this time, I never knew that the two young lovers were my deceased great-grandparents. It still gives me chills that my whole life, I thought I never had much family, but they were all around me, and I didn't even know it.

I always wondered why no one else never noticed them. Or anything strange, for that matter. Curiosity can be dangerous, but mine just happened to let me know things about myself that I never knew before. It was never my telepathic abilities that allowed me to see the dead. I looked around the dismal train at everyone looking gloomy as usual. Perhaps, I thought, people just need to pay more attention.

The train stopped at the downtown station, and now I would have a short walk to the diner. I walked down the same tired streets of a ragged town—building after building of vacant businesses that used to be booming. I came to the corner of the little diner that sat at the end of a row of empty buildings. I walked into a quiet atmosphere. An older couple was seated at one of the tables near the door and appeared to be the only customers. "Hello, are you dining in?"

"Um, yes, I'm expecting another person to be here shortly. Is it okay to have that table back there?" I pointed.

She looked around at all the empty tables. "Anywhere you would like." I followed her to the table, and she gave me two menus. "Can I start you out with a drink?"

"I'll just have water, and my date will have a lemonade." I sat and waited for Asher to arrive, but he was running later than I expected, or maybe I just got here earlier than I had planned.

I sat staring at the wall decorations and drinking my water when a man caught my attention. He was reasonably tall, average height for a man. He wore a navy-blue trench coat with a matching fedora on his head. By his attire, I could tell he was relatively wealthy. He went up to the bar, and a waitress came up to him. He asked for something, but I could not hear what he ordered. He turned and looked around the small space, waiting for his order. His face was severely burned, as were his hands. He took off his hat to wipe what I assumed was sweat off his head. His hair was neatly pushed back, and it was a bright white blond.

The waitress quickly brought a small cup of coffee, and he turned around to leave. He must have caught me staring at him, as he looked me straight in the eyes with a shocked look. He looked at me as I looked at him like we knew each other but couldn't quite place who either of us was. He looked at me as if he was seeing a ghost. But I believe I knew exactly who he was. After a short time, but what felt like a long time, he broke off his stare and headed out the door. I perked up when I saw Asher walk by the window. Asher held the door open for him, and he nodded in gratitude. Asher returned his nod with a smile and entered the diner. My heart was beating quickly as I watched this man walk down the sidewalk.

"Oh, you already ordered my drink, thank you." Asher sat down across from me. But I did not look at him. I kept my eyes on the man until he was out of my view.

"Is something wrong?"

"No, sorry. I just thought I saw someone I knew."

We both ordered a grilled cheese sandwich and fries. We could barely breathe after the large quantity of food we had eaten, but we decided to get dessert anyway. We shared a large cherry milkshake, which came in the tallest glass I'd ever seen. After we finished, we decided to go back to my apartment and watch TV, which was our favorite thing to do. As we walked down the old, cracked sidewalks, we passed the mysterious alleyways and vacant buildings, and for once, I was not scared.

I still feared matters I did not understand, but that was a normal reaction. Fear is an emotion, just the same as happiness or sadness. We can't feel happy if we never felt sad. The same, we can't feel brave if we never experienced fear. Without the chaos life puts us through, would we ever really become stronger? People we love die, things get lost, and our eyes cry tears from the pain we feel. Maybe someday we'll be reunited with the ones who are gone, find whatever we lost, and eventually, our eyes will dry. All these trials make up our own story, and I guess I'm still writing mine.

We reached his beat-up yellow truck and got inside. I pushed soda cans out of my way on the floor, which I did every time. On the way to the apartment building, we sang at the top of our lungs with the windows all the way down. People stared, but we didn't care. This was our time, and no one was going to take that away from us. When we pulled into the driveway, my throat was sore. As soon as we got in, we both jumped on the couch. I turned the TV on to our favorite show. I laid my head on Asher, and he wrapped his arms around me. There was no other place I'd rather be in the world.

I could hear the TV in the background, but I found my mind wandering, as it always did. A lot of me had changed over the last two months, except for my overactive imagination, which I discovered to be a trait that ran in my family. As I lay there, I thought about how much of my life had changed. *Life*, wow, that's the most complicated word I know. It never works out the way we planned, but isn't that the beauty of it? Knowing that each day will be a new chance. I am going to keep looking for the unknowns, because I know there are many more out there for me to discover. But mostly, I am going to find what makes me happy, remembering that the most beautiful things can be found in the strangest of places.

EPILOGUE

August 1997

Almost a year had passed since I had learned about my family's past. I felt I still only knew a fraction of what there was left to know. Asher and I left Fathorne and moved to the city. But I knew someday I would be back to visit my hometown. Sometimes in my mind, I would travel the dark, foggy streets. I had become an author of two popular novels and the true story of Fayland Park. I always knew that writing would be my ticket to being someone in life. I wrote inspirational stories, I guess, and love stories based on my grandparents' and great-grandparents' love.

I loved the busy streets and opportunities the city had to offer, something I had never really experienced. But there was something about my hometown. It was an old, sleepy town, but something made it unique that nowhere else could offer. It was depressing, quiet, and dilapidated, but it would be my forever home, no matter where I was. I just couldn't stay there; I had more of the world to explore. I was right about returning to Fathorne one day, though. I had purchased a train ticket, and today I was returning to my home.

I was finishing up unpacking the last remaining boxes. We moved into a small Victorian-inspired apartment building. It was very similar to our old residence. Yellow paint was splashed through the house with floral wallpaper. It was indeed a fixer-upper, and Asher and I were willing to put our time and effort into its walls. I unpacked the last box and looked at my new bedroom. It was strange living somewhere other than Fathorne. I zipped up my already-packed suitcase and headed for the door. Asher came from out of the kitchen to bid me goodbye.

"Are you sure you want to go?" Asher asked with a pouty face.

"Yes, I think it's time I pay a visit to our old town." I was devastated that Asher wasn't coming along, but it wasn't feasible with his busy work schedule. "I'll be back in just a few short days, I promise."

"You better be. I don't know if I'll make it," he said with a smirk. I don't think we have been separated since we started dating.

"That's true. This is something I have to do. I can't seem to get Fathorne out of my mind. I have to go now. Bye! I love you!"

"I love you too. Have a safe trip." With another peck on his cheek, I was gone and on my way.

On the train, I began to grow bored. I had already read my magazine and a short book I had brought. It was a three-hour trip to Fathorne. I could have driven, but it would have been even longer. Fathorne was in the middle of nowhere, and the fastest and most practical way to get there was by train. I laid my head on the window and looked out as we quickly passed rolling green valleys and trees. The simplicity of the scene was what made it stunning. I was already starting to miss Asher every passing second. I decided to focus and try to think of our living room. Soon, I saw him walking down the aisle of the train, looking like he was digging stuff out of a box. I knew he really wasn't there, but in the living room, unpacking more boxes.

I sneezed, even though I tried to hold it in, which made him quickly turn around. He had a puzzled look, and he reached out his arm; he must have seen me, well a silhouette of me. I snapped out of my focus, and he disappeared off the train. I was still perplexed and overwhelmed by my abilities. I would always use them for good, unlike my great-grandfather, Roger Merriam. I was glad I had this ability, but still, to this day, it bewildered me on how it worked.

After a drawn-out and tedious train ride, I stood on the large patch of dirt where an old arch used to stand proudly, even when the park was just a tragic reminder of the past. I could feel my chest swell as I prepared myself to step into the woods. This time, I wasn't going to find answers. I just wanted to see what was left behind. I wanted a formal goodbye instead of running out of here like the last two previous times. There weren't really any woods anymore, just a few trees that got lucky.

Most of the forest was burned to the ground, and it was just an open field with charred trees. I continued to walk and tried to get a perspective of where I was. As I stared at the nothingness, sadness began to fill my heart. What a place this must have been. I knew of the misfortunes that took place here, but it still held that fantastical charm. Even though I stood on vacant land, I felt that somehow I had escaped reality. I walked deeper into the property on the broad concrete path. A cola sign sat propped up against skeletons of a building. I looked over to see a pile of wood, metal, and debris. I could tell it was the Ferris wheel, by the art on the side of a wooden plank. It was astonishing how my great aunt's artwork had survived something as menacing as a fire. The flowers and cherubs were still evident.

I looked a little further up, where a scorched carousel resided. It had mostly fallen down, and the horses were spread out underneath it. I knew they were inanimate objects, yet they looked as if they were about to cry. Their beautiful colors were not stripped from them either. The various colors and artistry on the horses were breathtaking. Those were the only remaining structures I could identify, so I decided to go somewhere else. There was more I wanted to see, but there was nothing left to see. Everything had burned to the ground, forgotten even by time.

I took the path back to the blue mansion. I knew there were be a vacant spot. That large home was no longer there as I expected; just burnt wood and rubble. All the flowers and crops in the large garden had rotted away. I passed the two gravestones of my grandmother and great-grandmother. I grazed my hand on the tombstones as I got down on my knees to pay my respects. Two people I had never met had seemed to make such an impact on my life. I hoped they were now resting in peace.

Feeling deep sorrow, I started to walk back toward the entrance without hesitation. Even though I wanted to stay longer, despondency had overtaken me. When I got close to the entrance to a large open area, I felt something odd under my shoe. I smiled at what I saw, giving me perhaps a small touch of hope. I looked down at one single pink rose resting on the ground of what once was.

THE END